# HALF SICK
## OF
# SHADOWS

# HALF SICK
## OF
# SHADOWS

## LAURA SEBASTIAN

ACE
NEW YORK

ACE
Published by Berkley
An imprint of Penguin Random House LLC

Copyright © 2021 by Laura Sebastian
Penguin Random House supports copyright. Copyright fuels creativity, encourages diverse voices,
promotes free speech, and creates a vibrant culture. Thank you for buying an authorized edition of this
book and for complying with copyright laws by not reproducing, scanning, or distributing any
part of it in any form without permission. You are supporting writers and allowing
Penguin Random House to continue to publish books for every reader.

ACE is a registered trademark and the A colophon is a trademark of Penguin Random House LLC.

ISBN 9780593200513

Printed in the United States of America

Book design by Alison Cnockaert

For teenage me, who started writing this story
And for adult me, who finally figured out how to finish it

# AUTHOR'S NOTE

*Half Sick of Shadows* explores sensitive issues surrounding mental health and suicide. I believe these themes were necessary to tell this story, and so I tried to handle them as delicately and sensitively as possible, combining my own experiences and research with notes and opinions from sensitivity readers. As careful as I have tried to be, some scenes may be triggering to some readers.

If you or someone you know is experiencing suicidal thoughts or emotional distress, please call the National Suicide Prevention Lifeline at 1-800-273-TALK (8255), or text the Crisis Text Line (text HOME to 741741) to connect with a crisis counselor. Both services are free and available twenty-four hours a day, seven days a week. The deaf and hard of hearing can contact the Lifeline via TTY at 1-800-799-4889.

# HALF SICK
## OF
# SHADOWS

# 1

I WILL DIE DROWNING; it has always been known. This was my first vision, long before I knew it for what it was, and I've had it so many times now that I know each instant by heart. Where most visions are ephemeral things, shifting and changing in different lights and at different angles, this one is always so solid that it leaves its bruises on my mind and soul long after it ends.

The water will be cold against my skin. It will rush around me like a storm, tearing my hair in different directions until it clouds my vision. I won't be able to see a thing. I will want to kick up to the surface, to breathe the air I know is only a few meters away, but I will stay frozen and sink lower and lower in my whirlpool until my feet finally touch soft sand. My eyes will be closed, and everything around me will be darkness.

My lungs will burn, burn, burn until I fear they are going to burst. The surface will be so close, I could reach it if I just kick up . . . but I won't. I won't want to.

In a week or a year or a decade, I will die drowning. When I do, it will be a choice.

T HERE IS PEACE at the loom, in the steady rhythm of my fingers dancing over the silk strands like a musician with a lyre, peace in the threads
weaving in and out, in the future revealing itself to me stitch by stitch, possibility by possibility. Such small movements, repeated again and again and
again, each one small and meaningless on its own—but when the tapestry
begins to take shape and tell its story, the infinitesimal becomes infinite.

As a child in Shalott, I learned how to change the color of the threads to
render an image, frozen forever in time, but now I use only white. The magic-
imbued strands glisten like opal in the afternoon sunlight that filters into my
workroom through the oversized window.

Outside, the staggering cliff my cottage sits on juts out over rolling, pearl-
tipped waves. They crash against Avalon's shore, the sound loud enough to
reach me even in my cottage, but I don't mind it. The steady sound soothes
my mind, turning it soft and malleable and blank, receptive to the magic that
buzzes its way through me from my fingertips to my toes.

I keep my eyes on the threads, watching them weave together tight and
solid, the waves pounding in my ears and chasing all thoughts away so that
nothing exists at all outside of me in this moment—not Avalon or my friends,
not the past or the futures fracturing before me like cracks in glass. Only me,
only now.

The expanse of whiteness begins to shift, like shadows dancing across it, rippling over its shining surface. The threads vibrate softly beneath my fingers, emitting a glow all their own. I feel the change throughout my body as well, something unnamable tugging at my skin and sparking in my mind, threatening to pull me into it, into whatever the Sight wants me to see.

Though I've had hundreds if not thousands of visions over the last ten years, I don't think I will ever grow used to this feeling: how for just a moment, my body and my mind cease to be my own.

A rattling knock yanks me out of it, my fingers stilling against the white silk strands. I settle into myself once more, and the world around me suddenly feels too sharp, too bright, too *real.*

I look up, letting my eyes focus and adjust, and find him standing on the other side of my window, his knuckles still resting against the glass and a mischievous smile playing on his full lips. In the light of the Avalon sun, he is pure gold.

"Come on, Shalott," he says, his voice muffled through the glass. He jerks his head backward toward the beach, windblown black hair glinting in the sunlight. Behind him, I can just make out the other three, all beckoning me to join them, to spend the day on the beach, enjoying the sunshine and the sea. "It's too nice a day to waste cooped up inside."

Every day in Avalon is too nice to waste cooped up inside, I want to tell him, but some of us don't have much of a choice in the matter.

"Give me an hour," I say instead.

His bright green eyes crinkle, as if he knows it's a lie, but he shrugs his shoulders and turns away from me, his hand going to rest casually on the pommel of the sword sheathed at his hip. When he reaches the others, the four of them wave to me and I wave back.

*You mustn't strain yourself,* Nimue always says when she finds me here in the mornings, bleary-eyed and dazed. *Seers go mad that way.*

But sometimes it feels like I'll go mad if I stay away from the loom too long. Sometimes it feels like scrying is the only thing keeping me sane.

I watch them walk down the beach with a pang in my chest. Arthur and Guinevere are hand in hand, and though I can't see his face, I know he's blushing, like he always does around Gwen. Morgana leans over to say something in her brother's ear, and Arthur gives her shoulder a shove, making her laugh, her head thrown back, ink-black hair spilling down her back. Lancelot watches the two of them, shaking his head before glancing over his shoulder back at me, his green eyes colliding with mine again.

"One hour," I say again, and though he can't hear me, he must read my lips, because he nods.

Part of me wants to run after them and leave the loom behind for today, even forever, before it ruins me. But I can't do that, so I go back to my weaving, picking up the threads once more.

This time when the vision takes hold of me, there are no interruptions and I tumble into it headfirst.

Morgana, don't do this, please."

The voice isn't mine, but it will be one day, panicked and desperate and frightened. The small room will be made from shadow and stone, lit only by a few scattered candles, burning down to little more than puddles of wax. In the dim light, the pupils of Morgana's eyes will be huge, making her look manic as she flits around her room, pulling bottles down from their shelves and uncorking them to sniff or pinch or dump completely into the bubbling cauldron. Her ink-black hair will be unbound and wild, following her around like a storm cloud. Whenever a piece of it drifts into her face, she will blow it away in an annoyed huff, but that will be the only sound she makes. She won't speak to me. She won't even look at me.

Cold air will bite at my skin, the smell of sulfur seeping into the air from the potion brewing. Without a word, I know that whatever potion Morgana is brewing isn't only dangerous. It's lethal.

"Morgana," I will try again, my voice cracking over her name. Still, she won't acknowledge me. Not until I touch her shoulder. She will flinch away, but at least she will look at me, violet eyes hard and distant even when they meet mine.

She will not be the Morgana I know now, the Morgana who was my first friend, who has stood by my side unfalteringly since I was thirteen years old.

"This cannot stand, Elaine." Her voice will be calm and resolved, at odds with the chaos in her body, the storm in her expression. "The things Arthur has done—"

The words conjure nothing in my mind—no memory, no image, no thought at all. I don't know what Arthur has done to earn Morgana's rage, but it must have been something truly terrible.

"He has done what he believes best." It's a line that will feel familiar on my tongue, like I have spoken it many times. I will believe the words with every part of me.

Morgana pulls away from me, making a sound that is half-laugh and half-sob.

"Then you think Arthur a fool, Elaine? You think he didn't know exactly what he was doing? What is worse—to have a foolish king or a cruel one?"

Her eyes on mine will burn until I have to look away, unable to defend Arthur for the first time in my life.

"Which do you think it was?" she will continue, and I realize the question isn't rhetorical. She wants an answer. "Is he stupidly noble, or is there a conniving side under all of that quiet erudition?"

"Arthur loves you," I say, because I won't know what other answer to give. It will be one of the only true things I will know, but that doesn't mean it makes her beliefs untrue. I don't know how the two things can be unassailable facts, but somehow, they are.

She will scoff and turn away from me, unstoppering a bottle and letting the shadow of a serpent slither out into the sizzling cauldron. It will die with a shriek that echoes in the silence between us.

"And you?" I will ask her when I find my voice again. "He's your brother, and I know you love him. How can you even consider doing this to him?"

She will begin to turn away, but I will grab her hands in mine, holding tight and forcing her to look at me.

"The boy you teased mercilessly when his voice began to change? The one who still turns red in the cheeks every time Gwen smiles at him? The one who has taken your side against every courtier in this palace who wanted you banished or worse? If you do this, Morgana, there is no coming back. I have Seen this path, I have Seen this moment, and I am begging you not to do it, not to break us into pieces that we will never be able to mend."

Her hands will go slack in mine, and she will falter. For an instant, she will look once more like the Morgana I have always known, her vulnerabilities like sunlight slatting through a boarded-up window.

She will open her mouth to speak and—

WHEN I COME out of the vision, my eyes take a moment to readjust, to take in the tapestry stretched over the loom, showing a jet-haired women bent over a cauldron, staring intently into its depths, while another woman with fair hair watches on, hands clasped in front of her.

It's easier to see it this way than to be in the vision itself. Like this, there is some stretch of distance, some ability to pretend that they are just two strangers, not Morgana and me. It's easy to pretend that they are brewing a love potion or a healing draught, that they are discussing the effect the recent storm will have on their crops.

The first time I had this vision was in a dream, before I mastered the art of channeling them onto the loom. It was disjointed and unfocused, difficult to remember when I woke up. Through the loom, I'm able to focus better, and when it is done, I'm left with this: an image, solid and real.

"The poison scene again," a voice says from behind me, and I turn to see Nimue standing in the open doorframe, leaning against it. Her silver gown spills over her umber skin like water, skimming closely over her curves and leaving her shoulders bare.

I've been in Avalon for ten years now, and I still can't help but think that if she were to wear something like that in Camelot, she would end up stoned to death. But we are not in Camelot, we are in Avalon, and Nimue is the Lady of the Lake. She can wear whatever she likes.

I step away from the loom to give her a better look, though she hardly needs one. She's right—I've had this same vision before, too many times to rightly remember. It's always a little different, a little broader or narrower, a little longer or shorter—a reflection in a rippling pond, Nimue told me during one of my first lessons—but the same shape, more or less.

"The potion smelled of sulfur this time," I tell her, closing my eyes to better remember the smaller details, the ones that matter the most. "And there was something she put into it—the shadow of a serpent, it looked like."

Nimue says nothing for a moment. In the bright room of my studio, the burnished silver circlet around her bald head glows. Her mouth turns down at the corners as she considers my words, considers the tapestry before her. She reaches out to touch it, and as she does, it begins to turn white once more, the image erasing as if it never existed at all. It is a dangerous thing, to leave such blatant evidence of visions lying about. If Morgana were to see it, she would have questions I would never be able to answer. Besides, the only people who need to know about the vision are Nimue and me, and the scene is likely burned into our memories by now.

But I told Morgana about what I'd Seen in the vision, or at least insinuated it. I always do, in every iteration.

"Davaralocke," Nimue says finally, interrupting my thoughts. "A poison—you were right. And among the deadliest when brewed correctly."

I shake my head. "That's just it . . . the way she was brewing it . . . I've seen Morgana brew potions before. You know, you taught her—she's meticulous to a fault. But this time, she was careless. Throwing ingredients in by the handful or jar even, not measuring, not following a recipe at all, really."

Nimue makes a thoughtful noise in her throat before turning to look at me.

"And the end of it?" she asks me. "Did it change at all?"

I shake my head. "It ended just as it always does: It felt like maybe I got through to her, like I'd changed her mind, but it ended before I could say for sure."

For a moment, Nimue doesn't speak. "Do you know why you keep seeing this vision, more than any other?"

"Because it's important," I say automatically. It was one of the first things Nimue taught me when I came to Avalon, but now she simply shrugs her shoulders.

"Yes, but that's not the entire truth," she says. "It's because everything comes down to a choice that hasn't been made yet, a choice the future of our world hangs on. One choice, from one girl."

I stare at the blank tapestry, at where Morgana's figure was only moments ago.

"I have faith in Morgana," I tell her.

"Then you are a fool," she says, though her voice is soft-edged and not unkind. "An oracle should know better than to have faith in anyone. People lie, visions don't. Maybe there are many versions of Morgana that would never make that choice, but there is at least one who would. Who does."

I open my mouth to argue but I quickly close it again. There is nothing I can say that hasn't been said already.

"Did you come to see if I had anything new for you?" I ask her, to change the subject. "I'm sorry you came all this way, but it's been the same recycled visions for months now."

Nimue shakes her head, giving a small sigh. "That is because our world is on a precipice and the future is holding its breath." She begins to unwind the stitches I made on my loom, unweaving it piece by piece. She doesn't look at me. "Uther Pendragon died three days ago."

It takes a moment for me to hear the words, longer still to make sense of them enough to respond.

"King Uther is dead," I repeat slowly.

I didn't know the man well, mostly by reputation, and that itself wasn't entirely pleasant. Still, he was Arthur's father, and I know that he will feel the loss keenly.

"Does Arthur know?" I ask.

Nimue shakes her head. "Not yet. There was some talk among the council as to what it means."

The thought of the council arguing over a man's death for three days instead of telling his son makes my skin prickle with irritation. I have to remind myself that the council is made up of fey and that, to them, three days is a single breath, a negligible amount of time. I have to remind myself that most of their own parents have been dead for centuries, that they don't truly understand the strength of the bond between humans and their families, no matter how complicated those bonds might be.

"And what does it mean?" I ask Nimue.

"It means that Arthur has a throne to claim," she says, finally looking at me. "It means that his legitimacy as heir is already being questioned, being fought for by others who would take his throne and bring the world we know to darkness. It means that it is time for him to leave Avalon—and for all of you to go with him."

Though I should have expected the words, they still feel like a slap. *Leave Avalon.* I have seen a future off of this island, I have seen the tragedy and loss and hopelessness that that future brings. It has always seemed so far away, a problem for another Elaine, an impossibility that I've never fully been able to believe would come true. But here we are now, about to be shoved into a world I only really know through my visions and a few distant memories.

"It's too soon," I say, shaking my head. "We don't know enough."

"You will never know enough, Elaine," Nimue says. Though her voice remains placid, there's a tightness to her expression that is new. "The only way you will learn more is to act, and you can't do that while you are swaddled like infants on this island."

"But we're safe here," I point out. "All of us."

"And you will always be safe here," she says, and now there is no mistaking the sadness in her, leaking out to color her voice. "But you were not raised to be safe, you were raised to be heroes."

WHEN NIMUE GOES, I sit back down at the loom, though I don't reach for the threads again. Instead, my hands bunch together in my lap. The room feels like it is pressing in on me, making it difficult to breathe.

Suddenly, I feel like I am back in Camelot once more, back in my room in the tower I shared with my mother. I was a different girl then—*a sheltered girl who is so afraid of her own shadow that she won't walk in sunlight*, Morgana called me once, *a girl who closes her eyes and takes all the injustices the world pushes on her without a word in response, a girl who does everything her mother tells her to and never questions why.*

She wasn't wrong, but I am not that girl any longer. Still, I can't help but fear what will happen when I walk through Camelot's gates once more. Not only because of the things I've seen, the dark futures looming over everyone I love, but because I left Camelot Elaine behind ten years ago, and I'm afraid that when I return, she will as well.

M ORE OFTEN THAN not, I had to remind myself of the reasons I
loved my mother. As a girl, I would count them off in my mind whenever she said something cruel. I smoothed those reasons over the wounds her
words inflicted like a balm that never lasted long enough.

"Elaine, you aren't listening to a word I've been saying," she scolded on the
day that everything changed.

We ate our breakfast together as we did every day, in our tower with its
gray stone walls and gray stone floors and the single window that let in just
enough light to see by, making everything appear dull and spectral.

When I first came to Camelot at the age of eight, I had thought it a marvel
of a place, loud and bright and buzzing with people of all types, but our tower
was another world entirely. Days—sometimes weeks—could pass without the
sight of a single person apart from my mother and our sparse staff. *Lonely*
didn't seem the right word for it, though. When you don't know anything else,
even that sort of isolation could seem natural.

"I'm sorry, Mother," I told her that morning, ducking my head and staring
at the plate in front of me. Like most days, breakfast consisted of biscuits and
butter because my mother couldn't stomach anything more flavorful. She'd
insisted that I eat only half a biscuit to ensure that my dress would fit for the
banquet at the end of the week. My stomach grumbled painfully, but I'd long

learned that my discomfort was far preferable to what would happen if I were to ask her for more.

Her eyes watched me, a gray so pale that, in certain lights, the iris was nearly drowned by the whites, leaving only a pinprick of black. "Are you ill?" she asked.

I shook my head. "I just didn't sleep well last night. I had a bad dream."

She gave a loud sigh. "Well," she said, a single word that felt like it weighed a ton, "if you remembered your medicine, your dreams wouldn't be so unpleasant."

I loved my mother because I knew she loved me more than anyone else in this world.

For a moment, I considered telling her that I did take my medicine, that I couldn't forget it if I tried. Every night, it slid down my throat like tar, thick and foul, leaving a taste that lingered well into the next morning. But I still took it without fail because it was what I was supposed to do. But the truth wouldn't do any good, so instead, I kept my mouth shut and my gaze focused on my plate and the crumbs remaining. I wanted to press my finger against the surface to pick them up and lick them off, but I could already guess at my mother's reaction to that. It would be better to endure the five hours of hunger until lunch.

"I cannot stress enough how important it is that you remember," she continued. "We can't afford another *incident*. People are still gossiping about the last time you made a spectacle of yourself."

I couldn't remember much of that night, but still I flinched from the word *spectacle*, wielded like a weapon. I wanted to protest, to tell her it wasn't my fault, but arguing with my mother was like kicking a boulder—she remained unchanged, and I was the one left limping. It was never worth it.

"I'll try harder to remember, Mother," I said instead.

I loved my mother because when we lived in Shalott, she would take me down to the river there and teach me how to make flower crowns. Now, it had been years since she'd been outside—even since she'd been out of our tower.

The air in Camelot made her head ache, she said. So did socializing with strangers and any kind of music, even birdsong. The food upset her stomach.

The sun, even on a cloudy day, hurt her eyes. And so she stayed hidden away in our tower day and night, getting too much sleep, plotting my future, and doing little else. She said that I was her eyes and ears, but I suspected she had spare sets to tell her the things that I didn't.

"How is Morgause?" she asked, jerking me out of my thoughts.

At the sound of that name, I took a particularly long gulp of tea to hide my expression, but she must have seen it anyway because she made a disapproving sound, shaking her head.

I loved my mother because once, she could make me feel safe just by holding my hand in hers.

"None of that, Elaine. She is the princess of Camelot. You could do worse than make friends with her. Perhaps you could even gather news about when that brother of hers is finally returning to us from Avalon?"

It seems silly now, but back then, the image of Arthur I had in my mind was that of a storybook prince, tall and golden-haired with broad shoulders and a strong jaw. A prince so perfect he'd been spirited away by the fey when he was barely old enough to walk, the final element of the truce between his father, King Uther, and the fey of Avalon, to put an end to the Fay War that had plagued Albion for half a century.

The official edict was that Arthur would return to Camelot on his eighteenth birthday, but I'd heard rumors that Arthur didn't exist at all, that he was only a rumor started to distract from the fact that Uther had no legitimate heir. Even Morgause was the daughter of his late wife from her first marriage, her claim not strong enough to make her a true heir.

My mother gave a dramatic sigh. "Perhaps Morgause knows more. You could find out, if you were kinder to her."

I loved my mother because when she read poetry aloud, she would always sing instead of speak.

"I am kind to Morgause," I told her, though I didn't know how true that was. I tried to be kind, that much was true, but Morgause always replied with cruelty, so maybe, I thought, I was doing it wrong.

"Well." She forced a brittle smile. "Perhaps Arthur will make a reappearance for Morgause's birthday."

If Prince Arthur hadn't come back when his mother died, he wouldn't come back for his half sister's birthday.

"You will have to look your best, just in case," she said, her gaze turning critical as it swept over my face, taking in my lank blond hair, my sallow skin, the way the cap sleeves of my too-small dress pinched at the flesh of my arms.

*What use do you have for new dresses?* she'd asked when I'd pointed out mine didn't fit right anymore. *You could make them fit, if you tried.*

I loved my mother because she used to smell like cinnamon.

I didn't argue. I knew she always got what she wanted. It was just a question of how much I lost in the process.

"Perhaps if you didn't speak so much," she said thoughtfully after a moment. She leaned back in her chair to appraise me as if she hadn't seen me in months. "Maybe it will give you an air of mystery."

"I don't speak much as it is."

I didn't add that it was difficult to carry an air of mystery when everyone knew you as the girl who ran down the halls at three in the morning, barefoot and screaming, waking up from a nightmare that had been too real to be only imagination. But of course, that was one thing my mother would not discuss, no matter how many times I had tried to broach the subject.

"There are different kinds of silence, dear," my mother said. "There's a mysterious kind of silence, and then there's the . . . well, the strange kind of silence. What was it Morgause has taken to calling you?"

I loved my mother because she used to call me Little Lily.

"Elaine the Mad," I said quietly. Beneath the cover of the table, I clenched my hands into fists, reveling in the bite of my nails on the soft flesh of my palms. Painful, yes, but less painful than the conversation had become.

My mother scoffed. "Darling, there's no need to be so sensitive. She only means it in jest."

I suppose there was nothing funnier than knowing that everyone around you called you names behind your back. Unless you counted the fact that they said them to your face as well.

I loved my mother because she didn't believe anyone was evil, even someone like Morgause. Despite all evidence I had provided to the contrary. Every arm bruised from her sharp pinches, every time I had come home crying because of something she said or did, every cruel nickname she'd bestowed upon me—my mother ignored them all, dismissing them with a comment about how girls behaved at our age.

I loved my mother because she was all I had—because I believed she was the only person in the world who could love me back.

My MOTHER WILL not be waiting for me when I return to Camelot, though I suspect there is nowhere I can go that her ghost will not follow.

# 4

THERE WERE TIMES when I envied my mother her solitude. She could stay in her tower all day long—and did so without fail. I, on the other hand, had no such luxury.

On the day that everything changed, I was forced out to meet the other girls my age to work on Prince Arthur's birthday tapestry. One daughter from each family had been chosen to contribute to it, and the idea was that when the prince turned eighteen, or whenever he happened to return—*if* he ever returned—it would be presented to him as a gift from all of the eligible young ladies of court, one of whom he would choose to marry.

It was a strange custom, but an old one. I wasn't sure I understood the concept. Was he expected to fall in love with my tiny, evenly spaced stitches? Would he somehow be able to tell mine apart from every other girl's? What was more, no one had seen Prince Arthur since he was two years old, and that had been more than ten years ago now. Back then, Arthur wasn't a real person to me, more of a ghost mentioned only in hushed whispers but never seen.

None of us knew then how fruitless our efforts really were. Even then, when Arthur was only just thirteen, he was already madly in love with Guinevere. No tapestry was going to change that.

One of the less formal sitting rooms in the east wing of the castle had been given over to our work, with the normal plush velvet furniture pushed to one side to make room for a large table surrounded by eight chairs and the brocade curtains drawn tight to protect our delicate skin from the midday sunlight. Candles were lit instead, large white tapers clustered about the room with trickles of wax dripping down. Still, it was never bright enough to see by, and I often found myself squinting, even as I heard my mother's voice in my head warn that I would get wrinkles that way.

Our work so far had been spread on top of the table, the center already stitched in but its edges only marked with chalk to guide us where to go next. The design was slowly taking shape, showing a white unicorn ridden by a knight whose face is hidden by his helm but who could only be presumed to be Prince Arthur.

I was the first one there that day, so I circled the table, reaching my hand out to feel the stitched area. It was so small for the six months' time it had taken us. It would be another year before it was done, maybe two.

"It's a bit silly, is it not?" a voice behind me asked, surprising me. I turned to see Morgause leaning against the doorframe with her arms crossed over her chest, lips pursed and eyes narrowed.

Though Morgause wasn't actually a princess—she was the daughter of the queen from her first marriage—she held herself like royalty, as if the very air belonged to her and the rest of us breathed only because she allowed it. She was beautiful in a cruel way, with luminous bronze skin, long, wavy hair the color of jet, a hawklike nose, and a wide mouth painted red as blood. That day, I thought she looked half-feral; her hair was a mess of curls, and freckles were showing on her cheeks. Morgause was normally so careful about the sun, never walking outdoors without at least three servants carrying parasols and trailing after her.

I remember thinking there was something strange about her dress as well. Its voluminous petticoat and bell sleeves were fashionable enough, but it was crafted from ink-blue silk—darker in color and lighter in fabric than was common among ladies at court. And though it was difficult to say for sure without staring outright, I didn't think she was wearing a corset.

"I don't know what you mean," I told her, taking a step back, my heart already beating quicker in my chest. I remembered coming across a deer once when I was a child, in the woods outside my father's castle. For a second, we had both been frozen, our eyes locked on each other, its ears quivering before it darted away. It had been afraid of me then, just as I was afraid of Morgause now. The only difference was that I hadn't meant the deer harm. Morgause, on the other hand, had never said so much as a word to me that wasn't barbed, and I was sure she was nudging me toward some kind of trap.

"I think it's coming along quite well." I cast a glance around, but the room was empty. Were her friends hiding behind the closed door, waiting for their cue?

Normally, Morgause wasn't there for our sewing group—she couldn't very well marry her brother, after all—but I thought perhaps she'd had nothing better to do.

"Arthur will be very . . . amused by it, if nothing else," she said with a smirk at the tapestry before turning her attention to me. Her eyes searched my face for a moment, and a frown tugged at her mouth. "Who are you?"

Morgause was often cruel, but this was a new prank. For a moment, I considered playing along, but I did not feel like games that day.

"I only want to get through this quickly so that I can go home, Morgause. Can't you leave me alone today?" I meant for my voice to come out strong and level, but instead I sounded like a mouse even to my own ears.

She laughed, but it wasn't the high, derisive giggle I'd always heard from Morgause while she and her friends exchanged gossiping whispers. This laugh was full and throaty and so loud that she had to throw her head back from the force of it.

"I'm not Morgause," she said when she recovered, a wry smile playing on her lips. "I'm her sister."

Once she said it, I noticed that there were small differences between them: the freckles for one, and her eyes had a hint of violet to them, not pure gray. But Morgause's twin sister had not been at court since long before I arrived, and mention of her was rare, restricted to salacious whispers when there was nothing else to talk about. Some said King Uther banished her to a nunnery because of her ill behavior, though she couldn't have been more than six at the time. Others said he married her off to some foreign king in his seventies. A few even said that she was quietly put to death because she used fay magic.

What I'd never heard was Morgause saying a word in her sister's defense, no matter how vicious the rumors got.

"You don't believe me," the girl—whoever she was—said when I didn't reply. "Maiden, Mother, and Crone, my sister must have grown into some kind of nightmare. How old are you?"

*Maiden, Mother, and Crone.* The expression was foreign to me then, though in time it would become familiar, and one I deployed regularly myself for everything from a stubbed toe to a bone-melting kiss to a particularly troubling vision. At the time, it merely struck me as something the fey would say. Even though Morgause's father, Lord Gorlois, fought against King Uther in the Fay War, on the side of Avalon, Morgause herself detested the fey, like everyone else at court. She would never have used one of their expressions. *Goodness*, she would have said instead, even as her voice dripped with malice. Or maybe *heavens* or *dear me*.

"Thirteen," I told her, my voice cautious.

"And when did you come to court?"

"Nearly five years ago."

"Ah, well I suppose that explains it," she said, leaning against the wall and tugging at her gown. My earlier suspicion was confirmed—she was not wearing a corset, and it was quite obvious through the thin silk bodice of her gown. I averted my eyes, though she didn't seem bothered by it. "I left a couple of years before that. Our paths never crossed before, but it's a bit disappointing my reputation doesn't precede me."

"Were you really in a nunnery?" I asked before I could stop myself.

The girl arched a thick black eyebrow. "A nunnery?" she repeated with a very unladylike laugh. "I would rather die. Who told you that?"

I shrugged, feeling my cheeks go warm. "It's what they say when they talk about you. One of the nicer things."

"I can assure you, I didn't go to any nunnery," she said, indignant. "I think I'd prefer the *less* nice things."

"Where were you, then?" I asked her. Cavernous as Camelot was, I could feel it pressing in on me from all sides, and I was hungry for someplace new, even if it was only secondhand.

She gave me an impish smile. "Avalon," she said, as conversationally as she might have if she were taking a holiday in the south. I, on the other hand, couldn't hide my surprise, which made her laugh again. "I'm only back for a few days, for my birthday," she added before hesitating. "*Our* birthday, I suppose, Morgause's and mine. Uther really wanted Arthur back, of course. I am merely a compromise. But you didn't answer my question."

"I didn't?"

"Who are you?" she repeated.

"Oh. Elaine," I said before remembering myself. I dropped into a shallow curtsy, wobbling slightly as I rose. I could hear my mother's admonishment in my head—*spine straight, head level, gracefully!*—but my body always seemed to have other ideas.

"Very well done," she said, and though I didn't think she was being sincere, I also didn't feel like she was laughing at me. She was laughing *with* me, like there was a joke between us. I laughed, too, even though I'd missed whatever joke there might have been.

She dipped into her own curtsy, somehow both brief and deep. I wasn't sure how she managed it without falling over. "I'm Morgana," she said before straightening up once more. "Morgause is being troublesome, you said? She's always been like that."

I frowned. It wasn't that I was unfamiliar with Morgause's cruelty, but Morgana wasn't like me. Even then, I didn't have the impression that she was someone to be easily bullied. "Like what?" I asked.

Morgana hesitated for a moment, something dark flitting across her expression before disappearing just as quickly as it came about.

"When we were children, she would lock me in closets until our nanny came looking for me. Sometimes it took hours and I would sit there in that dark, cramped space, crying and afraid." She turned over her left hand so that I could see the puckered skin of a thick scar slicing across the skin of her palm, all the way from the heel of her hand to the first knuckle of her smallest finger. "And when we were six," she continued, tracing the scar with her finger, "she was angry with me for eating the last piece of cinnamon cake at dinner, so she bided her time and waited until we were out in the meadow and our nanny

turned her back. Then she took a sharp rock and dragged it across my palm."
She closed her hand over her palm, making the scar disappear. "She used to
terrify me."

"She still terrifies me," I told her.

Morgana wavered for a second. "What you need to understand about Morgause is that she doesn't like people she considers to be different. She used to
hate me for it."

"Used to?"

She shrugged. "Now that I've been away for a while, I've realized that
Morgause hated me because she feared me. So now, I've decided to make sure
she is too busy fearing me to remember to hate me."

"Why would she be afraid of you?"

Though Morgause was terrifying, there was something about Morgana
that I liked, even then, before I knew more about her than a name and a scar.
She intimidated me, I couldn't deny that, but I wasn't afraid of her, certainly
not in the same way that I was afraid of Morgause.

Morgana didn't answer right away. Instead, her eyes slid to the tapestry,
and she tilted her head to one side thoughtfully. "Are you particularly fond
of this?"

I looked down at the tapestry I'd spent the last month working on and
realized that I wasn't. It was well made enough, but when I looked at it, all I
saw was the hours of silent sewing I'd done while the other girls talked and
laughed among themselves. To me, the tapestry just looked like loneliness.

"It isn't for me, it's for Prince Arthur," I said instead of answering. It was
the expected answer, and the correct one, but Morgana only laughed.

"And Arthur will be mortified if he ever sees it," she scoffed, still staring
hard at the tapestry. "You would be better off giving him a book or an ancient
scroll if you want to endear yourself to him. You do know that the unicorn is
symbolic of a woman's virginity, don't you?"

"Virtue, I thought," I said.

She gave a rude snort. "I suppose *virtue* is the term used in polite conversation, so that well-bred men can pretend they aren't concerned explicitly with
what goes on between a girl's legs. I would hate to destroy your illusions, but

no one particularly cares about how virtuous your heart is. They care about how virtuous your body is, and the better term for *that* is *virginity*." She didn't wait for me to answer, instead plowing forward as she paced around the table, letting her fingers run over the stitches. "So . . . if the unicorn is for virginity, what can we make of this gallant young knight—meant to be Arthur, I suppose, though he isn't nearly so tall—riding the unicorn?"

It took a moment for her meaning to make sense, but when it did, embarrassment clawed over my skin, and I could feel my neck and cheeks flush. I looked around the room to make sure there was no one to hear her speaking so bawdily.

"At least you aren't so naive that you don't know what I'm speaking of," she said with a laugh, though she didn't so much as glance at me. All her attention was focused on the tapestry. She circled it like a wolf stalking its prey.

I followed her intent gaze and noticed a thin spiral of smoke coming from the center where the unicorn's horn was. At first, I thought it was only a trick of the light, but it began to grow quickly, thicker and thicker. I still remember the moment I realized what was happening, like a fog clearing before my eyes, leaving only one possible explanation: magic. Morgana was using magic.

As soon as I realized, I could suddenly taste it in the air—the faint scent I would later come to recognize always accompanied Morgana's magic, one best described as jasmine and fresh-sliced oranges.

It would be what I smelled when she brewed a potion to help Guinevere focus, when she fixed Arthur's favorite book after he'd read it to pieces, when she sent a gust of wind to knock Lancelot off balance mid-joust because he was getting a little too full of himself. It is what I will smell in the future as well, when she brews the potion to kill Arthur, on countless other nights to come.

There was a quiet but distinct pop, and a small flame appeared. I jumped back and gave an involuntary shriek, turning to Morgana, who was watching the flame with a mild interest as it grew bigger, spreading slowly over the unicorn's head.

"Did you . . . ?" I started to ask, but I couldn't find the words to finish the thought out loud.

Magic had been outlawed in Albion since the end of the Fay War, when I was just a baby. I'd heard stories of it, told in hushed whispers, as if even speaking of it could get a person executed, but I had never seen it myself. The only person who was allowed to perform magic in the country was the king's sorcerer, Merlin, and his power was reserved for the king himself, to keep peace. Never for show.

But Morgana had summoned flame as easily as she exhaled, as if the magic and the flame were an integral part of herself, a part that couldn't be smothered or ignored. As if the small act wasn't a death sentence for her, should anyone find out, but as if it were the only thing keeping her alive.

"You'll want to run along home, Elaine," Morgana said, pulling me out of my shock. "It's safe to say that your little sewing circle is off for today, and you don't want to be lingering about looking suspicious when it starts to spread, do you?"

By THAT EVENING, Morgana was the only topic of conversation. When I took my nightly walk through the castle to stretch my legs, I heard her name whispered by everyone I passed, spoken with the same tone I've heard people use when discussing the rats that were rampant in the streets or the plagues that swept through the countryside every couple of years.

"I heard she was spotted coming out of the east wing just a moment before the drawing room caught fire," Duchess Lancaster murmured to her husband, the corners of her pinched mouth turned down in a permanent frown.

"They say she set fire to the nunnery as well," the Earl of Bernswick said to his companion, Lord Newtrastle. "That was how she escaped."

"The abbess was found with a letter opener through her heart," Lord Newtrastle replied, his eyes glinting. "Of course, no one can prove Lady Morgana had anything to do with it, but . . ."

"*I* heard she did away with Prince Arthur," a girl younger than me said, the daughter of some lord I couldn't quite remember the name of. "She wants the throne for herself—as if *that* would ever happen."

That, it seemed, was a rumor too far, because her older sister pinched her arm hard, eliciting a yelp of pain from the girl.

"Don't make up rumors, Lewella," the older girl snapped. "If she killed Prince Arthur, do you really think the king would want her here?"

Lewella rubbed her arm, scowling at her sister. "He would if he didn't want anyone to know the prince was dead," she replied.

"Hush, before I tell Mother you were spreading lies."

But as the rumors spun wilder and wilder, painting a portrait of a monster in an uncorseted gown, I couldn't forget the Morgana I'd met. Ferocious and intimidating, yes, but just a girl. At the time, I didn't understand why they were so angry, so vicious toward someone they didn't know the first thing about, but now I know—there was nothing more terrifying in Camelot than a girl who refused to follow the rules.

I rounded the corner, ready to start back to the tower for dinner with my mother, when I nearly walked into a couple walking arm in arm.

The boy I didn't recognize at the time, though later, his face would haunt my nightmares—both the ones that might come true and the ones that were only dreams. He was tall with a sharply angled face and a hooked nose, with close-cropped sand-colored hair and gray eyes that glinted like cold steel. I couldn't explain it then, but when his eyes met mine, I felt a chill all over my skin that I couldn't get rid of. I was so distracted that it took me a moment to notice the girl next to him.

This time, I was sure it was Morgause. There was no mistaking her scowl, or the way she held herself, like there was a heavy crown resting on top of her pinned-back black hair that she couldn't let fall.

"Elaine the Mad," she said, drawing out my name in a long purr that somehow sounded like a threat to my ears. Of course, everything Morgause said had the sound of a threat to me.

"Lady Morgause," I said, trying to step around them, but she moved so that she was standing just in front of me.

"How fortuitous," she said. "We were just speaking of you."

Anything that was fortuitous for Morgause certainly wouldn't be for me, but I forced a smile and steeled myself, waiting for the inevitable attack.

"Oh?" I said.

Morgause glanced at her companion, then back at me. "Rumor has it that you were in the east wing when my sister set that fire," she said, choosing her words carefully. "In fact, I've heard it said that you came out of the room just before the smoke was spotted."

I forced a laugh, but even to my own ears it rang false. "I don't know anything about that," I told her. "I was on my way to the sewing circle when I was told about the fire. I don't even think I made it to the east wing."

I'd practiced the lie dozens of times over the course of the day, playing it over and over in my mind. But somehow, it still didn't sound convincing.

"You're a terrible liar," Morgause said before her expression softened into a smile. I'd seen her cruel smiles before, with bared teeth that might have resembled fangs. I'd seen her tight-lipped smirks. But I'd never seen a smile like that from her. At first glance, it almost might have seemed sympathetic.

"She's a wretched creature, isn't she?" she asked, dropping her voice to a murmur. "I don't blame you for being frightened of her. But if you tell us what really happened, we can see to it that she pays for her crime."

Her crime. Yes, starting a fire was a crime, of course, but the weight in Morgause's voice made me sure that wasn't all she was talking about. She knew about Morgana's magic. She knew, and she would see her sister die for it. A shudder coursed its way down my spine.

I was tempted to tell her exactly what she wanted to hear—more tempted than I'm proud to admit. It would have been the right thing, wouldn't it, to simply tell the truth? Magic was outlawed for a reason, it was dangerous, *Morgana* was dangerous. The laws we lived by said that what she'd done was a crime punishable by death. Who was I to say otherwise? And if telling the truth earned me kindness from Morgause, if it made her a little less cruel to me, why shouldn't I do it?

But Morgana had been kind to me when she had no reason to be. She might have been guilty of using fay magic, and of arson besides, but I couldn't believe she deserved death. Especially not when the same might have been said of me. I couldn't bring myself to offer her up to Morgause for a few words of kindness, with hooks lurking just beneath.

"I don't know what you're talking about, Morgause," I said. I had to force myself to meet her eyes, not to wither beneath her gaze like a thirsty fern. I imagined how Morgana would say the words, how she would hold her own next to her sister.

For a moment, Morgause only stared at me, her eyes narrowed and mouth twisted. Eventually, she tore her gaze away and turned to her companion.

"I told you she was a loon, Mordred," she said with a heavy sigh. "But *someone* must have seen it."

It was the first time I heard his name. Mordred. In time I would learn he was the king's bastard son, that he had a thirst for power that rivaled even Morgause's. I would learn that even then, as a youth, he was courting favor in the castle, promising things he had no business promising, making allies out of those who would scorn him. Later, I would learn to fear him, to see the ruin he trailed behind him, the threat he posed not just to me but to everyone I loved, but that day I was only wary, as I was of anyone in Morgause's company.

He watched me for a moment more, his own gray eyes thoughtful. "Perhaps you're right," he said slowly. "Whatever the case may be, she'll be gone before long."

They continued on past me, leaving me alone in the corridor, but even when they were out of earshot, I still heard Mordred's voice in my mind.

*She'll be gone before long.*

It was a fact, plain and simple, one Morgana had said herself. She was here for only a few days and then she'd be gone. She was even looking forward to it. But the way Mordred had said those words sounded like a threat. They worked their way under my skin until I could think of little else.

# 5

MORGANA TAKES THE news the hardest that night, when Nimue sits us down in her room after dinner. Even Arthur, the father he barely knew dead, doesn't carry on as dramatically as she does. But Morgana isn't mourning Uther—I doubt she'll spare him another thought. She's mourning Avalon, the only place she's ever called home, the place she once told me she wouldn't leave even after her body had turned cold.

"I won't go," she tells Nimue now, her violet eyes hard and defiant. Though she's nearly twenty-five, she could practically pass for a child again now, on the cusp of a temper tantrum. But beneath that bravado, there's something else that I understand all too well: fear.

I remember the way they treated her in Camelot before, the way they hated her because they didn't understand her. I thought it didn't bother her then, the whispers and sideways glances, the wide berth everyone gave her, as if they thought even the air around her were lethal, but maybe I just didn't know how to read her then.

"Avalon is my home," she continues, each word hardened to steel. "The Maiden, Mother, and Crone brought me here, and I belong on this island as much as anyone."

Nimue remains unfazed by her outburst. I suppose she's used to them by now. She's seen Morgana—seen us all—through childhood, through adolescence.

Even if she weren't an oracle, I doubt there is much any of us could do at this point to surprise her. I remember my mother, had thirteen years with her, but the others have been under Nimue's care since they were young children. To them, I imagine she's the closest thing to a mother they have.

"Until the Maiden, Mother, and Crone decide to walk among us once more, it is up to me as Lady of the Lake to carry out their wishes as I see fit," she reminds Morgana, patient but tired. She rubs her temples and leans back in her armchair. "Would you like some tea to soothe your mind?"

"No, I would not like *tea*," Morgana snaps. "I would *like* an explanation."

Nimue's eyes flit to me for only an instant before darting back to Morgana. "I have given that to you twice already, but what's once more?" she says with a heavy sigh. "Arthur is king of Camelot now." She nods toward Arthur, sitting in silence beside Guinevere.

He hasn't said a word since Nimue started speaking, since she told him his father was dead. Looking at him now, he doesn't look like a king. He looks like a boy who has just felt the earth shift beneath his feet and is no longer sure of anything. He is twenty-three now—not a boy any longer, not even the youngest king Camelot has had—but it's difficult not to think of him as the boy I met half a lifetime ago.

Beside him, Guinevere has his hand folded between both of hers. She usually isn't one for affectionate gestures, but that makes it all the more meaningful. I don't doubt she would do the same for any of us if we truly needed her, but there is an unspoken undercurrent to anything that passes between her and Arthur, as if they exist with one foot in this world and the other in a plane just big enough for the two of them.

Nimue continues. "He'll return to Camelot to claim his throne and rule there, and all of you will have to go with him."

I keep my eyes on Arthur while she speaks, while she outlines a future that he has always known will one day be his. His expression barely changes, but I know him well enough to see the flicker of uncertainty in his amber eyes. A good thing, I think. It means that he understands the weight of the burden he is shouldering. It means that he will not wear the crown lightly.

"Why?" Morgana asks, her voice breaking over the word. I tear my gaze away from Arthur to look at her instead, and there is no uncertainty there, just anger and fear. Even though they are half siblings, they couldn't look more different. Where Arthur is pale and russet-haired, with broad shoulders and long limbs that haven't quite lost their adolescent awkwardness, Morgana is lithe and graceful, with hair as dark as the moonless sky and skin the color of burnished bronze. The only similarities between them are their smiles and the freckles dusted over their noses and cheeks.

"I can stay here, help him from afar. I'm sure I would be of more use here than at court," Morgana continues.

Though I don't say anything, I agree with her. Especially knowing what Nimue and I do about her and Arthur's relationship, how everything we've seen shows it being the first to fracture, how it leads to everything else. I don't know why Nimue is so insistent on sending her back to Camelot. She could keep her here, happy and out of trouble. But I'm not foolish enough to believe that Nimue tells me everything she knows. I am a part of this web, my future as tangled with theirs as Morgana's, and she has every reason to keep things from me, for the same reason that I keep some visions from her.

It is a dangerous thing, to know too much of your future. Nimue told me that once. It has driven many oracles mad, stuck between the present and future and unable to take a step in any direction.

"It's what the Maiden, Mother, and Crone believe is best," Nimue says, her voice even and placid.

"Oh, they told you that, did they?" Morgana snaps.

Nimue ignores her, instead turning to Guinevere and Arthur. "You two have been quiet," she says. "But it's your future we are discussing, as much as it is Morgana's. Surely you have your own concerns."

Arthur is still too lost in his thoughts to speak, but Gwen looks up at Nimue, her green eyes pensive.

"Will I go home first?" she asks. Though she's spent most of her life on Avalon, she never lost her Lyonessian accent, the hard lilt of her vowels, the soft consonants. "I haven't seen my father in fifteen years."

I haven't seen my family since I came to Avalon, either, but unlike Guinevere, the thought of seeing them again fills me with more wariness than longing.

"You will go back to Lyonesse, Guinevere," Nimue says. "The betrothal between you and Arthur will need to be solidified by your respective countries. Once it's settled, you'll join him in Camelot. It shouldn't be long—a month, maybe two."

Gwen nods, relief flitting over her expression. She squeezes Arthur's hand tightly in her own, but he barely seems to feel it.

Finally, he looks up at Nimue. "When do we leave?" he asks her. His voice doesn't sound like his own. It is a hollow thing that cracks and echoes.

"Tomorrow morning, before dawn," she says, looking between all of us. "There are reports that several nobles are already making plays for your throne—your bastard brother chief among them."

She doesn't say his name, but I hear it all the same. *Mordred.* Though I met him only once, I've seen enough of his future that the mere mention of him crawls over my skin like the fingers of a cold shadow, raising goose bumps in their wake. "We received word that he's married Morgause, which will only strengthen his claim. It's important you act quickly."

I look to Morgana, searching for some reaction to the mention of her sister, but she gives nothing away. Her thoughts are sealed behind the seething thundercloud of her rage.

"If you make me leave," she tells Nimue, biting each word out, "I'll never forgive you. I'll hate you for it until I draw my last breath."

Vicious as the words may be, they slide off Nimue's back like water from a duck's wing. Maybe because she's heard them before, maybe because she's already come to terms with how true they are.

"You'll understand one day," she says, though I'm not sure she truly believes that.

Then she turns and leaves us alone. The door behind her closes firmly, decisively, but not quite with a slam—slamming doors and shouting and any kind of spectacle is strictly human behavior, after all, and Nimue would never indulge such a base impulse.

"Did you know?" Morgana asks me when she's gone. I feel guilty before realizing she's not asking if Nimue confided in me first. Her voice is tentative, like she's asking something forbidden. She's asking if I Saw it.

"No," I tell her honestly.

For a moment, she stares at me and I think she might push the issue, but instead she only nods.

"I can't go back there, Elaine," she says quietly, her words only for me.

And they are, because I am the only one who truly understands what she's saying. Gwen and Arthur will adjust well to the world outside of Avalon. They are personable and easy to like, and they get on well with pretty much anyone. Morgana and I don't, for very different reasons.

We are, as my father once said about me when I was young, acquired tastes.

I take her hand in mine and squeeze it hard, but I can't form any words of reassurance. She would see right through them. And besides, I don't think she really wants to be reassured.

"I'll be there too," I say instead. "So will Arthur and Gwen. You won't be alone."

Her expression remains taut and troubled, but she squeezes my hand back.

Arthur stands up abruptly, and in that instant, I see the torment in him plain as the moon shining through the window. He looks adrift.

"I don't know how to be a king," he says, shaking his head.

"You won't be alone either," I tell him. "You'll have us."

He nods slowly, turning the words over in his mind. I can see the gears spinning, like the mechanism that brings up a drawbridge.

"We have to tell Lance," he says suddenly. "He doesn't know yet. He should know."

I don't say anything in response to that. I've Seen Lancelot in Camelot, but as with most things, the timeline is murky, hinging on choices that have yet to be made—I don't know if he gets there at the same time as we do or not for years. A small, ugly part of me hopes he never comes at all because it would be so much easier for me if he doesn't. But I know that he's needed there, as much as any of us.

O NE DAY, A couple of days after she'd set the tapestry on fire, I came downstairs from my room to find Morgana alone in the sitting room, standing by the unlit fireplace, dressed in a lilac silk gown that hugged her figure but belled out around her knees and elbows. I couldn't find a single gem on it, unlike Morgause's dresses. Even though it likely had been made for her by the royal seamstress, she looked uncomfortable in it, fiddling with the only adornment she wore—a large, circular black diamond that hung around her neck on a plain gold chain.

"What are you doing here?" I blurted out before my thoughts could catch up with me. I never had visitors in the tower, but I imagined she should have been announced or sent word, not simply appeared in the sitting room like a specter.

She glanced up when she saw me, and a slow smile spread across her bloodred painted lips.

"You're a hard girl to track down, Elaine Astolat," she said, rather than answering my question. "Did you know that there are six Elaines at court in Camelot?"

I had never counted them myself, but the number sounded right.

"How did you get in here?" I asked again, sitting down in the velvet high-backed armchair. I could still smell the sweet smoke that had clung to it since my father's last visit.

She sunk down into the matching chaise across from me, primly crossing her ankles, though the ladylike effect was ruined when she slouched against the arm, propping her head up on her bent elbow.

"It turns out being the stepdaughter of the king gets you just about any-where," Morgana said with a shrug. "I deduced fairly quickly that you weren't Elaine the Old. Then there was talk of Elaine the Sour-Faced, which I also assumed not to be you. A little more narrowing down and I realized you must be Elaine the Mad."

Heat rose to my cheeks, though it wasn't the first time I had heard it said. With Morgana, though, there wasn't a trace of the malice that usually accom-panied the name, or any apology for that matter. When she saw my expression, her dramatic eyebrows arced even higher. "I'm sorry, I'd gathered it was an old epithet."

"It is," I admitted before pausing. "Did anyone tell you where it came from?"

Even now, I can't explain why I said it, why I offered up that part of myself to a stranger. I think perhaps the name bothered me more than I let on, even to myself. I think maybe I knew, even then, that the truth of it wouldn't scare her, that she might even prefer it to the more demure lies my mother had covered it up with.

"I overheard different tales," she admitted, her eyes on me, appraising. "Each more ridiculous than the last. But you've heard what they say about me by now. Morgana the Evil, Dark Morgana—"

"Morgana the Fay," I supplied before I could stop myself.

She looked surprised for a second before her mouth curved into a wide grin. "Yes, I'm quite fond of that one, you know. I certainly prefer it to the nun-nery story."

"Is it true, then?" I asked. I wasn't sure where the boldness was coming from. Maybe hers was contagious.

"Are you truly Elaine the Mad?" she replied.

There it was. The question I'd been waiting for. I thought back to the night I'd gone screaming through the corridors. Years had passed, but I could still feel the cold stone floor under my bare feet like it had happened the night before, could still feel my throat raw and hoarse from screaming. And then there had been the other nights, nights when I woke up drenched in icy sweat without a memory of what I'd dreamt. Other nights when I'd dreamt of drowning.

"Yes," I said after a moment. "I suppose I am."

"Well then," she replied, sitting up a little straighter. Her red mouth curved into a grin as dangerous as a knife's blade. "Tell me about it."

THE ONLY OTHER person I'd ever told about what I'd dreamt that night was my mother, after she brought me back to my room and tucked me into bed. It wasn't the first dream I'd had that felt real, but when I woke from a drowning dream, all I could remember was a feeling. This dream, I remembered every detail of. I rattled them off to my mother, who listened in stoic silence. Her face had turned ashen by the time I was done, but she forced her mouth into a strained smile before kissing my forehead, her lips icy against my skin. Then she pulled back a couple of inches to fix me with the sternest look I'd ever seen from her.

"You must never tell anyone what you just told me," she had said, her labored expression betraying her soft voice.

"But shouldn't someone warn the king?" I had asked her, thinking of the queen's face as I'd seen it in my dream, lovely as always but pale with a sheen of green to her skin and angry red slashes of color over her cheekbones. I had known, deep in the pit of my stomach, that she was mere breaths from death. It was only a dream, I knew that now that I was fully awake and back, safe in my own bed, but it hadn't felt like a dream. It had felt the way my dreams about water felt—like a memory, which was impossible.

"And say what?" my mother had asked. "That the queen will become ill? How do you think he would respond to that, Elaine?"

I had to think for a moment. I had spent the last eleven years of my life being told that honesty was the best course of action, but suddenly my mother was contradicting that, and I didn't understand why. But that wasn't the answer she was looking for, so I tried to think of an alternative.

"He might suppose it was my fault?" I said slowly. "That I had made it happen, somehow? That I had magic?"

The last word came out in a whisper, so dangerous that I half expected armed men to leap out from the shadows of my bedroom to arrest me for merely speaking it. My mother seemed shaken by it as well. She didn't speak for a long moment, but I knew by her expression that I was right.

"The past has not been kind to oracles," she told me finally, her voice fragile. "Even before the Fay War, when other types of magic were commonplace and unrestrained."

"Oracles?" I asked, unfamiliar with the word.

"It is an old term for those with a sight that allows them to glimpse beyond the present and into the future. You come from a long line. With some of us, it manifests itself as subtly as a strong intuition. The rest of us are not so lucky."

"I think it's happened before," I told her.

Pieces I didn't realize I had were falling into place to form a picture I could only barely make out. A strange sense of having seen something before, been somewhere before, met someone before. Our tower at the castle, for instance. When my mother had brought me there for the first time just before my birthday, I was certain I'd been there before. Upon seeing my room, I'd found it suddenly hard to breathe, and tears welled up behind my eyes, though I hadn't been able to explain why.

I opened my mouth to tell her about all of it, but her cold index finger came to rest against my lips again.

"Hush," she said, her voice managing to be both soothing and barbed with a threat. "Elaine, I need you to listen to me very carefully. You mustn't speak of this ever again, not to anyone, not even to me. If they discover what you are, they will try to use you, and when they realize that nothing they do will make any difference, they will blame you. I have seen it happen before, and I will not see it happen to you. Do you understand?"

With her finger still pressed against my mouth, I could only nod, though

I *didn't* understand. These visions were a kind of magic—if anyone found out, they wouldn't use me or blame me or any of that. They would kill me.

Her smile softened and she drew her hand back, going to the pocket of her nightdress, from which she pulled a vial the size of my forearm. She pressed it into my open hand.

"From now on, every night before you go to bed, you will take a sip and it will keep your Sight at bay. It will keep you sane, just like every other girl. Do you understand?"

I didn't, but again that seemed like the wrong answer, so again I nodded. She smiled, satisfied, before standing up and starting toward the door.

"Mother." She didn't turn back to look at me, but she did linger. "Is it going to come true? What I saw of the queen?"

"Yes," she said after a few strained seconds. "I'm afraid it will, though I don't know when or what the illness might be."

"But . . . then shouldn't we try to change things?" I liked the queen. I had met her only a couple of times, but she had a soft voice that sounded like honey and a kind smile. I didn't want her to die.

She gave a heavy sigh, still not turning to look at me. When she spoke, I thought I heard tears in her voice. "By the time you See things, they are already too far gone to change."

I'll never be sure if she was lying to me or if she was simply telling me the truth as she knew it. My mother and her mother and her mother before her had smothered their visions, not tried to use them, to understand them, to try to manipulate them. They hadn't had Nimue to explain what a vision was, how some were solid as stone, yes, but others were always changing, like the tides of the sea.

Either way, I suppose it doesn't matter. I believed her all the same.

"Take your medicine, Elaine, and try to sleep," she told me. "Things will seem better in the morning."

It had been more than two years since that night, but things never had managed to seem better. My mother refused to speak of it ever again, even after the queen did die, just as I had foreseen. And in the two years after that night, I'd kept my promise. I hadn't told a soul the truth, even after they'd all started calling me mad. I did exactly as my mother told me, taking a sip from the bottle each night and telling her when I ran low.

I had always done everything my mother told me to do.

Until I didn't. Until I broke my promise and told Morgana everything.

WE HAVE ORACLES on Avalon," Morgana said when I finished, her tone far more casual than I expected. There I was confessing the moment my world had turned inside out, and she was reacting as simply as if discussing the behavior of an odd but harmless neighbor, a curiosity rather than a curse.

"Only a couple, though. It's a rare gift," she continued. "Was that the first time you had your monthly blood as well?"

The question took me aback, and I could feel my cheeks heat up. I nodded. "A day or two later," I admitted. I remembered a pale pink dress, a luncheon, my stomach cramping so terribly I thought I'd eaten something rotten, the dampness on my thighs I'd mistaken for sweat, getting up to excuse myself only to hear the entire room burst into laughter at the blotch of red that had ruined my skirt.

"They tend to start around the same time. It was the same with me and my magic. Have you noticed any changes in your visions since? Depending on where in your cycle you are?" she asked without so much as a twitch of discomfort.

I shrugged my shoulders. "Perhaps? It's hard to say. The medicine stops them for the most part, just as my mother said, though now that you mention it, I suppose my sleep is always more restless around then. I assumed it was only the pain." For a second, I'd considered telling her about my dreams of drowning, how those, too, got worse around the time of my monthly blood, but I couldn't make my mouth form the words. Saying it out loud would have given the nightmare even more power, and I didn't want that.

"And you actually take the medicine?" she asked, looking truly alarmed for the first time. "Every night?"

I frowned. "My mother said it was important."

She leaned forward. "But weren't you ever curious? What if you saw that you were going to fall down the stairs and break your neck tomorrow?"

"But my mother said—"

"Yes, I know what your mother said." Morgana gave a loud and dramatic sigh, shaking her head. "But she doesn't know everything, does she?"

It was a new concept for me. Before that moment, I had never considered the fact that my mother might not know everything. Wasn't that why she had so many rules, why she always seemed so cautious? Because she knew things that I didn't?

"You don't do everything your mother tells you, do you?" Morgana continued, reading my expression. It was an innocuous enough question, but I remember how the corners of her mouth quirked up, in a way that was almost taunting. I remember the question feeling like a challenge.

"Didn't you?" I asked before I could stop myself. After telling that story, the queen was fresh in my mind.

Morgana didn't lose her smile, but her eyes narrowed. When she spoke, her voice was level and calm.

"Ygraine was Morgause's mother, and Arthur's, and she was a wonderful mother to them. But she never really felt like mine. Morgause was always her favorite—she took no pains to hide that fact. And it was just as well since I was my father's favorite, at least for the year we were on this earth together. Or so I've been told—I can't remember him myself. You probably haven't heard much about him. No one likes to remember the losers when a war is done.

"My father loved me best because he knew I had his blood in my veins," she said. "My mother was afraid of me, though, for the same reason everyone else in this damned place is. And for the same reason they're afraid of you." She inclined her head toward me, taking me by surprise.

"No one's afraid of me," I said, unable to keep from laughing at the thought. "They laugh at me behind my back and call me names and—"

"And why do you think they do that?" she interrupted. "They do those things because they know that you are different. They knew it that night, and they know it now, even with your mother's potion keeping you caged and docile. You are different and it terrifies them, so they try to push you down and keep you small and manageable. They know that if they keep you huddling in your corner, you will never stand to your full height. They know that if you ever do, you'll be great enough to ruin them."

She seemed so certain of me, even then when we were little more than strangers. To this day, I'm not sure why. Whenever I ask her about it, she just shrugs and says she thought I needed her. She was right, but I don't think that's the whole truth. I think that there was a piece of her soul that recognized mine, just as a piece of mine recognized hers. Maybe it was destiny. Maybe it was just that we were both so terribly lonely. Perhaps she needed me too.

"That's not me," I told her. "Surely you've seen that by now."

"What I have seen is a sheltered girl who is so afraid of her own shadow that she won't walk in sunlight, a girl who closes her eyes and takes all the injustices the world pushes on her without a word in response, a girl who does everything her mother tells her to and never questions why." The words pierced me through like well-aimed arrows tipped in poison. I suppose that was how I knew they were true. "I was the same way, before Avalon."

She said the name like a caress, like a solemn promise. That alone was enough to make my stomach clench with a yearning I didn't understand. It was like the way I missed my father and brothers and our home in Shalott. But how could I have felt homesick for a place I had never been?

"You would like it there, Elaine," she continued, looking truly happy for the first time since I met her. "There's an island off the coast of the Great Lake, but you can't see it from shore. You can't see it unless you know it's there, unless you know its secrets. And there are no castles, or towers, only homes built into the branches of the trees and little cottages built into cliffsides. No courts or kings or queens, and you can be free there. You can run through the forest and swim in the lake and the river, and do anything you want and there's no one to tell you no. Well, apart from Nimue, I suppose," she admitted, almost as an afterthought.

"Nimue?" I asked. It's strange to think now that there was a time when Nimue was a stranger to me. That first time I said her name, I stumbled over the strange syllables. *Nim-way.*

Morgana smiled. "She's the only one who understands. She helped me realize what I was capable of, what it was about me that made everyone fear me so much. And she helped me control it. She's the Lady of the Lake." She gave the title the reverence most people used when talking about the king—or even a god.

"I saw what you did with the fire in the tapestry room," I said.

She laughed. "That's the very least of what I'm capable of. It's fay blood—on my father's side," she says. "You must have some on your mother's side, I imagine."

The thought left me flabbergasted. "But I'm not . . . I'm not fay, I'm just . . . me."

She gave me a look that was half exasperation and half pity. "Oh, Elaine. Do you doubt the things I've told you?"

The strangest part was, I didn't doubt them at all. The outlandish, impossible things she had said all felt like things I already knew, deep down somewhere.

"I believe you," I said finally.

"So you see?" she said, leaning forward and taking my hands in hers, squeezing them tight in her grasp. "This is wonderful."

A laugh wrenched its way from me, bitter and hysterical. "How is it wonderful?" I asked her. "Not only am I insane, now I have fay blood? My mother *was* right, if anyone found out—"

"They would kill you," she finished, her expression calm. "They won't, of course, if you keep taking your medicine. You can pass as normal for the rest of your days. The vision incident will blow over eventually, once they realize you aren't a threat to their way of life. You'll be quite pretty someday soon, with a healthy dowry, I'd imagine. You'll make a lovely match. And then you'll have children of your own, maybe a daughter for you to pass your gift on to. And then, one day, you'll teach her to fear it, to stop it with potions and lies. Is that what you want? To become your mother?"

"No," I said, the force of the word surprising me. It didn't feel like my voice, too loud, too harsh.

She smiled, gripping my hands tighter. "Then, you see, it is good that I've found you. Now, you can come back with me to Avalon and meet Arthur, and Lance, and Gwen, and they'll love you right away like I do because you're one of us. There are oracles there who can teach you to control your gift so that it isn't frightening anymore. Isn't that what you want? To belong?" she asked.

It was. The idea of belonging somewhere—of having friends—was dizzying. But as wonderful as it sounded, it wasn't that simple.

"I can't just leave, Morgana," I told her. "My mother is here, and I have my father and brothers to think about. If I just left—"

"They would be fine," she said. "Everyone would think that we became such fast friends that I insisted you come back to Avalon. Uther would have to favor your family quite a lot for that to happen. Your brothers could end up with their own titles and lands if they played their cards right."

"But my mother," I said. "She would know the truth."

"I expect she would puzzle it out, yes."

I knew that my mother, with all her rules, would never understand my choosing to live without them. She was already so fragile a strong gust of wind could shatter her. I would be that wind. And yet . . . I wanted it more than I could put into words: a place where I belonged, where I would have Morgana to talk to and an island full of people who understood me. I didn't want to live in fear that I would make a misstep and bring my entire life to ruin. I didn't want to live where people whispered about me behind my back and made jokes at my expense. I wanted a home, not a lonely tower where I felt more ghost than human. I wanted Avalon so terribly it made my chest ache.

"My mother needs me," I said.

"She's touched in the head, Elaine," Morgana said, her voice surprisingly delicate. "And I wouldn't be surprised if it was that medicine that did it to her. Your power isn't meant to be dulled. Suppressing it can't be healthy. Not for her and not for you."

The thought hadn't occurred to me, but it didn't change anything. But in that brief instant, Morgana saw me hesitate. She found her opening. "Don't take your potion tonight," she said, almost desperately. "I'm leaving in two days, after my birthday banquet. Abstain from your potion until then, and if you still don't want to come with me, I'll understand. But it is an important choice, and you should have all of the information before you make it."

"Morgana—"

"Just promise me that much," she interrupted. "Two nights. Can you do that?"

In hindsight, I don't suppose I had much of a choice. I've never been good at saying no to Morgana.

# 7

I T WILL BE raining so brutally that each drop will feel like a tiny icicle digging
into my skin. A cacophony of waves will crash, pounding against my eardrums.
Every few heartbeats will be punctuated by a clap of thunder. Each time it will
sound like war. Each time it will sound like death. I will run, my bare feet sinking
into the sand with each step until my legs burn with pain, but I will know that I
have to keep running. If I stop for even a second, everything will be lost.

Cliffs will rise up from the shore in front of me—jagged, sharp things full
of nooks and crannies big enough to house entire families. When I get closer,
my eyes will find what they are looking for: a large, broad stone jutting out
over the tumultuous water where a dark, cloaked figure stands over a cauldron,
stirring with a wooden staff. As I get closer, lightning will strike, and I see her
face cast in sharp relief.

"Morgana!" The voice will be mine and yet not mine. Too old, too loud,
too sure. "Morgana, stop!"

If she hears me, she will give no sign of it. She will continue to stir the
cauldron, eyes bright and intent. I will start to climb up to her, scrambling up
the craggy surface of the large rock, scraping my hands and feet until I feel
blood, but still I won't stop. When I pull myself up to her ledge, I will see her
take a piece of white cloth dappled with dark red and drop it into the cauldron
before stirring it again.

"Morgana," I will say again, struggling to catch my breath as I get to my feet. "You can't do this. They are our people."

Her violet eyes will flash over to meet mine, and I will realize with a jolt how old she is—she's aged at least a decade, but her hollowed-out cheeks and sunken eyes will make her look even older.

"No. They aren't," she will say. She will sound like darkness, cold and harsh. Like death itself. She will continue to stir, but there will be tears streaking down her face, and her lips will press into a thin line. Her hands will tremble, but they will not cease their movement. "And if I don't, who will?" She will look up at me, her expression empty. "Will you, El?"

The thought will leave me chilled. I will want to help her, but my hands will stay stuck to my sides as I watch her work. When she pulls out the cloth again, it will be pure white, and I will see that it is, in fact, a shirt. A man's shirt, the kind my father and brothers often wear under their armor when they host jousting tournaments in Shalott. She will throw it to me, and out of instinct I will catch it. It will already be dry, but that won't seem strange to me.

"You might as well make yourself useful, it will be a long night," she will say.

"Tomorrow will be longer," I will warn, but I will oblige and fold the shirt neatly, setting it at my feet.

We will continue in tense silence for a few excruciating moments. It won't be until I feel wetness course down my cheeks that I will realize I am crying as well. Each time thunder strikes and war echoes in my mind, my hands will clench, digging my nails into my palms.

I have to stop it.

I can't stop it.

I am powerless in this.

"How do you do it?" I will ask her, so quietly I don't think she will actually hear me.

But she will and she won't need to ask what I mean.

"I try not to think about it," she will say, her voice hoarse. "I don't think about the names, or the faces. Just the shirts, just the blood, just the cleansing."

I will look at the dozens of piles of shirts left to go, each pile tall as I am and each shirt more red than white. I will feel like I am going to be sick, but I will swallow it down. If I break, Morgana will, too, and then we will both be useless. And we will both be too needed for that. Morgana will be right: There will be a job to do and someone must do it.

Morgana will reach for the pile again and come away with a white shirt that looks, at first, like any of the others. But it won't be.

A foreign, strangled cry will erupt from my throat, and I will launch toward her, trying to grab it out of her hands.

"No," I will say, sobbing as I tug at it, trying to free it from her grip. I will feel the stitches pull, close to breaking. Stitches I will have made with my own hands. "Not him, you can't. Morgana, please. Anyone else."

She will let go of the stick, and both of her arms will come around me, holding me tight against her so that the top of my head will tuck under her chin. Her hand will trace circles on my back.

"Elaine," she will murmur. "It is already decided. You know that."

I will struggle against her, but her grip will be too strong. "You can't take him," I will say, my voice cracking around the words.

"He made his choices," she will say quietly in my ear. "This is where they led him."

Still sobbing, I will clutch the shirt to my chest, and Morgana will clutch me to hers. I will be hollow with loss already; there will be a hole where my heart should be. I won't be able to stand this. I won't. I will have given enough to this world, I will not give him up as well.

THAT WAS THE first vision I had willingly, that night when I kept my mother's potion stoppered and on its shelf, when I fell asleep with Morgana's words echoing in my mind, mingling with thoughts of the image of Avalon she'd painted for me.

I woke up drenched in sweat, grasping for the potion, desperate for oblivion again, desperate to drive that image of Morgana, of the dark cliffside, of my own desperate anguish from my mind.

But I didn't take the potion. Instead, I stood there in my nightgown, my sweat-drenched hair plastered to my forehead and my heart thundering in my chest. The bottle was grasped in my white-knuckled hand while a war raged inside me, until I finally forced myself to place the bottle back on the shelf.

By the time I crawled back into my bed, my decision had been made. I knew that I would go to Avalon, no matter how my mother felt about it. The path was decided.

I think about that again now as I walk through the woods with Morgana. Arthur and Gwen have run ahead, looking for Lancelot. I'm sure they are both sad to be leaving Avalon, but they're excited as well. Excited for new lands, for new adventures, for their lives to truly begin out in the wild, unknown world.

Morgana isn't excited, though, and having seen what those adventures bring, what that world does to us, I can't bring myself to be excited either.

"Will we come back, Elaine?" Morgana asks me after a moment. She's hesitant, wary—as she should be. She knows by now not to ask me about my visions, how dangerous it is to know what your future holds. She remembers, as I do, what happened the last time I shared what I'd Seen.

I press my lips together and don't look at her. If I do, I fear I'll see the Morgana from my cliff vision, with her spectral eyes and gaunt face and a voice like death itself.

My mother was wrong about visions—they can change. Nimue told me so. She explained to me how visions shifted and changed over time, how the future was molded by choices, how the more a vision shifts, the less solid it is.

But that's the thing—my vision of us on the cliffside has never changed. I've seen it dozens of times by now, the same scene, over and over again, exactly the same down to the rhythm of my breath. Solid as the ground beneath my feet.

"Yes," I tell Morgana. "We'll come back."

I don't tell her any more. I don't tell her that when we do return to Avalon, we will no longer be ourselves. That the humanity she has now, the humanity that makes her who she is, will be long gone.

8

I SAW LANCELOT BEFORE I met him, though that vision was cloudy and incomplete—a product of an act of violence and twisted love I never expected. Some nights, I still feel her cold hand at my throat, feel her other hand forcing the mouth of the potion bottle between my lips. I wake up sputtering and unable to breathe, like I'm choking on bile. On nights like that, I almost wish for a drowning vision, to be haunted by the future instead of the past.

But I'm getting ahead of myself now.

ONE DAY, NOT long after I'd arrived in Avalon, I found myself alone with Lancelot for the first time, trekking through the woods at the northern edge of the island, a place I hadn't yet explored. The others had been called off to lessons, but as I would find out, Lancelot's lessons had ended the summer before. He was fifteen, and the fey had decided there was nothing more for him to learn that he couldn't teach himself.

Most mornings, he was up before dawn, running or riding his horse or practicing sword fighting. And even as the day went on, it seemed he was always moving, always training, always striving toward something I couldn't begin to fathom.

After we wound through the trees for almost half an hour in silence, the sound of rushing water started to underscore the birdsong, and soon a river came into sight, weaving through the forest. Some parts were shallow enough to be only ankle deep, water dancing over smooth stones that lined the bottom. As we followed it farther up, though, it appeared to get deeper, going from crystal clear to a more ominous ink blue, its depths obscured.

I heard the waterfall before I saw it, the unending sound of crashing water that tied my stomach into knots. The tightly wooded forest opened up into a field of pale purple flowers. The smell of them hit me before I could identify them by sight—lavender. I breathed deeply, the scent draping over me like a warm blanket. As we waded through the meadow, the flowers brushed at my bare calves, making them itch, but I forgot that altogether when the waterfall came into sight.

The water cascaded down over the craggy side of the mountain on the far side of the meadow in a pure wash of aquamarine, glittering in the midmorning sun in a way that I recognized even then wasn't strictly magical but didn't look quite real either. It was too blue, too pure, a color that almost seemed unnaturally pigmented, but wasn't. It was nature, pure and distilled.

There was a small pond at the bottom of the waterfall that gave birth to a stream disappearing into the woods we'd just come from. Though the water crashed violently in my ears, bringing up memories of visions, I somehow knew there was nothing to fear there—the water was different than in my visions, too bright and open to be the same place. Still, I hung back when Lancelot walked up to the bank, shucking his shoes and sitting down at the edge to dangle his feet in.

I suppose he did know I was there in the end, because he looked back at me over his shoulder, eyebrows raised.

"Everything alright?"

I must have nodded a little too quickly for it to be convincing. "I think I'll stay back here. The flowers are lovely," I said.

He gave a snort and rolled his eyes. "*The flowers are lovely*," he echoed. "Does everyone talk like that on the mainland?"

"Like what?" I asked, frowning.

"Like they're trying to fill the space without saying anything meaningful," he said. "You say, *The flowers are lovely*, when what you mean is *I'm too scared to get any closer to the water*."

"I'm not . . ." I started, but trailed off, my cheeks growing hot. "How did you know?"

"Your heartbeat sped up as soon as we got close, and your breathing became more shallow. Both are classic signs of fear."

I took an involuntary step back. "You can hear my heartbeat and breathing from all the way over there?"

He shrugged his shoulders. "Fay gift," he said, as if this were commonplace. I hadn't been on Avalon long enough to realize it was. "Do they not have water in Albion either?"

"We have water," I said, surprised at how snappish it came out. He was right, I realized. My heart was racing and my breathing was short. It made it harder to focus and harder to hold on to my composure. "Albion has water and trees and mountains and everything else you can find here. And if you must know, we don't talk to try to fill the space. It's called polite conversation, and you could benefit from learning the art of it yourself."

I regretted the words as soon as I said them, but if he was offended, he didn't show it. Instead, he shook his head, an irritating smirk tugging at his lips.

"You won't drown in the water here, if that's what you're afraid of," he told me after a moment. "Even if you can't swim, the water will just spit you back out onto shore. I've seen it happen before to children who swim too deep."

"I'm not worried about drowning here," I told him, but I didn't go into any more detail, and he didn't seem to expect me to.

He looked, for a moment, like he wanted to push the matter, but finally he nodded. "Do you miss it? Albion?"

In the week that I'd known him, he'd never asked me anything, at least nothing so genuine. I didn't realize until that moment that he had only ever asked questions he already knew the answer to.

"In some ways, I suppose I do," I told him after a moment. "But I never really belonged in Albion. It was . . . it was like wearing shoes that didn't fit right. They looked perfectly fine, but they pinched my toes and rubbed my heels raw until it hurt to even move. On other people, they fit perfectly. Just not me."

The confession felt like surrendering something, like handing him a knife to turn back on me.

"You don't feel that way here?" he asked.

"No," I admitted. "It's only been a week, but I already feel more at home here than I ever did in Albion."

For one brief moment, I thought we'd come to an understanding, the kind I'd found with the others but still eluded me with him. He looked at me for a long beat like he saw straight through to my soul.

And then he laughed, the sound of it cruel and sharp enough to cut through my bones.

"You don't belong here," he told me. "This isn't your home. You're a visitor here, just passing through. Eventually, you'll go home with enough wild stories to make you seem interesting for a few years. We won't miss you when you're gone."

I stared hard at him, trying to fight the tears springing to my eyes. "You don't know a thing about me," I told him.

"No?" he asked, lifting his eyebrows. "Tell me which part, exactly, was the lie then, Shalott."

But I couldn't. There was a part of me—a large part—that suspected he was right. That was what made the words hurt as badly as they had.

"Come on," he said after a moment with a beleaguered sigh. "We should head back down for lunch."

It was my turn to laugh, and I wiped a hasty hand under my eyes to catch any tears that might have seeped out. "I'm not going anywhere with you," I told him, but even to my own ears I sounded like a petulant child.

"Oh, so you're going to stay here, by yourself?"

"I'm going back to my cottage," I said, hoping I sounded more certain than I felt.

"And how are you going to get there?" he asked.

I turned away from him and started in the direction we'd come from, but as soon as I took a step down that path, nothing looked familiar. I didn't stop, though—getting lost in the woods felt like a preferable fate to spending another minute in Lancelot's presence.

"Where are you going?" he called after me, but I ignored him, walking into a copse of trees that looked like the one we came from.

Footsteps thudded, and Lancelot fell into step next to me. "You're going the wrong way," he said, sounding amused.

"Oh?" I said. "Well, I suppose it'll make a good *story* then, won't it?"

"Not if you aren't alive to tell it," he pointed out. "About half a mile this way is a pit of quicksand. It's a bit difficult to tell where solid ground stops and the quicksand begins, but if you're feeling lucky . . ."

I stopped short. "Well, that sounds foolishly dangerous," I said. "Why would you have a pit of quicksand where people walk?"

He looked surprised at the question. "For the quicksand fey," he said, like it should have been obvious.

I stared at him agog for an instant before closing my mouth and straightening my shoulders. "There are no quicksand fey," I said.

He grinned. "Look at you, learning," he said, taking hold of my elbow and turning me to the right. "Now, if you're really set on storming off, I would recommend doing so in that direction. You might still find yourself falling into a river or off the edge of a cliff, but if you do manage to make it through, you should run right into your cottage."

I gritted my teeth. "I'd imagine my peril would only serve to amuse you," I said.

"Depends on what sort of peril it is," he said. "But I doubt Morgana would be amused if I let you die on my watch, so I'd rather that didn't happen."

He started walking again and I tentatively followed, glancing sideways at him.

"You're afraid of Morgana," I said wonderingly.

He glared at me, but I could see the truth of it in his eyes. "I'm not afraid of anything or anyone," he snapped.

I laughed. "I can hear your heartbeat speed up. I can feel your breathing grow shallow," I said, doing my best impression of his moody scowl.

He was thoroughly unamused. "From me, that's a simple observation. From you, that just sounds strange," he said.

YOU TERRIFIED ME," he told me, years later. The words were a whisper against the bare skin of my shoulder, a prelude to the soft kiss of his lips a second later.

We were lying together in my bed, the stars glittering down through the skylight. White sheets were tangled around bare limbs, damp with sweat. My fingers traced the terrain of his bare chest, over the hills and valleys of muscle—cartography I already knew by heart. When he spoke, though, my fingers stopped short and I laughed.

"I did not," I told him, sitting up to look at him fully, though his face was open and guileless. It would never stop feeling like a rare sight to me, his expression unguarded as it was during those long, languid nights together.

"You did," he insisted. "Because I knew you didn't come alone. You brought change in your wake, and I knew the day would come when they would leave me behind." He didn't specify who *they* were, but he didn't need to. I knew he meant Arthur and Gwen and Morgana. Even in those private moments, they had a way of lingering on the edges, not intruding, but present all the same. "I said you didn't belong here, but the truth is, none of you do. And one day, all of you will leave and I'll still be here, alone."

He said the words simply—a fact stated, not meant to incite sympathy or pity or reassurances. I wasn't sure how to respond, though part of me wanted to tell him then that he could join us, that I'd seen that possibility. But the future still seemed so far off then, impossibly far away, a quandary for a different Elaine and a different Lancelot. There would be many of those, I knew; it couldn't hurt to add one more to the pile.

I brought a hand to rest over his heart, feeling it beat against my fingertips like the wings of a caged bird.

"It seems I still terrify you," I said, shifting so that I was leaning over him, hands braced on his shoulders. My hair fell in a curtain of gold around us, blocking out the stars above shining down from the open roof, blocking out

Avalon and the others, blocking out the future pressing in around us. The world narrowed to just him and me, narrowed further to the rhythm of his heartbeat and my own, to the breath held between his lips and mine.

"I can hear your heartbeat speed up," I told him, doing my best imitation of his deep, wry voice. My impression had gotten better since that early day when I'd first tried. By then, I knew his voice as well as my own. "I can feel your breathing grow shallow."

He held my gaze, his laugh a soft rumble in his chest that reverberated through my whole body. Then he tilted his mouth up to catch mine in a kiss, and our world narrowed further still.

WE FINALLY FIND Lancelot on the beach, collecting shells for his mother, Arethusa.

There are many stories about Arethusa, and they have a habit of changing each time they're told, shifting colors like the patches of opalescent scales that still cling to parts of her skin. Lancelot never talks about it himself, but from what I've gathered, her story goes something like this.

Before Lancelot was born, Arethusa was a water goddess whose domain stretched over the rivers and ponds of every land and through all the seas that connected them. Even the dirty puddles that dotted Camelot's streets were under her reign, and she could travel between each body of water as easily as I could take a single step.

Her power was great and her hold was strong and she was happy. Mostly. The water could be a cold and desolate place, after all, and Arethusa grew lonely.

She showed me her scales, once, the first time I had tea at her cottage. They cling in patches to the undersides of her arms, her stomach, her thighs, and she usually wears long, flowing dresses to cover them, though I didn't understand why. They were iridescent and glittering and delicately beautiful.

Once, she said, they covered most of her skin. Once, she had gills in her neck so that she could breathe underwater. Once, her legs ended in fins instead of feet.

From the river one day, she saw a man in the woods. She didn't say he was handsome, but she didn't need to—men in stories like this are always handsome. It is both the bait and the hook.

Maybe he loved her back, for a time. Maybe the promises he whispered in her ear were made in good faith. Maybe he never intended to leave her alone, her belly swollen, her scales falling away from her gilded skin because she had been out of the water for too long, waiting for him to return. Maybe it was all an accident. Arethusa still believes that, and I suppose she would know better than the rest of us.

Maybes don't matter, though, because he did leave her, she did lose her scales, and a few months later, she did give birth to Lancelot, alone and mostly human in a world she did not understand.

Nimue brought both of them back to Avalon, and for a time, everyone was certain that her scales would grow back, that she would be able to return to the sea, but that never happened. Some say it's a punishment by the Maiden, Mother, and Crone for abandoning her duty for a mortal man, but others say it's no punishment at all but Arethusa's choice to stay on land with her son.

I can't say what the truth is, and I doubt Lancelot could, either, if you asked him.

Now, the seashells are among the only tethers Arethusa still has to the sea. She showed me once how they contain messages, whispered into them hundreds of thousands of miles away. She showed me how to make my own, to toss them into the sea and trust that they would find their target in time.

I tried it myself after I first arrived here, whispering messages for my mother every day for a month, but they all went unanswered, so I finally stopped trying. I wasn't doing it right, I told myself, the messages never reached her, though I think some part of me has always suspected that was a lie.

"Any gossip from the mainland?" Morgana asks Lancelot when we approach, trying to keep her voice light.

Lancelot raises an eyebrow—a talent I've long envied. Every time I try to mimic him, I only succeed in looking like I have to sneeze. "These are important missives, M," he says. "Not gossip."

Morgana says nothing and after a moment he sighs.

"Lady Ducarte of Lyonesse is trying to seduce a shepherd two decades her junior with little success and everyone at court is laughing at her," he says. "Happy?"

"Thrilled," Gwen puts in. "Lady Ducarte once told everyone at court that I was raised by beasts."

I frown at her. "*You* tell everyone you were raised by beasts. How is it an insult if it's true?"

She shrugs her shoulders, glancing away. "It was in her tone."

I shake my head and look back at Lancelot. "We came to say goodbye," I tell him.

Lancelot shoots me a bewildered look before leaning down to pick up another shell, drying it off on his homespun tunic, already splotched with salt water.

"You didn't need to come all the way out here," he says. "I'll see you at breakfast."

I glance at the others, unsure how to say the words, but Arthur gets there first.

"We won't be at breakfast," he says, his voice coming out more certain than I expected. "My father's dead; I'm king of Camelot now."

It's the first time he's said the words out loud, and he says them like a question, as if he expects someone to correct him. No one does.

Lancelot looks between us, waiting for someone to jump in and proclaim it all a joke, but when he realizes that won't happen, his expression clouds over and he looks away, out to sea. Somewhere, past the horizon, Albion awaits.

"Well," he says slowly. "We knew this would happen eventually, didn't we? Safe travels."

He sounds so calm about it that I want to slap him. And I'm not the only one.

"That's it?" Gwen asks with a harsh laugh.

Lancelot keeps his eyes on the horizon. "What do you want me to say, Gwen?" he asks with a sigh. "We aren't children anymore. We have futures, and now those futures go in different directions."

*But what is your future?* I want to ask him. *Collecting shells for your mother when she is perfectly capable of doing it herself? Playing at sword fights you know you'll win? Running through the same woods you know like the back of your own hand, crossing the same paths again and again and again? Is that what you want? A life unchallenged and easy?*

"This is goodbye then," Arthur says, his own voice wounded. "There's no need to see us off—I know how much you value your sleep."

At that, Lancelot flinches like Arthur actually did hit him, but after a moment he nods. "I'll miss you all," he says finally, turning to look at us again. "You've been good friends."

And there it is, the crack in his armor, no wider than a hairsbreadth but wide enough to remember that even though he was raised among the fey, even though he shares half his blood with them, he is human as well, mortal, and sometimes his emotions push their way past the calm and stoic surface.

"I'll meet you all back at the cottage," I tell the others, not taking my eyes off Lancelot. "I just need a moment."

The others don't protest, they don't say anything as they walk back toward the edge of the woods, leaving Lancelot and me alone. Maybe they think they know what this conversation will entail and want no part of it. The thought makes my cheeks warm and I try to ignore it, even when Lancelot turns his eyes to me and one corner of his mouth turns up in a smirk.

"If you're looking for a more romantic goodbye—" he starts.

"I'm not," I interrupt, crossing my arms over my chest. "Come with us."

The words are out of my mouth before I can stop them, but so quiet I think he may not have heard. His shoulders tense, though, and I know he did. I clear my throat.

"Come with us," I say, louder this time. "To Albion. To Camelot. To court."

It sounds ridiculous when I say it out loud, especially like this. Standing ankle deep in the water with his trousers rolled up and his white tunic wet and unbuttoned, with his mussed black hair overgrown and curling around his ears—he doesn't belong on the mainland, doesn't belong at court. I try to imagine it: him in a stiff velvet suit buttoned up to his throat, stuck in a dimly lit castle, surrounded by stone and wood and stale air. I imagine him at a ball, dancing tensely to the delicate and restrained string music—so different from the wild drums of Avalon—twirling around the dance floor with a girl who looks something like me.

Even in my imagination, he looks miserable and out of place.

He must realize it as well, but he doesn't say no right away. Instead, he stares at me, suddenly looking so much younger than he usually does. I catch a glimpse of the man beneath the bravado, and suddenly he's only twenty-five, torn and confused and losing his only friends, insistent on fighting everyone because he doesn't know what will happen if he stops.

"Avalon is my home," he says softly. "It always has been."

"So make a new one," I say. "Home isn't a place, it's people. Your people are going to the mainland and you should be coming with us."

He shakes his head. "My mother needs me here."

It's the same excuse I gave Morgana a decade ago when she asked me to come to Avalon. I understand his hesitation better than I'd like to, but I push on anyway. "Your mother is stronger than you give her credit for. She is perfectly capable of taking care of herself, and you know that," I say, and it's the truth. Arethusa isn't my mother. She will survive on her own, and she has never held Lancelot too tightly. She will let him go with a kiss on his forehead and words of love in his ear.

"She doesn't need you," I continue. "Not in the same way. Arthur needs a friend, someone who isn't afraid to speak the truth, never mind his crown. Morgana and Gwen will need you, especially in that viper pit of a court. Both of them will feel so out of place, they'll need all of the familiarity they can get. Without you, it will always feel like something is missing."

Lancelot is quiet for a moment, his eyes heavy on mine. They are no longer stone walls; now his expression is open again and all the more terrifying because of it. I want to look away, but I can't. Tentatively, he takes a step closer to me, dripping water onto dry sand. I've never seen Lancelot tentative about anything, but suddenly he walks like he's worried the earth will collapse beneath his feet. He stops a few inches away from me.

"And you?" he asks softly, reaching out hesitantly to touch a strand of hair that's come untucked from behind my ear. He pushes it back into place. Small a gesture as it is, it undoes something in me. I try not to show it. "Do you need me there, too, Shalott?" he asks, as if he's afraid of the answer.

No, I want to say. I know Camelot, after all. I won't need a warrior or a sparring partner or a tether to Avalon. I won't need any other friends—three will already be three more than I had last time I was at court. No, I don't need him, because I've seen shades of our future, the soft pastels and the sharp, jarring hues that clash, and I know that one cannot exist without the other so I want none of it at all. I want none of him.

But I'm not a good enough liar to believe that myself, and so the words die on my tongue.

"Yes," I say instead. The word forces its way past all of my defenses. The sound of it surprises me, wrenched from the deepest parts of me like something ugly and shameful and necessary. How awful it is to need someone, but more awful still to admit it out loud. It feels like I've cut myself open and set myself out for the crows to pick at. I am fragile and weak and desperate. I am not so different than the girl I was before, in Camelot, the one who needed so much love and never got any of it. I never wanted to be that girl again, but here I am—needing something I know I won't get.

For his part, Lancelot looks as surprised by the admission as I am. All we can do is stare at each other.

After what feels like an eternity, he nods once, sharp and decisive, but he doesn't look at me. His eyes are focused over my shoulder, where I know he can see the candle flickering in his mother's cottage window.

"You can always come back," I tell him, but even as I say the words, I hate myself. Because I know in the deepest part of my soul that there is no truth to them. In all the visions of the future I've seen, Lancelot returning to Avalon has never been among them.

9

A T BREAKFAST THE morning after I first had the cliff vision, I had to force myself to eat, though with the vision still lingering on the outskirts of my mind, every bite I took felt likely to come right back up.

"Elaine," my mother said, her voice cutting through the fog of my mind as she idly stirred her morning tea, though there was nothing idle about the way she watched me. "I heard that you had a visitor yesterday."

I couldn't bring myself to be surprised that my mother knew about Morgana. After all, she always seemed to have eyes everywhere.

"Yes, Mother," I said, choosing my words with care. "Lady Morgana and I took tea in the sitting room. It was a lovely afternoon."

She digested this information with a placid expression, squeezing a lemon wedge into her cup of tea. "Morgana Tintagel is nothing but trouble. *Everyone* says so," she said, her voice crisp at the edges. "You would do well to keep your distance from her—we wouldn't want people to think you're anything alike, would we?"

"No, Mother," I said quietly, because it was what I was supposed to say. Even though the truth was that I would very much have liked being thought of the same way people thought of Morgana. It was certainly preferable to be feared than ridiculed, I thought, but I knew better than to say so to my mother, who would rather be ignored than either.

"I've heard she was always volatile, even as a child," she said. "I don't want her putting ideas into your head."

"She hasn't put any ideas into my head," I told her, though I realized a second later that it wasn't strictly true. She had put many ideas into my head during our brief acquaintance, but they didn't feel like her ideas. Morgana had merely taken a feather duster to my own thoughts and uncovered them.

"Elaine," my mother said again, setting her cup down on its saucer with a rattle that echoed in the cavernous room. She fixed me with an unwavering look. "Did you forget to take your potion last night?"

I chose my words carefully so that they wouldn't really be a lie. "No, I didn't forget."

But my mother looked at me in that way she had, and I knew she saw straight through me.

"Really, Elaine. Sometimes I think you behave this way to spite me. All I have ever wanted is what was best for you, and yet you seem to want to throw happiness away with both hands. It's too much for my poor heart." She clutched her quivering white hands over her chest in demonstration, like she might claw her own heart out to show me the proof.

"Maybe . . ." I started, before biting my lip, courage already wavering. I pushed forward. "Maybe my happiness means something different than yours does."

For a moment that stretched on for eternity, she was silent, staring at me with milky blue eyes as if I were a stranger to her. Her mouth bowed down, then pursed before she let out a beleaguered sigh.

"You are a child, Elaine," she said, each word sharp as glass. "You know nothing about life, so how can you know anything about happiness? Has Morgana been filling your head with lies?"

*No*, I thought. *Many things, but not lies.*

THAT NIGHT, MY mother slipped in through my bedroom door as I was getting ready for bed. I didn't even hear her come in at first. I was sitting at my vanity, running a brush through my unruly blond hair, when I saw her in the mirror, standing over my shoulder like a ghost. I jumped, snagging the brush in a particularly painful knot.

"Ow," I said, extracting it from the tangle. "You frightened me."

Silently, my mother extended her hand for the brush and I passed it to her, unable to meet her eyes. I felt like if I did, she would see all the secrets I had been keeping.

"I am worried about you, Elaine," she said after a moment of silence. Her low voice prickled dangerously at the back of my neck. "You've been acting strange."

Looking at her reflection, I realized with a jolt just how old my mother was. How much had she seen? And how much had she Seen? Maybe Morgana was right and my mother didn't know everything about the world, but I felt then that she must have known more than most.

"I'm still me," I assured her. "It's only . . . I'm questioning some things that I've never thought much about before."

Her eyes turned sharp. "Some things aren't *meant* to be questioned," she said. With one last, sharp tug through my hair, she set the brush aside. "It's time for bed."

I stood up from my vanity bench and turned to face her, struggling to smile pleasantly even as something prickled beneath my skin. It felt like fear, but that was ridiculous. I had nothing to fear from my mother. "Good night," I told her, trying to push the feeling aside.

But she remained standing there, making no move to leave. "Don't forget to take your medicine," she said, eyes heavy on me. A warning.

Every muscle in my body went taut, and the prickling feeling beneath my skin grew stronger. *Run*, a voice whispered through my mind.

"I won't," I told her, struggling to keep my voice level. Still, she didn't move. She wouldn't, I realized. Not until she saw it with her own eyes.

I crossed to the shelf and took the bottle down, unstoppering it, feeling her shrewd eyes tracking my every movement. I met her gaze as I lifted the bottle to my lips. The noise of the little liquid left sloshing around the bottle sounded impossibly loud in the dead quiet that enveloped us. I kept my lips sealed tight against the opening, not letting even a drop get past.

"Elaine," my mother warned, giving me a stern look. Before I could do anything, she closed the distance between us and took hold of the bottle herself, pinning me between her body and the wall behind me. "Drink."

I shook my head, trying to get away, but she held tight to the bottle and to me, keeping me in place. She reached up to pinch the bridge of my nose so that I couldn't breathe unless I opened my mouth. Her eyes had grown hard and impassive, until it felt like she was no longer my mother at all, but a stranger. When she spoke, her voice was distant and gravelly and so unlike the voice that sang me lullabies as a child.

The words she spoke burned themselves in my memory that night, strange and nonsensical as they seemed at the time. Some mornings, when I wake up from a dreamless sleep, I hear them again, whispering through my mind in her voice and lingering throughout the rest of the day.

"Beware, beware three maidens fair. With bloody hands. Trust not . . ."

She jerked her head to the side as if an invisible hand slapped her cheek hard. "Help not . . ." Another jerk of her head in the other direction. She clenched her jaw tight, like she was fighting the words, but they came forth anyway.

"She'll burn the world to ash and flame."

The words didn't make sense and her eyes had grown faraway, like she might have been half-asleep. *This must be it*, I thought through the cloud of panic, what I had seen and felt in my dreams. Drowning, but not in the way I had expected. Finally, I had no choice, I had to open my mouth. Immediately, the potion flooded in, but still she didn't let go of my nose.

"Swallow," she said, but she sounded like herself again at least. I had no choice. I swallowed, the thick, bitter liquid oozing down my throat.

Immediately, she softened and her hand released my nose, brushing against my cheek and smoothing down my hair.

"Good girl," she said, brushing papery lips against my forehead. "Get some sleep now." She pressed another kiss to the top of my head, and then she was gone and I was left alone.

As soon as the door closed behind her, I ran to my washbasin and hunched over it, willing the potion to come back up. I had never thought that I would actually want to be ill, but that night I thought I would give anything for it. I had only just gained some measure of control over my life, and I was not ready to give it up again. I pounded my fists against my stomach, hoping that would work, but it only made it ache. After trying for a few minutes, my legs gave out and I collapsed to the ground. Tears came freely and I didn't make any effort to stop them.

WHEN I WOKE the next morning, I was keenly aware for the first time of the lack of a vision. I'd taken that potion countless times, and in the mornings all I remembered was dreamless sleep, unless I'd dreamt of drowning. It hadn't quite been peace, but it was close enough.

But that morning, I knew enough to feel the absence of the vision. It was like the space left behind by a lost tooth—I couldn't resist prodding at it, feeling for any sense of what might have been there.

And *something* had been there. I was sure of it. I could feel its absence, feel something dancing just out of my reach, teasing me like a forgotten dream. The more I tried to remember, the more it slipped away. After I lay in bed for the better part of an hour, the only thing I could remember was a set of unfamiliar green-gold eyes, locked on mine.

Later, I would realize they were Lancelot's. The first time I saw him on Avalon, the pieces would click into place.

Sometimes I wonder what that vision was. Have I seen it again since? Maiden, Mother, and Crone know I've had enough visions of Lancelot. Or was it something else, a vision now lost to time? On days I am less kind to myself, I am convinced that it was a vision that could have changed everything, if only I'd been smarter, stronger, more determined to fight off my mother somehow.

I never saw her again.

When I eventually dragged myself from bed, I packed up a few things—dresses and shoes I would never wear on Avalon—and slipped out of the tower without a backward glance. I left a note behind, only seven words long.

*I love you, but I'm not sorry.*

Then I found Morgana and we left for Avalon right away, the birthday banquet be damned. She didn't need much convincing on that count—I suppose she'd gotten what she'd really come to Camelot for after all. She'd gotten me.

THE NIGHT BEFORE we leave Avalon, I dream of my mother.

I know right away it's only a dream, not because of some oracular sense but because she's outside, sitting by a rushing river, with the sun on her face and her silver hair loose around her shoulders. I know it's a dream because she's smiling and rosy cheeked and happy, dangling her bare legs in the crystal water, her dress bunched up around her knees.

We are in the woods outside Shalott, where we used to picnic when I was a child. Back before the sun became too bright for my mother, the sound of the birds chirping too loud. Before everything became too much for my mother, every facet of life so unbearable that she never left her room, no matter how I used to beg her to play with me.

"Come, Little Lily," she says now, taking my hands in hers and pulling me down to sit beside her. Her hands are warmer than I remember. I pull my own dress up to my knees and dangle my legs in the cold river. "Rivers are funny things, aren't they? Always running, never getting anywhere. I suppose you understand that better than anyone."

Her voice is its own kind of ghost, familiar and foreign in a way that clutches at my gut. I never heard my mother like this, though, with a smile in her voice, a lilting cadence that might give way to laughter at any second.

I know it's a dream, but it's one I want for a change, so I tilt my head back and enjoy the sun on my face, enjoy her presence beside me, solid and sure. For a moment, I forget to fear the water rushing about my legs.

All too soon, though, a cloud passes in front of the sun, and the world becomes gray.

"Change is coming," I tell her as the river rushes faster, churning so hard that whitecaps appear on the current.

"Change is here," my mother replies, in that voice I'm far more familiar with. It is full of omens and warnings, reproachful and fearful and bitter all at once. That is the voice of the mother I remember, and even now I flinch from it, feeling like a child again. A child who will always be a disappointment.

She gets to her feet and helps me stand beside her. I'm taller than her now, I realize with a jolt. How did that happen? I still feel like a child, clinging to her skirts.

My mother's hand lifts to touch my cheek, her fingers cold against my skin.

"I wonder what will be left of you," she muses, "when all the people you love have chipped away their pieces."

I jerk away from her, but she doesn't seem to notice. Her attention has returned to the river, which has begun to churn like the sea in a storm, the water turning black as the midnight sky, capped with streaks of white foam.

She takes my hand, but this time it has gone cold. Her flesh melts away until her grip is all skin and bone, then only bone.

"It is all coming now, Lily," she tells me. "You must choose your path."

She rasps out the same prophecy she told me that night long ago, but this time, it is complete. This time, I understand every terrible word of it.

*Beware, beware three maidens fair*
*With bloody hands and divine air.*
*Help not the girl whom others blame*
*She'll burn the world to ash and flame.*
*Trust not the girl with the golden crown*
*She'll take what's yours and watch you drown.*
*And my Lily Maid will scream and cry.*
*She'll break them both and then she'll die.*

And then my mother falls away altogether, and the past becomes the future, where I will drown. The water will fill my throat and lungs, and there will be a part of me that will want to struggle and a part of me that won't. I will stare at the moon shining through the surface above like a beacon beckoning to me, and I will ignore its call.

# 10

THE LAST TIME I stood on Camelot's shore, I was a frightened girl of thirteen, running away from a shadowed life of solitude. I remember how the storm lit up golden veins in the sky, how the wind whipped through my tangled hair, carrying the scent of honey and charred oak. I remember Morgana's hand in mine, solid and warm, as she urged me forward, toward the waiting boat, toward Avalon and away from the mother who would have rather killed me than set me free.

When I left, I didn't imagine I would ever come back to this place. But here I am.

Silhouetted against the pale light of dawn, the towers of Camelot's castle look beautiful—spindly and delicate like they've been crafted from spun sugar. There is nothing beautiful about that castle, though, and ten years away wasn't enough to let me forget that.

Morgana appears at my side like a shadow, slipping her hand into mine just like she did so long ago, when we were still children, practically. There's comfort in the gesture, an anchor that holds me here, now, to the present.

Resentment still rolls off her in waves, and she keeps glancing back at the shore over her shoulder as if, at any moment, Nimue might appear to say she's changed her mind.

"Arthur needs us," I tell her, drawing her attention back to me and

Camelot. It's not the first time I've said that to her, either, and she rolls her eyes.

I suppose I understand it, her irritation. It can't be easy being Arthur's older sister, always adjacent to greatness, to constantly be asked to put his needs before her own—though she has always done so without hesitation. But of all the parts of herself she's given up for Arthur, I don't think she ever expected Avalon to be one of them.

For all of us, it was home; for Morgana, it was her very heart.

She turns to look at me, her violet eyes more gray in the early-morning light. "It's not going to be like before, you know," she tells me. "*You* aren't like you were before."

Maybe I should be surprised that she sees through me so well, that she can read my thoughts as easily as I think them, but I'm not. Even when we first met, she understood me, like we were two facets of the same jewel.

"I know," I tell her, though I wonder how much truth there is in that. Part of me feels like as soon as I step into that castle, I will become that same girl all over again, the one who didn't know who she was or what she was capable of or how to stand up for herself.

"If you two are done whispering," Lancelot shouts behind us. "Gwen's done with the horses."

The others were relieved when I told them he was coming with us. I'm relieved, too, though I know there are plenty of reasons I shouldn't be. And Nimue . . . well, when he appeared on the shore with a packed bag and his sword at his hip, she wasn't surprised, whatever there is to make out of that.

I give Morgana's hand a squeeze before releasing it and turning back toward the shore, where five horses stand in the water beside Lancelot, Guinevere, and Arthur. Sea-foam still clings to the horses' legs, sinking into their skin to become white markings against their glistening wet black hides.

What were they before? I wonder. Did the water birth them, or were they constructed from the water itself? They stomp their hooves and toss their heads impatiently, alive as any horse I've ever seen, but I know just how misleading magic can be. I can't begin to understand Gwen's power of manipulating nature any more than she can understand my Sight.

Guinevere drops her hands to her sides and smiles, satisfied with her work. A breeze blows through her loose red hair, and the sight of it sends a pang through me. Once she's joined us in the castle as Arthur's betrothed, she'll have to start binding it in plaits and chignons. In Camelot, only children wear their hair loose like that.

"They'll get us to the castle?" Arthur asks her, brow furrowed as he examines the horse closest to him, even reaching a hand out to touch its flank. He is mildly surprised when the creature doesn't dissolve beneath his fingertips.

Gwen glowers at him. "*And* take me to Lyonesse *and* make it back here before the magic fades," she says. "I know what I'm doing, Arthur."

The irritation in her voice makes his cheeks redden, but only for an instant. We all know Gwen's temper—quick to burn, but over in a flash. In a moment or two, she won't even remember that she was annoyed at him.

Nimue always said that Gwen was like a cat—just as likely to nuzzle and purr as she was to hiss and scratch, but she never specified if she was a tabby or a tigress. I suppose it varies from day to day.

"You shouldn't be traveling on your own," Arthur says, but that only makes her laugh.

"And why not? The horse knows the way, and you have a throne that needs warming."

He looks ready to argue but decides against it. Instead, he shakes his head and lets it go. We all have short tempers right now, I think, not just Gwen. We all are heading into an uncertain future. We've all lost the only real home we've ever known.

As if sensing my thoughts, Lancelot looks over his shoulder at the horizon. From here, all that can be seen is the lake itself, the morning mist dancing over its surface, but somewhere in the distance is Avalon. It's where his mother is still, where he was born, where he's lived his entire life. It's where Nimue waits, watching us from afar, the chess pieces she spent years painstakingly setting in place.

"There's no more time to waste," Lancelot says, all brusqueness, bringing a hand down onto Arthur's shoulder. "Gwen's right—Arthur has a throne to claim."

I have to bite my tongue to keep from correcting him because we're all tense and anxious, and there's no point in fighting with each other when there will be enemies aplenty once we're at court.

Still, I doubt getting Arthur on the throne will be the real challenge—he is his father's only heir, the rightful king of Camelot. No one can contest that. Keeping him there, however, will be another matter entirely.

As we mount our horses and start toward the castle, I can't take my eyes off those delicate spires.

*You aren't like you were before*, Morgana said. I know her words were true, but I also know that there are ghosts waiting for me in the halls of that castle, and the girl I was is only one of them.

WHEN WE REACH the fork in the road where Gwen's path separates from ours, we pause to say our goodbyes, dismounting from our impatient horses, who stomp their hooves and whinny, eager to keep going.

Arthur and Gwen say their goodbyes first, and the rest of us avert our eyes, trying to give them some semblance of privacy, though I'm not sure how much good it does. Besides, very little of their courtship has been private. We were there the first time they kissed, during their first quarrel. And what's more, there will be very little privacy when they're ruling Albion together. Perhaps it's better they don't grow accustomed to it now.

With that done, Gwen hugs Lancelot and Morgana, kissing both of their cheeks and murmuring words I don't hear. They both laugh, and I think I see Morgana hastily wipe a tear from her eye. It seems they're always at odds with each other, but Gwen has been more of a sister to Morgana than Morgause ever was.

And then it's my turn. When Gwen folds me into her arms, my mother's words from my dream last night come back to me.

*Trust not the girl with the golden crown, she'll take what's yours and watch you drown.*

The thought sends a shiver down my spine. There is no doubt in my mind that the girl she spoke of was Gwen. I know it in the same bone-deep way that

I know the other girl she mentioned was Morgana. The three of us have always had a tangled future, but we aren't there yet, and no matter what my mother told me, I know that prophecies can change. This one will have to.

"Keep Arthur safe," Gwen tells me when she pulls back, her freckled hands tight on my shoulders. Behind the usual ferociousness of her green eyes, a touch of fear lingers. She bites her lip. "Please," she adds.

"Of course," I tell her. "Of course I will."

"They'll try to tear him to pieces, you know," she says. "He's not made for that."

Sometimes, I forget that Gwen arrived in Avalon only a year before I did, that she remembers the mainland better than Arthur and Morgana. She remembers court life and the politics behind the power of the throne. She remembers the games.

"I know," I say. "And you'll be with us soon enough, Gwen. He'll need you at his side."

Gwen nods, but she glances away as she does. It's such a brief thing that I almost miss it—I might have missed it if I weren't looking for it.

"Hey," I say, tugging her attention back to me. "Arthur needs us."

Those words are almost as familiar to her as they are to Morgana, repeated over and over by Nimue until they became an integral part of all of us.

Arthur needs us. Arthur needs us. Arthur needs us. He has a destiny to fulfill, after all.

I see the twinge of bitterness flash through Gwen's eyes as clearly as I feel its echo deep in my soul. But that, too, I push away.

"I'll see you soon," I tell her.

She embraces me once more before stepping back and climbing onto her horse. The rest of us wait, watching her ride away. It's only when she disappears down her path that we mount our horses and start toward Camelot once more.


BACK ON AVALON, Gwen rarely slept. She would roam the island instead, as the moon arced its way over the sky above. The lack of rest never seemed to affect her. She was always alert during the day, her eyes always bright, with none of the dark circles that I would see beneath my own after a sleepless night. It was just how she was, she said.

One night, I'd gotten so caught up in a vision that I emerged from the Cave of Prophecies long past dinner. The moon was directly overhead, a large, silver half circle surrounded by more stars than sky. My stomach rumbled, and I crossed my arms over it. I wouldn't be able to eat until breakfast, but that was likely just as well. I don't remember anymore what vision I had seen, exactly, but I remember it was a bad one, that it had left me feeling too nauseated to stomach anything.

It wasn't until I was walking through the woods alone in the middle of the night that I realized I should be frightened. At that point, I had been on Avalon for more than a year and her woods were familiar to me, but in the dark they had become strange and dangerous once again. The island may have been asleep, but the woods were as awake as ever.

A wind rustled through the trees. Insects chirped. A river ran somewhere out of sight. But it was the silence that was the eeriest thing because it was *too* silent. A pregnant pause that raised the hairs on the back of my neck.

Suddenly, a golden orb flickered into view, weaving between trees not far ahead. Tentatively I took a step closer, then another until I caught sight of her telltale red-gold hair—a rarity even among the fey.

"Gwen?" I said.

The orb stilled and Gwen turned toward me, dressed in a white nightshirt that fell down to her knees and holding a sphere of warm light in her cupped hands. Her hair was piled on top of her head so messily that pieces had already sprung free, sticking out at strange angles.

"Elaine," she said with a tired smile. "What in the name of the Maiden, Mother, and Crone are you doing out at this hour?"

A stab of annoyance wedged into my gut. Did no one notice I wasn't at dinner? Did they not miss me at all? Even after a year, it still felt like that sometimes. Like I would never be able to truly fit in with her and the others, that I would always be a newcomer and an outsider.

"I got caught up in the Cave of Prophecies," I told her. "I lost track of time."

Gwen shook her head. "We thought that's what it was," she said. "We wanted to go fetch you, but Nimue said it was important you not be disturbed."

That made me feel a bit better. Though I wasn't sure where she was going, I fell into step beside her.

"And you?" I asked. "Another bad night?"

Gwen's face clouded over but she only shrugged her shoulders. "Not so bad, I don't think," she said. "But no, I couldn't sleep, if that's what you mean."

"Surely one of the fey can brew you something," I said. "Even on the mainland we have sleeping draughts."

She shook her head. "Well, they can," she said. "But either they don't work at all or they work too well. I would take something to sleep, and the next thing I knew it was three days later and I had no memory of the time in between, though apparently I was awake and functioning for much of it. It's a scary thing to hear, that your body is working without your mind. I didn't care for it. I'd rather not sleep at all, so I stopped taking anything."

I thought of the potion my mother used to give me—different, but similar in some ways. Both took something from us while masquerading as cures.

"Besides, I've found I quite enjoy these nights," Gwen continued. "There's something peaceful about being awake while the rest of the island sleeps."

"I didn't think you cared much for peacefulness," I said, which made her laugh.

"No, I don't think I do most of the time," she admitted with a sheepish smile. "I like a good, noisy world. I like it to be so loud I can't hear myself think. Usually. My thoughts aren't too interesting anyway."

For so long, my thoughts had been all I had. The idea of trying to drown them out was strange to me.

"I don't think that's true," I told her.

"Maybe not for you," she allowed, laughing. "People like you and Arthur must have very interesting thoughts. I imagine your thoughts have fascinating conversations with one another, multiplying enough to keep you occupied for hours on end. But that's never been the case for me. What thoughts I have force their way out of my mouth before I can grow too attached to them. That's why Arthur will make a far better king than I will a queen."

I shook my head. "Don't be silly, Gwen."

Guinevere gave me a serious look. "Everyone says so—Arthur is more level-headed and strategic and diplomatic. Apparently those are qualities that make for a good ruler in Albion."

"Not in Lyonesse?" I asked.

She frowned. "In Lyonesse, it is about strength. Strength to take a throne and strength to hold it. Our dynasties aren't the same as other countries'. Power shifts far more often. My father is the longest-reigning king, you know, and he's only been on the throne for two decades. Disagreements aren't settled with diplomacy and polite debate there—they're settled with blood. Wonderful a king as Arthur might be, he wouldn't survive a week in Lyonesse."

I wasn't sure I could disagree with that assessment, but I still wanted to defend Arthur. Back then, he'd been merely infatuated with her—an infatuation we'd all believed was one-sided. He wanted so badly to be thought well of by Gwen—hearing that she thought him weak would have shattered his heart.

"Arthur's brave, though," I said.

Guinevere looked at me like I had just sprouted green hair. "Well, of course he is," she said. "He speaks his mind and defends his actions, which is the kind of bravery that matters most in a ruler, no matter what kind of ruler they are. He has the other kind of bravery, too—the sort that's tied to his pride and temper that most boys seem to have. It's just that to lead Lyonesse, you have to be fearless."

I had always heard *brave* and *fearless* used interchangeably, but when I said as much to Gwen, she laughed.

"A person is brave in spite of their fear, but being fearless is another beast entirely. Arthur could never be fearless. The wise ones know that there is much to fear in the world; it's the foolish who claim that nothing frightens them and only because they don't have the foresight to know what to be afraid of until it's too late. You aren't fearless, are you, Elaine?"

She said it like a challenge, though I wasn't sure what the right answer was. I shook my head. "No, not at all. I think I fear too many things."

"Because you and Arthur are the same," she said. "Wise and brave, yes, but never fearless."

I don't think anyone had called me brave before, and at first I wanted to correct her. I wasn't brave, after all. Most days, I still felt like the frightened girl I was in Camelot, hiding in shadows and keeping my head down. But even when I was that girl . . . I left. I walked away when it would have been easier to stay and suffer in silence. Maybe that had been a kind of bravery.

Gwen was right, though, I would never be fearless. I don't think there has ever been such a thing as a fearless seer.

I followed Gwen out of the woods, past the last of the great oak trees, greeted by a fresh sea breeze that ruffled my hair, carrying with it the scent of salt water and serenity. The bright moon shone down on the jagged cliffside that overlooked the beach below. At first, I thought it was the one from my vision with Morgana, but this one was much lower and more narrow. Gwen must have come often, because she went straight to the edge and sat down, letting her feet dangle over precariously. She closed her hands and extinguished the light she carried, the moon overhead bright enough to make up for it.

I stopped a step short, standing at her shoulder. Even that felt too close to the edge for me and I wanted to take a step back, but I forced myself to hold my ground.

"Are you fearless?" I asked her, though looking at her sitting at the edge of the cliff like it was the most natural thing in the world, I think I knew the answer already.

Her smile turned to a grin, and her eyes lit up with mischief. "Oh yes," she said. "I'll be a fearless fool to my last breath. There is no saving me from that."

## 11

CAMELOT IS QUIET. In my memory it is a bustling city at all hours, full of shopkeepers hawking their wares to harried shoppers, children playing in the streets, and the smell of roasting meat and potatoes in the air. Now, though, there isn't a soul in sight. The streets are empty; the air is still and silent. It is a ghost city.

Finally, as we approach the castle, a lone man crosses our path, dressed in a dirty gray cloak and hunched over a crooked cane.

"You, sir," Arthur calls out, pulling his horse to a stop.

The man looks up, bewildered at our presence.

"What're you doing out and about?" the man demands.

Arthur looks at us and shrugs his shoulders before looking back at him.

"We seek the sorcerer Merlin. Do you know where he can be found?" he asks.

The man stares at Arthur for a moment, agog, before he begins to laugh so hard his whole body shakes.

"Merlin?" he echoes. "You're looking for Merlin?"

"Do you know him?" I ask hopefully.

"Aye," the man says through laughter. "Just as I knew King Uther. Good friends, we all were."

Arthur still looks perplexed, too used to the straight answers of the fey to recognize the man's sarcasm. I shake my head.

"He can't help us," I say. "Come on, someone in the castle should—"

"Hold on, miss," the man interrupts, straightening up and stilling his laughter. "It's true, I don't know Merlin personally, but it just so happens I do know where the sorcerer can be found."

"Where?" Morgana asks.

The man gestures around the city with his free hand. "The same place everyone else is—the coronation of the new king, taking place in the throne room. Would've gone myself, but bah, once you've seen a couple of coronations, you've seen them all—"

"Coronation," I interrupt, my voice growing shrill even to my own ears as panic overtakes me. "That's impossible. Whose coronation?"

The man lifts his bushy eyebrows.

"Why, the crown prince," he says slowly, as if we are the mad ones. "Prince Mordred."

To the others, the name is only passingly familiar, mentioned briefly by Nimue as Arthur's bastard brother and Morgause's new husband. I, on the other hand, know his name and know his face. I've Seen it in visions, seen it stitched into shimmering tapestry before picking it apart, as if that simple act is enough to erase his actions, his great innumerable treasons. I saw it in person, only once, but that was enough for me.

I dig my heels into my horse's sides and urge her on, quickly, to the palace rising in the distance.

"Come on," I shout to the others over my shoulder. "There's no time to lose."

MORDRED WILL BE the death of Arthur.

Or at least he'll deliver the final blow.

Really, Arthur will start dying the second Morgana betrays him. Or maybe it's more accurate to say it will start when he betrays her. When Gwen and Lancelot betray him, he'll die a little more. He will charge into battle a shell of himself.

It will be in the middle of that battlefield swarming with the shadows of men. A thousand screams will pierce the air around them, but Arthur's won't join them. He won't scream or cry or beg for mercy. He'll only stare at Mordred, empty and determined, as if he could kill him with his gaze alone. But there will be something else in the look—a dare.

*End it*, the look will say. Its own kind of plea. Because he will know that this isn't a battle he will win. He will know that death is close and that, in its own way, it will be a mercy.

He will only wish that he didn't have to die alone.

Mordred's blade will slice through Arthur's chest, and though the battle still rages, I hear the noise it will make. I feel it in my own chest as if I've been stabbed as well.

His eyes will search the world around him, desperate for a familiar face in the hell he's found himself in, but there will be no one left.

*I'm here*, I want to tell him. *I'm with you. You are not alone.*

But I'm not there. I'm not with him. And he will breathe his last breath alone, a single unuttered word on his lips.

A name, maybe.

THE THRONE ROOM is overflowing with people, all clamoring to get a look at the man they believe will be their new king, though not if I can help it. It's the poorest of Camelot's citizens who cluster in the back, dressed in their finest clothes, plain and worn as those might be. They are all so tightly packed together that there is no getting through them, no matter how we try.

"Morgana," I say, grabbing her arm. "Use a spell—clear a path."

Morgana doesn't need to be urged twice to use magic. The words are barely out of my mouth before the air around her begins to shift, smelling of jasmine and oranges.

And just like that, people shuffle to the side—not far, there's not enough room—but enough to create a narrow path.

"Lance, you first, and shout as loud as you can," I say to him. My heartbeat thrums in my ears, blood rushing through me like I'm running. Every nerve feels alive at once—it is a frightening feeling, but one I would drown in if I could. It is an addicting thing, to have a purpose. "They'll listen to you. Announce Arthur's presence. Herald him in."

Lancelot looks unsure, but he nods, shouldering through the crowd. He stands far taller than most, and with his broad shoulders squared and his head held high, he cuts quite an imposing figure, making way for Arthur to follow in his wake, with Morgana and me close behind.

"Make way for Arthur Vendragon," he shouts. "Rightful heir to the throne of Camelot."

"*Pen*dragon," I whisper. "It's *Pendragon*."

"Right," Lancelot says. "Arthur *Pendragon*, rightful heir to the throne of Camelot, coming through, if you don't mind. Make way for the true king, please and thank you."

I'm sure his mother would be quite proud of his manners, but no one else seems terribly amused by them.

"Louder," I say. "More commanding. You have to tell them, not ask them."

Lancelot shakes his head but complies, lifting his voice high enough to be heard throughout the throne room.

"Make way for the true king, Arthur Pendragon," he shouts. "Make way for the king."

Finally our group breaks through the throng of commoners and steps into the throne room itself, more spacious and less crowded. Everyone here is dressed in elaborate brocade dripping in jewels and pearls and crystal flowers, with hair that's been coiffed and braided and powdered. A single silk slipper here would pay for a whole peasant family to eat for a year.

Where the peasants stared at us warily, these people are outwardly hostile, and Morgana has to work her spell even harder to urge them out of our way, though there is far more room now than there was before.

Finally, we reach the front, where a young man with dark hair and a hooked nose sits on the great golden throne while a man stands behind him, white hair tied back from his sharp-featured face, fingers all ringed with gold and silver. He holds a crown, hovering it just over the dark-haired man's head. Mordred is ten years older than the boy I met in the corridor with Morgause, but still a few years shy of the man I've Seen kill Arthur, trapped somewhere between a king's unwanted bastard and a fearsome and desperate warrior.

And the white-haired man—Merlin. I'd seen him often at court, though always from a distance. Somehow he looks younger than he did then. He must be hundreds of years old, but just now he looks barely forty.

"Stop," Arthur calls out, stepping in front of Lancelot and drawing himself up to his full height, even taller than Lancelot, taller than almost everyone around him.

"How dare you interrupt the ceremony with your theatrics," Mordred says, glowering. "Continue, Merlin."

"We come from Avalon," I blurt out, though as soon as the words pass my lips, I realize they might have been the wrong ones to say. I clear my throat and change paths, looking only at Merlin. "I don't know if you remember me, sir."

Merlin pauses, eyes on me. The crown in his hands hesitates, hovering still above Mordred's dark head.

"Elaine Astolat," he says slowly, recognition sparking in his eyes. "The Lady of Shalott."

At the sound of my name, the crowd behind me erupts in hushed voices. Most of those whispers must be about my father and brothers, I'd imagine, but there are some here who must remember me, must remember my mother. I hold my ground and keep my eyes on Merlin.

"You were here, sir, when Morgana came to court." I gesture behind me, where Morgana stands. "You were here when we left together. Do you remember?"

"I do," Merlin says, looking at Morgana, then at me. "I did not think to see you again."

I reach into my pocket to pull out the sealed letter, holding it out to him. "Nimue sent us back, with Prince Arthur, to take his rightful throne."

"This is ridiculous," Mordred says, looking between Merlin and me. "Prince Arthur disappeared as a baby. He's dead."

"Perhaps," Merlin says slowly, his eyes moving from me to Arthur, appraising.

"Prince Mordred is right," a man behind me says, his voice booming, echoing in the cavernous space. "This boy—whoever he may be—looks nothing like Uther. He is far too skinny, too fair, to be his son. This is nothing more than a trick, like all those other imposters who have shown up since Uther's death."

"Perhaps," Merlin says again, but he sets the crown down on the pedestal beside the throne and comes toward me, taking the letter from my fingers and unfurling it. As I suspected, the seal breaks under his touch, and the spell with it dissolves in a puff of white smoke. As his eyes scan the missive, I pull the signet ring and the other letter from my pocket as well.

"I also have this ring and the original letter Uther sent to Nimue, the Lady of the Lake, when he entrusted Arthur to her care."

That leads to a new eruption of protests.

"King Uther would never give his son to the fey," one man shouts.

"It is a trick—the boy is a changeling sent to be the fey's puppet," a woman adds.

"We will have no puppet king."

"Long live King Mordred."

The shouts multiply until there is nothing but a din of protests, but Merlin holds up a hand and the room falls silent.

"This boy may indeed be the lost prince," he says, and though his voice is quiet, it carries throughout the room so that even the peasants gathered outside can hear. "But then, he may not be. The letter is indeed from Uther—I was present when it was signed. The ring, too, is genuine, and I have no reason to doubt the authenticity of the letter from the Lady of the Lake as well."

Relief surges through me, but before it takes too firm a hold, Merlin continues.

"However," he says, "the fey are tricksters. It is known. And it may be that they have sent us an imposter in the place of the prince."

"All I am hearing is *may*s," Mordred says with a scowl. "Nothing solid enough to interfere with my coronation. Continue."

For an instant, I worry Merlin will agree, but after a moment he shakes his head. "I fear that would be unwise, Prince Mordred," he says, his voice low. Now, it doesn't carry. In fact, I would doubt that anyone farther back than us could hear him. "To ascend to the throne amid conflict is to wear the crown too briefly. We must do our due diligence to assure everyone the claim of the king is a true one."

Though he speaks to Mordred, his eyes are on Arthur, and I understand that the words are meant for us as well. I understand that Merlin could declare Arthur king, but to do so would leave many unconvinced, that the crown would pass to him with uncertainty that could fester and spread.

"I propose a series of three tests," Merlin says, louder now, to everyone gathered. "The first is simple and can be performed here and now to test this so-called prince's blood." He holds up the crinkled letter, marked with a spot of Uther's blood, turned brown with age. "If he is Uther's son in body, a simple spell should declare it so."

He gestures Arthur up onto the dais to stand beside him. When he is there, Merlin takes Arthur's hand and the dagger at his hip, using the point of it to prick Arthur's thumb. When a bead of blood wells up there, Merlin touches it to the letter, just over Uther's bloodied mark. He holds the paper up so that everyone can see.

"If these two are of the same blood, the mark will turn blue, to show that this boy is of the same royal lineage."

For a moment, everyone in the room holds their breath, their eyes stuck to the parchment. The change happens like ink blossoming across water, spreading out slowly, then all at once.

"There," Morgana says, her voice triumphant. "That proves it—Arthur is the rightful king of Camelot."

Merlin makes a sound in the back of his throat. "What it proves is that Arthur is indeed of Uther's blood—reassuring, yes, but not enough. Before his death, Uther declared Mordred his legitimate son and his heir, and so it isn't enough for Arthur to only be of the same blood as Uther—Mordred is as well now. He must also be of the same mind and of the same spirit. As I said, there will be three tests."

Three tests, but one already done in a matter of seconds. "Whether it's three tests or a hundred, it will be done," I say. "What is the next? Whatever it is, Arthur will pass them all as easily as he passed the first."

But as soon as Merlin smiles at me, I realize I've made a mistake, though I don't know what it was. "Three will be enough, but the next will not be as simple, I'm afraid." He turns to address the crowd again. "As many of you know, what should have been King Uther's greatest legacy eluded him in his life. A true son would be able to fulfill it."

The crowd begins to cheer and jeer, knowing what is coming next, though I can't begin to guess.

Merlin claps Arthur on the shoulder. "King Uther sought to unite all of the kingdoms of Albion under a single reign. He very nearly succeeded, but even in his last days, a lone kingdom eluded him."

The pieces fall into place, and I have to resist the smile pulling at my lips. Arthur's eyes find mine, understanding.

"The second test is to fulfill your father's legacy and defeat the beasts in the North to bring Lyonesse to heed under Camelot's rule."

# 12

M ERLIN GIVES US a week to rest before we're to leave for Lyonesse with an army of only fifty knights. As he announced these rules in the throne room, I watched as Mordred's smile grew and stretched over his face like an uncoiling snake. Fifty knights to do what hundreds—even thousands—hadn't been able to do. It was, to his ears, an impossible task.

It strikes me as unfair as well that while Arthur was meant to move mountains to take the throne, Mordred was able to inherit it by default. But destined as Arthur might be to rule Albion, we are at a distinct disadvantage—few people seem to believe that. To most, he is a stranger, shaped by enemy hands. Mordred has had years to curry favor and build loyalty. Arthur hasn't.

But it doesn't matter because when Arthur, Morgana, Lancelot, and I are alone in Arthur's childhood bedroom, we all let ourselves celebrate. One week of rest, but we could leave tomorrow if needed. No need to leave at all, certainly no need for knights—all it would take is a letter and Gwen would come to Camelot, marry Arthur, and bring Lyonesse officially into Albion.

"That won't do, though," I say as Arthur examines the room he can't possibly remember.

I'd thought the room would be too small for him, but it isn't. The bed he slept in as a toddler prince is still large enough to comfortably sleep an entire family, and the room itself is spacious, with a large oak wardrobe in one corner that is inlaid with a pattern of white bone. Wide windows open to the east, letting in plenty of sunlight, and the polished marble floor is laid with a crimson wool rug. The only things in it that will need replacing are the desk and chair, both of which look doll-sized next to Arthur's tall and lanky frame. If he were to try to sit in that chair, his bent knees would come up to his shoulders.

"This test is meant to show your mind, yes, but no one will tell stories about you bravely writing a letter. No one will want to sing songs about you bravely asking your betrothed to save *you*."

"Though, I do recall Gwen saving you a fair bit in Avalon," Morgana points out with a snort of laughter from her spot sprawled on the velvet chaise.

"It . . . was about even, I'm sure," Arthur says with a measure of indignation before looking at me. "So we'll put on the show, you're saying. Actually ride all the way to Lyonesse. Act like Gwen and I don't know each other. Isn't that a bit dishonest?"

I shrug. "Perhaps, but stories will spin on their own," I say. "Believe me, they'll all be far more interesting than the truth. And the fact that you are going into Lyonesse at all will make you brave in their eyes. Most knights wouldn't dare."

"And for good reason," Morgana says, propping herself up on her elbows. "I know Gwen loves her home, but you've heard the stories—it's a country overrun by monsters and savages. Wolves who walk upright. Children with fangs who howl at the moon. I certainly won't be tagging along on this ridiculous quest."

"So you would like to stay here instead?" I ask her. "Alone at court?"

That gives Morgana pause, and she rolls her eyes before flopping back against the overstuffed arm of the chaise.

"Fine," she says. "I suppose I'll come. Better monsters who *know* they're monsters than ones who insist on wearing pretty masks."

"We can stop by Shalott on the way," Arthur says, looking at me. "Stay the night, if your father will have us."

*My father.* Even before I left for Avalon, I hadn't seen him in months, hadn't lived with him in years. He's a stranger to me now, and my brothers are as well. They'll be old enough now to have married, to have children of their own. I try to summon their faces in my mind, but I can't quite manage it.

"You're the true king of Camelot, and of Albion as a whole," I tell him. "Of course he'd be honored to have you."

Arthur must hear what I don't say, because he offers me a small smile. "It'll be good for you to see him again," he says. "I came home to a dead father—one I'll never have the chance to know. Yours is still here."

I nod and shift my attention to the desk and chair. I don't want to think about my father. Yes, Arthur's right—I will have a chance to know my father, to build a bridge between us. But thinking about him makes me think about my mother, about the bridge I destroyed, destroying her in the process. Arthur didn't know his father. He can only miss him in the abstract sense. But I knew my mother—I loved her and I hated her and I will never have the chance to forgive her, or to ask her for the forgiveness I need.

Lancelot appears at my side without a word, his shoulder brushing against mine even though the room is spacious enough that there is no reason to. He looks at me sideways, and there is a question behind his eyes that I don't want to answer.

After a second, he clears his throat and changes the subject.

"I can't believe you were ever small enough to fit in this chair, Arthur," he says with a laugh. "These will need to go; we'll get you something your own size."

Arthur looks over at us from the bookshelf that stands by the wardrobe, his hand resting on the spine of a well-worn tome.

"No need for that before this quest, I'd imagine," he says with a sigh. "I doubt I'll be spending enough time in this room to warrant it."

He looks at me as he says it, as if looking for confirmation.

"No," I agree. "Even when you pass Merlin's tests, there will be plenty who oppose you. We need to ensure that your path to the throne is smooth and unhindered. Mordred has a lot of allies—we need to try to woo them over to our side."

I pause, running my hand over the small chair, the cherrywood back of it only coming up to my hip.

"And besides, they don't need replacing," I say, tracing the dragon that's carved at the top of the back, curling around where Arthur's shoulders would have been. "We can get rid of them entirely. Set up your office elsewhere in the palace. You will likely be there often, knowing you, and it will do well for the rest of the palace to know how hard you work, to wander by and see it with their own eyes from time to time."

Arthur snorts, pulling a slender volume from the shelf and turning it over in his hands. I'm too far away to make out the title, but there is an illustration of a lion on the front, faded with age.

"Will I be a dancing bear? Performing tricks for an audience?" he asks, and though his voice is wry, there's a note of real bitterness beneath it.

"You'll be a king," I remind him, softening my voice. "Making decisions for a country of people who will, more often than not, fail to see the effects of your work because they will be too small to affect them in any tangible way. If you have to dance to assure them that you're working—"

"I'll dance," he says, sounding resigned. He opens the cover of the book in his hands, scanning the first page. "This was one of my favorites as a child," he says.

"What is it?" Lancelot asks, moving away from me and toward Arthur.

Arthur shakes his head. "I can't remember all of it—something about a lion cub who wants so badly to be a lamb."

I know that story, I remember it from my own childhood. "He does," I tell him. "The cub gets adopted into a family of lambs, but when he gets older, his true nature becomes undeniable and he eats them all up."

Morgana sits up, looking at me with arched eyebrows.

"That's horrific," she says, though her eyes are bright.

I shrug. "Most children's stories were, from what I remember. Lots of oblique warnings and ominous messages hidden beneath the friendly facade of talking animals."

"I don't think that's the version I heard," Arthur says as he flips through it. "You're right, that's what it is, but the version I remember wasn't so bleak. I think my mother made up her own story as she read it to me."

At that, Morgana looks away. "That does sound like her," she says. "She was never good at the macabre."

I can count on one hand the number of times Morgana has talked about her mother in the ten years that I've known her, and even then none of it has been kind. This time, though, there's an undercurrent of tenderness to it. Arthur must hear it, too, because his brow creases and he puts the book back on the shelf firmly, as if he can shelve the ghost of the mother he can barely remember along with it.

But ghosts aren't so easily pushed aside, and I know that better than most. Which is why I straighten up and force a smile at Arthur.

"You should take the night to settle in, and Lancelot should stay with you," I say, nodding toward him. "Mordred seemed happy enough that Merlin posed such an impossible challenge, but he might decide to hedge his bets and dispose of you altogether."

"You really think he would kill Arthur?" Lancelot asks.

Morgana interrupts with a laugh. "Him personally? Not a chance. Did you see his hands? Not a callus on them. But I agree with Elaine—he wouldn't hesitate to hire someone else to do it if he thought Arthur was a threat."

Arthur and Lancelot exchange looks. "I'll get a guard outside the room as well," he says, sounding resigned but diplomatic. "I am officially blood of the royal family, if nothing else. That should entitle me to some guards."

Lancelot looks affronted. "Do you not think I could handle any assassin on my own?" he asks.

Arthur shrugs. "Not if you're asleep," he says. "You sleep hard enough that it would take an assassin's blade just to wake you up."

Even Lancelot has to laugh at that. "What about you?" he asks me.

I bite my lip. "I should check in on my family's tower. I don't think anyone has been there since . . ."

The words stick in my throat. *Since my mother died.* It's been almost three years since whispers made their way to Avalon in Arethusa's shells, but I still don't think I've ever said the words out loud. I still don't think I'll ever truly believe them, and certainly not before I see our empty tower with my own eyes.

"I'll come with you," Morgana says, getting up from the chaise and smoothing her violet silk gown down over her legs. It's wrinkled now, but she doesn't seem to notice or care.

"You don't have to," I tell her, but I think she must hear the relief in my voice because she smiles, linking her arm through mine and squeezing it.

"Of course I do," she says, as if it's the most natural thing in the world.

As soon as we step into the hall outside of Arthur's room, we almost run straight into a familiar face. Though it's the same face Morgana wears, with the same jet-black hair, the same hawkish nose, the same square jaw, there is nothing of Morgana's warmth reflected in Morgause. It is like seeing Morgana mirrored in ice. When she smiles with Morgana's full mouth, it is a sharp and mocking thing. It is a smile that has been practiced and rehearsed in front of a mirror until there is no true joy left in it.

All of a sudden, I am thirteen again, flinching from her words like they are the physical strike that usually accompanied them—the sharp-nailed pinch to my arm that drew blood, the shove down a dark hallway, the tug to my hair that was hard enough to pull out clumps of it. Every time, it was followed by a spark of glee in Morgause's cold eyes, a true but brittle smile stretching taut over her mouth.

It took a long time for me to understand how deeply some people enjoy inflicting pain on others, whether physical or emotional, but I don't think I've ever seen anyone equal Morgause in that.

This time, though, she is barely even looking at me. All her attention is focused on her twin, and Morgana does not flinch from her.

"Hello, Morgause," she says, her voice level.

For a tense moment, Morgause sizes her sister up like a general taking stock of an enemy across the battlefield, searching for weaknesses. After what feels like an eternity, she takes her sister by the shoulders and leans in to kiss her twice on each cheek. There is no one around but me, but it still feels like a show. Maybe she intends me to be the audience, but if so, she fails. I can clearly see how her fingers dig into Morgana's shoulders hard enough to leave bruises behind, how she doesn't quite touch her lips to Morgana's cheeks but instead hovers just above, how her smile is frozen and tight-lipped.

"It's been so long, my dear sister, but you look . . ." She pauses, dragging her eyes from the top of Morgana's head all the way to her toes. I imagine her taking inventory, noting Morgana's wild and unbound hair, the constellations of freckles that cover her cheeks and nose, her thin dress that bares her shoulders and a scandalous amount of her chest, her worn muslin slippers. Her eyebrow raises a fraction, and her smile widens. "Well," she finishes finally, but somehow that single innocuous word contains an ocean of insults.

Morgause is well versed in the art of court-speak, in saying one thing but ensuring your target hears something else entirely. I was on the receiving end of it so often that I became fluent in it myself, but Morgana never did. She left too young, stayed away too much. She sees her sister's barbs but doesn't know how to volley them back just as delicately. She only knows how to lob cannonballs. Effective, yes, but wielding more damage to herself than to anyone else.

I see her open her mouth, see the brash, ugly words forming on her lips, see Morgause about to get exactly the reaction she wants, see her telling everyone at court how feral her sister is, how Arthur must be as well, fay-raised and fay at heart. I see her using this to put chinks in his armor before he even has the chance to pass Merlin's tests. Before I make a conscious decision to do it, I am stepping into the line of fire.

"And marriage seems to be suiting you, Morgause," I cut in with a sharp smile of my own. "I have to say—I didn't think a king's bastard would find such a highborn wife, but it was so selfless of you to offer yourself up. You must have had better prospects, no?" I ask, frowning.

Morgause blinks at me for a moment, speechless. I want to relish the stunned look on her face, but I continue.

"And that dress," I add, looking at her dark green velvet gown with its trumpet sleeves and gold-embroidered bodice. It's the same dress she wore earlier, to what should have been her husband's coronation. I would imagine she put a lot of thought into it, a lot of effort. After all, once Mordred was crowned king, she would rise with him. She had to dress the part of a queen. It's a beautiful gown—Morgause's gowns always have been—but that makes it easier to sense her self-doubt and feed on it. "Well, it's very . . . *brave* isn't it?" I ask with a smile.

Morgause looks at me like she's smelled something strange that she can't quite put her finger on.

"Elaine the Mad," she says, her voice thick and sweet as syrup. "Why, I almost didn't recognize you. I didn't know that you were still tagging along in my sister's shadow, but I suppose I shouldn't be surprised. Birds of a feather and all of that."

I return her syrupy smile. "You wouldn't be looking for Arthur, would you?" I ask, stepping sideways to plant myself between her and Arthur's bedroom door. "I'm afraid he's busy, but if you would like to set up an audience with him, I'm happy to schedule something for you. He has a busy few days before we depart for Lyonesse, but I will try to fit you in, of course. Come see me in my tower tomorrow, once I've settled in, and we'll try to arrange something."

The smile slides off Morgause's face like butter out of a hot pan. "He's my brother," she says. "Surely he can see me."

I click my tongue in mock disappointment, even as a thrill of pleasure runs through me. It isn't that I think she's dangerous, at least not firsthand. Morgause, like Mordred, is not the kind to do her own dirty work. And I'm sure that if Arthur did see her, he would embrace her and speak kindly. But still I bar her. It truly is something, after all, to hold power over someone who'd previously choked you with theirs.

"I'm afraid not. He's very busy and, of course, he's still in mourning. Today is simply out of the question, but if you come see me tomorrow—"

"And what authority do you have?" she interrupts, her voice jumping up an octave. "Why should you keep me from my brother?"

I keep a firm hold on my serene expression, though I'd like nothing more than to laugh in her face.

Morgana, though, has less self-control, and her grin turns malevolent at the edges. "My darling sister," she says, linking her arm through mine. "Don't you know who you're talking to? Lady Elaine of Shalott—Arthur's closest adviser. He trusts her judgment implicitly, and should you try to go over her head . . . well, I wouldn't recommend it."

Morgause glares daggers at both of us, her eyes darting to the door behind me as if she's genuinely considering shoving past me and going in anyway. But that story would make its rounds through the palace in a matter of hours, and that is certainly not a story she wants told. After a moment, she smiles again, but it's brittle, fracturing like spider cracks on cold glass.

"Very well," she says, inclining her head, her eyes lingering on me, bright and simmering with fury. "We'll speak again tomorrow."

Before she turns to leave, though, she pauses, looking me over and tilting her head to one side. "It's wonderful to see you again, Elaine," she says, her voice syrupy once more. "Power doesn't suit you, but not to worry, yours will be short lived. Never fear—when you find yourselves in my court, I'll ensure you're treated justly."

The threat hangs in the air long after she walks away. It's an empty threat, I tell myself. Arthur will pass Merlin's tests with ease—he has to. But nothing is certain, not even the countless visions I've had of Arthur as king. He can still fail. And if he does, Mordred will become king and—perhaps worse still—Morgause will be queen.

# 13

EVERYTHING IN THE tower is covered by a thick coat of dust, casting the place in a silvery pale glow. A ghost of a place with ghosts of its own hiding in each corner. It hasn't been touched since shortly after I left, I'd imagine, after my father came from Shalott to bring my mother home. Arthur's great-grandfather gave it to mine when the castle was first built, and it's been in my family ever since. My father and brothers could have stayed here whenever they came to court, but I doubt they'd want to stay in a place so haunted by my mother's spirit. I don't want to stay here myself.

It doesn't look so different from the day I left, really—the velvet curtains still drawn closed, the teacups still set out on the table, the couch pillows still indented from where my mother would always lean against them.

If I try, I can see her there again now, the chenille blanket drawn up to her throat as she surveyed me in my gowns, critiquing the way they fit my figure, the way my hair was done, my posture. I always felt as though I left her presence several inches shorter—another thing she would no doubt find fault in.

Where my Sight is best channeled through the loom and Nimue's worked best through a scrying pool, my mother's prophecies took the shape of words, their meaning twisted and veiled and open to interpretation—every oracle is different, I've learned. Nimue told me that if my mother had received the proper training, it wouldn't have consumed her so fully, that she could have learned how to handle them, but as it was, each time she had a vision, it took something of her mind, something of herself. I saw it with my own eyes that night, how she became someone else, a stranger with my mother's face, but with hands that hurt instead of held.

*Beware, beware three maidens fair*, she'd murmured under her breath as her fingers pressed into my throat until I couldn't breathe. *With bloody hands and divine air.*

I touched my fingers to my throat, suddenly breathless. As if my mother could reach me even through death.

"Are you alright, El?" Morgana asks, drawing me out of the past and back into the present.

She walks along the edge of the sitting room, running a finger over the dusty windowsill and holding it up to inspect. The pad of her fingertip is almost black with grime.

"I'm fine," I tell her with a smile, though she sees right through it.

"You'll have to hire a staff," she says. "But even then, you shouldn't stay here alone. It's too big, too empty."

"Are you offering?" I ask her.

Her smile broadens. "The royal wing of the palace is too stuffy for me, and heavily populated by a never-ending flood of simpering simpletons who will no doubt be clamoring for my demise," she says. "I would much prefer solitude with you."

"People will talk." It's exactly what my mother would have said if she were here, but I don't mean it scornfully, or even as a rejection. Just a simple fact.

Morgana shrugs her shoulders. "People will talk if you're living here alone as well. They'll talk no matter what," she points out, which I can't argue with.

Instead I nod, crossing to the overstuffed sofa, piled with pillows and blankets that were never enough for my mother to find comfort. The indent from her body is still there, as if she rose only a moment ago to fetch a cup of tea, as if she'll return any moment and chide me for slouching.

"I want new furniture in here as well," I tell Morgana, my voice coming out surprisingly level. "All of it."

She doesn't protest, doesn't tell me I'm overreacting. Instead, she nods. "And how will you pay for all of this—the new furniture, the staff, the gowns you'll likely need? It won't come cheaply, and until Arthur is crowned, you won't get a salary for advising him."

"My father has an account with most everyone in the palace. He won't protest my using it, if he notices at all," I say. My father has always had too much money and little interest in it. "I'll write to him, let him know I've returned. Let him know that we'll be arriving in Shalott soon."

She doesn't say anything for a moment. "When was the last time you saw him?" she asks me.

"It must be close to eleven years now," I tell her. Saying it out loud knocks the wind from my lungs. Eleven years is such a long time—almost half of my life—but in many ways, the time has passed in the space of a single breath. Will he even recognize me on sight? Will I recognize him?

"I'll write to him as soon as I'm settled," I tell her, though I'm already dreading it. Not because I don't love my father—I do, even with all the distance between us—but because I don't know what to say to him, how to begin to build that bridge. "When Arthur's crowned, I'll bring one of my brothers to court—the Crone knows we'll need all the allies we can get in this viper pit."

Morgana nods, turning the information over in her mind. "And are they . . . handsome, these brothers of yours?" she asks with a grin. Though I know she's trying to lighten the heavy atmosphere hanging over us, I don't doubt that she is, at least somewhat, earnest. Morgana has rarely met a soul she didn't hope to entice, even if she had no interest in them herself.

I laugh. "I couldn't begin to tell you that for a number of reasons," I say. "But I would be surprised if they weren't married by now. They're both close to thirty."

Her expression sours at that. "Marriage," she says with a disdainful scoff. "I'd hoped to have avoided that particular trap by staying in Avalon."

"It's not as though you have anyone to force you into it," I point out. "Your parents can't very well marry you off, and Arthur wouldn't dream of trying."

"He definitely has more sense than that," she says, shaking her head.

"What about you? Surely the prime adviser to the king will be a bride in high demand."

I glance away so she can't see my cheeks turn pink. There was a time when a husband and children were all that my future contained, when even as a child myself, my mother was scheming and laying traps to catch me one. There was a time when it was all I thought I was capable of.

"I think you're greatly overestimating my appeal on the marriage market," I tell her. "My proximity to the king might be a boon, but it comes with my own power, which Camelot men don't tend to find appealing, not to mention the fact that my Sight makes for a strange and frightening trait in a wife."

Morgana shakes her head, looking out the wide window and leaning on it, likely coating her dress in dust, though she hardly seems to notice.

"And Lancelot?" she asks, almost tentatively. "You brought him all the way here, after all. Might as well make an honest man out of him."

I shake my head. "Lancelot is here for Arthur, not me," I say, though even as I say the words, I hear him back on the shore. *And you? Do you need me there, too, Shalott?* "Besides, he hasn't been raised for monogamy."

"He hasn't been raised for court, either, but here he is."

I swallow, but Morgana must see there is more I'm not saying. She's always known me too well.

"I imagine it must be difficult for an oracle to make commitments," she says after a moment. "I suppose you can't help but see the myriad of ways they go wrong. How do they go wrong?"

I bite my lip. There's always a risk, discussing visions with others, but in these visions, at least, Morgana had no part. So I tell her the truth.

"Oh, the ways you'd imagine, really," I say, trying to keep my voice casual. "I've seen him have his affairs, seen him leave me, seen us hurl words at each other designed to do nothing but maim."

"Affairs," she says, tilting her head to one side.

*Trust not the girl with the golden crown, she'll take what's yours and watch you drown.*

Part of me wants to tell Morgana about what I've seen of Lancelot and

Gwen, to tell her about my mother's prophecy, but the words die on my tongue. Speaking them aloud will give them power.

"It's Lancelot," I say instead, shaking my head. "The affairs can't be the most surprising bit. You know how he is."

"A couple of years ago I might have believed that," she says, her violet-gray eyes surveying me in a way I don't think I will ever grow accustomed to. "But there hasn't been anyone else in some time."

It's true, as far as I know. In the beginning, when we were mostly stolen moments and passionate kisses, neither of us made any bones about the fact that there were others—not just for him, but for me as well. And there was never a moment, in my memory, when we decided to see only each other. It just happened—no one else held my interest anymore, and it seemed to be the same for him.

"I've Seen my heart break," I tell her, keeping it as simple as I can. "More than that, I've Seen the rest of me break as well, and I've Seen the world break around us."

Morgana smiles, though it doesn't reach her eyes. "That's a bit dramatic. Everyone's heart breaks, El. Just because you can see it coming doesn't mean you can avoid it altogether. Besides, I'd wager you've seen more than just the bad bits."

That I can't deny, though it almost makes it worse, in a way.

"It's good to see Morgause is as vile as ever," I say to change the subject. "I thought for sure you were going to hit her."

"Oh, I likely would have," she says, laughing. "But I must admit, the face she made when you insulted her dress was somehow even more satisfying. How did you do that? It *sounded* like a compliment, but it wasn't."

I shrug my shoulders. "It's easy to pick up on once it's been directed at you a few too many times."

"I don't want to pick up on it, though," she says. "I miss Avalon already. But one day, we'll go back. You said it yourself."

I move to stand next to her by the window, staring out at Camelot, at the tall border walls, at the taller trees peeking over the tops of them. Somewhere out there is Avalon, far in the distance and cloaked in mist, but there all the same. I feel its presence in my soul, the faint tug of home.

"Yes," I tell her, thinking about the vision I had of us on the cliff, older and utterly changed but still us. "One day, we'll go back."

For better or worse, we'll go back.

# 14

THE FIRST DAYS at court pass in a blur, so busy and overstuffed that by the end of each day, my mind is too exhausted to scry at the loom, and instead I tumble into my childhood bed and a deep, dreamless sleep that is never quite long enough.

Morgana hires a staff to clean and cook, and though they are perfectly competent at their jobs, I suspect she chose them largely because they don't seem to fear us. They bow and curtsy and always put a *lady* before our names, but they also hold our gazes and talk and don't skitter in the shadows every time either of us enters the room. It's quite possible they go home to their families each night and tell them stories of the witches they work for, but if they are afraid of us, they hide it well, and that is all I can ask.

When I lived in this tower with my mother, I never had a single guest before Morgana, and my mother didn't either. Besides the servants, the tower was a lonely wasteland, and my mother and I were little more than two ghosts floating through it.

Now, though, the tower is never empty. From morning on, if I'm here, there is someone waiting to speak with me. When I do leave, I always return to a queue that winds down the steep stairway. I discuss Arthur while I eat breakfast, while I visit the seamstress, while I take my exercise walking in the gardens. I construct the history of his life for them, painting a picture vivid enough that he ceases to be just an upstart boy who appeared out of thin air and begins to at least resemble a living myth—a lost prince, returned home to take his rightful place on the throne. I spin a story they want to believe—and, more importantly, a story they want to repeat over and over and over again until the great myth of Arthur becomes larger than life.

I don't lie about Arthur—there is little need to, after all—but I am careful about what information I give and what I withhold. I am conscious of the fact that once these stories leave my tower, they will begin to twist and change with each retelling. I try to ensure that they twist in a way that is beneficial to us.

When I tell the Duke of Northam about Arthur's bravery, I tell him how he fought the dragon that lived in the northern caves of Avalon. I tell him how it was a fierce battle, how hard Arthur fought. I tell him that, should he ask his prince, he might even get to see the place on Arthur's forearm where the dragon singed his skin. The duke listens, enraptured, as I tell him what the dragon was like, how tall and fierce, with fangs sharper than daggers and fire spewing from its mouth.

All of that is true. But what I don't tell the duke is that it was merely sparring, that neither Arthur or the dragon—Meerla was her name—intended to do the other harm.

And by the end of the day, the story has multiplied. The overexcited daughter of an earl told me in hushed tones over dinner that she'd heard Arthur had vanquished an entire legion of dragons, completely on his own. That his sword shot bolts of lightning. That he fought with the strength of fifty—no, *one hundred*—men.

The next morning I do it all over again, this time with stories of his wisdom.

It's tiring work, but the most unexpected part is that in Arthur's meetings, almost every lord or earl or duke who comes before Arthur doesn't come alone. They always bring their daughters along, or if they have no daughters, their nieces or sisters or granddaughters. The girls all stay silent during the meeting, but their eyes rest on Arthur, hungry and confident and promising.

"I wish they wouldn't bring them," Arthur says to me in the brief break between two audiences. "It makes me uncomfortable—like they want something from me that I don't know how to give."

I look up from my sheet of parchment, littered with splotches of notes I'm not sure I'll be able to decipher later. We're sitting in the office I had set up for him, sparsely decorated with a large oak desk and shelves of books I borrowed from the royal library. There is a map of Albion hanging on the back wall, though it is more work of art than strategic tool, with its curling ornate script and the country covered with gold leaf. Avalon is conspicuously missing from it.

Arthur sits behind the desk in a high-backed leather chair that resembles a throne while I sit in an armchair off to the side, a book balanced on my lap with the parchment over it to give me a hard, flat surface to write on. The empty chair on the other side of Arthur's desk is smaller than both of ours and a few inches lower to the ground, so that anyone who sits on it is dwarfed by Arthur, and even by me.

"You can't be that thick, Arthur," I say with a laugh. "You know exactly what they want—you. Or, rather, your hand. Even if you fail Merlin's tests, you're still Uther's son. And since Mordred is already married, that makes you the most eligible bachelor in the country."

Arthur slumps down in his leather chair, ducking his head, as if that can hide how red his face grows. "I'm not eligible, either, though. I'll be coming back from Lyonesse with Gwen."

"I know that," I say, shaking my head. "But they don't, and honestly, it's better to keep that from them as long as we can. Mordred has had years to curry favor with the nobles. You haven't. Take whatever advantage you can. When you do return with Gwen, everyone will be pleased enough. Bringing Lyonesse into Albion is what they all want. *But*, in the meantime, giving the court the illusion that one of their family might end up on the throne beside you will give them a reason to support your claim."

The furrow doesn't leave Arthur's brow. "You want me to lie?"

"You don't have to lie," I say with a sigh. "You don't have to do anything. They believe you're looking for a wife—for a queen—let them believe it. That's all."

"Like you let them believe I've vanquished an army of dragons single-handedly?" he asks. "Or that the High Lady of Wisdom sought my guidance on Avalon? She asked me for directions to the loo once, and I provided them."

"That is guidance," I say, but I don't look at him, instead focusing on my notes.

He doesn't reply, looking out the window that overlooks the forest to the east of the castle. "I didn't think it would be like this," he admits. "I mean, I didn't think it would be like anything in particular. I never thought about it, coming back here, but if I'd had to imagine it . . . well, it wouldn't have been like this."

"What would you have imagined?" I ask.

He shrugs his shoulders, and for a second, I think he doesn't have an answer, but finally he speaks, his voice soft.

"Like a story, I suppose," he says. "Where the prince is welcomed home with open arms and crowned and becomes a benevolent king who sits on his throne and uses his power to help people."

"Stories make it seem easy," I say. "The king always has unlimited power and is loved by everyone. They never show how he gets that power, how he earns that love. They don't show that no one can be universally loved, that there are always those lurking near power, waiting for their chance to yank it away because everyone believes themselves to be the heroes of their own story."

He nods, but his eyes are still heavy and troubled. "I wish Gwen were here," he says after a moment. He looks at me and half smiles. "No offense to you—I would be utterly lost without your help, and you're one of my closest friends. I love you. But—"

"Well, I'm sure I'm not as good at kissing you," I say with a laugh.

His face turns red again, and he laughs. "Apples to oranges," he murmurs, which makes my own face heat up.

That single kiss had been a clumsy thing, borne of adolescent curiosity and frustration that the others always treated us like we were inexperienced children compared to them. It had lasted only a few seconds before we broke apart, laughing until our stomachs ached.

It was a perfectly fine first kiss for both of us, all things considered, but Arthur was right, it was incomparable to a kiss with a person you truly want in that way. And that has never been what Arthur and I are to each other, simpler as it might have made things.

Which is why I take one of the pillows from my armchair and throw it at his head.

He catches it deftly with a grin. "I'm not talking about that, though . . . well, not *just* that. I just miss her, especially here. This place isn't what I expected. It's so gloomy and cold. I think it needs her, in a way. It needs her light."

The yearning in his voice tugs at my heart. He isn't the only one who misses Gwen.

"We leave for Lyonesse in two days. If our travels go to plan, we'll be there in a week. And then there will be only one test separating you from the throne."

He nods slowly, and when he smiles, he doesn't look like a king. He doesn't even look like a prince. He just looks like a boy, the boy I've known since I was thirteen years old, with his freckled face and curious eyes.

"I trust you, El," he says.


THE THING ABOUT Avalon is that no one can truly prepare you for it. A million words—even a billion—might paint a vivid picture, but there is no combination of words in this world that can do it justice.

On the boat ride there, Morgana tried to describe it to me, and she did as good a job as anyone was capable of. She told me about the rolling fields full of every flower imaginable, the forests so lush that not a single sunbeam could get through the leaves, the beaches where turquoise waves rolled in, bringing shells that shone like jewels. She told me it was the most beautiful place in the world.

All of that was true, but there were things no amount of explanation could have prepared me for—like the way the paths that wove through the forests would often change depending on the time of day or the weather or the mood of the sprites who called it home. Or how mermaids lived in the lakes and rivers and sea, how they were just as likely to give you pearls as they were to pull you into the water and drown you. Or about the fey themselves, how some looked as human as Morgana and me, but others had skin in a rainbow of hues, or wings sprouting from their backs, or cloven feet and horns. Some, in fact, had all of that and more.

I don't think Morgana really understood that those were things she should have told me. Avalon was home to her, and so the things that seemed strangest to me were perfectly commonplace to her. Many times, I would ask her something and she would respond with a blank stare and a bewildered explanation that left me with more questions than answers.

I learned quickly that there was no one better at answering questions than Arthur.

At first, he intimidated me, even though he was younger and barely came up to my shoulder. He was quiet and soft-spoken, a whisper among the shouts of the others and easily lost in any crowd, but he was still *Arthur*. Still the lost prince I had heard about so much he was more myth than anything else, and there he was—just a boy with his nose buried in a book and his head always in the clouds.

He didn't know what to make of me at first, a strange girl in a strange land where he had grown up knowing everyone, and I suppose that feeling was mutual. I never knew what to say to him. What does a person say to someone they know to be their future king? I stuttered and stumbled over my words. I always felt like I should curtsy or call him *Your Highness*, though the first time I did, he looked like he wanted to die of embarrassment and Morgana continued to mockingly call him that for the rest of the day.

One day, though, I asked him a question and that changed everything.

"Is it always this cool here?" I asked. "It was the middle of summer when I left Camelot and sweltering hot."

We were at lunch, and Morgana, Gwen, and Lancelot hadn't arrived yet, so it was only the two of us. Arthur was reading a book about the flora and fauna of Avalon, but when I spoke, he looked up from it, blinking like he'd just been dragged out of a deep sleep. When he registered my question, though, he put the book down spine up and leaned forward, resting his elbows on the table. His eyes grew wide and bright.

"It's a fascinating phenomenon, really," he said. "Part magic, part science. You see, because we're so close to the water, we get the benefit of the ocean breeze, which you don't get in Camelot because it's so landlocked. But it's also to do with the island itself. It regulates its temperatures all on its own—you'll see it more when winter comes. The most you'll need is a light cape to ward off the chill."

I considered this. Even though I'd been on Avalon a week at that point and seen magic with my own eyes plenty of times, the idea of it was still strange and intangible to me.

"Is it some kind of spell?" I asked him. "Does Nimue cast it?"

He shook his head. "I don't think so, no," he said. "There was a book I read—mostly a log of tide patterns from a few hundred years ago, but there was a section in it about the weather. It claimed it was the island itself that regulated the weather. It's why the rain is so controlled here as well—we never have droughts, but we also never have floods. Sometimes you'll see a storm far out in the distance, but it never comes here. It actually moves *around* the island, as if there's some sort of barrier protecting it."

His face lit up as he spoke, and I found myself leaning forward, desperate to hear him speak more, even if it was only about the weather.

"Do you ever get used to it?" I asked him. "Magic, I mean?"

As far as I could tell, Arthur was the only one on Avalon without a drop of fay blood, without a hint of any kind of magic. Morgana had her spells and potions, Gwen had her control over nature, Lancelot was faster and stronger than any human could be . . . but Arthur was only Arthur, hopelessly human in every way.

He shrugged. "I think a person can get used to anything if they're around it enough," he said. "And I've been around it for as long as I can remember."

"You don't remember Camelot at all?" I pressed.

He frowned at that, as if trying to search his memory. "I remember . . . shadows of things. Hazy images, flashes of feelings. Every so often, something comes back, but it usually slips through my fingers again. I was only two when I left."

I nodded, unsure of what to say, but before I could say anything, he looked up at me, something shy and tentative in his expression.

"Will you . . ." He trailed off, chewing on his bottom lip. "Will you tell me about it?" he asked. "Camelot, I mean. Or Albion in general. There are so many books in the library here, but most of them are about Avalon or magic or the fey. The ones that are about the mainland are mostly old, and even when they aren't, there's a distance to them. They're all written by fey, so they read like an observer's account of a place and its people. It's hard to get a real feel for it through them."

"You want me to tell you about Albion," I said slowly.

He shrugged, giving me a small, secret smile. "It's my home, after all. Why shouldn't I be curious about it?"

As I would find out, Arthur was curious about everything. Anytime I answered one question, he always had five more at the ready. And as I told him about Albion, about Camelot, about court, he told me about Avalon. He showed me the island in a way that Morgana hadn't been able to, with patience and a sense of wonder.

# 15

THE DINING ROOM in the royal wing is large and airy, anchored by a table that holds only six people, as opposed to the five long tables in the banquet hall that can hold fifty people each. For all the grandeur of the room—the large windows overlooking the forest, the tapestries threaded with gold and silver, the crystal chandelier overhead, the gilt plates and bowls that set the table—this is a space that few people in the palace ever have the opportunity to see.

I never thought that I would be one of them, but here I am, sitting at Arthur's right hand, just across from Lancelot.

Though there is nothing strange about the three of us eating together, the surreal nature of the surroundings is only amplified by the presence of Morgause and Mordred.

The seat next to me remains empty, though I'd expected Mordred to take it. I admit I was relieved when he didn't, opting instead for the foot of the table directly opposite Arthur. It was an unmistakable show of power, a way of asserting himself as Arthur's equal, and I'm sure even Lancelot with his limited knowledge of court etiquette can feel the chill that hangs over the table.

Arthur is the first to speak, lifting his gold goblet of wine with a congenial smile.

"It is so wonderful to be back home, with family," he says, nodding toward Mordred and Morgause. "Thank you for coming tonight. I did feel terrible for interrupting your coronation like I did. The timing was regrettable."

Mordred returns Arthur's smile. "Regrettable, yes, but as Merlin said, it is important to be thorough."

"Of course," Arthur agrees.

Morgause sips from her own goblet with pursed lips. "And yet . . . we aren't with *all* of our family, are we?" she asks, her voice lilting and slippery. "My dear sister couldn't join us?"

"Morgana was feeling indisposed," I say, which is true enough.

*If I have to have dinner and watch those two hold hands or kiss or whatnot, I'll be sick*, she'd told me when I invited her. *Maiden, Mother, and Crone, he's our* stepbrother.

From what I'd gathered over the last few days at court, Morgause and Mordred's marriage barely raised an eyebrow when it happened two years ago. Even though they shared no blood, they were related through marriage, and were siblings at that. Mordred's natural father had raised Morgause as his own since she was practically an infant. Still, at the time, Uther was without a proper heir—only a ward and a bastard. It made perfect sense for them to consolidate that power.

"Pity," Morgause says, though there is no pity in her voice. Only boredom and a thimbleful of venom.

"I'm glad that your girl could finally make room for us in your busy schedule," Mordred says with barely a glance at me. He slouches down in his high-backed chair with his goblet held carelessly in his hand. Though tonight's dinner is a casual affair, he wears a gold-trimmed doublet with heavy rings on all his fingers and a jewel-encrusted chain around his neck.

When they walked in, Lancelot leaned in to whisper to me, *If I threw him in the moat, I reckon he would sink straight to the bottom.*

*By the end of the night, we may need to put that theory to the test*, I'd whispered back, fighting a bout of laughter.

"Lady Elaine is my adviser," Arthur says, and though his voice is smooth enough, there is a sharp edge to it. "Not my *girl*."

If we were on Avalon, I would put a hand on his arm to calm him. Mordred is trying to get a rise out of him, that's all. But such a gesture—small as it may be—would lead to wagging tongues in the morning, and those rumors would do neither of us any favors.

"It has been a very busy few days," I cut in before Arthur can say more. I try on an apologetic smile, though I don't bother trying to make it look genuine. "It seems that everyone at court is eager to offer Arthur allegiance since his return. It's been very tiring, I'm sure you can imagine."

Mordred's smile is tight, his gray eyes darkening until they are nearly black. "I'm sure I can," he says before turning back to Arthur. "When do you leave for Lyonesse?" he asks.

"The day after tomorrow, at dawn," Arthur says. "It's a week's journey, so we should return just outside the fortnight."

Morgause's eyebrows arch. "So soon?" she asks. "Lyonesse has been resistant to joining Albion for decades. Surely it will take longer than a few days to persuade them, far longer if you have to resort to force."

Arthur shrugs his shoulders, a small smile playing on his lips. "You'll forgive me, dear sister, if I don't divulge my plan quite yet."

Mordred sips his wine, watching Arthur over the rim of the goblet, calculating. "As Uther was fond of saying, a strategy is only as good as the men you have at your side. I have to say, I do worry in that regard. After all, you have no men at your side—just two women and one of the fey."

Lancelot blinks, surprised to find so much attention suddenly on him. I suppose he's gotten used to largely fading into the background and letting Arthur and me do the talking while he merely looks intimidating.

"I beg your pardon?" he says, sitting up.

"I'll thank you not to insult my advisers," Arthur interrupts before Lancelot can say something he'll regret.

"Your advisers," Mordred says with a scoff, the thin veneer of gentility slipping away. "Your advisers are a lady with a reputation for madness, a witch so cowardly she won't leave her tower, and one of our own enemies."

"I didn't realize I was anyone's enemy, *my lord*," Lancelot says, derision dripping from his voice. "If you're referring to the war with Avalon, I was only just born at the end of it. And at least in Avalon, I was raised not to insult women without cause. I'd heard Albion was a chivalrous place, but I'm beginning to think I was mistaken."

Lancelot keeps his voice level, but as he speaks, Mordred's face turns red. Before he can reply, Morgause gets there first.

"And here I always believed that to the fey, a stretch of twenty years was little more than a blink," she drawls. "There are many in Albion who believe the truce that ended the war was nothing more than a child's promise to the fey, that they are lying in wait, biding their time. That they, perhaps, insisted on raising a human king to be their pawn so they could one day take their revenge." She pauses, idly toying with the stem of her wineglass, her eyes falling on me as her smirk widens. "And I do believe that Albion and Avalon have very different definitions of womanhood."

"That's enough," Arthur says, his voice too full and booming to have come from his lanky body. "I'll hear no disparagement of any of my advisers or Avalon in my presence, not even from family."

The hairs on the back of my neck prickle, and I want so badly to reach out and clamp my hand over his mouth, to stop him from speaking, from giving them exactly what they hoped for. On Avalon, I would have, but here all I can do is clench my teeth and clutch the arms of my chair and wait for it to be over.

Mordred smirks, running his finger around the rim of his goblet while looking at Arthur with glittering eyes.

"Spoken as a true champion of the fey," he says.

For a second I think Arthur might snap at him, might throw all of his regal behavior out the window and leap across the table to pummel him. Instead, though, he takes a deep breath.

"Spoken as the future king of a country with citizens who are both human and fay, as well as a good amount who are both. I don't intend to be king of the humans, or king of the fey for that matter. I intend to be king of Albion and everyone who calls it home. Otherwise, we run the risk—no, the absolute certainty—of finding ourselves at war again. That, Lord Mordred, is why my father sent me to Avalon, to ensure that I had one foot in each domain so that I could rule over both.

"And you were right, sister," he adds to Morgause. "The fey have long memories. If war comes again, make no mistake: They will wipe us out. I don't intend to let that happen."

Silence follows his words and lingers for the rest of the meal, though my stomach is so tied in knots that I can't eat more than a few bites. When the dessert wine is poured, Mordred drinks it down in a single gulp before setting the goblet down so hard that I fear he'll have left a mark on the oak table.

"You get ahead of yourself, brother," Mordred says finally. "You have two tests left, and the last few battalions we've sent to Lyonesse haven't returned. I wouldn't start picking out my coronation robes yet, if I were you. You might be better off picking out a funeral shroud."

WHEN DINNER ENDS and the others disperse, Lancelot lingers. Suddenly, the cavernous dining hall feels too small, its wall pressing in on every side of me. Though there are servants who will sweep in at any moment to clear the table, I busy myself with stacking the plates, gathering the goblets, anything to keep from facing him.

It is one thing to talk to him with Arthur as a buffer, when we are only a group of friends and neither of us can say anything beyond that. But alone? With wine and fury and fear of what Lyonesse will bring rushing through my veins? That is another story entirely.

His hand comes over mine, over the plate I'm holding, and I drop it. It crashes to the stone floor below, shattering into gold-painted shards.

"Sorry," Lancelot says. "I didn't mean to . . ."

He trails off, dropping down to gather the broken pieces. As I watch him, a strange thought occurs to me: He's as nervous as I am. Cool, collected Lancelot, who never stumbles over words, who never trails off his sentences and rarely apologizes, and here he is, all aflutter.

"Be careful, it's sharp—" I say, but as soon as the words leave my mouth, he lets out a hiss of pain and drops one of the pieces. A line of red wells up on his palm, and he closes his hand tight over it.

I take a clean napkin from the empty seat next to me and drop down beside him, holding out my hand. After a second, he gives me his, and I wrap the napkin around his palm.

"It isn't too bad," I tell him softly. "It should be fine by tomorrow. Tonight, even, with your fay blood."

He doesn't say anything for a moment, his brow furrowed. "What Mordred said . . ."

I bite my lip. "I'm sorry for that, but he isn't alone in his suspicion of you. It will take time, but you can bring them around."

He smiles wryly. "I wasn't talking about him insulting me. What was it he called you?"

I glance away, feeling heat rise to my cheeks. It's easy to forget sometimes that Lancelot never knew me then, he didn't know the girl I was in the eyes of Camelot, unsettled and unsettling.

"*A lady with a reputation for madness,*" I repeat. "Quite a delicate description, all things considered. I think I got off the easiest, compared to you and Morgana."

He laughs softly. "I wish Morgana had been here," he says. "Unwise as it might have proved, it would have been fun to see her response when he called her a coward."

"She would have strangled him with that hideous jeweled chain," I say, laughing myself. After the laughter subsides, I bite my lip. "Before Avalon, I knew I was an oracle, but I didn't understand what that meant. I wasn't trained. I was prone to visions that manifested as hysterics. It . . . earned me a reputation. I'd hoped ten years would have been enough to rid myself of it, but it seems people have long memories."

He smiles, one corner of his mouth lifting higher than the other in that infuriatingly charming way he has.

"We've only been here a few days," he says. "A few more and I doubt anyone will be mocking you. By the time Arthur's crowned, I daresay you'll be running this whole place. You're good at it, you know. Far better than I am."

Though he says it lightly, there's an undercurrent of bitterness to his words. In Avalon, Lancelot was the golden child, excelling at whatever task was put in front of him. He was the best hunter, the best swordsman, the best jouster.

Even when we were helping his mother gather shells on the shore, he was always determined to collect the most—and he always succeeded.

"It's hard for you, isn't it?" I ask. "Not being the best at everything?"

"It's torture," he admits before pausing. "That wasn't what I wanted to talk to you about."

"No?" I ask, hating how my voice breaks.

He considers his next words carefully, staring over my shoulder as if he's afraid to look at me. When his eyes do meet mine, though, it is a spell all its own, and I am powerless to break it.

"You've been avoiding me," he says. "Ever since we got here."

"I've been busy, Lance," I say, shaking my head and avoiding his eyes because he's always quick to know when I'm lying. I start to stand, but Lancelot's unbandaged hand comes to rest against my cheek, and just like that, I freeze.

"So if I want to talk to you, I should make an appointment?" he asks, voice low.

"What is there to talk about?" I ask him, but my voice doesn't come out the way I mean for it to. It wavers and fractures and betrays me.

"Fair point," he says, pulling me closer to him. Automatically, my hands go to his shoulders, the muscles there hard and familiar. It feels like we're dancing again, on Avalon, the lure of the fay music weaving enchantments in the air. "We don't have to talk."

The instant he kisses me, that spell tightens, tightens, tightens, before breaking all at once. I push him away gently, one hand on his chest, but it's enough. His hooded eyes open, focusing on me, full of questions.

"We aren't on Avalon anymore, Lance," I say quietly. "We can't just sneak around together. In Camelot, no one does . . . *that* . . . I mean, I suppose they do, but only married couples. We aren't even supposed to be alone together now, not unless we're wed."

For an instant, he looks confused before he realizes what I'm saying.

"Well," he says, the word heavy. "We could be."

His tone is so blasé that for a moment all I can do is stare at him.

"We could be . . . what, married?" I ask him slowly. "Are you . . . proposing?"

He shrugs his shoulders. "It makes sense, doesn't it? You said it yourself, rules in Camelot dictate that if I lie with you, I have to marry you," he says.

I shake my head, unable to hold back a laugh. It's too ridiculous. "Camelot's rules didn't apply back in Avalon. Don't worry, I won't hold you to them. You don't have to do anything."

Lancelot shakes his head. "That's not . . . that's not what I mean," he says. "You asked me to come with you. You said you needed me here. So then why are you pushing me away now?"

*Because the needing is terrifying. Because I've seen how it ends. Because I don't want you to break me, and I don't want to break you either.*

"I'm not pushing you away," I say instead. "But it's complicated."

"But you love me," he says.

My cheeks are burning now. "I never said that. Neither of us did."

"Because we didn't need to, Shalott. No point in wasting time saying things that everyone already knows to be true."

That gives me pause. "Do you love me?" I ask, though as soon as I say the words I regret them. It's a dangerous question, and one with no good answer.

The corner of his mouth quirks up in a smile. "So much I think it'll kill me sometimes. And I know you feel the same."

He hasn't the slightest idea, though, how literal the killing is for me.

"That was on Avalon," I say finally, though my voice wavers. "Whatever value love held there, it doesn't hold the same here."

"The rules have changed," he says, nodding. "That's what I'm saying. There are no bonfires here. You're saying I shouldn't do this . . ." He trails off, snaking his arm around my waist and turning me to face him, our bodies so close that I can feel his heart beating, quick as a hummingbird's. "Not with a woman who isn't my wife," he murmurs, his lips close to mine. "I want to keep doing this, Shalott. I want to keep doing everything, with you. And if I have to play by Camelot's rules to do it, I will."

He's so close that I can feel his breath against my cheek, so close that his eyes don't look green or brown or hazel anymore, they are an undeniably inhuman gold, and I can't look away. He smells like Avalon still, like smoke and lavender and honey and that implacable scent of magic that always lingered in the air.

If I tilted my head up just an inch, my lips would find his, and the yearning to do just that consumes me until I can't think straight, until I can't think about anything but him—his closeness, and how he is still too far away from me.

But that way lies a thousand heartbreaks. I've Seen them, the million ways he could betray me, the ways we will almost undoubtedly betray each other. I've felt it—the fatal blows to us, the loss of him like the loss of a limb, the utter helplessness as my life crumbles around me without him to hold it upright.

I want him, there is no denying that, but I do not need him. Not yet. Not ever, if I can help it.

He moves to close the distance between us, but I stop him, placing my hand on his chest, just over his rapidly beating heart.

"No, Lance," I say, so quietly that I'm not sure he heard me at all. But he stops, so I suppose he must have. I clear my throat, taking a step back, out of his embrace, hoping the distance will help me think clearer. It doesn't, really.

"That isn't what marriage is," I say when I find my words again. "You don't marry someone because you want to . . . because you want to bed them. People here marry for many reasons—for money, for titles, for power."

I swallow, readying a weapon I know will sting, though sting *less* than what will come if I let him touch me again.

"You don't have anything to offer. No money, no titles, no power."

He goes still, and the hurt that flashes over his expression hurts me just as terribly. I want to take the words back, to tell him I don't mean them, that I don't care about those things, and besides, soon I'll have enough of all three for the both of us. Before he can speak, to argue, to inevitably convince me of some terrible idea, I take another step away from him, as if the air between us is any kind of barrier.

"And here I always thought you were something of a romantic, Shalott," he says finally, his voice dry and sharp, though I know it's all a defense. I've wounded him, and he won't allow me to do so again.

I shrug my shoulders. "The thing you need to understand about Albion, and Camelot specifically, is that it demands more of its women than it does of its men. There are different rules. I know how to play them, but you still have to learn."

I turn to go, but his voice stops me.

"I do love you, Elaine," he says, so quietly I almost miss it. "Maybe I should have said it before. I've loved you since that bonfire—maybe even earlier. I love you, but the truth is that sometimes, loving you feels like trying to hold a billow of smoke in my hands."

I pause, lingering in the doorway. I suppose he's right—I already knew he loved me, but hearing him say the words out loud undoes me.

"You're right—I don't have money or a title or any kind of power here," he continues. "I'm sure there are dozens of lords and earls and dukes here in Camelot to offer you those. But my offer stands, should you change your mind."

# 16

THAT BLASTED BONFIRE. They were a monthly occurrence on Avalon to celebrate the full moon—I must have attended close to a hundred. But still, I knew immediately which one Lancelot was referring to.

The full moon bonfires were riotous parties, with freely flowing wine and thin inhibitions and so much close dancing and bare skin that any of the old matrons of Camelot would have fainted to have seen it.

The first one I attended had been overwhelming to me. The fey with their wine-stained mouths and drunken laughter, whirling together in frantic but graceful movements that looked too far from the carefully choreographed dances in Camelot to possibly be called the same thing. A quartet of forest nymphs played instruments I couldn't name—some version of pipes and violins, drums and flutes perhaps, but different. Like they'd been carved from the trees but were somehow alive still. The effect of it all was terrifying, but before long the rhythm of the music worked its way into my own blood like the spell it was, making it impossible not to dance as well.

Before long, I was dancing with the rest of them. I twirled under Arthur's arm so many times I became dizzy and light-headed, both of us giggling madly, leaning on each other for support. I swayed with Morgana, our cheeks pressed together as we pretended to be stiff Camelot courtiers, unable to keep from laughing every few seconds. I held Gwen's hands and spun in mad circles, round and round and round until we couldn't hold on anymore and collapsed on the sand, breathless and giddy. I even danced with strangers, fey whose names I didn't know. In the energy of the night, they all stopped seeming so scary. Instead, I thought them all beautiful with their gemstone skin and wings and horns.

I danced until the night became a blur and the next thing I knew I was waking up in my own bed without any idea how I got there.

I learned quickly how to pace myself, to rest between dances to keep the music from getting too firm a hold on me.

But that wasn't the bonfire Lancelot had meant—if he'd been at that one, I don't recall seeing him. More likely than not, he'd spent the night in some other girl's arms, dancing with her and not thinking of me at all.

No, the bonfire in question was a year later. I was seventeen and found myself sitting on a boulder at the edge of the fray, my knees drawn up to my chest and my sheer cerulean silk gown spilling over the rock like a waterfall. A glass of fay wine was warm in my hand, and I sipped it slowly, biding my time before diving into the madness.

The wine was sweet enough to drink in a few gulps, but that was another thing I'd learned the hard way to pace myself with—fay wine wasn't like wine in Albion, where I'd seen courtiers drink entire bottles in single sittings. In Avalon, wine was far more potent. If you weren't used to it, a few sips would be enough to undo you, and the less fay blood you had, the more dangerous it was. Arthur never had more than a sip.

The gowns worn at bonfire nights were longer than the usual day dresses worn on the island, but elegant in a way that would have gotten us stoned to death in Albion. That night, mine left my arms bare and dipped low enough to show the shadowed space between my breasts. It was unstructured, without layers of petticoats and corsets beneath, loose enough to breathe freely and deeply. I knew that when I stepped closer to the light of the fire, my legs would be clearly visible through the silk.

But still, mine was relatively tame. There were bare legs and arms, sheer shimmers of fabric that didn't do much to hide skin underneath, dresses that dipped so low in the front they show the women's belly buttons. The quartet of fey playing their strange instruments next to the fire wore matching floor-length skirts but nothing above their waists. Their yellow hair was pulled forward over their shoulders and falling just long enough to hide their bare breasts. By comparison, my own dress felt practically matronly.

I spied Morgana dancing in the thick of the crowd, her own gown black lace that swathed over one shoulder, see-through in more places than not. Even though the skirt was long and flowing, I could see her legs quite clearly through the material, all the way up to her hips. She felt my gaze and grinned, beckoning me to join her, but even with the music pulling at my skin, I shook my head.

"Five minutes," I mouthed to her, holding up my hand.

She rolled her eyes and turned back to her partner, a handsome fay boy with horns that twisted up through his curly black hair. She twined her arms around his neck and they danced even closer, until they looked like one being instead of two.

"It's her blood," Arthur said, surprising me by joining me on the rock. His hair was messier than ever, bits of it sticking straight up like russet dandelion fluff. His white shirt was askew, an extra button undone, and there was a high pink flush across his cheeks, whether from the heat or the wine I couldn't tell. When he saw my confusion, he laughed.

"The music doesn't affect her as much as it affects us," he explained. "You usually last longer than I do, which I take as a testament to your own fay ancestors."

"What does that say about Gwen?" I asked. It was easy to find her in the crowd with her red-gold hair. She danced with a group I didn't recognize, her ivy-green gown twirling around her legs like flower petals, one sleeve slipping down over her freckled shoulder, though she didn't bother pulling it up.

"Gwen likes the oblivion she finds in the music," Arthur said after watching her for a moment, his gaze lingering a little longer, a little heavier. "She told me once it reminded her of the heat of a hunt in Lyonesse, when the mind quiets and pure instinct takes over. All action, no thought."

I glanced sideways at him. His feelings for Guinevere were so obvious, even then. She ignored them, in hopes that they would go away on their own, but there was never any chance of that. I think I would have known it even if I hadn't seen glimpses of their future. Arthur's infatuation was never destined to be a simple thing, like Lancelot and the countless girls he fell in and out of love with, or Morgana and her infinite partners. It wasn't a quick-burning flame. Arthur didn't fall in love easily, and I didn't expect falling out of it would come any easier to him.

"You and Gwen are very different," I said carefully, elbowing him to add a lightness to the words. "I can't imagine you ever giving up your thoughts. You cling to them, Arthur, like a child who insists on carting his blanket with him everywhere."

He laughed, shaking his head.

"I like logic," he agreed. "But logic on Avalon is a scarce thing—even when you think you have a hold on it, it slips right through your fingers like grains of sand. You must be finding that out as well, now that you've been here awhile."

Awhile. It felt like an eternity and a moment at once. I finished my glass of wine in a single gulp and set it aside.

Arthur held a hand out to me, and we both slipped off the boulder. He led me into the crush of fay and human bodies. It became easy to let my guard down and let the music in, to let it work its way through me until my heartbeat became just another part of the song. In Camelot, Lady Grier, the dancing teacher, called me a gelding because of my clumsy steps, but when my body moved of its own accord to the fay music, I didn't feel clumsy at all. I felt light and graceful, like my body wasn't quite mine anymore but a part of the island itself, guided by wind and tides and stars.

I never let it take me too far, though, even if it meant pinching the soft underside of my arm every few minutes to clear the fog that draped over my mind. The crowd pulsed in time to the music, like we were one heart, one body. The faces blurred together—most of them strange and fay, their eyes gliding over me like I wasn't quite there. I was grateful for Arthur's hand around mine, an anchor in the madness. Even when I couldn't see him, I knew he was there.

Every so often, among the shifting crowd, I caught a glimpse of Morgana's violet cat eyes or Guinevere's red mess of curls. I tried to pull Arthur toward them, but they slipped from view whenever we got too close.

Arthur's hand was pulled from mine by the pulsing crowd, and panic flashed through me, laced with the dull haziness of the fey's energy. It was both terrifying and intoxicating, too much and not enough. My body moved to the music without my mind's consent, drawing me into the moment and blurring everything before and after. My mind grew fuzzy, but the edges were still sharp enough to cut, sharp enough to know that there were too many people—too many strangers—too little space around me. I couldn't breathe, a weight on my chest forcing the air from my lungs. The world around me spun. Faces blended together. Everything moved slowly and jerkily.

I swayed on my feet.

And then, a hand circled my wrist, tugging me toward the edge of the crowd. At first, I thought it was Arthur, but when we pulled through the crowd I found Lancelot instead, his grip on my wrist surprisingly tight.

When we were clear of the crowd, I yanked my arm from his grip and he cleared his throat, glancing away from me uncomfortably. I looked down and realized that in the whir of the dancing, the shoulder of my gown slipped off, causing the neckline to plunge lower than even Morgana wore it. Hastily, I yanked it back up.

"Easy there, Shalott. You looked ready to pass out," Lancelot said, his voice calm and aloof as it always was when he spoke to me. "If you got trampled by that crowd, I don't think the others would ever let me hear the end of it."

"I'm fine," I said, crossing my arms over my chest. "I suppose I should thank you," I added after a moment, but I didn't actually say the words, and I think a part of him was glad for that. I doubt he'd have known what to say in response.

He surprised me by taking hold of my hand again and pulling me close to him, letting his other hand come to rest on the small of my back.

"What are you doing?" I asked, alarmed, even as years of dance training took over and I brought my hand to rest on his shoulder.

"Dancing with you. I would have thought that was obvious," he said drily as he began to guide me to the music. This far away, the music didn't have as firm a hold on me. My mind stayed my own, which made the situation feel all the more absurd.

"But . . . why?" I asked.

"Because you seem determined to," he said, as if it were obvious. "And at least here you aren't in danger of being trampled to death."

As we turned, I caught sight of a girl lingering on the edge of the crowd, watching us. A cloud sprite with a mess of silver curls and a white gown that clung to her skin like a dense fog. Her name was Eira, maybe, but it was hard to say for sure. Lancelot went through girls so regularly that it was difficult to keep their names straight.

"You don't have to do this," I told him. "And besides, you've got someone waiting for you."

Lancelot followed my gaze and sighed, giving me a rare smile that disappeared before it reached his eyes.

"Well, in that case you might be doing me a favor. I've been looking for a way to end things with her."

I laughed. "Again? Just two days ago, you were saying you were madly in love with her."

He shrugged. "I was then."

"Your feelings change like the tides, Lance," I said, and though I was mostly joking, he must have heard the part of me that wasn't.

"At least I embrace mine," he replied evenly.

He didn't say it cruelly, but I felt the sting of the words all the same.

"You embrace a lot more than your feelings," I snapped.

For a moment he didn't say anything. "You know what the biggest difference between humans and fey is?" he asked finally.

"Magic," I said, without hesitation.

He shook his head. "It's the life span. The way humans live, it's as if every moment is their last, because you have so few of them that they very well might be. But fey see life like a long chess game. It isn't about their next move, it's about what they're going to do in ten moves, twenty, thirty. There's no end in sight for their lives, and so their actions are largely meaningless in the scope of things."

"I don't see what that has to do with anything," I said.

"Because, Shalott, I have one foot in each world, neither human nor fay. I've been raised fay, with this idea of a great sprawling life full of everything, and I want that . . . but I will, in all likelihood, have a human life span. A hundred years, if I'm lucky. Why shouldn't I fill those few years with what I want?"

I wasn't used to Lancelot being so candid, and it took me by surprise.

"Because there are consequences to your actions," I told him after a moment. "There are real people who get hurt by them."

"Like Eira?" he asked, laughing. "She's immortal. Years pass like breaths for her—in a few she won't even remember my name."

Even though he tried to put a smile on it, there was a wound hiding beneath the casual words. A wound I had never realized he carried. I looked up at him, feeling like I was seeing him truly for the first time. Lancelot was not the sort of person who showed his vulnerabilities. He was not the sort of person to look at someone with openness and understanding and an intense searching—at least not in the present. But that was exactly the way he looked at me that night, and there was something familiar about it that worked its way beneath my skin. It was the way he looked at me in my visions, the way he would look at me in whatever future came our way.

"Thank you," I told him, to break the silence. "For getting me out of the crowd. For staying with me."

The heaviness of the moment grew to be too much, and he looked away from me, his usual sardonic smile tugging at the corners of his mouth. He stepped back so we weren't so close, opening up a narrow chasm between his body and mine. "Is this how they dance in Camelot, Shalott?" he asked.

I cleared my throat and reached down to adjust his hand, moving it farther up on my back and widening the space between us even more.

He laughed, but there was no morose undercurrent to it now. It was just his usual laugh.

"That's not as fun," he told me, his voice low in my ear. It sent a shiver down my spine that I tried to ignore.

I felt heat rise to my cheeks, which made him laugh harder.

"I swear to the Maiden, Mother, and Crone, Lancelot, if you don't stop laughing at me, I will shove you into the fire myself," I murmured.

The threat was hollow, and he knew it. He looked down at me with lifted eyebrows and an amused smile.

"I can't promise anything," he said. "But if you decide not to throw me in the fire, maybe you'd like to keep dancing with me."

I almost laughed before I realized he was earnest. I swallowed and nodded my head.

"Alright," I said. "But I reserve the right to throw you into the fire after we dance if I still want to."

He smiled. "That sounds fair, but since we're in Avalon and not Camelot . . ." he said before pulling me closer so I was flush against him, and moving his hand down low on my waist.

I felt my cheeks heat up, and I tried to ignore the way dancing with him made me feel. It was like being back in the crush of the crowd, with the fay music loud in my ears and heavy in my bloodstream.

*Both terrifying and intoxicating*, I thought. *Too much and not enough.*

It was hard to ignore how close he was, the smell of smoke and honey and lavender clinging to his skin. It was harder to ignore the feel of his calloused hand in mine, warm and tight, like I might slip through his fingers. His other hand was pressed against my back, anchoring me. It was impossible to ignore his face looming over mine, moonlight turning his hair silver. It curled around his ears, just slightly, annoyingly too long.

I wondered suddenly what it would be like to run my fingers through it.

It was his eyes that undid me, though. They held mine, and all of that irritating arrogance was gone from them. He looked unsure, tentative for the first time since I met him, but there was a frantic energy there as well. He was nervous, I realized, though he looked as surprised by it as I was.

That first kiss was inevitable, but it still took my breath away. I wasn't sure which of us moved first, who kissed whom, but one moment we were Elaine and Lancelot and the next we were sinking into each other, a blur of hands and hair and skin, of lips and tongues and teeth.

Our breaths became one.

Somehow, we remained standing.

Somehow, the world kept on moving around us, the same as before.

It wasn't the same, though, because even when Lancelot and I broke apart, dazed and breathless, he was still looking at me with nervous topaz eyes, dark and bright and intense.

The world shifted, but we were the only ones who felt it.

THE VISIONS BEGAN after that, tapestry after tapestry woven showing all the ways we could bring each other pain and misery. Sometimes I saw him walking away from me, sometimes I was the one who left him. Sometimes I saw his heart breaking, sometimes I saw mine, sometimes I saw the things that would spiral from that heartbreak—other decisions and betrayals that would feed one another and grow larger and larger.

In some versions of our future, I saw how our story would play into the larger story of both Arthur's triumph and his ruin. I saw the small part our own story would play in the future of Albion.

Every time I saw these things, I swore to myself that it wasn't worth it, that I wouldn't let it happen. Every time, I ended things with him. I told him that it wouldn't happen again. But at each bonfire, I found myself in his arms, kissing him until the sun peeked over the lake and painted the sky in streaked pastels.

And then it wasn't just bonfires anymore. It became stolen kisses in the woods and alibis for our absences that our friends only pretended to believe. It became nights spent together in my cottage, limbs entwined and hearts beating together. It became lunches with his mother and long languid talks. It became the slow peeling back of layers, the revealing of vulnerabilities, the acceptance of each other, inside and out. It became love.

As a child, my brother Lavaine had taunted me by telling me there was a python loose in the castle. He told me if I weren't careful, it would wrap around my neck and strangle me, and that the more I struggled against it, the tighter its grip would become. It was a lie, of course, a fancy Lavaine had made up to torment me after reading about pythons in some book or other. Still, the idea of it had never left me.

That was what it felt like, falling in love with Lancelot. I knew how it would end, but the more I tried to resist it, the harder I struggled, the stronger the hold he had on me. There was never going to be any fighting it. In that, I suppose, I never had a choice.

But marriage? That was a choice. That wasn't something that would happen by accident. That I had a say in; that I could still control—and I intended to do just that.

# 17

"I DON'T SEE WHY I'm needed at the Choosing of the Knights," Morgana says with a heavy sigh. "And all of that pomp and circumstance make it so incredibly, bone-achingly boring."

Though the sun has been up for two hours already, Morgana is still in bed, in her nightgown, her hair loose and messy around her shoulders. It looks like she hasn't brushed it in a week at least. And the more I look at her nightgown, the more sure I am that it's the same one she wore yesterday, and the day before that. And as I rack my memory, I realize that I haven't seen her in anything *but* her nightgown since we arrived here.

"You're Arthur's sister. If you aren't there, people will talk," I say, riffling through her wardrobe for something presentable. I find a cream dress with embroidered roses, but when I hold it out to her, she makes a face and shakes her head.

"I don't care if people talk," she says, rolling her eyes and falling back against her mountain of overstuffed white pillows, her jet-black hair radiating around her, making her look like a painting of some long-forgotten deity.

"I do. And so does Nimue," I say, diving back into her closet and pulling out a spring-green muslin dress, trimmed with white lace and pearl buttons. It's a cruel card to play, her desire for Nimue's approval, but Morgana has forced my hand.

"Ugh, no," she says, scowling at the dress. "That looks like something Morgause would wear."

"Say what you will about your sister, she always dresses fashionably," I point out, but I hang the dress back up and try again. I doubt I'll find anything she'll like. They're all court dresses—pastels and lace, flounces and ribbons. It's hard to picture Morgana in one at all. Maybe that's why she hasn't left the tower.

"If Nimue cared, she would have been in touch," Morgana says after a second. "If she cared, she wouldn't have banished us from Avalon in the first place."

Nimue's words come back to me. *You will always be safe here. But you were not raised to be safe, you were raised to be heroes.*

It was enough for me, but Morgana is different. She has never wanted to be a hero, never craved glory or admiration. She cares about her own happiness first and foremost, and there is something admirable about that, especially in a court where women are happy to fold themselves up tight to be more easily manageable, to swallow arsenic to be thought of as just a little bit sweeter.

Though I worry it'll lead to a fight, I take a steadying breath and ask the question I've been dreading.

"When was the last time you left the tower?"

She doesn't answer right away, instead burrowing further beneath the covers, as if she might disappear into them altogether.

It's strange. In the years that I've known her, I've never seen her try to disappear. That's always been me, trying to fade into the background or fall away into the pages of a book. Morgana has always been the one who pulls me out and forces me into the world. I don't know what to do now that our positions have switched.

"I don't know what the point of that would be," she mutters. "There's nothing for me there. There's nothing for me *here*, either, but at least it's quiet. At least I don't have to worry about those people, whispering behind their hands about every breath I take."

"And here I thought you didn't care if people talked," I say.

"I don't," she says quickly—too quickly to truly be believed. "They're welcome to talk all they want, about whatever they want. I won't try to stop them. But that doesn't mean I have to hear it. It doesn't mean I have to feel their judgmental eyes staring at me. It doesn't mean I have to smile and pretend I don't notice that they're all plotting how best to bring me to ruin."

I roll my eyes. "You're so dramatic," I tell her. "And they aren't that bad anymore, for the most part. Teenage girls are always vicious, but they grew up just like we did."

Morgana glowers. "Girls like that never grow up," she says. "That ugly meanness is always lurking under the surface. They've only grown smarter about it—biding their time and waiting to attack."

I can't help but snort. "You overestimate them," I say.

"Or you *underestimate* them," she corrects.

"I don't underestimate anyone," I say, though her words wriggle under my skin. I pull out another dress for her inspection. Like the others, it has a flounced skirt and lace trimmings, but it's dove gray, without any other embellishments.

She doesn't reject it right away, but her gaze is distasteful.

"There's nothing black?" she asks.

"Not before sundown," I tell her. "Pastels only. It's customary."

"Says who?" she mutters, but she climbs out of bed. I suppose she didn't actually expect an answer, but that's just as well because I don't have one.

There are so many silly rules for women in Camelot—pastels only before sundown, necklines above the collarbone, never lift your skirts high enough to show your ankles, hair up unless you're a maiden, never dance more than twice with the same man unless he's your betrothed, avoid being alone with men who are not familial relations. I don't know where they came from, and before, I never really questioned them—it was just how things were. But none of those rules existed in Avalon, and after living without them for so long, I can't deny the restrictions are chafing.

Morgana takes the dress from me and stalks behind the painted screen to change into it.

"Do you know how the Choosing will go?" I ask her.

"I imagine a good many speeches about bravery and valor?"

"Just the one, really, and it's Arthur's. We've been working on it for days now. Then he'll name the knights he's chosen, they'll accept and swear fealty to him, and it'll be done. Only fifty, which is intended as a laughable challenge, but Lance has watched them train, and he's given us a list of the best. We'll make do. Then that'll be followed by a feast to bid him—bid *us*— goodbye."

Morgana snorts. "That's kind. No doubt most hope we won't return."

"So you'll come to the Choosing then," I say. "And the feast."

"I would rather swallow rat pus."

"Do rats have . . ." I trail off and shake my head. I haven't even had break-fast yet—it's far too early to be discussing rat pus. "Never mind. But you should come. Just because you aren't around to hear the whispers doesn't mean their whispers don't touch you."

Morgana steps around the screen again, wearing the gray dress. It looks strange on her, and not just because it's unlaced. I don't think I've ever seen her so covered, or so restricted. I don't think she could lift her arms over her head without the silk tearing. She looks miserable in it as well, tugging at the skirt uncomfortably as she looks at her reflection in a tall looking glass.

"You look lovely," I tell her, but she only scowls at me, gesturing for me to lace up the back.

"What are they saying?" she asks me, her voice quiet. She doesn't want to care what people are saying about her, but she does. There's some relief in that, in knowing that she's as human and vulnerable as the rest of us, even if she likes to pretend otherwise.

I tighten her laces, earning a groan from her, though I leave them loose enough. Not the way my mother used to tie mine, so tight that I could scarcely breathe. Some nights, there would be bruises on my rib cage when my maid stripped off my dress, a watercolor of blues and purples and greens.

"They say you're hiding," I tell her, tying a neat bow at the small of her back and looking at her in the mirror, looking at us, standing together. Two sides of the same coin, just as Nimue said. So different, but with the same heart. "They say you're frightened. That you're ashamed of something—though what you're ashamed of changes depending on who's doing the telling. Warts, sometimes, or a sixth finger. I heard someone swear that you returned to court impregnated with a fay child and that the pregnancy has turned you blue."

She gives a snort of laughter. "People are morons, El," she says, but her eyes are guarded and hard.

"Maybe," I say, wrapping my arms around her waist and resting my chin on her shoulder. "Last night, Mordred called you a coward for not attending dinner."

She frowns, the energy between us shifting.

"He said that?" she asks, her voice low and dangerous. "He called me a coward?"

I nod, making her wince when my chin digs into her shoulder. She doesn't shrug me off, though.

"Fine," she says through gritted teeth. "I'll attend this ceremony, but don't expect me to be happy about it."

I squeeze her waist and plant a quick kiss on her cheek. "I would never dare."

I'D BEEN TO Choosing of the Knights ceremonies before, though they always felt more like excuses for a banquet than events in their own right. In my memory, they were tedious affairs, but at least quickly done with. I remember King Uther overseeing things, instructing whichever lord or earl or foreign prince he was sending on a quest to choose his men.

Though the choice, I felt, had always been made beforehand. Whoever was leading the quest knew who he wanted and listed the names one after the other. When each knight heard his name, he would come forward to bow and swear fealty to the leader and vow to see the quest through to its end, no matter the outcome.

As I follow Arthur down the palace steps and into the bustling courtyard, I hold a worn piece of parchment tightly in my hand. It had been folded and unfolded so many times over the last few days that it was in danger of falling apart altogether. On it, Lancelot had scrawled the names of fifty men who, in his estimation, would make the best team to venture into Lyonesse with.

*Fifty men.* That was all we would be given. Merlin expected us to conquer a wild, monster-infested country with only fifty men.

Or maybe he didn't expect that at all. Maybe he expected we would fail, and didn't intend on throwing any more soldiers than necessary into the mix.

It didn't matter, though, if we had fifty men or a thousand; the treaty with Lyonesse would be signed either way.

Still, I would have preferred a larger team. A larger team would mean more men—many of them the sons of noblemen—to give their loyalty to Arthur, to follow him, to call him king. It would have meant more support, which is something we desperately need.

But fifty men is all we will get, and so we will make do.

The courtyard is full of people—noble, judging by the array of fine silks and jewels that glitter in the light of the afternoon sun—all gathered around the arrangement of knights in polished armor, lined up in too many rows to count, shoulder to shoulder.

We seem to be the last to arrive. Merlin is already waiting on the dais at the center of the square, dressed in ink-blue velvet robes, his white hair bound back with a leather tie.

Before Arthur joins him on the dais, I press the piece of parchment into his palm, and he gives me a grateful if somewhat anxious smile. As natural as Arthur has always seemed when he speaks before a crowd, I'll never understand how he gets so nervous beforehand.

"You'll do fine," I say. "It'll be over before you know it."

He gives a quick nod before turning away and starting up the steps of the dais to join Merlin while Lancelot, Morgana, and I gather at the front of the crowd, so close to the gathered knights that the smell of their sweat is nauseating. I try to hide my discomfort, but Morgana makes no effort to do the same. She covers her nose with the sleeve of her gray gown.

"Thank you for joining me this morning," Arthur says, looking around at the crowd. I take a moment to do the same, my eyes catching on some familiar faces. Several of the dukes and lords and earls I've dined with the past few days, the young ladies they tried to present to Arthur during audiences, all dressed up in gowns a touch too elaborate for the occasion, various jewels and beading glittering in the pale morning sun. My eyes linger on Mordred and Morgause, standing a few feet to the left of me, both wearing cloaks trimmed in ermine, a matching set of dolls—the kind whose eyes seem to follow you eerily across the room.

"Tomorrow I will embark on a quest to fulfill my father's dying wish—for a united Albion. I will not return to Camelot until that quest is completed and I have truly earned the right to be called his son and heir."

He scans the rows of knights with alert eyes, though he can't make out any of their faces. They are all wearing helmets with the visors down.

"You are Camelot's best and brightest," he continues. "The pride of our kingdom, the heart of our country. It will be an honor to have you by my side in this quest, and I wish that I could take all of you with me, but I will limit my group to fifty men."

He unfolds the parchment, and I hope that I'm the only one who notices how his hands shake ever so slightly.

Clearing his throat, he looks out at the crowd once more and announces the first name.

"Sir Caradoc."

Lancelot leans toward me, his voice low as we both watch a knight in the front row step forward.

"He's one of the best I've seen," Lancelot says. "Plus, the younger son of another king of some kind. Nates, I think?"

I nod. Nates is a small island kingdom off Albion's eastern coast. Their king swore fealty to Uther before I was born, and they've been part of Albion ever since.

Sir Caradoc pushes up his visor. "I thank you, sir, for your request. It humbles me. But I must decline."

I jerk away from Lancelot. In all my years of seeing the Choosing of the Knights, I have never seen a knight *decline*. I didn't even think that was permitted. A quick sideways glance at Mordred and his insufferable and unsurprised smirk, though, and the truth of it hits me—Sir Caradoc is his.

For his part, Arthur doesn't stumble. He inclines his head toward Sir Caradoc, who lowers his visor once more and steps back in line.

"Sir Palamedes," Arthur calls next.

Another knight steps forward, and again, Lancelot leans toward me.

"He's older—in his forties, perhaps, but he's good and the men all respect him."

I barely hear him, though. All of my attention is on Sir Palamedes as he lifts his visor. Even before he speaks, my stomach is sinking. I don't need to scry to know what will happen next.

"I thank you, sir, for your request. It humbles me. But I must decline."

There's no denying Mordred's grin now. He is practically beaming as uncertainty works its way into Arthur's features. He shifts his weight from one foot to the other and frowns at the sheet of parchment as if maybe he's misreading it.

"You didn't plan this, did you?" Lancelot asks me.

"Of course she didn't," Morgana hisses before I can answer.

"I didn't ask any of them if they would join Arthur. Should I have?" he continues, frowning.

"It's never been necessary," I say, though all of my attention is on Arthur. "It's a formality—knights always go where they're told. They don't *choose* their assignments based on politics or familial loyalty."

"But that's exactly what they're doing," Morgana says, peering around me to glare at her sister and Mordred. "He must have offered them something significant."

Arthur tries three more names, but each knight—Sir Dinadan, Sir Ector, and Sir Safir—all say the same as the other two. They thank Arthur for his request. They are humbled by it. They must decline.

After Sir Safir steps back in line and lowers his visor, Arthur crumples the piece of parchment in his hand. Though frustration and mortification are burning through every inch of me, Arthur looks calm. He gazes out at the assembly of knights.

"There are many admirable qualities in knights," he says. "Bravery, valiance, a strategic and sharp mind. I have no doubt that none of you would be standing before me if you didn't possess each of those qualities in abundance. And so the only quality that matters to me today is this: a willingness to follow me, to see my father's wish fulfilled, to unite our entire continent under one flag, one crown, one rule. I know that I ask a lot—traveling to a dangerous land where few have ever dared go and from which fewer still have returned. I know that I am only asking for the bravest of men to follow me."

A glint of admiration flashes through me. *Well done, Arthur*, I think, using their pride against them. *Let it be said the men who refused to follow you are cowards without ever actually saying the words yourself.* I didn't know he had it in him.

Arthur continues. "If you are willing to accompany me, please step forward. The rest of you are dismissed."

Silence follows his words, and fear coils in my belly. No one will join him. Mordred wooed them all to his side. He orchestrated this whole event not just to kill Arthur's chances at succeeding but to fully humiliate him, to tell Arthur and the entire court that he does not belong here, that he is not someone who is worth following.

Morgana's hand finds mine, and she squeezes it tightly, her eyes glued on Arthur.

"They're all fools," she says through tight lips. "They should be falling all over themselves to follow him. Oh, what I wouldn't give for just one strike against my sister, one opportunity to rake my claws over her fa—"

"Shh," I say, my eyes finding one knight who steps forward on uncertain feet. He isn't in the front row, or the second, or the third. He stands back in the fifth row. He pushes up his visor, and the sight of his face feels like being struck by a bolt of lightning.

I know that face, even though I've never met him before, not in person.

"I will fight beside you," the knight says, and I recognize his voice straightaway as well. I've heard it in my visions, swearing loyalty to Arthur; I've heard him scream like death itself when he's held Arthur's cold body in his arms.

Arthur smiles. "I would be honored, sir. Would you tell me your name?"

"Gawain, Your Highness," he says. "Our mothers were sisters, but we never had the chance to meet."

"Well, cousin, I am glad to rectify that now. Are there any others?"

One by one, more knights step forward, pushing up their visors. I catch a few names here and there, but not close to all of them. I do see, though, that none of them are in the first few rows—most lingering near the back, where I assume the newest recruits stand, or the ones who have already been tested and been found lacking.

"How many is that?" I ask.

Lancelot, the only one of us tall enough to manage a good view, does a quick count—too quick—in his head before frowning.

"Nine," he says. "Only nine knights."


WHEN THE CHOOSING is over and the crowd dissipates, I linger between Lancelot and Morgana, watching Sir Gawain. He must feel my eyes on him because he turns and meets my gaze. I hold it until he disappears into the crowd, trying not to think of another time I felt those eyes on mine, desperate and wild and bright with unshed tears.

"Elaine?" Lancelot says, drawing me out of my thoughts, his expression perplexed.

"What did you observe of him?" I ask Lancelot. "Sir Gawain?"

He considers it for a second, shrugging his shoulders. "He's green, but he has promise, I suppose. Passion but not precision—but precision can be learned and he's young."

"Not so young," I say. "I would wager he's around Arthur's age."

"He wasn't on your list?" Morgana asks him.

"No," Lancelot says after a pause. "None of them were, the ones who offered. A few of them have some promise, but none of them are trained. None of them are ready for Lyonesse."

"Well, they'll have to be," I say, as if it's that simple. "And it isn't as though we're bringing them to war, are we? They're an escort party, nothing more. They can manage that, I assume?"

Lancelot hesitates before nodding. "They'll do," he says.

"Good," I tell him. "Will you fetch Sir Gawain and bring him to breakfast?" I ask, stepping down from the dais with both of them at my heels.

"*Why?*" Lancelot asks.

*Because he's important. Because when the rest of us fall, he will remain. Because he is a missing piece and we need him.*

But I can't tell him any of that.

"You heard him—he's Arthur's cousin, and Morgana's as well, for that matter. He is one of our only noble connections, and after Mordred's display of power out there, we need all the connections we can get."


AFTER THE BATTLE is won, after Arthur is betrayed, after that sword plunges into his back, cutting clear through to his stomach, Gawain will be the one to carry him. He will support him, all on his own, for miles. He will do his best to clean the wound, to keep Arthur awake, to lessen his pain, but he will know it won't be enough. Which is why he will bring him to the shore, why he will call for me.

Sometimes, I come alone. Other times it is Guinevere or Morgana with me. Sometimes, it is all of us, together, who bring our boat to the shore. It will be a hard journey through the mist, but it's for Arthur, and so we won't hesitate to make it.

In a low, hushed voice, Gawain will tell me what happened, but he won't need to. I'll have seen it already myself, with my own eyes, but I will know that they are words he will need to say himself in order to make sense of them, in order to believe them.

When he asks me to save Arthur, his voice will crack like an adolescent's. When I tell him I'm not sure I can, he will shake his head.

"You can," he will say, his voice unwavering. "You will."

I won't correct him, but I won't make promises that I can't keep either. Even if I wanted to, the words wouldn't pass my lips.

Together, we will lift Arthur into the boat. If Gwen and Morgana are there, they will stay with him, stroking his hair, murmuring comforting words, uttering spells that are barely more effective than a mother kissing her child's scraped knee.

Numbness will overtake me as I steer the boat back out, back to Avalon. The feelings, the emotions, will shove at me, begging to be felt, but nothing will quite make it through. All I will know is that I have to get back to Avalon, that time is running out, that everything hangs in the balance.

It will be just as well—if I could truly feel the weight of the moment, I would become paralyzed by it. Better to let the shock take hold of me, to push myself forward without feeling anything but cold logic.

But as we sail away, I will look back over my shoulder to where Gawain stands on the shore, his shoulders slumped and head hanging low. All of the life will have gone out of him, but he will stay standing. He will fight another day for Arthur and his legacy, even if Arthur himself is no more. He will mourn, yes, so much that it might just break him, but it never will.

No matter what, Gawain will be the only one who will never betray Arthur, the only one who will never run, never cower. In many ways, he might just be the best of us.

We need him or we have no chance.

## 18

ARTHUR AND GAWAIN are fast friends, which surprises me more than it should. Though I've seen him fighting at Arthur's side, ready to give his life to protect his king, I also know firsthand that we are a tightly knit group and that it is not easy for another person to work their way between our threads. Gawain, though, manages it as naturally as breathing. As soon as Arthur and Lancelot arrive and Gawain sees the book Arthur carries with him, they launch into a discussion about it, and the rest of us are left outside of their bubble.

Morgana seems to take to him as well—like the servants she hired, he doesn't fear her, and that is enough to endear him in her eyes. Before our morning tea has cooled enough to drink, she is already teasing him the same way she does Arthur, and I half expect her to ruffle his hair or tug his ear in jest as she gently mocks the two of them. But to everyone's surprise—including Morgana's—Gawain manages to elicit a promise from her to read the book.

"I've been trying to get her to read something for ages," Arthur exclaims, hitting the table with his hand. "She has no interest in anything that isn't covered in spells or potion recipes."

At the mention of Morgana's witchcraft, I hold my breath. Magic is still illegal in Albion, and though Morgana hasn't cast a spell that I know of since we interrupted the coronation, there is no telling how Gawain might react to that.

"Now that I'd like to take a look at," he says to Morgana. "Though I doubt it would be more than gibberish to me."

"You never know," Morgana says, sipping her tea. "We are cousins, after all—the same blood runs through our veins. You might be surprised at what you're capable of."

"Not again, Morgana—you already tried that on me when we were children," Arthur says with a laugh before turning to Gawain. "She managed to convince me that I could levitate rocks. Really, she was the one doing it, but I was so proud that I insisted on demonstrating my newfound gift in front of the Lady of the Lake and her council, to convince her to let me take lessons with Morgana. And of course, I made a fool of myself in front of them when my powers suddenly disappeared as suddenly as they came on."

Gawain laughs so hard he spits out his tea, covering his mouth to hide it, but of course that makes all of us laugh even harder.

Well, almost all of us.

As the conversation continues over poached eggs and toast topped with butter and pomegranate arils, my eyes keep drifting to Lancelot, seated beside me. He stares at his plate, chewing each bite of food slowly, without his usual voracious appetite. When he does look up at Gawain, his eyes are guarded and suspicious, as if he's searching for his strengths and weaknesses and imagining how those will match up against his own, should it come to that.

It's a look I know well—not so different than the way I saw fay girls look at Gwen on Avalon, not so different than the way Mordred looked at Arthur yesterday. Not so different than the way many people look at Lancelot himself, whether he's riding or fighting or merely standing at Arthur's side.

Still, seeing Lancelot jealous is a strange and surreal sight.

AFTER BREAKFAST, I pull Lancelot aside and let the others go out of the room. Lancelot glances after Arthur, but we both know he won't go too far without him. He's so deep in conversation with Gawain, though, that I don't think he really notices that Lancelot is missing.

"He's a good person, Lance," I say, keeping my voice low. I remember how thin these walls are, how sometimes they seemed so thin my mother could even hear my thoughts.

Lancelot shrugs, his shoulders stiff. "I don't know him, not really, and I suppose I'm not as trusting as the rest of you are."

That makes me laugh. "You think I trust easily?" I ask him. "How could I possibly, seeing the things I've seen?"

Lancelot considers that for a second, but he doesn't look at me. Instead, he looks everywhere else, his eyes scanning the table with its dirty plates, the windowsill, the stained glass window. I try to imagine it through his eyes, what he sees in this place with his fresh gaze. Maybe he thinks it pretty. To me, though, it is too full of ghosts. To me, it will always feel like a prison of sorts.

"I think," he says carefully, tasting the words slowly, "that you seem to trust him after knowing him for less than a day far more than you trust me after knowing me for half of your life. Why is that?"

I don't know how to answer that. Arthur and Gwen and especially Morgana have asked questions about my Sight before, even though they know I can't say anything. Still, they've all asked at some point. I don't even blame them for it. Curiosity, as Nimue liked to say, is as much a blessing as a curse.

But Lancelot has never asked me about the things I've Seen. He's never come close before. I suppose, growing up among the fey, he understands the rules better. He knows what can come of breaking them.

Now, though, he's dancing on the edge of doing just that. He must know it, he must realize exactly what he's doing. He must understand that I won't answer him.

But still, he's asking.

"Arthur can trust him," I say instead. "And so I trust him."

"Are you saying Arthur can't trust me?" he asks, taking a step back.

I open my mouth and close it again. There is no way to answer that question, no way to respond that won't break something, in some way. I bite my lip and decide that maybe honesty is truly the only way forward.

"I don't know," I say quietly.

Lancelot stares at me, his expression unreadable, but I suspect if I tried to dig beneath that blank exterior, I would find a deep well of hurt.

"Why did you ask me to come, Elaine?" he asks, and it's the fact that he calls me by my first name that feels like a punch in my gut. There is no playfulness in his voice, no joking, no lightness that is so characteristically Lancelot. "You told me that I was needed here—that Arthur needed me, that *you* needed me. That's why I came."

"No," I say, the hard edge in my voice surprising both of us. "You came because you knew your life on Avalon would have bored you. You came here for Arthur, yes, maybe you've even told yourself you came for me, but that isn't the whole truth of it, Lance—you can lie to yourself about this, but you don't have to lie to me. You came here for you, for adventure, for glory."

Lancelot stares at me for a long moment, his jaw slack and eyes wide. It isn't often that I've been able to render Lance speechless, but I take no joy in it. After a moment, he straightens up again.

"I was wrong," he says finally, turning and walking toward the door. "It's no wonder you don't trust me, Shalott—you don't know me at all."

HE'S WRONG. I know Lancelot as well as I know Morgana or Arthur or Gwen; I know him as well as I know myself. But after he leaves, his words stay with me, digging beneath my skin like shards of glass that I don't think I will ever be able to pry out.

I shouldn't have said that about Arthur not being able to trust him. I'm not sure it was a lie, exactly, but it was only one possibility. Still, that one possibility can be enough to drive a person to do unthinkable things. I learned that lesson myself not long after Nimue began training me on Avalon.

Arthur's and Gwen's days were spent in lessons more often than not, learning about various aspects of being rulers. Morgana always called them "crown classes" with a roll of her eyes, but I liked to join in when I had some free time. The lessons on decorum and the complicated forest of Albion family trees were more familiar to me than anything else on Avalon—comforting, in a strange way—but the strategy lessons were my favorites. They were taught by a fay woman named Galina who looked almost human apart from the thin-leafed vines that wound their way over every visible inch of her skin.

One day, before I learned to control or truly understand my visions, I Saw Galina slip off a rain-slicked cliffside and break her leg. And even though Nimue had told me never to tell the subject of a vision what I Saw, I couldn't put the image out of my mind—the pain in her eyes, the bone-shattering scream.

All I told her was to avoid the cliffsides in the rain—no more than that. But Galina, like all the fey, knew that I was an oracle. She took the vague warning for what it was.

Two days later, after a rainy night, her body was found in the woods. Instead of taking her usual route home, along the cliffs, she had heeded my words and walked the long way through the woods instead. It was difficult to say for sure what had happened, but she appeared to have gotten lost on the unfamiliar path and, as the night got darker, tripped over a protruding tree root and struck her head on a boulder.

Morgana was the only person I ever told about that, and though she told me it wasn't my fault, I don't think either of us believed it.

So I know the consequences that can come of telling someone their future. I know that it wasn't fair to put even the haziest idea of betrayal in Lancelot's mind, but it takes me a moment to understand why I did it anyway, why I just couldn't help myself.

Because I don't like being the only one who knows it. Back in Avalon, I at least had Nimue to share my visions with, my fears and hopes for the future, the paths that twisted out in front of us like writhing snakes. And now? Now there is no one. Only me, to bear the weight of everyone's futures alone, and it is too much.

Still, it wasn't fair of me, and I know I owe him an apology. After all, I know better than almost anyone that Lancelot is the opposite of selfish, that even if he keeps most things close to the chest, he cares deeply, loves deeply, protects with everything he has.

*It's not enough, though*, a voice whispers through me. I tell myself that's why I don't go after him.

LANCELOT GREW UP half-human, half-fay, with one foot in both worlds but no traction in either. His mother's blood made him faster and stronger than any human I knew. He could see as easily in the pitch dark as he could in broad daylight, and, as he'd pointed out to me himself, his senses were inhumanly sharp, making him able to hear a rabbit's footsteps from a mile away or smell when lunch was ready from the opposite side of the island. Even when I found him insufferable, I could never deny that he was an exceptionally gifted boy.

The fey disagreed. They didn't see anything exceptional about Lancelot—to them, he was slow and weak and fragile, hindered by his human blood. He looked human, after all, and he could perform no magic. In all likelihood, they said, shaking their heads and clicking their tongues in some show of mock sympathy, he would live a mortal life.

He hated that, the reminder of his mortality and his humanity. Given the chance, he wouldn't have hesitated to trade it to be entirely fay, or at least possess some kind of magic. He never said anything outright, but I knew he resented Morgana, Guinevere, and me. How could he not? The three of us all had less fay blood than he did, but with ours came gifts. Tangible, magical gifts.

Arthur was the only person on Avalon with less magic than Lancelot. And if the fey pitied Lancelot for his dormant blood and short life span, they despised Arthur for it. After all, his father was the reason they'd been banished to Avalon, the reason they'd lost family and friends in the Fay War. Arthur was a symbol of everything that had been taken from them. Of course they despised him—Arthur never even seemed to hold it against them.

But Arthur had Nimue's protection, and so the worst the fey ever did was glower at and ignore him, and the rest of us, as best they could. That was fine by Arthur, and Gwen, Morgana, and I were happy enough with our small group. But Lancelot was different. He never stopped yearning to be accepted by them, to be truly able to stand in their world, tall and proud, despite his innate humanity.

That was where the Challenging came in. It was a tournament that lasted a full week, but one that took place only once every decade.

"The fey live for hundreds of years," Lancelot explained once, when I asked why it happened so rarely. "For them, ten years is nothing."

But for Lancelot, ten years was everything. He saw his first tournament when he was only nine years old, watching the string of events at his mother's side, watching the competitors with hungry eyes.

"They were heroes," he explained to me as the next tournament drew close and he began to practice even harder. "The crowd cheered and applauded, and the winner just basked in the glory of it."

He pointed out the winner to me at dinner that night, a broad-shouldered man with long white hair tied back from his face with a leather cord. He was surrounded by people, the center of the conversation. He was admired, accepted, even worshipped. And as Lancelot looked at him, I looked at Lancelot and saw the envy there. And beneath envy, there was something else simmering: cold, hard determination.

Lancelot was going to win the next Challenging. He was going to prove once and for all that he belonged with the fey, that he was one of them, that he mattered.

He'd practiced for the last decade, trained every day, sometimes all the way from sunrise to sundown. The fey might have been naturally more skilled, but they hadn't worked to hone their talents as dedicatedly as Lancelot had. He was ready to meet them in speed, strength, and sense. He was ready to *beat* them.

And he did, in the first few events. If he didn't come in first place, as he did in archery and broadsword fighting, he came in the top three. Only in tracking did he falter, and even then he still placed fifth. By the time the last event came around, he was the top competitor and the one to beat.

Maybe some of the other fey were afraid; maybe they were bitter or petty or just angry about it. Maybe they didn't care about Lancelot at all and he was merely collateral damage in an attempt to take a rare strike at Arthur. There's no way to know for sure.

The last event was a footrace around the entire island, and it was an event Lancelot felt confident in. He ran around the island every morning, honing his speed and agility as he climbed through the cliffsides and jumped over streams. His timing was excellent—most days he managed it in just an hour.

The race took place just before sundown. Morgana and I were the only two of our group not competing, but we saw the other three off and then sat down to wait for their return. Lancelot had a very good chance of winning, we said while we waited, but Gwen had also had a good showing at the first few events, though she lacked Lancelot's hard determination. She would likely still be somewhere at the front of the pack. Arthur, though, just wanted to have fun. By human standards, he was a good warrior, a fast racer, a decent archer. By fay standards, though, he was dismal. He'd come dead last at most events, and we had little reason to believe the footrace would be any different.

But even as the race started, he'd given Morgana and me a cheerful smile and a wave before taking off, amiably settling into the back of the pack of runners.

I remember the first runners returning just after dark had fallen—a good hour later. I remember my heart sinking when Lancelot wasn't the first, when he wasn't the second or third. When Guinevere came in twelfth in the race, fifth overall. When she shook her head and said she hadn't seen Lancelot.

In the end, he and Arthur had tied for last place, finally crossing the finish line when all the other spectators had ambled off to celebrate with the victors in the dining hall. Morgana, Guinevere, and I were the only ones left.

"I was nearly to the end when I heard a couple of fay boys behind me— Cillorene and Tolias," Lancelot said, like the names might mean something to us. They didn't. "Cillorene is an illusionist. He was bragging about how he'd cast a charm on the cliffs to change the paths and get other racers lost."

"That's cheating, though," I said.

Lancelot shrugged. "It's not actually in the rules. After all, those charms only work on humans," he said, his gaze sliding to Arthur, whose cheeks had gone red.

"There was no reason to ruin Arthur's chances," Guinevere said through gritted teeth. "It wasn't as though he was a threat to them." She realized what she'd said as soon as the words were out of her mouth. "No offense, of course, Arthur. You were doing quite well."

Arthur shrugged his shoulders and glanced away. "I just wanted to finish the tournament," he said. "I didn't much care about places."

"It was a prank then," Morgana said, looking at Lancelot, who nodded.

"A cruel one," Lancelot said. "I suppose, since no one would be watching and no one would be able to prove it afterward, it was a rare chance to strike out at him."

Arthur swallowed, shaking his head. "If Lance hadn't come back for me, I'd have been stuck in those mountains until morning," he said.

"That's the best-case scenario," Morgana said, her voice sharpening. "In the dark, you could have fallen right off the cliffs. Arthur, you could have *died*."

Arthur's shoulders hunched, and his cheeks grew even redder. "Yes, well, I didn't, did I? Because Lance came back for me."

As we headed to the dining hall, I fell into step beside Lancelot at the back of the group. The others were talking among themselves, Morgana threatening all manner of ways to get revenge on Cillorene, and Arthur begging her not to.

"I'm sorry," I told him softly. "I know how much you wanted to win."

Lancelot didn't deny it—didn't say anything at all. After a moment, I caught his hand in mine. I remember the decision to do it, the fear that he might pull away from me. It must have been early on in our romance, when things were still uncertain between us. But he didn't let go of my hand. Instead, he held it back, squeezing it tight.

"I did," he said, the words coming out choked. "There was a moment, El, when I considered not going back. I could have finished the race first, then doubled back and found him. I don't know that another half hour would have made much of a difference."

"But it could have," I said. "You chose not to risk it. You chose Arthur."

He didn't understand why I was making such a fuss about it, but even then I had seen futures where he betrayed Arthur in a number of ways. That glimpse of his heart, the fact that he'd put aside his greatest desire to protect his friend—to me, that was worth making a fuss over.

"In any event," he said, shooting me a half smile, "there's always the next one, isn't there? I waited a decade before. I can do it again. The next time, I'll win. Just you wait."

I hadn't known what to say to that, so instead I'd held my tongue. How could I have possibly said that in all my visions, every different path we'd taken, none of us had ever seen another decade?

# 19

I'S A PRETTY memory, I suppose. A good story I tuck away to use when scrutiny inevitably shifts from Arthur to Lancelot, a tale to show how loyal Lancelot is to Arthur, fay blood or not. It won't even need exaggerating like Arthur's stories—it is perfect just as it happened. No one could hear that story and doubt Lancelot's devotion.

Except for me, it seems. I lived the story, I know it to be true, but it's not enough to counteract the visions that cloud our futures, an array of countless betrayals, minute and major, intimately personal and public.

As much as I try to cling to that version of Lancelot, the one who selflessly sacrificed his own dreams to protect his friend, it grows more and more difficult with every vision of him in the future doing exactly the opposite—betraying Arthur in a million different ways. Betraying me too.

MAYBE IT WILL happen at high summer, when the Camelot heat will be so overwhelming that my gown will be plastered to my skin, my pinned-back hair heavy and itchy with sweat, every step feeling like I'm walking knee-deep in sand.

Arthur will be beside me, his arm linked through mine as we stumble away from the banquet hall. Muffled strains of harp music will follow down the hall, and my mind will be fuzzy at the edges. But if I will have had one glass of wine too many, Arthur will have had three, and he will wobble on his feet, his words slurring and louder than he means for them to be.

It won't do for the courtiers to see him like this, unable to hold his wine even though he's approaching his late twenties now. Which is why I will be leading him away from the gathering—a summer solstice banquet, perhaps? Or is it someone's birthday? That changes often enough, but what happens next is always the same.

There will be voices, hushed and frenzied farther down the dark corridor. Moonlight will pour through one of the narrow windows, illuminating an entwined couple in pale light, just enough to make out the shape of them.

"At least someone is enjoying themselves," Arthur will whisper to me, his breath smelling like wine as he leans further on me.

"You seem to be enjoying yourself plenty," I will reply, adjusting his arm around my shoulders so that I can support his weight better.

But something will be wrong. I will know it, but I will not be able to put my finger on what it is. Whether it is the alcohol or some strange oracle sense, I'm not sure. Still, no matter how many times I have seen it happen, I am always surprised when the light shifts and the color of the scene comes into focus.

Pale arms scattered with constellations of freckles.

Coal-black hair, overgrown and curling over his collar.

The embellished green silk gown fit for a queen.

A deep blue velvet jacket that I will have picked out myself, with neat gold buttons that I helped do up only hours before.

"They're too small," Lancelot will have groused when we got ready earlier that evening, frustrated as his large fingers fumbled with the tiny buttons.

"Here," I will have said, laughing as I stepped closer to him, slipping each button into its corresponding hole.

"What would I do without you, Shalott?" he will have asked.

I will have answered with a kiss that had stretched out into far more, until we were quite thoroughly late to dinner.

But now it will be someone else's fingers on those buttons—long pale fingers, one ringed with a familiar stone.

"It will go well with her eyes, don't you think, Elaine?" Arthur will have asked me what feels like an age ago, holding up the ring for my inspection.

*Yes,* I will remember agreeing. *Gwen will adore it.*

Even incoherently drunk, Arthur will not be stupid. I will try to pull him away, to distract him—even then my concern will be to protect Arthur's heart, even as my own will be shattering. But it will be too late and he will be unmovable, rooted to the stone floor like a centuries-old oak tree.

"Gwen?" he will ask, his voice suddenly going quiet. "Lance?"

They will break apart as if burned, scalded by horror and shame, but they will have no words. None of us will. Instead, we will stare at one another, the four of us locked in a moment that will feel like it is perched on the edge of a cliff, a mere breath away from falling over.


THERE HAVE BEEN other visions, other betrayals. Sometimes Arthur and I find them together like that, but other times it is only me, sometimes it is only Arthur, sometimes neither of us at all but some other friend reporting seeing them together. When it is the last, Arthur refuses to believe it. He sends the friend away for daring to lie.

In several visions, it is Gawain who comes to me, telling me in carefully phrased words what he saw.

"Do you think he loves her?" I will ask him as we walk through a rose garden, the smell from the blooms sickly sweet and almost noxious.

His gaze will cut to me, brow furrowed. "What does it matter?" he will ask me.

But it will matter, because that is one thing I never managed to figure out from my visions, and I'm not sure why I care about the answer as much as I do. Would it be better if he loved her, if she loved him? Or would that make it so much worse?

"Arthur will find out," Gawain will say, his voice low. "These things never stay secret for long. No matter how he will try to protect you from the fallout, you will still be the wife of a traitor."

"The wife of a traitor," I echo. "The friend of two other traitors too," I add, because by this point, Morgana will have already gone, chased away from court by shame and vengeance.

"Camelot is turning more volatile by the day," he will say. "And with your . . . connections. And your ties to Avalon. There will be plenty who will want to see you executed with the others."

I will swallow. "You think Arthur will have them executed? It's Gwen and Lance, Gawain—no matter what they've done, he still loves them."

"I don't think he'll have much of a choice in the matter," Gawain will say softly. "When word gets out, they will label her an ungrateful monster, him a traitorous fay. What will they label you?"

A dozen possibilities will whisper through my mind, and I will know he speaks the truth.

"You should leave this place," he will continue. "As soon as you can. *We* should leave."

That will take me by surprise, and I will turn to face him fully. "You would leave too?"

He will try to shrug in some sort of nonchalant manner, as if he is offering something simple and easy—a coat to keep me warm, the dessert he is too full to finish. But it won't be simple and easy. He will be offering to break his vows to Arthur, the loyalty he prides himself on. For me.

"Arthur needs you," I will remind him. "And he needs me as well."

Gawain will shake his head, a small, bitter smile rising to his lips. "I was afraid you would say that."


IN THE END, it is always Mordred who strikes the death blow against Arthur. It is always the blade in his hand, the hate filling his gray eyes until they are nearly black. But who puts Arthur there, facing him alone in the middle of a battlefield strewn with bodies? Who puts that sword in Mordred's hands? Who brings us to that battle, with Arthur ill-prepared and desperate for something I'm not even sure he understands?

Mordred might be the one to take Arthur's life, but we all will have a hand in it. The moment will have been shaped by Morgana's betrayal, forged by

Guinevere breaking his heart, strengthened by Lancelot ruining his trust. It will even be wrought by me, in some ways. In ways I don't understand, can't put a name to, but that I feel all the same, in the deepest part of my soul. After all, when Arthur falls, he will fall alone. I will not be beside him.

So perhaps it is unfair of me to hold Lancelot's failings against him—his possible failings, I remind myself. If Arthur cannot trust him, he can't trust any of us. And if that is the case, he is already lost.

It isn't difficult to find Lancelot—all I have to do is look for Arthur. As always, Lancelot isn't far away. Just now, he's standing guard outside of Arthur's study, spine straight and chin lifted so that it's parallel to the ground. He doesn't acknowledge me as I approach, and though I know I deserve it, the gesture still makes my face heat up.

"He's with Lord Eddersley," he says.

"Lord Endersley," I correct. "And I know. I made his schedule, remember?"

Lancelot makes a brusque noise in the back of his throat. "You can go in if you want," he says after a second. "I'm sure he'd welcome your trusted counsel."

Another barb that hurts more than I'd like to admit.

"Lord Endersley is harmless," I say. "I think Arthur can handle him alone. Besides, I came to see you."

At that, his eyes finally slide to me—still cold, but at least he's looking at me. I tell myself that's an improvement. I open my mouth to apologize but quickly close it again. *I'm sorry.* Two words. They should be easy to say, but they stick in my throat. They don't feel like enough.

"I hate this place," I say instead. "I hate who it's turning me into. I shouldn't have said what I said to you, it wasn't fair."

"No," he agrees before hesitating. "But was it the truth?"

I should have known he'd ask that, should have prepared something to say in response, but instead I just shrug my shoulders. "The truth is that there are versions of you that hurt him," I say slowly. *There are versions of you that hurt me,* I want to add, but I hold my tongue. "But there are versions of me that hurt him too. And Morgana, and Gwen. That's what scares me. It isn't only you, but it's a possibility. One we can avoid."

For a long moment, he doesn't speak, turning the words over in his mind. "You've seen everyone betray Arthur," he says finally. "But have you ever seen Arthur betraying any of us?"

"No," I say immediately before faltering. It's not the entire truth, is it? The big betrayals and abandonments have all been ours, it's true, but smaller things, perhaps. Raindrops that might gather enough to cause avalanches.

He sees the answer in my eyes, and his mouth hardens into a grim line. "Love goes both ways, El," he says after a second. "So does betrayal. You're looking at Arthur as a victim, and you aren't doing him any favors there."

"He's a piece of the puzzle, as much as any of us," I say, something sliding into place—something small, admittedly, but another piece that makes the picture just a little bit clearer. "Do you love him?"

He blinks at me slowly, considering it. "Yes," he says. "Of course I do."

"And Morgana?" I ask him.

One corner of his mouth lifts in a smirk. "Maiden, Mother, and Crone help me, but I do."

I hesitate. "And Gwen?" I ask him.

He seems to expect the question, but beyond that there is no response, no flash of lust in his eyes, no hidden passion in his gaze. He only shrugs his shoulders. "Of course. Arthur, Morgana, Gwen. I love them all. I wouldn't be here if I didn't."

I nod slowly. "Good," I say. "That's all I need to know."

When I move to turn away from him, he stops me with his voice. "You're forgetting someone," he says.

I turn around. "I know you love me, Lance," I tell him. "No matter what happens, I don't think I will ever doubt that."

He holds my gaze. "But you doubt me," he says.

I shake my head. "I doubt that it's enough."

# 20

THE NIGHT BEFORE we leave for Lyonesse, a banquet is thrown in Arthur's honor. At least, that is the official reason, though even before I arrived, I'd heard murmurs and snickers that referred to tonight as Arthur's good riddance feast.

"Like the meal you give a lame horse before putting it down," one man said, not realizing I was walking just behind him.

It's nothing I didn't already know—most of Camelot doesn't expect we will return—but the words burn in my veins all the same, and the anger simmers even as I enter the banquet hall with Morgana. The large room is already overflowing with people and filled with the smell of cooked meat and the sound of harp song.

Long tables in the banquet hall are already piled high with a feast for a king, even if Camelot is currently lacking one. I try to scan the hall for Arthur, but it's too crowded to see much of anything. Everyone is talking, and as I walk through the crowd, I catch bits and pieces.

"Did you see his face when Sir Caradoc refused him?" one man in a crushed velvet doublet asks his friend. "I thought the boy was going to faint on the spot."

I frown. Arthur held his composure well, I'd thought, but I suppose that hardly matters. Gossip thrives not on what is true but on what people wish to believe. Maybe they wish to believe Arthur is weak and overemotional.

"Surely he must have known," an old woman with white hair held back in a long braid says, clicking her tongue. "This is not his court. Those were not his men. If he wants an army, he should get one from Avalon. The sooner the upstart is gone, the better off we'll all be."

By my side, Morgana turns toward the woman, ready to say something undoubtedly rude, but I loop my arm through hers, keeping her at my side.

"Let them talk," I say, though I hate it as much as she does. "The more you try to stop it, the worse it'll be."

"Speaking from experience, El?" she asks, glowering at the woman over her shoulder. "How well did ignoring them work for you? Did they simply stop when you didn't respond?"

"They stopped when I left," I say pointedly. "And now that I've returned stronger and more powerful, they haven't dared start again. We leave at dawn, and Arthur will return stronger. That is the only thing that will stop their wagging tongues, I promise you."

"I can think of quite a few spells that would have the same effect," she points out.

Though I would love to see that, I shake my head. "They already view the fey as the enemy—you using magic against them wouldn't serve to change their minds."

"They don't need to know it was magic," she says. "Just a touch of tongue sores? A mysterious case of throat rashes? The possibilities are truly endless if you get clever enough."

"Yes, well, the trouble is, you aren't quite as clever—or subtle—as you think you are," Lancelot says, appearing on my other side with a goblet of red wine already in hand. He lifts it to his lips, but before he can take a sip, Morgana pulls it from his grasp and claims it for herself, draining it in one long gulp.

"You take that back," she says, wiping her hand across her mouth in a most unladylike fashion that draws all manner of raised eyebrows and glares. "I don't care for subtlety, true, but you can't take my cleverness from me."

Lancelot glowers at her but doesn't complain. Instead he shakes his head and lets his gaze scan the crowd again.

"I haven't been able to find Arthur. He sent me ahead, said he'd join in a minute. Perhaps I shouldn't have left him alone, but there were other guards to see to him," he says. "I saw Mordred and Morgause and Merlin, but there's no sign of him anywhere."

The foreboding feeling in my stomach grows larger. "Something's not right," I say, as much to myself as to them.

"He had guards," Lancelot says again, firmer this time. "Gawain was one of them. You said you trusted him."

"I do," I say. If Gawain is with Arthur, he must be safe, but the nagging feeling in the pit of my stomach doesn't subside.

Before I can say more, a boy no older than ten approaches, stopping before me and bowing deeply at the waist. "Lady Elaine, the mage, Merlin, requests you join him at his table for dinner."

I open my mouth to turn down the invitation, my mind still spinning with all the reasons for Arthur's absence, but when I truly hear the boy's words, I hesitate. I've been hoping to speak with Merlin since we arrived, but the opportunity hasn't arisen. This may be my last chance before we leave for Lyonesse. I glance at the others.

"Find Arthur," I tell them. "I'll meet you when I'm done."

As I turn to follow the boy, Morgana calls after me.

"Bring more wine, will you?"


IN MY VISIONS, Merlin has always existed as a blank spot. There are scenes where I *know* he has been present, where I hear his name mentioned, but the instant I try to focus on him, to see what he is doing or hear what he says, the scene goes topsy-turvy and a splitting pain erupts behind my eyes, strong enough to draw me out of the vision entirely.

Nimue, I would later find out, had the same issue when she scried. As did every other seer on Avalon, dating back to Merlin's birth some five hundred years ago.

He is nothing short of an enigma.

Now, HE SITS at the head of the smallest table, placed on a dais that holds it above all the others. When I step up the stairs, he rises in one fluid motion, inclining his head toward me. Part of me still flinches the second his eyes meet mine, a ghost of a headache sprouting up out of pure habit. As I look at him now, though, the scene doesn't go wonky. I see him clear as anything, and he sees me and the strangest feeling comes over me.

Fear.

"Lady Elaine, thank you for joining me," he says, his voice jovial enough as he pulls out the chair next to him. For his great age, he moves nimbly, something that shouldn't surprise me after being around Nimue, but I'm not sure I ever grew used to Nimue either.

They're the same age, thereabouts, but where Nimue is ageless and eternal, there is something at odds about Merlin, something that makes him a contradiction. He appears middle-aged, but at the same time he's all knees and elbows, like an adolescent, and on top of that, his hair is the white of an elder and his voice reminds me of my grandfather's, soft-edged and lightly rasping.

"Thank you for the invitation," I tell him, ignoring my uncertainty and taking the seat he offers. "I've been hoping for us to speak."

"As have I, but I fear we've both been quite busy the last few days," he says.

He reaches for a crystal decanter of red wine and pours some into my golden goblet. "In her letter, Nimue mentioned that you were an oracle."

"I am," I say, taking the goblet. Something tells me that this conversation is one I will need my wits for, so I'm careful to take only a small sip.

"Actually, what she said was that you were the most gifted oracle she'd ever taught," he continues.

I almost spit out the wine in my mouth but force myself to swallow. "She said that?" I ask.

The thought of Nimue paying such a high compliment to me causes heat to rise to my cheeks, even if it doesn't sound like her. In our lessons in the caves of Avalon, I always felt like I was lacking in some way. I could never See enough, and when I did, the details were always beyond what she asked me. She pushed me hard every day and never once seemed entirely satisfied.

"She's quite demanding, I remember that well, but trust me, she was quite proud of you," Merlin murmurs, as if reading my mind.

"You knew her personally?" I ask, surprised. "What, on Avalon?"

"Oh no, my dear," he says, mouth bowing into a rare smile. "I haven't set foot on those shores—it is a place for fey, after all, and their chosen friends. I have never been called either."

It's an easy thing to forget—that Merlin, with all his magic, isn't fay as far as anyone has been able to see. No one knows exactly what he is or where he came from, but when the Fay War came about, he gave his loyalty to Uther and the humans. The fey never forgot it—even when I'd been there, the fey would curse his name. Except for Nimue, of course, but then I never heard her curse anyone.

Now, though, I wonder if there was more to it. If she didn't simply refuse to speak badly of him, but if she actually liked him.

"But you knew her," I say.

His smile grows faraway.

"You are young, but as unfathomable as it might be, there was a time when there was no Avalon, when there was no Albion. There was only home, and home had no edges or borders. It was infinite."

"And it was peaceful," I say, because while it might be unfathomable to me, it is not an unfamiliar tale. I heard the same from Nimue more times than I could count. But Merlin surprises me, shaking his head.

"It was not," he tells me, a snort in his voice. "You think such a thing as peace exists when fey and humans walk together?"

"But for centuries, there was peace," I say.

"For the fey, there was peace," he corrects, casting me an amused glance. "Of course they found it peaceful. They were the ones in power. They held the reins. How could they not be at peace? The humans, however, were certainly never peaceful. They lived lives of fear and cowering. That much, I'm sure you understand."

There's a draft in the banquet hall, but despite the chill, heat still rises to my cheeks.

"There were no wars," I say, pushing forward. "No violence, no plagues. Fields grew plentiful, and no one went hungry. The united world was a utopia."

"For the fey," he says again. "But this is where Nimue and I have always disagreed as well, and you are her pupil. But that is the answer to the question you wanted to ask." When I frown, his smile grows wider. "Why I am here, and she is there. It's because the drawing of the lines was inevitable. Her protecting the fey was inevitable . . . as was my protecting the humans. And so here we are."

"You've made quite a fortune here," I say, looking out at the great hall, all the people talking and dancing and eating. Though they may not know it, and they would doubtlessly resent him if they did, Merlin has had no small amount of dominion over their lives, and their ancestors' lives before them. He has shaped them all—*us* all—shaped this court, shaped this country.

"I made Uther's great-great-grandfather a king of a feral and barren land," Merlin says, following my gaze. "Everyone thought I was mad. But Owain didn't. So together we built a country and I made him a king. That was what they called me then—the Kingmaker. After all this is done, they might call me that again."

My eyes find Mordred in the crowd, standing beside Morgause and holding court with a band of noblemen and noblewomen clamoring for his attention.

"And what a king you've chosen," I say, pursing my lips. "Mordred will be the death of everything you've built."

Merlin clicks his tongue and shakes his head.

"Come now, Elaine. You know better than to share visions," he says mildly.

"It's not a vision," I say, turning to look at him. "It's a deduction. Mordred is selfish and vain. Put a crown on his head and power in his fist, and he will bring us all to ruin. You don't need to be an oracle to see that."

Merlin considers this for a moment, his head cocking to one side. "Perhaps," he allows. "And if I put a naive boy on the throne? One led by his pure heart and gilded ideals, with Nimue pulling his strings? Do you not think that would bring the country to ruin just as quickly?"

"I don't think you give Arthur enough credit," I say. "He knows his own mind. And yes, he's young and idealistic, but he's also bright. He's brave. He's determined."

"Perhaps," Merlin says again. "But none of this is proven. I'm not the only one who sees him that way—look at them, Elaine. They smell it on him, like starving wolves catching the scent of fresh meat."

I shake my head. "There are plenty of noble families who have told me their support is with Arthur."

At that, Merlin laughs, and the sound is so loud and full I fear it will break him, but he is stronger than he looks.

"Child, you have spent too much time among the fey with their truth-cursed tongues. You've forgotten just how gifted humans are at lying," he says. "Most of the people you see down there, they don't care a whit about a pure heart or a valiant spirit. They don't even care, really, who sits on the throne. All they care about is how they can benefit, and their whims can change in an instant, as you saw at the Choosing of the Knights."

I shake my head. "You let Arthur walk into a trap," I say. "Was it not enough to set him an impossible task? You have to make it even harder however you can?"

Merlin's laughter subsides, but his smile lingers, brittle at the edges. "Oh, Elaine," he says sadly. "The task is easy, compared to what he will face if he actually succeeds. I have no desire for him to fail, or for him to succeed for that matter. I'm not one of the fey, it's true. And though I'm not human, either, I will admit I have this in common with them: The only thing I care about is how my goals stand to benefit."

My mouth goes dry. "And what are your goals?" I ask. "To keep the fey banished and bound to their island?"

He doesn't answer, only continues to smile like I said something amusing. After a second, his gaze slides over my shoulder. "I believe the Lady Morgana is requesting your attention."

I follow his eyeline to the far side of the room, where Morgana stands by the entrance, waving toward me. It might be the lighting in the banquet hall, but she looks paler than usual.

"You should go," Merlin continues. "I'm sure we'll speak again if you return from Lyonesse."

IT TAKES A moment for me to place the expression on Morgana's face as I approach her across the banquet hall because it is one I don't think I've ever seen there. I've seen her giddy with happiness, I've seen her angry enough to kill, but I've never in all our years of friendship seen her truly frightened.

A handful of courtiers try to stop me, but I barely notice them, hurrying past with nothing more than a smile or a hasty promise to speak soon, but all my attention is on Morgana. Maybe Nimue was right—maybe we truly are two sides of the same coin. Because her fear seeps into me before she even says a word.

"We found Arthur," she tells me when I reach her, wasting no time on a preamble. "He's in his room."

"In his room?" I ask, lowering my voice. "The banquet's important. He needs to be here. People will say he's embarrassed about the Choosing of the Knights—"

"I don't think he cares what people are saying at the moment," Morgana says, biting her lip before jerking her head back to the entrance and the shadowed hallway beyond. "Come, you should talk to him yourself."

# 21

LANCELOT AND ARTHUR sit on the edge of his bed, huddled close together. There is a crumpled letter in Arthur's hand and an open bottle of wine in Lancelot's, though they seem to be passing it back and forth. When Morgana and I enter, Arthur's eyes find me, and all of a sudden, he looks like a lost child.

He opens his mouth once, then closes it again, shaking his head. He holds out the paper to me instead and I take it. Lancelot passes Arthur the bottle of wine and he takes a long drink, wiping away the excess on his sleeve, staining the white cotton red.

"What I wouldn't give for good Avalon wine," he mutters. "This stuff is practically water."

I unfold the letter, glancing up at him. "Careful, we leave for Lyonesse at dawn tomorrow," I remind him. "Last time you tried to ride after a night of too much drink, you vomited all over yourself."

Arthur grimaces before shaking his head. "Read the letter, El. It came just an hour ago."

The first thing I notice is the broken seal of a wolf's head. The next is Gwen's unadorned signature at the bottom, a rough scrawl without flourishes or loops. The message itself is similarly simple.

*A—*

*I can't. I'm sorry.*

*—Gwen*

I turn the letter over as if more might be written on the back, perhaps, but it's bare. Four words. Six, if you count the address and signature.

"You don't know what it means," I say, folding up the letter again, though I hear how my own voice raises.

"It's pretty clear to the rest of us, Shalott—and to you as well, I'd imagine," Lancelot says. "She's ended things. There is no betrothal."

I sit down on Arthur's other side, handing back the letter and taking the bottle of wine in return. I take a long drink.

"Gwen's flighty," Morgana says, pacing the space in front of us. "This shouldn't surprise any of us. She changed her mind. She'll change it back. It's just what she does. In fact, if she hadn't broken the engagement at least once, I'd suspect there was something wrong with her."

Arthur winces, and I shoot Morgana a look. That doesn't help.

"I don't think any of us know Gwen's mind," I say, glancing back at Arthur. "We don't know where this came from or why now. The last time we saw her, she had no doubts, but that was a week ago. A lot could have changed since she returned home."

Arthur laughs. The sound is jarring, cutting through the heavy air in the room like a sharpened sword. The rest of us stare at him, but he doesn't stop laughing for a full minute, his face turning red and tears beginning to stream down his cheeks.

"The quest," he manages between laughs. "The men. *Nine men*. Nine men to take a country of monsters, and now Gwen isn't even with us."

"She will be again," Morgana says, but even she doesn't sound sure.

Arthur shakes his head, his body still quivering with laughter. "Is that something to risk nine lives for?" he asks. "I should call the quest off."

"You don't mean that," I say to him. "Even if you wanted to, you couldn't. If you do, Mordred becomes king and you get branded a coward."

That stills his laughter. "And if I don't want to be king?" he asks quietly. "Every time I've pictured it, every time I've thought about it, it's always been Guinevere and me on that throne together."

I don't know what to say at first, so I just take hold of his hand.

"You're upset," I tell him finally. "You're heartbroken. You have every right to be. But you don't mean that. I can assure you that you will be a great king with or without Gwen."

"I don't see how we'll be able to put that theory to the test," Lancelot says softly. "Without Gwen . . . this quest is truly hopeless."

I think about what Merlin said at the banquet, how the quest was almost impossible, yes, but no more difficult than being king would be. I believe in Arthur as king—I believe it with every ounce of myself. So of course he would be able to complete his quest. Somehow, we would find a way.

"This letter doesn't change anything," I say, taking it from Arthur and crumpling it in my hands. I rip it to pieces once, twice, three times, until her words are illegible. "If taking Lyonesse is what we have to do for Arthur to become king, it's what we'll do. We'll leave tomorrow, as planned, and when we get there, Arthur will talk to Gwen. We'll fix things."

For a moment, no one says anything, though I hear the unasked question they are all thinking. Morgana is the one who finally gives it a voice.

"And if we can't?" she asks.

I purse my lips. "If Gwen won't be our ally, then she'll become our enemy," I say, though the words make me feel sick. "One way or another, we are taking that country, and you, Arthur, are taking your crown."


It was never any secret that Arthur fancied Gwen. He wore his feelings for her plain in the stumbling of his words and the red in his cheeks whenever she looked his way. In fact, within moments of meeting Arthur, there were three things I knew about him with utter certainty.

He was brilliant.

He was kind.

He was completely infatuated.

Arthur had been only thirteen at the time, but here we were after a decade of friendship, and if you were to ask me to list three things about him here and now, my answer wouldn't change.

He is brilliant.

He is kind.

He is completely infatuated.

YOU SHOULDN'T TEASE Arthur so much," Morgana told Gwen one afternoon. The three of us were sitting together in one of the northern meadows, this one so overrun with bright bursts of poppies and chrysanthemums that the ground was nearly more red than green—the sort of poetic metaphor one might choose when describing a battlefield for those with delicate sensibilities.

We were meant to be gathering poppy seeds for the kitchen—one of the chores Nimue came up with to keep us busy when our days couldn't be occupied by lessons. It had worked when we were younger, but by then we'd learned that Nimue didn't care about poppy seeds. She merely wanted us out of the way for a few hours, and it didn't matter how those few hours were spent.

It was too pretty a day to spend working, Morgana had reasoned, and Gwen and I didn't put up much of an argument. We sprawled out together in the meadow, skin warm from the sun, talking about everything and nothing at all.

"I don't tease him," Gwen said, frowning as she pushed herself up to her elbows to fix Morgana with a glare.

"Elaine?" Morgana said, looking to me. Gwen and Morgana were often at odds with each other, and since Arthur and Lancelot had learned long ago not to get caught up in their arguments, I'd had no choice but to assume the role of mediator when I'd arrived. Surprisingly, the role fit me quite well.

"You were teasing him a bit," I said. "This morning. His hair, that mark on his face. Remember?"

Gwen gave a dramatic sigh and flopped down on her back. "Well that doesn't count. He'd fallen asleep on a book again, and you saw it yourselves—his hair was ridiculously mussed up, and the book had left its imprint on his cheek."

"Of course we saw it. We laughed at it. We made fun of him for it. But you were the only one to muss his hair further, weren't you? The only one to touch his cheek like you could iron out the mark."

Gwen didn't speak for a moment, and the only sound to be heard was the soft chirp of birdsong in the distance.

"I touch everyone," she said. "I'd have done the same if it had been either of you."

"Yes, but neither of us is in love with you, are we?" I asked softly.

Gwen turned her face toward me and grinned. "Really? Not even a little bit? Careful, Elaine, or you'll hurt my feelings."

A year earlier, her flirting might have made me go red in the cheeks or stutter, but like magic, it was the kind of thing one built up a tolerance for. I met her gaze and leveled my own look at her.

"I love you. And so does Morgana, though you know she'd never say as much—" Morgana broke in with a snort of disapproval. "But not the same way Arthur does. You know that, and you're trying to deflect."

The grin slipped from her face, and she looked away from me, tilting her face back up to the sun. She was bound to get more freckles like that, but we weren't in Albion—no one would criticize her for it. I rather thought they suited her.

"He's always been mad about you," Morgana said after a second. "But it isn't a childhood infatuation anymore. He's sixteen now, growing whiskers and everything. You mustn't let it stick, Gwen. You'd do better to break his heart now, ruin him for you, than to let him believe there's hope when there isn't."

Gwen didn't reply, instead rolling over onto her stomach and pillowing her arms beneath her head.

"Gwen?" I asked, turning on my side to face her. "There isn't hope for him, is there?"

She opened her eyes to look at me, a cloud hovering over her face, obscuring her usually open and readable expression. Before she could answer, Morgana cut in with a laugh.

"Of course not, El," she said. "I know you've the heart of a romantic, but you know Gwen and you know Arthur. If there are two people more ill-suited for each other, I've never met them."

Something flickered in Gwen's expression, almost like a flinch, but it was gone before I could read it.

"Gwen," I said again, reaching my hand toward hers, but she gave it only a brief squeeze before releasing me.

"Morgana's right, El. We're ill-suited. Laughably so. You've been to Camelot, you know exactly the sort of woman who will end up at his side. Am I that sort of woman?" she asked.

"No," I admitted.

She shook her head. "No, I will belong in Lyonesse, with my kin. Free to run wild and live unrestricted by corsets or court etiquette or all manner of those *should*s and *should not*s you've talked about. That is happiness for me."

She said the words with conviction, like she believed every word she spoke, but they still rang false to my ears. Morgana must have heard it too.

"Then you'll stop it? Hurt him now to save him later?" she pressed.

Gwen didn't speak for a moment, but then she nodded.

"Of course," she said. "You're right. It's kinder in the long run."


IN GWEN'S DEFENSE, I do believe she tried. In the weeks that followed, she put more distance between herself and Arthur. She didn't tease him, or touch him, or even speak directly to him most days, but as much as that seemed to hurt Arthur, it hurt Gwen just as much. As the moon waxed and waned overhead, Gwen seemed to fade before our eyes.

I don't think the casual observer would have noticed it. She didn't mope or sigh mournfully or hide away in her rooms to sulk. But to me, and to Morgana, Arthur, and Lance, the difference in her was marked and frightening.

It started with her laugh. Where it was once a full-throated force of nature, it became quiet. Tight-lipped. Half-hearted.

She slept even less than usual, and where she had always found herself at the center of conversations, she slipped to the outskirts of them. She was still witty, still clever, still able to utterly disarm a person with a single word or even a look. The main difference, I suppose, is that it began to feel like she was merely going through the motions. Saying what she felt she ought to say, smiling when she thought she ought to smile.

She became a player in the farce of her life.

And that, more than her coolness toward him, was what truly seemed to break Arthur.

"Something is wrong with her," he told me while we roamed the shelves of the library one afternoon. He pulled a fat, leather-bound book from a high shelf, bringing a thick cloud of dust with it.

I coughed, waving my hand in front of my face. "It's Gwen," I told him, though I knew even as I said it that the words were anything but convincing. "You know how she is, Arthur. She's moody, but she always bounces back."

Arthur snorted, his eyes scanning the page. "Moody? I would give my right arm for Gwen at her moodiest just now. My lungs for her to snap peevishly at me and glower. My heart itself for a withering stare—a cutting remark even. This isn't moodiness. You know that. What's wrong with her, El?"

Guilt swam through me, but I forced myself to shake my head. "What makes you think I have any idea?"

He looked up from the book and raised a single eyebrow. "Because you know everything about everyone. Isn't that your gift?"

"You know it's not," I said, taking the book from him and flipping through it myself. I can't remember now what we were looking for, but I remember we were trying to settle some sort of debate between us. It happened often enough—one of us would recall some fact, the other would call it a falsehood, and we would debate it back and forth until we resolved to find proof, one way or another. "I know the future, Arthur, at least parts of it."

"I wasn't talking about your oracle gift," he replied. "It isn't a magical gift.

It's just you. You understand people. And you understand Gwen. So what is it? Did I do something?"

"Of course not," I said quickly. Too quickly.

"Elaine," he said, his voice softening.

I sighed. "She's trying to figure some things out, Arthur," I said.

"About me?" he pressed. "She barely looks at me anymore. I was so lost in my thoughts yesterday that I tripped over my own feet in front of everyone in the dining hall and she didn't even make fun of me for it."

I didn't answer, but that seemed to be all the confirmation he needed.

"I didn't ask anything of her," he continued. "I know she doesn't feel the same way about me as I do about her. I've never held that against her. I just . . . I just miss my friend, El. I know you miss her too."

"I think she doesn't want to give you false hope," I told him, my voice quiet. "But, Arthur, I don't think it would hurt her so much if it *was* false hope. I think, in doing what she believes is best for you, she's breaking her own heart."

Arthur frowned, trying to make sense of my words. "You think she loves me?"

I considered my next words carefully. "I think she knows she could, and that scares her."

"But . . . why? She must know I feel the same way. I've never been good at hiding it."

I bit my lip, trying to figure out how to put it into words. "I think that she's afraid it will change her."

"But it won't—"

"It will," I corrected, because that, at least, I'd Seen. All the ways loving Arthur would change her, all the ways it might destroy her in the process. "It will change you too. That's the very nature of love. Gwen likes her life as it is, she likes the future ahead of her, she's content with her path. Loving you would throw everything into chaos."

He was quiet for a moment. "Funny, I always thought Gwen thrived on chaos," he said, though there was no humor in his voice.

"Controlled chaos. Chaos of her own making. But this? This means trusting someone else enough to give them some measure of influence over her life. You must know how much that terrifies her."

Arthur nodded slowly, but his eyes were far away, already formulating a plan, I knew, already solving the problem he'd been presented with.

"I concede defeat," he told me. "You were right."

"About what?" I asked him.

He thumped his knuckles against the cover of the book in my hands. "Whatever we were arguing about. You were right. I'll see you at dinner."

And then he was gone, leaving me alone in the library. At least, I thought I'd been alone, but then Nimue appeared beside me like a summer breeze. First there was only still air, then she arrived.

"Was that wise?" she asked, her voice idle enough, but I heard the undercurrent.

"I don't know," I told her, shrugging my shoulders. "But my friends were hurting and it hurt me."

She clicked her tongue. "If you cannot tolerate your friends' pain, there is a difficult road ahead of you."

My stomach clenched. "If you'd hoped to keep Arthur and Gwen apart, you would never have brought her here. You would have done everything in your power to keep them as far away from each other as possible. But if they truly love each other, if they come to terms with that now, if I can find a way to bind them together irreversibly . . ." I trailed off.

"Then you think you can save them."

"I think I can make it harder for them to hurt each other," I said.

Nimue's hand grazed my arm, a comfort and a warning.

"You know nothing about love, Elaine," she told me. "But you will."

I'D WORRIED ARTHUR might do something foolish after our conversation, that he might take the sliver of hope I'd thrown his way and let it overwhelm him into making some sort of grand romantic proclamation, that he might end up pushing her too hard too soon and scaring her even more. Though I'm sure she would have protested the comparison, it was easy to think of Gwen as a skittish horse, and I thought if Arthur tried to do something quintessentially stupid and Arthur-like such as telling her he loved her, she would bolt off into the sunset, never to be seen again.

But he didn't.

If I didn't know better, I'd forget we'd had that conversation in the library at all. He let Gwen retreat from him and all of us, he didn't push her or try to goad her. He didn't even stare at her when she wasn't paying attention like he usually did, like she was some kind of puzzle he couldn't figure out. He simply gave her the space she needed.

And then one day, about a month or so later, when Arthur, Morgana, Lance, and I were eating stolen lemon cakes together in a forest clearing, Gwen appeared seemingly from nowhere, brows drawn and eyes focused.

"Gwen," Arthur said as she approached, her gaze trained solely on him with such intensity the rest of us might as well not have been there at all. "Are you al—"

She didn't let him finish. She dropped down to her knees beside him in one fluid motion, took hold of his face, and pressed her lips to his.

It happened so suddenly that for a moment, no one moved; no one even breathed. And then, just as suddenly, Arthur was kissing her back, his own hand coming to rest on the back of her neck, tangling in her red-gold hair and anchoring her there.

Perhaps it should have been embarrassing for me—and for Morgana and Lance too—to witness that kiss, to see the relief and wariness and desire mingling together in two of our closest friends. But it wasn't embarrassing. It wasn't awkward. I didn't feel the burning need to avert my gaze and pretend I didn't notice it happening right before me. Instead it just felt right, like something that was always meant to happen that way.

After a moment, Gwen pulled away and sat back on her heels, her eyes searching Arthur's dazed face and her swollen mouth slightly open. She looked at him like he was a problem she was on the cusp of solving but hadn't quite figured out yet. Then she rolled to her feet and held her hand out to him.

"We're going to go talk," she told him. It wasn't a request, but it wasn't a command either. Instead it was simply an acknowledgment of fact. Arthur nodded and took her hand, letting her pull him to his feet and lead him out of the clearing and away from the rest of us without so much as a goodbye.

# 22

SLEEP DOESN'T FIND me, even though we leave for Lyonesse in the morning and I know I'll need all the rest I can get. When the moon is high and full in the sky, I throw off the coverlet and climb out of bed. In the pitch dark of my room, I have to fumble around before I find a candle, and it takes longer still for me to light it. With trembling hands, I carry the candle across the room to where my loom has been set up, a basket of skeins of pearlescent white thread beside the seat. I set the candle in the window and sit down, tracing my fingers over the threads already warped on the loom, watching them glimmer in the candlelight.

I know that we will succeed, one way or another, in Lyonesse. I *know* it.

But I don't—not really. I haven't had time to scry since coming to the castle. I haven't been able to See how the strings of fate have adjusted in the space of a week. Maybe, if I had, I would have Seen Gwen's letter before she sent it, I would have Seen Arthur's failure to procure more than a handful of second-rate knights. If I could have Seen them, maybe I could have done something to circumvent them before the possibilities became facts.

But I won't make that mistake again.

Though sleep pulls at tired limbs and my mind is a fog of wine and exhaustion, I reach into the basket and draw out a skein, feeling the soft thread between my fingers.

In a few hours we will be leaving for a land feral and unknown. In a couple of days I will be seeing my father for the first time in more than a decade. In a week, my friends and I will step into a land of monsters where Gwen is the crown princess.

None of that is in my control. But, in some ways, this is.

GWEN WILL STAND at her window, her red hair unbound and wild, her feet bare, her dress several sizes too big. The hem of it will be caked in mud, the same mud that will clump in the ends of her hair and streak her ruddy cheeks. She will peer past a velvet curtain with wide, impassive eyes.

Below her window, a battle will unfold, if it can truly be called that. There will be a handful of scrawny boys in shining armor, swords in hand. Even with their helmets on, I know a few on sight—Gawain, Lancelot, and Arthur. A ways back from the action, Morgana stands in a black lace gown, her hands raised as she summons magic, but even that will not be enough.

Fifty men will fight against them—though *men* does not seem to be an accurate term. Though they will walk on two legs, they will be disproportionate, their arms and legs strangely bent so that they look almost broken. They will wear no armor, no helmets, and their bare faces will be sharp and tufted with fur. Not hair—*fur*. They will have ears like wolves, snouts like wolves, teeth like something altogether *other*. I have never seen teeth so sharp in nature; each one will be filed to a rose thorn's point.

The swords of the knights will be useless against the monsters. Even when they draw blood and red runs thick over the silver blades, mats itself in the monsters' fur, it will seem to have no effect. The monsters will not feel the blow, will not even feel it when an arm is cut clean off, or a leg. They will keep fighting, keep striking, keep sinking their unnatural teeth through the metal of the knights' armor and into the skin below.

The screams that pierce the air will be so loud that even through time, they rattle my bones. But Gwen will not flinch from them. She will have the power to end the fighting with a word, but she will not say it. She will stand in the window and she will watch the bloodshed unfold, her eyes locked on one knight in particular, on Arthur.

When one of the monsters pins him to the ground and rips off his helmet, when he lowers those teeth to Arthur's bared throat, Gwen will not look away. She will not regret what must happen. But she will mourn him all the same.

ARTHUR WILL KNEEL before the king of Lyonesse—though I cannot see his face, I see that he has the same wild red hair as Gwen—and he will propose a treaty. He will promise trade agreements that will make the king richer than his wildest imaginings, he will offer an army to drive back the monsters that overrun the country, he will swear to make Gwen his queen so that their offspring will one day rule the whole continent.

The king of Lyonesse will smile and lean forward in his throne, and then he will order Arthur executed on the spot, his head returned to Camelot to send a message that Lyonesse answers to no ruler but him.

ARTHUR AND GWEN will make up, but they will have had enough of crowns and politics and quests. They will run away together to live in the woods, all alone, and they will live to old age, happy and fulfilled and at peace, blissfully unaware of Mordred bringing Albion to ruin a hundred miles away.

ARTHUR WILL BE so distraught after speaking to Gwen that he will go for a walk in the woods and fall off a cliff.

GWEN WILL HAVE already eloped with a man I don't know, and Arthur, brokenhearted, will fall ill and die.

———✦———

ARTHUR WILL HAVE his sword drawn, facing Gwen, who will wear a torn silk gown, her hands slick with blood, hair matted with dirt. She will snarl under the light of the moon, and her eyes will be hungry. She will have no weapon, no shield, no armor, but he will be the one to look at her with fear while she looks at him with only hunger.

Lightning will streak through the air, echoed by a rumble of thunder, and just like that they will spring toward each other and Arthur will raise his sword to strike.

WE WON'T EVEN make it to Lyonesse. We will get lost in the wild woods between Shalott and the border. Only Gawain will make it back to Camelot to tell the story.

ARTHUR WILL SPEAK to Gwen. She will tell him about her fears, about her father, about all the reasons she became afraid to leave home, to make a new life in Camelot. She will tell him that she loves him. He will tell her they can figure things out, together. She will take his ring back and slide it onto her finger.

We will return to Camelot, with Gwen and a signed treaty. The people will cheer. Mordred will glower. Morgause will turn puce.

ARTHUR WILL CHALLENGE one of the monster men to a duel for Gwen's hand, though Gwen will roll her eyes at the prospect. They will fight. The monster man will win by decapitating Arthur with a single blow.

ARTHUR WILL CHALLENGE one of the monster men to a duel for Gwen's hand, though Gwen will roll her eyes at the prospect. They will fight. Arthur will win, but Gwen will refuse to marry him all the same because she would never marry a man who treats her as a prize. Arthur will be executed on the spot for disrespecting the princess so.

THE VISIONS GO on and on, a blur of *maybe*s and *could be*s and *might*s until I can't quite tell where one vision ends and the next begins. I try to hold on to the one outcome, the one future where we return to Camelot triumphant, but in the shadow of all the other futures, it shrinks. It almost disappears altogether.

But as pale, dusky light begins to seep through my window and I hear Morgana awaken in the next room, I clutch that vision so tightly, clinging to it like a life raft in a storm. The only thing keeping me afloat. The only hope we have.

It isn't likely. But it is possible. And that has to be enough.

# 23

MY BAG IS already packed when Morgana knocks on my door, poking her head in to ask if I'm ready. She's still in her nightgown, and her ink-black hair is a wild mess with pieces that almost seem to stand on end, so I assume it will be at least another twenty minutes before she's ready to go.

"I'll be ready long before you are," I tell her with a laugh. "I'm sure Arthur assumed we would be late anyway."

Morgana shakes her head, a small smile tugging at her lips. "My brother knows me well," she says before turning and going back to her room.

I wait until the sound of her footsteps fades down the hall before I approach my vanity. It feels too small for me now, the ivory paint peeling from the wood in places. Even after being cleaned, the cushion on the stool before it still smells of must.

I remember sitting here while my mother brushed out my hair every night, her fingers merciless against the tangles. I would always go to bed with a sore scalp.

Now, though, I sit before the gilded mirror and braid my own hair, but my mother's words echo through my mind all the same. *They will try to use you,* my mother warned me once. She was talking about Camelot's courtiers, and I'm sure that in that, she was correct. But now, I can't stop thinking about my conversation with Merlin. I can't stop thinking that humans weren't the only ones who might have used me—not just me, but the others as well and Arthur in particular.

*You think such a thing as peace exists when fey and humans walk together?* Merlin asked me.

I had thought just that. The fey couldn't tell lies, after all, so what reason did I have to disbelieve Nimue? But truth is like fine lace, full of open loops to slip through if you're clever enough, and Nimue has had centuries to hone her cleverness. As I think back over everything she's told me of the World Before, I realize that when she spoke of peace, she spoke of peace for *us*. I interpreted the *us* as being general, peace for everybody, but perhaps she only meant it as "us, those with fay blood."

I tie off the end of my single simple braid with a pale yellow ribbon. When that is done, I gaze at my reflection in the mirror and take a deep breath.

"Nimue," I say, my voice coming out level and clear.

For a second, nothing happens. Then, slowly, the surface of the mirror ripples, like a once-still pond when rain begins to drizzle. When the surface stills again, it is not my own face looking back at me, but Nimue's.

It's strange—I saw her only a week ago, but I think I'd already begun to forget her face. Seeing her again now takes me by surprise. I suppose when I saw her every day, I grew used to the sheer inhumanity of her, but now after a week of humans, I'm taken aback by the sight.

Her features are too sharp and, at the same time, too full. Her eyes too large. Her obsidian skin too luminous.

"Elaine," she says, when I don't speak. "Is everything alright? You know to be careful about calling on me. Arthur has been crowned, yes?"

"No," I say, biting my lip. Though I know the complications we've faced since arriving have been well outside of my control, I still feel like they are my fault somehow. Like I've failed her.

"Arthur hasn't been crowned," I say. "When we arrived, Merlin set him a quest, and I'm starting to suspect it might be an impossible one."

Nimue frowns. "You delivered my letter?"

"Yes."

"He read it?"

"Yes. He sought me out last night and said . . . well, he mentioned that the two of you have had your differences. He said that a united world would not be in the best interests of humanity. I don't know that I agree with him, but I would like more information."

Nimue considers this. "Of course you would," she says after a moment. She isn't angry—I don't know why I expected she would be. I don't know that I've ever seen her truly angry. I'm not sure she has it in her to be. "Merlin and I have not always stood on the same side of things," she says slowly. "It was my hope that Arthur would be able to convince him that the fey are not malevolent. A human child, raised among us. I think you would agree that Arthur was never treated as anything lesser."

I flinch, thinking about the footrace, about the other fay children who reveled in bringing Arthur low, who never saw him as an equal. When I tell Nimue about this, her expression clouds but she does not falter.

"Hate is learned, Elaine," she says, her voice level. "The way those children acted was inexcusable, and I wish you had told me of it earlier. But inexcusable as it is, I do understand the impulse, as I'm sure you do as well. They were exiled by humanity, bound to an island; in some cases their families were broken up in the process. There are many differences between humans and fey, but I'm sorry to say our adolescents are every bit as rash and emotional as human adolescents are. More so, perhaps. They were angry, and they were taking out that anger on the representation of someone they were raised to view as the enemy. But, if our plan succeeds—if Arthur succeeds—there will be no need for bitterness any longer, no need for hate. We will have peace."

There it is again, the *we*.

"And humans will have peace as well," I press.

Her smile is nothing but open and guileless.

"Yes," she says, her voice emphatic. "Arthur's reign will mean peace for everyone—humans, fey, and everyone in between."

I search for the holes in the lace, but there are none. Except the major one, that is. Which is that she is telling the truth as she believes it. Whether or not that is the objective truth is something no one can truly know. She must see my hesitation, because she leans forward, as if there isn't a sea between us and she might reach out to touch me.

"You have more questions," she says, her voice softening. "Of course you do. I would expect nothing less of you, Elaine, and I will answer any question you can think to pose, as best as I am able. You have my vow in this. But for now, there is only one truth that matters—I wish for Arthur to succeed, as do you. We are on the same side. Do you believe that?"

I don't hesitate to nod. That much I know to be true.

"Good. Then tell me—what has happened?"

As quickly as I can, I tell her about what has occurred since we arrived, the quest, the knights, Mordred's scheming, and Gwen's letter. Lastly, I tell her about my scrying last night and what I learned.

Nimue purses her lips when I finish. "What was the first thing I told you about scrying, Elaine?" she asks quietly.

I think back to a cave on Avalon, Nimue standing behind me while she showed me her scrying mirror and how she used it to summon visions. I hear her voice, low and melodic, in my ear like a lullaby. I feel her hands on mine, guiding but also cold and unlined and not quite human.

"The future is not set until it is the past," I say.

She nods. "Maybe a hundred—a thousand—versions of Arthur will fail. But you know now that one will succeed. Do you know how?"

I shake my head. "Not really. I know more of what not to do. I know not to let him duel for her hand. I know not to let it come to a battle. I know there are things he shouldn't say, shouldn't do."

"That will have to be enough, to start," she says.

"But Gwen—"

"Gwen is human, mostly," Nimue says with a sigh. "Which means that she is always a variable."

"More of a variable than the rest of us, I think," I say.

Nimue laughs loudly at that, shaking her head. "You might think that," she says. "But I assure you it isn't the truth. You are all variables. If anything, Gwen's flightiness makes her more of a constant—at least you know to expect it."

"I thought I could at least count on her love for Arthur, but in some of my visions . . . she just let him die," I say. "It was like she didn't care for him at all, like he was a stranger."

Nimue's smile goes straight, and she gives a sigh. "I believe she does love him," she says after a moment. "But love is never a steady force, and it is always relative. She loves Arthur, yes, but what does she love more?"

I wait for her to continue, but she doesn't. "Is that all you'll tell me?" I ask.

Nimue gives me a sad smile. "Oh, Elaine," she says. "I haven't told you anything you don't already know. I've trained you well. All I can do now is wish you luck. You mustn't reach out to me again unless it is an emergency."

I bite my lip and nod. "I . . . I didn't think it would be this difficult, Nimue," I say. "I imagined Arthur would be welcomed back with fanfare, that the people would cheer for him. But it's getting to him, and it's getting to me as well. How can he be any kind of ruler if he can't keep everyone happy? His throne will always be in jeopardy no matter what."

"Yes," she says plainly. "But that is a problem for another day, Elaine. In order to keep his throne, first you must get him on it to begin with."

WE LEAVE AS the sun rises over Camelot, painting the gray stone in shades of bleeding pastel. With the nine knights and a cook, we are a party of only fourteen. A scouting party, practically, not a royal delegation by any stretch of the imagination, and certainly not an army if it comes to it.

The cobblestone streets are quiet this early, but the few people already out wave as we pass. Arthur waves back, shouting greetings and well-wishes. The people return them, their smiles growing. I imagine it isn't often they're spoken to kindly by a nobleman. One man calls him Prince Arthur. Another bows and calls him king.

It was a smart thing to do, court the common people. We won't find much support with the nobles, after all, and we need people on our side. But even as I think it, I know that isn't why Arthur showed them attention and kindness. He did it simply because he's Arthur.

Simple a thing as it is, his goodness bolsters me. Maybe Nimue is right and humans are fickle creatures, forever changing and unpredictable, but there are some things I believe are solid, and chief among them is Arthur's goodness, his selflessness. He won't fight for Gwen, he won't duel over her, he won't offend the king there. And not because of any warning I might give but because it's just not in his nature.

A million ways this could go wrong, but I believe in Arthur. That has to be enough.

# 24

WE STOP FOR the night in a thicket of woods about halfway between Camelot and Shalott, all of us exhausted and grouchy—apart from Lancelot, whose inhuman reserve of energy only serves to further sour the mood in the air. Especially when he suggests we keep on riding and try to make it to Shalott tonight.

"We wouldn't get there before sunrise," Arthur points out mildly before I can snap at Lancelot. "And besides, we need food and sleep—well, maybe *you* don't. But the rest of us do. Not to mention the horses."

"We can just make do on bedrolls for the night, but the women should have a proper tent," Gawain says, glancing at Morgana and me. "I'll pitch it."

"No need," Morgana says with a smile. She reaches into her saddlebags to pull out the folded tent. The material leaps from her like it's possessed by a spirit. It makes a large arc through the air and then hangs in the clearing in the shape of a tent, large enough for the two of us.

"Morgana," I hiss.

Morgana looks at me with wide eyes. "What?" she asks. "If we return triumphant, Arthur will be crowned king, and magic will no longer be a death sentence. And if we don't . . . well, we're dead anyway, aren't we?"

I look around at the others—the knights are eyeing Morgana with a blend of awe and wariness, but no one speaks for a long moment.

Finally, the cook clears his throat. "I don't suppose you can help me get the fire started as well?" he asks.

He's a mysterious figure, our cook. Overgrown black hair covers his eyes more or less, and he wears a red kerchief around the lower half of his face due to what he described as a fear of illness.

*If I fall ill,* he said earlier when Lancelot asked him why he wore it, *all of you will surely fall after me.*

Now, Gawain gives him a suspicious look, but Morgana only laughs and follows him to where he's set up wood for a fire.

"Are you alright?" I ask Gawain.

He tears his gaze from the cook's retreating figure and looks at me sheepishly. "It's nothing. His voice just sounded familiar for a second is all. I'm more tired than I thought."

Everyone begins to unpack their own bedrolls and other necessities, but there's little for me to do since Morgana set up our tent.

"Do you need help with anything?" I ask him. "I don't have Morgana's gifts, but I can be an extra pair of hands at least."

He glances at me and smiles. "If you really don't mind," he says.

"Elaine," Lancelot calls from the other side of our camp. "I think we need more firewood."

I look at the fire and the collection of wood beside it. I might not know much about fires, but it looks like enough to last us until morning. When I say as much, though, he just shrugs.

"It might be enough," he allows. "But I'd rather we don't find out it's not when it's dark as pitch out and we can't find more."

The last thing I want is for exactly that to happen—not because of the cold, but because it would mean I'd have to listen to him gloat about being right, so I send Gawain an apologetic smile before starting into the woods around us.

A few moments later, as I'm picking through the underbrush, a twig snaps behind me and I whirl around, dropping the two pieces I'd already found.

"It's just me," Lancelot says, coming toward me, holding his hands up like I'm a wild animal who might flee or attack at the slightest provocation. It's not an unfair gesture, because for an instant I'm tempted to do just that. "I thought you might like some help."

I crouch to pick up the wood I dropped. "I don't see why you didn't just come then," I say. "This isn't a two-person job."

Lancelot shrugs, coming toward me and taking the wood from my arms. "Maybe I wanted to walk in the woods with you, Shalott," he says with a slow smile. "Maybe I thought it would be romantic."

"In the last seven years, you've never been one for romantic gestures," I point out. "But I suppose on Avalon, there was no one you found worthy of jealousy. I don't belong to you, Lance."

"You made that perfectly clear, and I've never argued it," he replies before pausing. "Do you like him?"

I shrug my shoulders. "I don't really know him. Courtship isn't high on my list of priorities at the moment, in case you didn't notice. But he's been nothing but kind, and I didn't see the harm in offering him kindness in return. He's one of us, Lance. Whether you like it or not."

He doesn't flinch from that, his eyes holding mine. "One of us," he echoes. "What do you mean by that?"

"Just . . . we were raised, in a sense, to support Arthur, weren't we? Raised to be his allies, his confidants. Gawain . . . is the same somehow. I can't explain it. He just is."

Lancelot shakes his head. "He isn't. The same, I mean. Us—you and me and Gwen and Morgana and Arthur—no one can touch what we have. Avalon bound us together in a way that I don't think anyone else would ever be able to understand. Other people are good, necessary, I know that. But at the end of the day, it will always be us against the world."

I look away, and he reaches out with his free hand to take hold of my arm.

"There it is again," he says, stepping closer. "You disagree with me. Why?"

I hesitate. "All I see is possibilities. Nimue said that there is nothing certain about the future until it becomes the past. But there are possibilities, possible futures, where you're wrong."

"Then don't let me be," he says, as if it's that easy. He releases my arm and reaches up to touch the side of my face instead. "Fate is all well and good,

Shalott, but it's nothing without us, without our choices. I know myself. I know what I choose, what I will always choose."

I step closer to him, closing the distance between us, but before I do something I know I will regret, Morgana's voice pierces the air, announcing that dinner is ready.

Grateful for the interruption, I step back, letting Lance's hand drop. "You should find a few more pieces of wood, since it was your idea," I say, surprised that my voice comes out level.

"Elaine—" he starts, but I shake my head.

"Right now, we need to focus on getting Arthur crowned," I say. "Nothing else matters until we do."

He holds my gaze, and in that moment, I swear he sees every one of my thoughts laid bare. All of the dangerous thoughts about him, all of the things I've Seen, every twisted and ugly part of me.

"Arthur is like a brother to me. Of course he matters," he says, his voice low. A secret spoken in the dim woods, lost to the trees. "But you, Shalott . . . you're the sun. Without you, nothing wakes. Nothing grows. It's just darkness."

I stare at him for a moment, unsure of what to say.

"And," he continues, a smile spreading over his features once more, "for what it's worth, I thought we had a few romantic moments in Avalon. The waterfall, for one."

Heat rises to my cheeks as I remember that afternoon, the memory warm with sunshine and the smell of grass and salt water.

"You were terrified to go anywhere near the water, remember?" he asks.

I remember the fear fluttering in my belly, the sound of the rushing water sending my pulse pounding, loud enough to drown out any thoughts. But I also remember his smile as he stood knee-deep in the churning river, his hand held out to me, palm up. I remember only a beat of hesitation before I slipped my hand into his and stepped into the river beside him. I remember the fear that felt primed to overwhelm me reduced to a simmer. I remember feeling safe and, at the same time, like I was standing on the precipice of something great and dangerous, something that for the first time had nothing to do with water at all.

It wasn't the stuff of the Camelot courtships I was raised around, the ballads about fair, demure maidens and valiant, pure-hearted knights who saved them from all manner of evil. But I had to admit, it was romantic.

I step closer to him, a movement so natural it doesn't even feel like a choice.

"You trusted me then," he says, reaching toward me, his hand coming to rest on my waist. "Did I let you drown?"

"Lance," I start, but before I can follow that train of thought—before I can say something I will likely regret—

"Elaine!" Morgana calls from the camp. Nimue's words come back to me. *Love is never a steady force.* It complicates everything—Arthur and Gwen are proof enough of that—and the last thing we need is more complications.

So I turn and walk away from him, back to camp, where I let the conversation among the others drown out my churning thoughts.


THAT NIGHT, AS Morgana and I get ready for bed, a single candle illuminating the tent in a hazy, dim light, she gives a loud sigh, tossing a rolled-up nightgown at me. It hits me in the face, taking me by surprise.

"Hey," I hiss, careful to keep my voice low. The walls of the tent are thin, and I can hear every move the knights outside make, each step, each breath, each snore.

She fixes me with a bemused look, one dark eyebrow lifted high. "You were quiet all through dinner. What's wrong with you?"

"Nothing," I say, pulling my traveling dress over my head. "I'm just . . . thinking about Gwen. And the quest. And seeing my father tomorrow. There's a lot happening."

Morgana says nothing as she helps me with the laces of my corset, and I do the same for her. When we've both changed into our nightgowns and gotten into our bedrolls, she turns over to face me.

"I don't doubt all of that is bothering you," she says, her voice a whisper. "But that's not all it is, is it?"

The candle flickers on the ground between us, casting her face half in shadow. Her violet eyes are darker than usual, the color of the amethyst that lined the walls of the Cave of Prophecies on Avalon.

I bite my lip and pull my quilt up to my chin before telling her what Lancelot said in the woods. She knows the rest of it already, everything apart from the specifics of my visions, though I would be surprised if she hadn't guessed the bulk of that as well. Though I've never said explicitly how I felt about him, I don't think I had to. She knows, just as Gwen likely does.

"Lancelot's heart is fickle, we know this," I whisper when I'm done. "Give it a few days—he'll find some wild Lyonessian girl, and next thing you know he'll be madly in love with her. It's what he does and it's for the best. Arthur and Gwen have already made enough of a mess of things with their feelings. We can't afford any more."

Morgana doesn't say anything for a moment, but her eyes stay on me, reading my features like I'm a book open before her. I hold her gaze, but of course, she sees through me anyway.

"I used to envy you, you know," she says.

The idea of that is so laughable that I don't know what to say. Ever since the moment I met her, I've envied Morgana. Envied her confidence and strength, her brazenness, her bravery. How can she possibly have ever envied me? When I don't speak, she continues.

"Seeing the future—it seemed like such a grand gift. That kind of knowledge . . . that kind of power. It used to be that I wanted it more than anything," she says.

"You certainly hid it well," I say with a laugh. "Besides, you can create things, change things, summon things."

"Yes," Morgana says. "Things. Gwen's power is over nature, your power is tied to people. But mine . . . it's only things. Inanimate objects. Maybe there is more of a scope to my gift, but the fact remains, I envied you. Both of you."

I don't say anything for a moment, still trying to wrap my mind around her confession. "Why are you telling me this now?" I ask.

Morgana rolls over onto her back, staring at the roof of the tent. "Because I never really considered how hard it would be," she says. "What that kind of knowledge would do to you."

I frown. "What has it done to me?" I ask her.

She looks at me again, smiling slightly. "It's made fear your constant companion," she says. "You look at a situation, even a happy one like a boy you're madly in love with saying he loves you, and you see only how that love might rot."

"Do you think it won't?" I ask. "You've seen him, Morgana. Love is weakness. That's what you've always told me: Exploit it in others—it's a useful trick to know—but guard your own heart with iron and steel. Guard it above all else. Because if a person has your heart, they have all of you."

Morgana frowns. "Did I really say that?" she asks.

I shrug. "More than once," I tell her. "Word for word. I remember it well."

"Maiden, Mother, and Crone, I can be prickly sometimes, can't I?"

"Sometimes?" I ask, earning a sharp glare.

"Well, I'm sorry at any rate," she says with a sigh. "You're the last person I should warn to caution. You're already far too cautious for your own good."

I snort. "Tell me, Morgana, do you really believe that Lancelot can be faithful to anyone?" I ask her.

She doesn't answer right away. "I think the danger in knowing someone as long as we've known one another is that it makes it harder to see when people change. It's harder to let people grow."

"You think he's grown?" I ask.

She must hear the skepticism in my voice because she gives a loud sigh. "I don't know, El. I'm only saying. He's in love with you, and you're clearly in love with him."

"For now. He's in love with me *for now*."

"Maybe," she says. "Maybe not. There's really only one way to find out."

"You mean when I'm brokenhearted?" I ask.

She rolls her eyes. "Heartbreak isn't as lethal as the name implies, you know. Maybe it feels that way at the time, but I swear it isn't. You've seen Gwen and me both rebound from it eventually. I don't regret anything leading up to it, and I doubt Gwen does either. It's life, Elaine. Getting hurt, picking yourself up, trying again. You're so focused on the ending sometimes that I don't think you know how to appreciate the *during*."

I don't know how to respond to that, but I feel her words burrow their way under my skin. If we keep talking about this, I'll drive myself mad, so I change the subject.

"Do you think Gwen regrets anything with Arthur?" I ask her. "That letter . . . it was so short. It didn't say anything, really. Nothing personal in it at all. It could have been a letter from a stranger."

Morgana doesn't say anything for a moment. "Gwen's emotions always run hot," she says after a moment. "Sometimes it's easier for her to turn them off completely to protect herself. Maybe to protect Arthur too. I don't know."

"What do you think we'll find in Lyonesse?" I ask.

Morgana's quiet for a moment, her brow furrowed. "I don't know," she repeats. "All I know for sure is that I miss her. The circumstances aren't ideal and I have no idea what to expect, but all of that aside, it will be good to see her again."

"I miss her too," I say, even as I remember the Gwen from my visions, cold and emotionless as she watched Arthur die. That isn't the Gwen I know, I tell myself. *But it is*, a small voice replies. That version of Gwen is a part of her, whether I like it or not.

"We should get some sleep," Morgana says. "I know you have mixed feelings about seeing your family tomorrow, but I for one am looking forward to sleeping in an actual bed."

She leans over and blows out the candle, shrouding us in pitch darkness. Her breathing slows almost immediately, soon replaced by soft snores, but sleep doesn't find me right away. Instead, I stare up into the night air, my thoughts a whirlpool of fear and dread and plots that can go wrong all too easily.

## 25

I MET LANCELOT AND Gwen for the first time on my first day on Avalon, over breakfast in the dining hall. Of everywhere on Avalon, the dining hall was one place that at least felt somewhat familiar. There were no constantly changing paths, no writhing trees, no rivers full of mermaids waiting to drown you. It was just a dining hall, like any that might have been found in Camelot, with only one large table that stretched the length of the entire building, made of solid, polished black marble. The chairs that went down either side of it were simple things, carved from dark wood, with straight backs and no arms. Painted porcelain bowls and plates piled high with food covered most of the table's surface. Some I recognized, like apples and toast, but other things looked strange to me: pastries shaped like daisies, and violets with petals that looked like they'd been crystalized, a round fruit the size of my palm with vivid green skin covered in spikes, a pot of jam the color of a new gold coin. There was a silver goblet at each place, filled with water.

Morgana led me by the hand to the far end of the table, where a girl close to my age was sitting alone. All I could see of her was a cascade of candlelight-orange hair that fell down to the middle of her back. It looked like it hadn't been brushed in months.

"Elaine," Morgana said as we approached. "This is Guinevere."

The red-haired girl turned to look at me over her shoulder, and I was struck for a moment. There were beautiful ladies back at court, tall and elegant with fine bones, luminous skin, and confident smiles, but next to Guinevere, they would have been plain at best. Though to look at each of her features individually, she was a collection of what I'd been raised to see as flaws. Her skin was the color of sun-warmed bronze, and there was a deep red flush across her sharp cheekbones. Thick eyebrows arched high over green eyes that looked like a cat's—though not the tame, housebound sort. More like the large wildcats I had seen only in paintings. Her jaw was too strong and square, her mouth full but undefined, her whole face covered in freckles—all flaws Camelot women would have gone to great lengths to disguise or fix through whatever means necessary. But Guinevere wore her flaws like they were assets, and so they somehow became just that.

"Hello," she said through a mouth half-full of apple, the word coming out garbled. She paused and swallowed before smiling, not quite sheepish, but more like we were sharing a private joke. "Morgana mentioned you in her letters. I hoped she'd manage to bring you back with her."

"I told Elaine a bit about you, as well," Morgana said, sitting down across from her and motioning for me to join.

"Morgana said you're from Lyonesse originally?" I asked Guinevere.

In the stories I'd heard, Lyonesse was a wild land, overrun with beasts who walked like men and men who ran wild like beasts. I imagined it to be dreary, a world bathed in sepia and gray. It was difficult to imagine a girl like Guinevere there, with her bright hair and eyes and smile. When Morgana mentioned her Lyonessian friend, I'd expected a hunched-over, toad-faced girl who would sooner bite me than smile. I expected a monstrous thing, raised by beasts and not quite human. At the time, I thought she looked like only a girl, much like me, but later I would see the more wild parts of her. She might not have had fangs in the literal sense, but they were certainly there, hiding just in the corners of her blinding smile.

At the sound of her country's name, Guinevere beamed.

"Yes," she said, sitting up a little straighter. "Do you know it?"

I shook my head, not wanting to tell her about the rumors I'd heard, especially since I was beginning to doubt the truth in them. "I was born in Shalott, though, and it's just across the border."

"You should visit sometime," she said eagerly. "It's so beautiful, and you could stay with me."

It struck me then as an abrupt sort of invitation to extend to someone you've just met, but before I could answer, Morgana snorted.

"Elaine, you would hate it there—so dark and wild. All overgrown forests and fog-draped moors—"

"And monsters?" I couldn't help but ask.

Guinevere laughed. "Monsters," she scoffed, "are in the eye of the beholder. Honestly, from what I hear about the so-called humans in Albion, I'm inclined to think *they're* the monsters."

"That I can't disagree with," Morgana said with a smirk, reaching across the table to take a piece of toast and a spoonful of jam. "But really, Gwen. Lyonesse is not for the faint of heart. I've heard stories of knights fleeing back across the border in terror."

Guinevere frowned, shrugging her shoulders carelessly. "Perhaps their king should train his knights better then," she said coolly, her eyes catching on a group of fey who stepped into the hall. "Here, we'll ask Lancelot," she said.

I followed her gaze to the cluster of fey, trying to accustom myself to the sight of so many. Scales covered bare arms, horns protruded from slicked-back hair. It was overwhelming, almost, to see so many of them at once, all so brazen, but I couldn't look away.

I guessed the Lancelot Gwen mentioned must be the only boy in that group who looked close to our age, who also happened to be the most human in appearance. He stood beside a woman with golden skin like his, but where her hair was seaweed green, his was a perfectly human black. The boy's eyes darted over to our part of the table before landing on me for an instant, confusion furrowing his brow, and I quickly looked away, embarrassed to have been caught staring. Out of the corner of my eye, I saw him bend down to kiss the woman on the cheek before starting toward us.

"Good morning," he said to Gwen and Morgana with a grin at each of them before sinking into the empty chair across from mine. His hair was windblown and messy, and his peculiar green eyes shifted focus around the table, settling on each person before finally landing on me, his brow creasing into a frown. "Who are you?"

"Elaine," I told him, a bit taken aback by his bluntness. Before I could say more, Morgana interrupted.

"I found her in Camelot," she said with a hint of smugness, like I was a toy she was showing off. "She's an oracle."

Lancelot's gaze turned appraising for a second before shifting to Morgana. "And Nimue . . . knows about this?" Lancelot asked.

"Of course," Morgana said. "She was very glad I found her."

It was strange to have people talk about me but not to me. I found I didn't care for it.

"Nimue was very welcoming," I said, which might have been a slight exaggeration. I could still hear her ominous voice in my mind, welcoming me to Avalon.

Lancelot's strange eyes weighed almost uncomfortably on me, and I looked away again quickly. "It's all very new to me," I admitted. "I certainly never thought it was something to be proud of."

I expected Morgana to jump in again, sharing my history as if it were some kind of exciting adventure story I never agreed to be a part of, but instead she only gave me a small smile, reaching over to take my hand. "Nimue will have a lot to teach you," she said.

That surprised me. "Nimue's going to teach me herself?" I asked, thinking about the way she looked at me like I was an equation she couldn't solve. It was discomforting, and I wasn't sure I wanted to be around her more than necessary. I certainly couldn't imagine taking regular lessons with her.

But Morgana only laughed.

"Nimue's the best oracle on the island," she said, as if that explained everything.

I suppose it did explain some things. But it mostly invited more questions.

"But she's the Lady of the Lake," I pointed out. "Surely she has better things to do than teach me."

Gwen shook her head. "An oracle from Albion? I can't imagine a pupil she'd be more interested in."

Gwen immediately went back to her breakfast, so I don't think she saw the fear that came over me. Lancelot did, though, his eyes thoughtful as they met mine. I expected him to say something, but instead he held my gaze for a second longer before tearing his eyes away.

As BREAKFAST WOUND down and Morgana and Gwen started to head off to their lessons, Morgana suggested that Lancelot give me a tour of the island.

Before I could respond, Lancelot did.

"I can't," he said, clipped and curt.

Gwen snorted. "What else do you have to do?" she asked before spotting something in Lancelot's face. "Oh, meeting up with . . . what's her name again?"

Lancelot cleared his throat, a flush working its way across his cheeks. He gave a name then that has long faded from my memory, replaced by countless names that followed it, blending together until one was no longer decipherable from the rest.

Morgana rolled her eyes. "Well, you can meet up with her some other time," she said. "You can't leave Elaine alone in a strange place where she doesn't know anyone."

"It's fine," I said. "Really, I probably need a nap after everything last night. And by the time I wake up, your lessons will be over anyway."

Morgana didn't budge, though. "Lancelot," she said, her voice a warning.

He held her gaze, and for a moment they were locked in a silent conversation before Lancelot finally looked away with a loud sigh. "Alright," he said, turning to me. "A tour it is."

Morgana kissed him on the cheek as she got up from the table, surprising Lancelot. "Arthur should take note. That is some chivalrous, princely behavior right there."

"Now you're just trying to cause a fuss," Lancelot grunted, glancing farther down the table, where a group of fay girls with candy floss hair and stardust skin watched on and whispered behind their hands. "Where is Arthur, anyway?"

"Early-morning lessons at the library," Gwen said, getting up as well. "I'm about to join him."

After they departed, I looked back at Lancelot.

"You really don't have to cancel your plans," I told him. "I'm not a child in need of a nanny. I'll be fine on my own."

For an awful moment, I worried that he might actually take me up on that, but he mercifully shook his head.

"It's fine," he said, waving a hand dismissively. "I was going to end things with her anyway. You're just giving me a day's reprieve on that unpleasant conversation, and Morgana gloating that she told me so."

"Oh," I said. "Well, if you're sure you don't mind."

"I'll mind if you faint from hunger halfway up the mountain. You haven't eaten anything."

I looked down at my plate, which was still piled high with fruit and pastries. The others all devoured their breakfast, but I couldn't bring myself to take a bite. Hungry as I was, the stories I'd heard about fay food lingered in my mind. How it could turn you loopy and delirious. How, with fay food, there never seemed such a thing as too much, and humans had a tendency to gorge themselves to death. The apple I cut into looked as normal as anything I'd find in Albion, though brighter and crisper than I thought possible. I blinked hard, half expecting it to turn to rot before my eyes, but it didn't. The pastries were just flaky layers of dough crusted with violet and rose sugars—inordinately pretty, but normal enough.

"Are you . . . checking for poison?" Lancelot asked me, watching as I poked and prodded at a rose pastry. I didn't know him well enough then to tell if he was amused or simply thought me an idiot.

I bit my lip. "In Albion there are stories about fay food being enchanted," I admitted.

"In Avalon, we say that human food tastes of dirt," he replied, a touch of scorn in his voice that rubbed me the wrong way.

"Food is food," I told him. "Some of it is good, some of it not. I don't think any of it tastes like dirt, though."

He leaned back again, looking a bit disappointed, though I wasn't sure why. "Well, our food isn't enchanted. Can't say the same for the water, though, so I'd recommend staying clear of that."

I gaped at my water goblet—the only thing I'd trusted enough to try. After all, water was only ever water—except in Avalon, apparently.

Lancelot managed to hold on to his somber expression for another few seconds before breaking into laughter. "Oh, you should have seen your face," he said. "The water's fine, and so is the food."

I felt my cheeks warm, though I tried to hide it by taking another sip of my water. I still couldn't bring myself to put a morsel of food into my mouth, though, which Lancelot noticed.

"You're going to have to eat eventually," he pointed out.

Hesitantly, I speared a violet pastry petal with my fork and lifted it to my lips. The sugar crystals melted against my tongue, and I realized they not only looked like violets but tasted like them as well—or at least how they smelled, since I've never thought to eat a violet myself. But somehow, with the buttery pastry flaking and the generous coating of sugar, the violet tasted like a treat of its own.

When I swallowed, I realized Lancelot was still watching me, waiting for my reaction. I took a moment to ponder the flavor and textures. I'd had hundreds of pastries in my life, but I had never had one quite like that.

I lifted my napkin to dab at the corners of my mouth.

"I suppose I understand why the fey think human food tastes like dirt," I told him. "It's edible, but nothing like that."

I went to spear another piece of it when Lancelot's laughter stopped me. The more he laughed, the less I found I liked it. He wasn't laughing with me, the way Morgana did. He was laughing at me. It reminded me of how Morgause and her friends laughed at me, and I felt myself shrink.

"You look so funny with your fork and knife," he said, folding his arms over his chest.

I looked down at my utensils and back at him, failing to grasp what was funny. I knew that I was holding them right—I had taken etiquette lessons at the palace for the last four years. Seeing my confusion, he shook his head.

"I've just never seen anyone eat like that, apart from things like meat." He unfurled his arms and reached for a pastry with his hands, breaking off a corner and popping it into his mouth with only his fingers before brushing the crumbs off onto the table. "It's a bit easier," he said after he swallowed.

I frowned, watching him. My mother would have fainted if she saw him eat with his hands like that—and if she saw me do it, it would simply kill her. That wasn't the reason I held tight to my fork and knife, though. It did appear easier, and a quick look around the table confirmed that everyone else was eating with their fingers as well. But I purposefully speared another piece of pastry on my fork because I didn't want to give him the satisfaction.

# 26

IT'S A STRANGE thing—I haven't called Shalott home in more than a
decade now, but as soon as we cross the river that separates my father's domain from Tintagel, my blood begins to thrum through my veins like a lullaby, sung in my mother's voice. The air tastes different here—familiar, in a
way, though I can't put my finger on exactly what about it I recognize. All I
know is that it smells like picnics in the meadow, my brothers laughing nearby,
my father's deep voice chiding them to behave, my mother's cool fingers comb-
ing through my hair.

"Welcome home, Elaine," Arthur says to me when we stand together on
Shalott's side of the river. The others are behind us, coaxing the horses across,
but all my attention is focused ahead. The rolling green hills, the open skies the
color of lapis, the thick patches of white lilies that stretch over the landscape.

*Lily*, my father would call me, after the flower on our family's sigil. The
first daughter born in my family in generations. *Lily*, my mother said the night
before I left, in the middle of her rambling, raving prophecy. *My Lily Maid will
scream and cry. She'll break them both and then she'll die.*

I shake my head, clearing away my mother's voice like cobwebs and turn
to Arthur. "It's not home, though," I say. "Not really. I spent only a few years
here. Avalon is home."

But even as I say it, I wonder how true the words are. Yes, Avalon is the first place that comes to mind when I think of home, but standing here on this shore, I can't deny the tug of yearning in my heart, the breath of relief I feel in my whole body, the sense of peace that can only accompany a homecoming.

"You can have more than one home," Arthur says. "Are you ready to see your father?"

I open my mouth and then close it again. I don't know how to explain, even to Arthur, that my nerves aren't about seeing my father, or my brothers for that matter. It isn't about whom I will be seeing again at all, it's whom I won't be. It's the fact that my mother's ghost will linger in this place, just as she lingers in the tower at Camelot. But this time, I will see that ghost in people instead of stone; I will see her lingering behind my father's eyes, in my brothers' smiles.

That is what I'm not ready for. That's what I'll never be ready for.

"It's been a long time," I say instead. "He's a stranger to me, and I to him. What do you say to a stranger that shares your blood?"

As soon as I ask the question, I wish I could take it back. Arthur's parents were both strangers, and he never got the chance to say anything at all to them.

But he smiles slightly at me, one corner of his mouth rising higher than the other. "I don't know, El," he says. "But I suppose you have to start with hello."

I DON'T REMEMBER SHALOTT being very heavily populated—especially when compared to Camelot—but when we cross over the moat and into the village that surrounds the castle, the streets are crowded with too many people to count, cheering our arrival. Parents hold small children on their shoulders to see; men and women wave and shout.

"Quite a welcome for you," I say to Arthur as we ride in, our horses keeping pace with each other. "I assumed that people would wait to meet you before deciding to oppose Mordred, but perhaps tales of your valor have preceded us."

Arthur looks at me, both amused and bemused. "They aren't shouting for me, El," he says with a laugh. "They're shouting for *you*."

Once he says it, I listen closer. It's hard to hear much of anything in the din of cheers, but there it is—"Lady Elaine," they shout, over and over. Some even cry out that old nickname, Lily Maid.

"The prodigal daughter returns," Morgana adds from behind us, her voice carrying over the crowd.

Heat rises to my cheeks as I look around. I left here a wallflower of a child—surely not one to be missed by anyone, and yet . . .

"Go on and wave," Arthur says, grinning now. "Isn't that what you always tell me? Wave and smile at your admirers."

My face grows even hotter at that, but I do as he says and raise my hand. The movement feels jerky and unnatural to me—how does Arthur always manage it so gracefully?—but I do my best. After only a few minutes, my arm begins to ache. Arthur must see the strain in my smile because he laughs.

"Not as easy as it looks, is it?" he asks.

I turn to retort, but before I can, my eyes catch on the stairs leading up to the palace, where the crowd clears to reveal a mere handful of figures dressed in pale blue—Shalott Blue—standing in wait as we approach.

My father is older than I remember him, which I expected, but he is sharper too. As if my memory exists only in the background of my life, blurry and out of focus. His face is broad and weather-beaten, with deep lines around his bright blue eyes and smiling mouth. When his eyes find mine, his smile widens and he lifts his hand in a wave.

*I suppose you have to start with hello*, Arthur said, and I know he's right. So I wave back.

When we reach the castle steps, Arthur dismounts and hands me down from my horse first so that I can lead our procession up the steps.

As I walk, I lift my dress so I don't trip over it, though it's also an excuse to drop my gaze and focus on the stones beneath my feet instead of my forgotten family waiting. When I do force myself to look up, though, I find my father walking toward me as well, throwing all decorum to the wind.

When we meet in the middle, he smiles at me, and that smile works its way into my blood, familiar and kind.

"Elaine." He says my name like he is giving thanks to a deity. "I feared you were lost to us."

The confession knocks the breath from me. "But you must have gotten my letter—"

"I did," he says. "But after all these years and no word . . . we began to think the worst. And your mother . . ."

It pains him to talk about her, even after all these years. I understand—it pains me too. Before he can say more, I place a hand on his arm.

"I'm here," I tell him. "I'm sorry you worried."

He pauses, looking me over. "And to think," he says with a laugh, shaking his head. "When you sent word you were coming home, I imagined I would be greeting the same child I saw last. You've grown up."

"Yes," I say, squeezing his arm. "But I am so happy to see you again."

He takes me by the shoulders and folds me into his embrace, kissing me on the forehead before pulling back.

"Welcome home, Elaine," he says before holding his arm out to me. I take it and let him lead me up the rest of the steps, my friends and the knights trailing behind me as we make our way up to the small group gathered.

My father makes introductions quickly—my brothers, Torre and Lavaine, who are now in their late twenties, with beards and wives and *children*.

Torre steps forward to embrace me first, but when I step into his arms, he ruffles my hair, and that simple gesture sends me back in time, and, without thinking about it, I bat his arm away playfully, making him laugh.

"You haven't changed at all, Elaine," he says, stepping back to introduce his wife, Irina, a reed-thin woman with a guarded expression, her pale blond hair pulled back in a tight braid. When Torre gestures toward her, though, she smiles warmly and steps forward to kiss me on each cheek while holding an infant bundled in her arms so that all I can see is a small pink face with round cheeks and wide eyes that find mine and hold my gaze.

"And our son, Hal," Torre continues, gesturing to the baby.

Lavaine is next, his embrace tighter than my father's or Torre's. He hugs me so hard I feel like my bones might break, but I hold him back just as tightly. He towers over everyone else—taller even than Lancelot behind me— and after a second, he lifts me off the ground so my legs dangle.

"Good to see you, Little Lily," he says when he sets me back down, his grin mischievous. He gestures to the woman behind him with deep ochre skin and black hair done in two braids that loop over her ears. Her swollen belly pushes against the flowing silk of her gown—I'm surprised she's out of bed in her condition; she looks ready to give birth at any moment. "This is my wife, Demelza," he says.

Demelza beams at me, stepping toward me with outstretched arms and a wide smile, pulling a girl of about six with her, clinging to her skirts and watching me with somber dark brown eyes. Though they are her mother's eyes, not my brother's blue ones, there is something unmistakably familiar about her.

"I am so glad to have another sister," Demelza says as she hugs me. When she pulls back, she takes hold of her daughter's hand and tugs her forward. "And this is your niece, Mathilde."

The name catches me off guard, stealing the breath from my lungs. I look to Lavaine to find him watching me.

"After Mother," he says when my eyes find his. "We thought it a fitting tribute."

"If this one's a girl, we've been planning on calling her Elaine," Demelza says, one hand resting on top of her stomach.

"I'm sure Mother would have been honored," I say when I find my voice. "Just as I would be. Thank you."

I look down at the small girl with her fearful eyes and my mother's name, something I can't place tugging at my mind. She looks at me like she recognizes me, her brow furrowed as her eyes scan my features, as if I am a puzzle she is trying to put together. It's a look I recognize—one I know I've given people myself.

Before I can follow that thought, though, Arthur clears his throat behind me and I remember myself. I look over my shoulder at Arthur and his knights, Lancelot standing on one side of him, Morgana on the other.

What do we look like to my father? I wonder. After two days of riding and a night spent in the woods, all of us look a little worse for wear—more akin to a band of rough nomads than a royal procession. I turn back to my father and gesture at my friends.

"And it is my honor to present His Royal Highness, Prince Arthur of Camelot and Albion, along with his sister Lady Morgana of Tintagel, and his loyal band of knights."

"Your Highness," my father says, his voice low. He wastes no time in dropping into a bow—not the shallow, effortless dipping of the head the courtiers at Camelot did, though—a surface courtesy and nothing more—no, my father bows deeply at the waist until his back is parallel to the ground. An instant later, my brothers follow suit, and Irina and Demelza drop into deep curtsies—or at least as deep as they can manage with a child in Irina's arms and another in Demelza's belly.

"Rise, please," Arthur says, glancing at me with discomfort plain in his eyes. He steps toward my father and holds out a hand, which my father takes in both of his. "Your daughter has been an invaluable friend and adviser over the last ten years, and it is truly an honor to meet you," Arthur continues. "I thank you for your hospitality on this leg of my quest."

My father lowers his head over Arthur's hand before rising and clapping Arthur on the shoulder, a gesture that strikes me as familiar—the way a father might greet a son. The others rise as well in my father's wake.

"You have my support and the support of my family, both in your pursuit of your throne and anything else you may require. Whatever you ask of Shalott, you shall have it, Your Highness," my father says, his eyes darting to me for an instant before finding Arthur again. "I hope that you enjoy our hospitality tonight. We've prepared quite a feast for you and your brave men, to show you the best Shalott has to offer. It is the least we can do for you after bringing my daughter—Shalott's greatest treasure—back home to me."

My father looks at me again, his gaze tender, and I try to smile back, but something has lodged in the pit of my stomach that makes it difficult to smile or even to breathe.

*Shalott's greatest treasure.* Grateful as I am to be with my father and brothers again, I've no desire to be their treasure or anyone else's. Maybe, in another life, I would have been exactly that. I would have grown up here, content and happy. But I am not that girl.

⟶ ✦ ⟵

As my father leads our group inside the castle, Morgana appears at my side, linking her arm through mine and leaning in to whisper in my ear.

"Your father does know you aren't staying, doesn't he?" she asks.

I'd had the same thought. With all his talk of my return and welcoming me home and thanking Arthur for bringing me back, I wonder if he thinks I mean to settle here. And if he does . . . how will I be able to explain to him that I don't mean to stay any longer than Arthur does—just for the night? Arthur needs me, after all.

*And what of your father?* a voice whispers in my mind. *Doesn't he need you as well?*

"I don't know," I tell Morgana, biting my lip. "I'll talk with him about it later. Once we're settled and we can speak privately."

I hesitate, thinking about the girl—Mathilde—and the nagging feeling that hasn't gone away since I saw her. That frightened expression, the way she looked at me . . . like she knew me somehow, like I knew her even though neither of those things were possible. But they are—I know that better than anyone.

"There's something else," I tell Morgana. "I think my niece is an oracle."

Morgana looks sideways at me, her eyebrows raised high. "Are you sure? You only saw her for an instant, and she's too young for her gift to have matured."

"Matured, yes, but it doesn't come all at once like that—I've had visions my whole life, I just couldn't remember most of them. They twisted and blended with my dreams and nightmares and imagination. Even looking back with what I know now, I couldn't tell you what was a vision and what was a dream." I shake my head. "But . . . the way she looked at me. I remember that look. Like she recognized me even though she's never seen me before."

"Perhaps she's just overimaginative," Morgana says.

"I hope you're right," I say. "Our family doesn't need another oracle—especially not one named for my mother."

For a moment, Morgana doesn't say anything. "And if your suspicion proves correct?" she asks finally. "What will you do with that information?"

The question wriggles under my skin. "I don't know," I admit after a moment. "But if she's inheriting the gift from my side of the family—which I would wager she is—her mother won't know what she is or what to do with her when her visions begin in earnest. At least my mother understood what was happening to me, even if her methods for helping me were flawed—her mother will be at a loss entirely. You told me yourself that people fear what they don't understand. What happens when her mother begins to fear her?"

"You can tell Nimue," Morgana says. "I'm sure she'd welcome another pupil, especially one from your bloodline."

I shake my head. "I left my family because staying was dangerous for me and I didn't have anyone who could help me here. She's a child—she can't be more than six. I don't want to pry her away from her parents unless it's necessary. I want to talk to her first. Maybe I'm overreacting—maybe I'm seeing oracles where none exist. Being here again . . . it's strange. Perhaps it's only my mind playing tricks on me."

"Perhaps," Morgana echoes, but she sounds dubious.

# 27

AFTER THE ELABORATE ten-course feast in the banquet hall, I feel like I can barely move, let alone dance, but when my father raises a toast and offers Arthur the first dance of the night with his daughter, I can hardly refuse. Arthur takes my hand and leads me into the center of the grand ballroom, beneath the great, glittering chandelier casting prisms of light onto the stone floor below.

In one corner, a string quartet begins to play, the melody light and cheerful and familiar, even after all these years. All of a sudden, I am back in dancing lessons, trying not to trip over my own feet and never quite succeeding.

"I don't know how to dance to this," Arthur murmurs in my ear.

"Not to worry," I reply. "The steps were more or less burned into my mind. Just follow my lead."

Though the steps of the dance are simple enough, with everyone's eyes on us, I find myself faltering, and Arthur faltering along with me. We stumble together, bumping legs and arms. His expression is so tense with concentration that I have to bite my lip to keep from laughing.

"Hush, or I'll step on your toes," he says, and I'm not sure if it's a threat or merely an earnest warning.

Luckily, after a moment, other couples begin to join our dancing, crowding around us and shifting some of the focus away.

"Not much like bonfire dancing, is it?" he asks with a half smile.

"No," I say with a laugh. "Do you miss it? Avalon?"

He considers for a moment, his eyes still stuck to his feet. "Not as much as I thought I might," he says. "I miss Nimue, of course. I miss the island, too, and the freedom that we had. But there was something about life there . . . like I was always lying in wait for something to happen. I'm not waiting anymore, and I am glad about that."

I nod. "I agree, in a strange way," I admit. "Are you nervous about seeing Gwen again?"

"Oh yes," he says without missing a beat. "Not just nervous—terrified. Don't tell anyone I said so, though."

"Of course not," I say. "We couldn't let anyone think their future king is so frightened of a girl."

"Not before they meet her themselves, at least. Once they do, I'm sure they'll understand."

I think again about the Gwen in my visions—the one who was by turns cold and cruel and foolishly romantic. Arthur doesn't even know about those versions of Gwen and he's afraid of her, though I wonder if it's a different sort of fear altogether. She turned him away already, but that was through a letter. A cold, impersonal thing, and even that crushed him. What will happen if she rebuffs him face-to-face, if he holds his heart out to her and she walks away?

"Just promise me one thing," I say as the song reaches its final trilling notes. "Promise you won't challenge anyone to any duels."

Arthur looks at me, bemused. "Of course not," he says. "Gwen wouldn't have any patience for that kind of chivalrous nonsense."

A dangerous thing begins to unfurl in my belly at his words. It is something that might best be called hope.

I TRY TO LEAVE the dance floor to find a place to sit down, but before I get two steps away from Arthur, Torre meets me to request the next dance. Lavaine takes the one after that, and then I dance with each of Arthur's knights. Only Lancelot stays away from the dance floor, leaning against a sliver of wall nestled between two floor-to-ceiling windows that overlook a rose garden. He doesn't so much as glance at me, and so I try not to look at him, either, but it's difficult. I find my eyes straying toward him every time I forget myself.

By the time Gawain—the last of the knights—releases me, my feet are aching, and all of the spinning has that ten-course meal ready to come right back up.

A man the age of my father, who dined beside him at the banquet, comes toward me, intention clear in his eyes, and I force myself to smile, knowing it would be unforgivably rude to turn down a dance.

Before he can reach me, though, Morgana approaches, hand in hand with my niece, Mathilde. The girl, so shy before, swings Morgana's hand and rolls back and forth onto the balls of her satin-slipper-clad feet.

"You look like you need rescuing," Morgana says, looping her arm through mine. "Doesn't your aunt look like she needed rescuing?"

Mathilde glances at me thoughtfully, as if she's still trying to size up who I am and why I've suddenly been forced into her life. She looks up at Morgana and nods, smiling shyly.

"You made friends quickly, didn't you?" I ask Morgana.

Morgana shrugs. "Children are never afraid of me," she says. "In fact, they seem to actually *like* me for some reason. That baby wouldn't stop *giggling* at me." She jerks her head over her shoulder to where Irina is holding a fussing baby Hal.

We make our way to a small seating area in the corner of the ballroom, where a velvet sofa sits empty. When we're settled there with Mathilde between us, Morgana gives her a light nudge.

"Go on, Mattie," she says. "Tell your aunt Elaine what you told me."

Mattie—it's easier to think of her that way than as Mathilde; it distances her somewhat from her namesake—looks at me with wide, dark eyes.

"I thought you were dead," she says matter-of-factly.

I glance at Morgana and then back at Mattie. "No," I tell her. "I was only away for a bit, but I couldn't write my parents and they worried. Did they tell you that I was dead?"

Mattie hesitates and shakes her head. Her eyes go to Morgana, and she shrinks back against the sofa cushions.

"I saw it," she says, so quietly I can barely hear her. But I do, and it sends a chill down my spine.

Morgana is equally spooked. This much, it seems, is new information to her. "You *saw* it?" she asks before looking at me. "She didn't tell me *that*."

Mattie sinks further into the cushions, as if she wants to disappear from view altogether.

"Morgana," I say. "Can you find some cocoa for Mattie?"

"But—"

"Please," I interrupt, before lowering my voice. "Whatever she has to say, you shouldn't hear it."

Morgana wavers, but her eyes are still locked on mine. "She saw you *die*, Elaine," she whispers.

"We all die eventually," I point out with an attempt at a smile. "And it's a possibility, not a certainty. But still, you can't know it."

For a second, I think she's going to protest, but eventually she sighs, shaking her head.

"Do you want some cocoa?" she asks Mattie, who nods. "Alright then. I'll be right back."

When she leaves, I turn to Mattie, but words don't come easily. I don't know how to talk to children. I don't know how not to frighten her or traumatize her. She's so small and fragile, it feels like I could hurt her by breathing too hard near her.

I try to smile, but I imagine it looks more strained than comforting. Though our corner is otherwise empty, the room itself is crowded with dancing couples and clusters of men and women, talking and laughing and sipping wine from ornately bejeweled goblets. The joyful energy permeating the room is at odds with the heaviness in the air between Mattie and me. We watch the dancing for a moment, watch Arthur gallantly twirl Irina around the dance floor. Without meaning to, my eyes slide to Lancelot, brooding in the corner, but this time his eyes meet mine and hold them.

I glance away before he decides to come over here.

"When you saw . . . what you saw," I say to Mattie, choosing my words carefully, "did I go underwater and not come up again?"

Mattie's eyes are wide and solemn as she nods her head. "There was a light," she says quietly. "And when you saw it you tried to scream, but nothing came out but bubbles."

I bite my lip, unsure of what to say next. I try to think about what I was like at her age, how I felt about those dreams that plagued me, what I would have liked to hear someone else say.

"Did you tell your mother about it?" I ask her.

Mattie nods. "She said it was a bad dream. That it wasn't real. But it felt real."

I nod. "Your mother was right," I say. "It wasn't real—you see, I'm here now, aren't I? I couldn't have drowned."

Mattie considers this for a moment before smiling slightly. "It was only a dream," she says.

I wish I could leave it at that, but it won't do. It would be a disservice to her. Not so different than the potion my mother gave me to dull my own visions. I always wished someone would have been honest with me—I just never imagined how difficult honesty was.

"Some people, like you and me, have dreams that aren't just dreams," I say carefully. "They aren't real—not yet. But one day, they might be."

Mattie considers this. "You mean, one day you'll go underwater and not come up?" she asks.

A comforting lie bubbles to my lips, but I push it down again. "Not for some time, I hope," I tell her. "And maybe not at all. Whatever you see in your dreams, it is only one possibility. The future is a fluid thing, it's always changing. The future isn't set until it's the past. Do you understand?"

Mattie shakes her head.

"No, I don't suppose you do," I say. "But there is nothing wrong with you, Mattie. Right now, your visions are uncontrollable, but one day, with practice, it won't be that way. One day, you'll understand. But until then, do you think you can try not to be afraid of the future?"

"I don't want you to die," she says, her voice cracking. "And I don't want Morgana to hurt that woman. And I don't want the bad man to . . ." She trails off, closing her eyes tight as if that can block out the images dancing through her mind.

*The bad man to . . .* what? Part of me wants to ask her, but a bigger part remembers what it is like to see things you are too young to understand, to have to make sense of cruelty and death instead of just being a child.

"Have you learned your letters yet, Mattie?" I ask her.

She opens her eyes, though they are still wide and frightened, like a deer in the woods separated from its herd. After a second, she nods.

"Then here is what I want you to do—anytime you see something that frightens you, I want you to write it down. However you want to write it, whatever you want to say. And when that's done, you can do one of two things—you can either put the parchment into the fire, or send it to me. It doesn't matter which, but it helps, I promise. Just writing the words down, getting them out of your mind. And when you do whatever you choose—burn it or send it—I want you to put it out of your mind and never think of it again."

Mattie considers this for a moment, her legs swinging back and forth anxiously, rustling her taffeta dress.

"But what if the bad things still happen?" she asks. "If I send them to you, will you stop them?"

I open my mouth to say yes, of course I will, but I have to quickly close it again. As much as I would like it to be the truth, it isn't, not entirely.

"I will do everything in my power to stop them," I say carefully, the closest thing I can make to a promise.

THIS IS THE Cave of Prophecies, where all Avalon's seers train," Nimue told me on my second day in Avalon. I hadn't been able to sleep much since arriving, my mind a never-ending blur of awe, excitement, and anxiety. For all of Avalon's unknowable splendor, my mind drifted back to my mother in her cold, lonely tower too often to give me a moment's rest. I'd already sent her a letter assuring her I was safe, but I knew my mother well enough not to hold my breath waiting for her response. Still, I'd hoped. And I'd worried.

And now, standing before the great glittering mouth of the cave, I stifled a yawn. The cave was on the far northern edge of the island, burrowed deep in the mountains there.

"Does it bore you, Elaine?" Nimue asked, glancing sideways at me as I lifted a hand to cover my yawn.

"No, of course not," I said quickly, forcing a smile. "I beg your pardon, the last couple of days have been so exciting I haven't been able to sleep much."

A truth but not a whole truth. Nimue's eyes searched my face, and I was sure she understood that—I'd never been a good liar, after all—but she didn't press me on it. Instead, she held up a hand and summoned a ball of flame to her palm, illuminating the small cave in a warm golden light. Though I'd seen bits of magic the day before and from Morgana before that, the casualness of the gesture still made me jump.

After my eyes adjusted to the sudden pop of brightness, I could make out more of the space. Stalactites hung from the roof of the cave, shining in Nimue's light and casting a prismatic, dancing glow on the gloomy space. There was nothing in the cave but a tall table with three legs and a burnished mirror resting on its surface, but I barely noticed that. Instead, my attention went to the walls of the cave, which were covered floor to ceiling in small white scrawl. Words and phrases in countless different hands, layered over one another so that some were obscured altogether, the white of the chalk faded and lost to time.

I wanted to ask Nimue what the words were, but she didn't give me the chance. Instead, she jumped right into our lesson with no preamble, instructing me to stand at the edge of the mirror and peer into it, summoning a vision. That was all the instruction I was given.

As I would later learn, the mirror was how Nimue best scried, and so it was easier for her to teach through it until an oracle found their own medium. At the time, though, I didn't know about any other mediums. All I knew was the mirror and that it did not speak to me the way Nimue seemed to expect it to.

Later, I would know that Nimue welcomed curiosity and questions, that I could express my own doubts freely, but at the time I was too intimidated by—and, to be quite honest, frightened of—Nimue, and I felt like asking any questions would only make me look foolish in her eyes. There was a deep-seated part of me that yearned to impress her and that worried that I would be sent back to Camelot if I were found wanting.

So I tried my best to do as instructed, staring into the mirror and focusing, though all I managed to see for more than an hour was my own face, staring back at me with frustration that increased with every passing moment.

When I focused so hard my head began to ache, I finally tore my gaze away from the mirror and looked up at Nimue, who was watching me with a critical furrow in her brow.

"I've only ever had visions when I've been asleep," I told her. "I don't think I can just summon them."

For a moment, she didn't reply, continuing to stare at me like she could see me both inside and out. Panic gripped me, and I wondered if it was a test, if failing it meant she'd send me back to Camelot.

"That is because when you are asleep, your mind is restful and empty," Nimue said after a moment. "You must learn to replicate that while you are waking if you are going to control your gift instead of living a life where your gift controls you."

Unbidden, I thought of my mother, her life led by and eventually ruined by her own gift. The idea of ending up like her . . . no, I wouldn't entertain that thought for even a moment.

"It isn't that easy," I told her, trying to push away my frustration, though it bubbled up over the edge anyway. "A person can't empty their mind completely."

"I can," she said. "And so can every other oracle I've trained in the last two centuries."

Her voice was sharp, but after another look at me, she seemed to soften and held her hands out toward me, palms up. Her palms were paler than I expected, only a bit darker than my own, but where mine had a web of creases and lines etched into the surface, hers were smooth as porcelain. "If you are more interested in palm reading, perhaps Avalon is not the best place for you," she said curtly.

Idle as that threat might have been, it still constricted around my stomach like a snake.

"I'm sorry," I said, sliding my hands into hers. Her grip was jarringly cold and smooth, like holding on to ice.

"I am going to guide you this time, to give you the feel for it, but you must try to keep your mind empty and focus only on the mirror. Nothing exists outside of it, not you or I, not your new friends, not your mother in Camelot. Do you understand?"

It felt like a steel corset tightened around my ribs at the mention of my mother. Morgana must have told her, though I wished she wouldn't have. My mother was just that—mine. Not a tool Nimue could use or a story Morgana could twist to suit her own needs.

With her holding my hands, the chill of her touch working up my own arms, it became easier to clear my mind. I kept my eyes on the mirror, letting them glaze over and lose their focus. After a moment of nothing, I was about to pull away when the surface of the mirror began to ripple like water. The image reflecting back at me shifted, slowly at first, then all at once. I knew I should feel surprise or alarm or relief, but I didn't feel anything at all. It was just as Nimue said—nothing existed outside the mirror any longer, not even my own mind.

MORGANA WILL BE standing over a rushing river dressed in a dirty black dress with wide, ratty lace sleeves and a low neckline. Though she must be more than a decade older than she is now, I will still recognize her, if only barely. Her dark hair will be overgrown and matted, and her eyes will look more animal than human, bloodshot and hungry. She will look like a story to frighten children; she will even frighten me.

She will hold a sword with a gold hilt etched with a word in a language I can't name, but I will understand what it means all the same. The sword will look like it could be one of my brothers', or my father's, but I know right away that it's nothing like theirs. There will be an aura of magic surrounding it. The word on the hilt, the sword's name, whispers through my mind, sending a shiver down my spine.

*Excalibur.*

A young man will stand beside Morgana, dark-eyed and sullen, his face all hard angles, sharp enough to cut. Though he will look like he would bite someone for looking at him the wrong way, his hands will shake, his eyes anxiously darting around the scene. He won't reach for the sword, though desire for it will be clearly etched into his expression.

Morgana will whisper to him, her voice low and seductive. "I know your anger, my darling. I can feel it rolling off you in waves. I can taste it in the air. It's delicious."

He will shake his head, feebly at first, then stronger. He will whisper a word so quietly that I won't be able to hear it, though I know what it is. *No.*

But Morgana won't be dissuaded. She will lean toward him, touching her hand to his cheek in a caress. He will lean into it, eyes fluttering closed, a fan of dark lashes over alabaster white skin.

"Just this one thing, Accolon," she will tell him, her voice weaving around him like a spell, though there is no magic in the air. "Then I'll take you to Avalon, just as I promised, and we can be together always."

She will paint a dream he will want so desperately to come true, no matter what he will have to do to get there.

"Always," he will repeat, his voice reverent. He will take the sword from her, holding it aloft so the midday sun glints off the blade. It will look wrong in his hands. Like the traveling fair I saw as a child that brought a bear dressed in a ball gown.

And then the boy will stalk off into the woods, and Morgana will stand alone by the bank of the river, eyes wild and roving, searching for answers that the river won't be able to provide.

The vision began to fade then, and I felt myself coming back into my own body, back to Avalon and the Cave of Prophecies, a slight tingle in my fingers and toes as if they had fallen asleep. I became aware of Nimue's hands around mine, cold and bracing. But then, just as suddenly, I was pulled back into the vision by a shifting wind.

The trees will rustle, the churning river will smooth to a standstill, the sky above will turn a violent indigo, streaked with veins of green lightning. Thunder will clap from miles away, but it will ring in my ears like it struck right beside me.

I will no longer be an observer in this vision. Somehow, some way, some version of me will be here too—here but not here. And I will not be the only one who realizes it.

Morgana's eyes will suddenly lock onto mine, as if she can see me through time and space. Broken as she will be, she should be powerless, but she won't be. Broken, she will have become a fearful thing to behold, because she will have nothing left in the world to lose.

And somehow, I will match her hate, her venom, though I can't rationalize it—it is not my anger, after all, not yet. But there will also be pity there, deep down. So much so that I won't know how to hold it back. Coursing through it all will be a power I never knew I could possess. A power that has brought me here but not here, something this future possibility of me will be surprised by as well.

"Is this a game you really want to play, Elaine?" she will ask. A shiver will run down my spine at the amount of hate in her voice as she says my name. "This is a clever trick, I'll admit, but you can't save him. I will win. This time, I will win."

Our eyes will remain locked, unblinking, unflinching, unyielding as the metallic sounds of a sword fight fill the air. But only one of us will succeed; only one of them will live.

WHEN THE VISION released me, I found that my hands were still clasped in Nimue's. Her grip had tightened painfully, turning my flesh to pins and needles. Her eyes were still closed, her mind still lost in the scrying mirror. I tried to carefully extract my hands from her grip, but before I could, she came to with the gasp of breath of someone who had been drowning, her pale eyes darting frantically around the cave before settling on my face. She looked at me peculiarly, her eyes unfocused before she dropped my hands like they were made of hot coal. She gripped either side of the mirror, knuckles blanching. The muscles of her back heaved violently. I thought she might have been ill, but nothing came up, and after a minute she went still.

"Nimue?" I said tentatively. I started to reach a hand out to touch her, but after the way she'd dropped my hands earlier, I thought twice and let it fall back by my side instead. "Do you need water?"

She took two more deep breaths before looking up at me like she'd forgotten I was there. "No," she said, her voice steadying. "You are not to speak of what you saw, do you understand? Not to Morgana or anyone. It does not leave this cave."

"I . . . yes," I said after a second. I hesitated again, trying to make sense of what I saw. "That was Morgana."

"Yes," she said. Her voice was calm again, devoid of surprise or emotion. "It's an old vision. At least it was an old vision."

"Was?"

She ignored me for a moment, picking up one of the candles and crossing to the far wall of the cave. She held the candle up to the wall, searching for something amid the scribbles.

"Ah. Here it is—*Morgana, Accolon, Excalibur, River, Death*," she said, tracing words with her finger. She set the candle on the ground there and pulled a stick of chalk from the air. I didn't have time to think on the peculiarity of the chalk appearing from nowhere before she started writing something there. She had a frantic energy about her that was frightening, especially when mixed with the placidness of her expression. I didn't know what was going on, I didn't know what any of it meant, but I knew I didn't want to interrupt her.

"The end is new," she said when she was done, turning to face me again. She dropped the chalk, and it disappeared from existence before it could hit the ground. "Before, it ended when the boy—Accolon—left."

I swallowed, thinking of the sullen young man with shaking hands and hungry eyes. "Who is he?"

She waved a dismissive hand. "The second son of a duke in Lyonesse—if we were to map out the web of complex family ties, he would be Gwen's second cousin, though I doubt she's ever met him. He doesn't matter," she said. "Just a quiet boy with a quiet life and a quiet hunger for more—until he meets Morgana, at least."

Morgana. Whoever that was in the vision wasn't the Morgana I knew. There was no laughter in her in that vision, no unrestrained vivacity. That girl was someone the world had broken and left for dead. And then there was the way she'd said my name—I had never heard her speak with so much hate, hate toward *me*. I wasn't sure I would ever be able to unhear it.

"How?" I asked, because it was the only word my mouth would form.

Nimue understood my question well enough. She gave me a sad, strained smile. "Morgana's descent has been long foretold, I'm afraid. I brought her here in hopes of altering that, but so far I haven't had much luck."

I thought of Morgana as I had seen her in my first vision, hard-edged and spectral on an Avalonian cliffside. For a moment, I was tempted to tell Nimue about that, but before I could, she continued.

"There are prophecies dating back centuries that speak of a king with the power to unite Albion and Avalon. King Arthur, born from war, destined for peace," she clarified. "But only if his wicked sister, Morgana, doesn't destroy him first."

I understood her words, but I couldn't quite make sense of them. I couldn't imagine shy, quiet Arthur as a great king any more than I could imagine Morgana as a villainess determined to bring him to ruin.

"Morgana loves Arthur," I said. "He's her brother and the only family she really has left. She would never hurt him."

Nimue heaved a deep sigh. "And yet, this vision is proof enough that it is not only a possibility, it is the road we are currently on. There is a version of Morgana that will turn against Arthur—against all of us. Many versions, maybe."

"But you said it changed," I said, eager to find something to grip that made any kind of sense. "If it changed—"

"Visions do not change, exactly," she said, frowning. "However, there are often many visions of any one event, showing many paths of possibility. Nothing in the future is truly settled until it becomes the past. This, however, was one of very few instances where I have seen an old vision extend. I imagine because a great change has come, rearranging things, altering things. I imagine it's because of you."

Her words, calm as they were, felt like a punch to my stomach. "Morgana hated me in that vision," I said. "You're saying that because I came here, we are destined to be enemies?"

Nimue didn't answer right away. She considered the question, turning it over in her mind. "Because you came here, your life and Morgana's have become entwined," she said carefully. "That much, I believe, is set. But what ties will bind you, how tight they will be, whether they will strangle you both—that remains to be seen."

She might have been unable to tell a lie, but there were ways for her to find the holes in the lacy truth. Ways for her to soften it at the very least, wrap it in layers of velvet and silk. But she didn't. She told it to me plainly. For all her flaws, I don't believe Nimue has ever been anything less than honest with me. Not even when I'd have welcomed it.

"But it may not happen," I said. "You said yourself you were trying to alter it."

Nimue looked back to the wall scrawled with prophecies and prophecies and prophecies. So many futures that it was dizzying.

"Trying," she echoed, shaking her head. "Arthur is Avalon and Albion's only hope for peace, and if Morgana is on his side instead of against him, he will truly be unstoppable—that future has been seen as well, though it is rarer, more . . . delicate. It is not only the future I want, or you want—but the future we all *need*, Elaine. Albion and Avalon need to coexist. If we stay separate, it won't be long before we are destroyed."

I considered this, searching for an answer, though the only one I could find was so painfully obvious I hesitated to even suggest it. "If you were to tell Arthur and Morgana about this, it could be prevented. Morgana loves Arthur," I said again.

Nimue made a noncommittal noise in her throat. "Or," she said, "it will sow seeds of doubt in Arthur and Morgana's relationship that will lead to fractures and breaks until it becomes a self-fulfilling prophecy. It would not be the first time an oracle tried to prevent a future only to single-handedly cause it. Visions are a tricky business, Elaine. There is a reason so many of us go mad."

I thought of my mother again, trapped in her tower by her own mind, frozen in a state of permanent fear of a hundred futures that might never come to be—so afraid that she'd stopped living altogether to keep herself safe, to keep *me* safe.

The echo of the night she forced the medicine down my throat came back to me, her voice faraway and unfamiliar as she whispered a prophecy in my ear. It did not sound like a pleasant vision, and it had been one about me. Could it have been enough to drive her to madness?

"I need your help, Elaine," Nimue said, drawing me out of my thoughts. She leaned against the wall covered in prophecies, watching me with imploring eyes.

"Me?" I asked, so surprised I laughed. "But I don't know anything about this—I can only remember three visions in my life, that one included. I couldn't be of any help."

Nimue smiled fleetingly, shaking her head. "Maybe I would have believed that before your arrival altered a vision that hasn't changed for decades. And the vision itself, someone who can reach through time and space like you did—like you will do—that takes great power. You might not possess it yet, but the potential for it must be in you. I can show you how to reach it. And you want to help, don't you? You want to save Avalon and Albion. You want to save your friends."

My heart leapt. I did want to save both worlds. I barely knew Morgana and the others then, but they were already my friends, closer friends than I'd had in thirteen years in Albion. I also wanted Nimue to continue looking at me like that, like no one ever had before, like I was important enough to make a difference. And though I was frightened to admit it out loud, I wanted the power she spoke of; I wanted to be powerful. I thought of Morgana, how she walked through Camelot with her head held high and that aura of strength around her, so dense it made everyone look on her with fear and a kind of respect. I didn't think I was capable of that, but if Nimue could show me how to find my own power . . . how could I possibly turn that down?

"What can I do?" I asked her, my voice hoarse.

"Practice," she said. "Every day. Here, whether I can join you or not. Whatever you see, write it on the wall, no matter how trivial you think it may be."

She turned to go, but before she made it to the entrance of the cave, I spoke again.

"Do you really believe it will be enough?" I asked her.

She froze but didn't turn around, the lean muscles of her bare back going tense. "It has to be," she said, before disappearing into the daylight outside.

Curiosity got the better of me in her absence. I crossed to the wall Nimue scribbled on earlier, picking up the candle she had left on the ground to examine what she wrote, what she deciphered from the new ending of the vision. It was easy to find, even among all the chaos, the chalk still pure white against the mottled stone and old writings that had turned gray with age.

*Hate. Death. Elaine.*

# 28

I SLEEP RESTLESSLY IN my childhood bedroom. Though the room is large and the bed plush, there is something suffocating about it, something in the cheery floral tapestries that drape the walls, the carved wooden furniture painted white, the rosy-cheeked dolls lined up on the windowsill, that makes me feel like I am being crammed back into a youth I left behind long ago. It feels like I only find sleep for a few blissful moments before the rising sun is streaming in through the lace curtains.

We will leave after breakfast, but before that there is one more thing I have to do. So even though my body protests each movement, I force myself out of bed. I find a dressing gown in my wardrobe—adult-sized, thankfully—and pull it over my nightgown before leaving my room and padding down the hallways, the stone floors like ice beneath my bare feet.

After so many years away from the castle, I thought I might have forgotten my way around, but somehow, I know exactly where I'm going, even though the layout of the castle is labyrinthine and bewildering to strangers. It's only a few minutes later that I find myself standing before the door to my father's study.

He always used to be here first thing in the morning, reading and responding to letters, going over tax ledgers, calculating castle expenses. *Boring things,* he'd told me when I was a child, but I'd still sat with him some mornings, playing with my dolls on the floor in front of his great mahogany desk, happy just to be in the comfort of his presence.

I knock now, tentatively. Perhaps this is an old habit, one he no longer indulges. My brothers are older now—maybe they handle the business matters of the estate. Maybe my father sleeps in.

"Come in," a voice says, unmistakably my father's.

I smile slightly and push the door open. My father is at his desk, just as I remember him, bent over a piece of parchment with a quill in hand, scribbling wildly. He looks up when I enter and sets the quill down.

"Elaine," he says, surprised. "I assumed you would sleep far later—I can rarely manage to wrangle your brothers out of bed before the clock strikes eight."

I step fully into the study and close the door behind me. "The fey on Avalon rise with the sun each morning," I tell him. "It's a difficult habit to break."

"But a good one to keep," he says. "It is something, to be done with work before anyone else has even gotten out of bed. It leaves the whole day to be enjoyed."

"I don't want to interrupt your work, but I was hoping we might speak before my party leaves," I say.

A small furrow appears in my father's brow, but he nods, gesturing to the chair across from his desk. "You are planning on leaving again, then," he says, shaking his head. "I had hoped you would stay with us awhile longer, but I can't say I'm entirely surprised. Prince Arthur does seem very . . . attached to you."

It takes a moment for me to understand the inflection in his voice. Yes, Arthur is attached to me, but the way he says it implies something more than just friendship.

"I'm only his adviser," I tell him. "Arthur is dear to me, and I to him, but we are friends and I have no desire to be queen."

My father laughs. "I thought every girl wanted a crown," he remarks. "You certainly enjoyed playing princess as a child."

"I liked the crown," I tell him, laughing. "But I didn't understand what would come with it. That, I don't think I will ever care for. Besides, our quest in Lyonesse will end in a marriage, I believe. Between Arthur and Princess Guinevere."

"A Lyonessian princess?" my father asks, bushy eyebrows raising. "Prince Arthur is indeed a brave man to want such a bride." He pauses. "Will you return to Camelot when this quest is through?"

I nod, looking down at my hands. "I would love to stay in Shalott—truly I would—but I'm needed more there. Merlin has a third test for Arthur, and then once he's crowned king, the challenges will only multiply. He needs me."

He takes a moment, searching for the right words. "I must admit, I feel . . . ambivalent about sending you back to Camelot alone. I made that mistake with your mother, and I don't want to repeat it with you. You're too much like her already."

He knows, I realize. He might not have the words for it, might never have spoken of it aloud, but he knows on some level what I am, what she was.

"It isn't the same," I tell him. "Mother wasn't well. She didn't . . . she didn't understand her own mind. I do."

He looks at me, understanding sparking behind his eyes. "Still. An unmarried daughter, alone at court. It isn't done, Elaine. And the thought of you in that tower, alone."

"Actually, Morgana is staying with me there. It keeps it from being too lonely," I tell him.

"That may be, but it doesn't provide me much comfort," he says with a heavy sigh. "I don't suppose I can order you to stay here?"

I smile, but it feels brittle. "I think you know better than to try," I say.

He nods. "Then perhaps we can reach a compromise," he says, leaning back in his chair. "Go to Lyonesse, help your prince on this quest of his—hell, take my troops with you. A hundred men at your disposal—you know you'll need it. Take your brothers too. They've grown soft, lounging about the estate unchallenged, but they're good men and strong fighters, when they've had need to be."

He isn't wrong. Even if we are only talking about appearances, Arthur's arriving in Lyonesse with a scant handful of men is an embarrassment. The show of an extra hundred people at his back could do us a lot of favors. And, a small voice whispers, it will be nice to have my brothers along.

"At what cost?" I ask.

He laughs. "Not a cost, Elaine. I'm your father—this isn't a transaction. Take the troops, they are yours without strings. But this is your home and I would be glad to see more of you." Before I can protest, he adds, "Not to stay, mind, I know better than to ask that. But to visit. A few times a year. *And* I will let your brother stay with you when the coronation is over, to keep you company and serve as a knight to Arthur, representing the support Shalott will put behind him."

I pause. "Which brother?" I ask.

He laughs, waving a hand. "Take your pick—they're both capable enough."

"Lavaine," I say without hesitation.

My father raises his eyebrows, and I bite my lip. My father knew what my mother was, that was clear in his reaction earlier. He knows what *I* am.

"You must know," I say slowly, "that Mattie is . . . like Mother and me."

My father blinks once before nodding. "I feared as much, but I wasn't sure yet."

"If she's in Camelot, I can help her, keep her from . . ." I trail off, unable to form the words. *Keep her from ending up like Mother.*

My father hears them all the same, though. "I fear the ghost of your mother will haunt me for all of my days, Elaine," he says after a moment, his voice quiet. "I will always wonder if there was something I could have done—if I should have kept you at Shalott, if I should have sought a different doctor, if I should have . . ." He shakes his head. "It just seems like I should have been able to do *something.*"

I lean across the desk and take his hands in mine. They are cold and wrinkled, his fingers bony.

"There was nothing you could have done," I say, as gently as I can. "There was nothing either of us could have done. I've thought about it too often, felt that guilt so heavily I feared it would drown me. But she was long gone before I was born, I think. Maybe even before you married. There was never any saving her, not for either of us. All I could do was leave before she dragged me down with her. I will always feel guilty for that, but I can never regret it."

His smile is brittle as he brings my hands to his lips and kisses my knuckles. "I am proud of the woman you've become, Elaine," he says to me before pausing. "No, not proud. I can't be proud—what did I have to do with any of it? But still, it has given me great joy to see you again, for however long it might be. I think she would have been glad to see it too."

AFTER BREAKFAST, OUR horses are saddled once more, and my father's troops are assembled to accompany us. There are so many, brought together so quickly—he must have arranged it in advance, before we had even arrived. Looking at our party now, even I have to admit we are an impressive sight.

Morgana is already flirting shamelessly with one of my father's squires, a handsome young man with bright eyes and a roguish smile. Nearby, Arthur watches them like he wants to be sick, and it is all I can do not to laugh at the lot of them.

I say my goodbyes to the family I've only just regained. Torre and Lavaine are saying goodbye to their wives, and I linger nearby, dropping down to crouch before Mattie, who wraps her small arms around my neck and squeezes so tightly I can't breathe, but I can't bring myself to pull away. I hug her back, lifting her up into my arms.

"Remember your letters," I tell her, and she nods.

When I come to my father, he pulls me into an embrace before holding me at arm's length. "Have a safe journey, daughter," he says, his voice a low rumble. "I hope I see you again soon."

"You will," I tell him with a smile. "We'll stop again on our way back."

His smile broadens, and he pulls me into another hug. "Then I will arrange an array of festivities to celebrate," he says before looking past me, at Arthur, his expression shifting into one far more serious.

"The only way from Lyonesse to Camelot passes through my domain, Your Highness. If you return without my daughter, you would be better off not returning at all. Am I understood?"

Arthur turns a bit green but nods. "Of course, sir."

THOUGH THERE IS no sign of any border markers, I feel it the moment we enter Lyonesse. The air is sharper, more acrid, and the wind picks up speed, blowing my hair in all directions and obstructing my vision. I could even swear the light is dimmer here, as if a bit of gray gossamer silk hangs over the sun.

Beside me, Morgana shudders, pulling her horse to a stop. I do the same, and together we survey the landscape around us. The ground is mostly barren, more dirt and rock than grass, with none of the lush forests of Shalott. Instead, only a few skeletal trees reach up from the earth like hands clawing toward the overcast sky.

"It's hard to picture Gwen here," I say, thinking of my friend with her bright red hair and wide smile and endless abundance of energy.

Morgana laughs. "And here I was thinking the exact opposite," she says, glancing at me. "It's a feral land, and it is difficult to think of a place that would suit her more."

I let Arthur and his troops ride past us, waiting until they are out of earshot before I give voice to the worry that I haven't been able to say in front of Arthur.

"What if she doesn't want to come with us?"

For a moment, Morgana doesn't answer, and the only sound is the hoofbeats of Arthur's troops beating against the dry earth.

"We are meant to be allies," she says finally. "It's why Nimue and the fey gave her impotent father an heir, why Gwen came to Avalon in the first place. She is meant to be our ally—Arthur's ally. If she refuses to be that now, when we need her, she's no longer an ally at all. She's an enemy, and she will be treated as such."

Morgana's voice is so cold that it takes me aback, but it isn't unfamiliar to me. It's the same way she sounded in visions of her I've seen. The same way she sounded when she stood beside the river and looked at me with nothing but hate.

"She's not just our ally, Morgana," I say carefully. "She's our friend. That means something." Though I don't mean for there to be, I hear the question in my own voice. I hear what I'm really asking—not just about Guinevere but about Morgana herself. If she'll turn on Gwen this quickly, how difficult would it be, really, for her to turn on any one of us?

Morgana shifts to look at me, her mouth straining into a tight-lipped smile. "I know," she says, shaking her head. "I love Gwen. I know she isn't our enemy. But I am angry, angry at her for that letter, for hurting him with so little care. I'm angry that the rest of us didn't even get that much from her—no goodbye, no explanation. Nothing. What kind of friend does that, Elaine?"

I don't have an answer to that, but the words lodge beneath my skin.

"I don't know," I say. "But it's *Gwen*. I don't like thinking about it, but I haven't been able to stop—but you are right. If it comes down to her or Arthur . . . it has to be Arthur."

Morgana swallows, her gaze focused on the horizon ahead. "Why are you telling me this? We don't know it'll come to that."

"But if it does," I say. "Lancelot will do what needs to be done—he'd take Arthur's side against anyone in this world or any other. But you . . . *me*, even."

"We have to keep one another on the path," she says. "That's what you're saying. Even if Gwen has fallen off it—"

"We can't fall off ourselves," I finish. "Not even to save her." I dig my heels into the sides of my horse to get moving again, Morgana following a second later. "No matter what happens, we aren't leaving without Lyonesse under Arthur's domain."

NO ONE WANTS to stop for the night in the wild moors of Lyonesse, but when the moon is high in the sky and there is still no sign of the castle ahead, Arthur makes the call to set up camp and resume the journey in the morning. There are whispers of monsters among the men, wolves that walk upright on two legs, beasts with fur and talons and teeth sharp as needle points, but not one person actually protests—after a day of riding under the hot sun, I think exhaustion manages to outweigh fear.

The cook gets started building a fire with help from a few of my father's men, including Torre, now that there are too many mouths to feed for him to cook on his own. More men set up tents, but when Morgana goes to help them with magic, I stop her with a hand on her arm.

"There are too many of them," I say quietly. "Chances are more than a few will fear you for it, and we don't need that kind of division right now."

Morgana looks at me, taken aback. "You want me to hide myself?" she asks, a dangerous edge to her voice that I tell myself is only because she, too, is tired.

"I want you not to flaunt your power in front of men who will resent you for it. I want you to not make enemies of those we need to be allies."

She looks away, wounded, and I squeeze her arm, drawing her gaze back to me.

"Not *yet*," I add, offering her a smile I hope is reassuring. "The time will come to show them who you are, what you can do. The time will come when they'll admire you for it. But old prejudices die slowly, and we need to proceed with caution."

Morgana's mouth is a tight, firm line, but she nods once. "Fine," she says, pulling away from me and walking off to the far edge of the camp with her arms crossed over her chest.

I watch her go with a pinch of dread festering in my stomach, though I know it was the right call and that she knows that too. Morgana's anger is always quick and fleeting—she'll be past it by the time dinner is ready—but every time I see a flash of her temper, I see the possibilities once more, of what will happen when her anger lingers, when it spreads and grows and consumes every inch of her.

"So," a voice says from behind me, drawing me out of my thoughts. I turn to find Lancelot watching me with guarded eyes and a pursed mouth. "You didn't want to stay in Shalott?"

We haven't spoken for two days now, not since the last time we made camp in the woods, and the realization sits strangely. There's been little time to miss him, but now that he's standing so close again, I realize I did just that.

I swallow, lifting a shoulder in a shrug. "You thought I might?" I ask.

"No," he says. "But I feared it all the same. You were offered a home, with people who love you and far less of a chance of dying horribly. You have to admit you were tempted."

"I'll be going back," I say with a shrug. "A few times a year, at least. I worried my father would be a stranger to me, but he wasn't. Not really. I didn't realize how much I missed him."

"It was good to see you happy, Shalott," he says after a second. "With your father and your brothers, with your niece. It was good to see you with family. It was good to see where you came from."

I bite my lip. "It was nicer than I expected, to be around people who didn't need me." As soon as I say it, I wince. "That didn't come out the way I meant. I love advising Arthur, I do. And I love helping you and Morgana and everyone navigate this future we've been thrust into. I wouldn't change us for anything."

"But it was still nice," he says. "To just be loved, without obligation."

He says it like he understands, and in that moment, I feel seen. I nod. "You must miss your mother," I say to him. "Have you spoken with her since we left?"

He shrugs, glancing away. "A few shells here and there," he says. "But it isn't the same. I do miss her."

Guilt nags at me. After all, I asked him to leave Avalon, to leave her. If not for me, he wouldn't have to miss her, and she wouldn't have to miss him. He must see my expression, because he shakes his head.

"She's proud of me," he says. "And, to be honest, I'm proud of me. Leaving home wasn't easy, but you were right—I needed to do it. I'm someone different out here, away from Avalon. I'm enjoying discovering who that person is."

There's something else he wants to say, but it doesn't come out. He glances away from me, a confession hovering in the air between us.

"I . . ." he starts before trailing off. He takes a deep breath. "I've been looking for my father."

For a moment, I can only stare at him, unable to form words. He shifts from one foot to the other under my gaze, uncomfortable.

"Your father," I say slowly. "Are you referring to the father who abandoned your mother when she was pregnant with you? That father?"

He pauses before nodding his head. "That's the one. Unfortunately, the only father I have, so I can't be too picky about him—"

"You can, though," I point out. "You can leave it be, refuse to unmask him. What good will it do anyone?"

He shrugs. "I don't know," he says with a sigh. "But . . . after Arthur returned home to find both his parents dead, after leaving the only family I've known behind . . . and especially after seeing you and your family . . . I've been feeling the need to find him."

"But Arthur's parents didn't abandon him," I say. "Neither did mine. It isn't only shared blood, it's a shared life, it's memories of love and family. You have that with your mother already."

"I'm not saying I know what will come of it, Elaine," he says, and I know he's earnest because he doesn't call me Shalott. "Maybe I'll find his name and that will be enough. Maybe I'll want to . . . I don't know. Challenge him to a duel for my mother's honor—that's how it's done here, isn't it?"

He tries to make it a joke, but it doesn't quite land.

"Or maybe," I say, looking at him carefully, "you'll find him and he'll tell you it was all a mistake, that he never meant to abandon your mother, or you. That he's never stopped thinking about you or trying to find you."

Lancelot glances away, but he doesn't deny it.

"Well, it isn't impossible, is it? And it's what my mother believes," he says, his voice quiet. "And I've always wondered, I suppose. I'd like to know for sure."

I glance around the camp, but no one is paying us any mind, so I reach out and touch his arm, his skin warm beneath my fingers.

"I don't want you to end up hurt, Lance," I say, my voice barely louder than a whisper. "And I fear the chances of this ending well are slim."

"I know that," he says with a lopsided smile. "But I suppose I have to find out for certain. Can you fault me for that?"

"No," I say after a moment. "I don't suppose I can. Have you found anything?"

Lancelot shakes his head. "A few scraps of leads, but nothing that's turned up anything concrete. It's difficult—all I have is a given name and a timeline."

"So you haven't asked Arethusa for more information," I say, which isn't surprising. Lancelot has always gone to great lengths to shelter his mother, as if she isn't an all-powerful water goddess with entire oceans at her beck and call. I'm surprised he even has a name to go on, since he usually tries to avoid all mention of his father around her.

"She doesn't need to know anything about it," he says, a low warning in his voice. "It's my foolish quest—I accept that—but she doesn't need to be concerned with it. The whole thing has hurt her enough already, and I won't add to that."

I nod. Though I don't want to think about it myself, I do know something about protecting mothers, even at great personal cost.

"Why are you telling me this?" I ask him. "You must know that my gift will be of little use—"

"I didn't ask you in order to use your gift," he says, before smirking. "I just . . . wanted to hear you tell me you think I'm an idiot, I suppose. I can't explain it, but you are awfully charming when you're insulting me, Shalott."

I squeeze his arm. "I don't think you're an idiot, Lance," I say softly. "I just think you're a bit more human than you like to let the rest of us believe. You have a fallible heart, unarmored by immortality."

He looks down at my hand on his arm for a moment before covering it with his own free one, linking his fingers through mine. His palm is warm and calloused against the back of my hand, and despite the heat in the air, I shiver.

"El," he says. Just a single syllable, but in his mouth, it sounds reverent.

I wait for him to say something clever, to break the moment with a snide retort or even just one of his smirks. But he doesn't do any of that. Instead, his gaze holds mine captive, his eyes molten gold in the light from the campfire. And for just a moment, I don't think about all the ways we will doom each other. Instead, I think of falling asleep beside him with his arms around me. I think of quiet days spent together in a home all our own, with him polishing his swords and me reading, neither of us saying anything at all but not needing to. I think of him lifting a lace veil from my face and looking at me the way he is now, like I am the sun and he is the moon and he will follow me across the sky for the rest of eternity.

I've seen good and bad, yes, but what was it Lancelot said about his father—*I have to find out for certain.* Maybe he is a fool for that, but maybe I'm a fool too. Because even though I know we are most likely doomed, part of me wants to find out for certain as well.

I open my mouth, but before I can even utter a word, a shout goes up from near the campfire, jerking me out of the moment.

"Gareth!" Gawain roars, angrier than I imagined him capable of ever being. I step away from Lancelot, letting my hand slip out of his, but he stays close at my heels as we go to see what the fuss is about.

Gawain has the cook by the back of his collar, the bandanna the cook wore around his face tossed aside, revealing a smooth-faced youth, no older than fifteen. Even at first glance, he looks like Gawain—the same umber skin, the same pale gray eyes, the same square jawline. But he hasn't quite grown into his features yet, and now his eyes are large and anxious, darting around the camp.

"Gawain, let him go," Arthur says, in the commanding tone I've come to think of as his king's voice.

Gawain scowls at the cook but obeys. "It's my *brother*," he says, shaking his head. "My youngest brother, who is supposed to be home with our parents, still in school. He's only fifteen. Do they know where you are?"

The boy—Gareth—flushes scarlet. "I . . . I left a note," he says. "They know I'm with you."

"Oh wonderful," Gawain says. "So I'm the one they'll blame when you get yourself killed."

"I won't," he protests, looking to Arthur. "I just . . . I wanted to see what court was like—what the knights were like. I'd heard so many stories, and I've always wanted to be one. I just wanted to see the Choosing ceremony, I swear, but then they were all such cowards. Not knights at all. And I thought . . . well, I *knew* I could be better. And you needed men, Your Highness. Why not me?"

Arthur's eyes shift between Gareth and Gawain. "You have to be eighteen to be a knight," he says finally to Gareth. "Your father was one, and his father before him. And now your brother—I imagine you knew the rules."

"I did," Gareth says slowly. "But that's why I came as a cook. Not a knight. I didn't break any rules, but I thought that if you needed me, I could be here to help. I'm good. Gawain knows it too—I've beaten him at sparring a few times."

"Only when I let you win," Gawain snaps, but his voice is too defensive for it to be the entire truth.

Arthur looks at Gawain. "If we were still in Albion, I would send him back," he tells him. "But there is no going back now, and I can't spare men to take him home."

Gawain shakes his head. "He's a child, he can't stay."

"And yet we have no choice. I'm sorry, but that's what it has to be." Arthur turns to Gareth. "But your disobedience cannot go unpunished. I'm sure your parents will be furious enough, but in the meantime, you'll be in charge of cleaning dishes and doing laundry. Gathering firewood. Chambermaid tasks and nothing more. If I see you with a sword in hand, I will assign a guard to nanny you, and you will never have the chance to be one of my knights when you are old enough. Am I understood?"

Gareth nods, his eyes still wide. "Yes, Your Highness. Thank you, Your Highness."

That settled, the rest of the camp goes back to their business, but a few feet away, Lavaine lingers. He doesn't watch the now quietly bickering brothers, though. He watches me, his eyes dropping to where my hand rests on Lancelot's arm, where his hand covers mine.

It was a private gesture, a simple comfort I hadn't thought twice about, but Lavaine's gaze prickles, and I pull away, jolting Lancelot's attention back to me.

"Shalott," he says.

I tear my attention away from my brother and force a smile. "Let me know if you discover anything about your father," I tell him. "If there's anything I can do to help . . ."

He nods curtly. "I know where to find you."

ELAINE, JOIN US," Lavaine says once dinner is served and I've collected my plate. He nods toward the patch of grass he's claimed for himself and Torre.

I can already guess what he wants to discuss, I am already dreading it, but they are my brothers and I've been hoping for the chance to spend more time with them. If this is the only way I will get it, I suppose I have to take it.

"I'll see you back in the tent," I tell Morgana before leaving her to join Torre and Lavaine, sitting down beside them and arranging my skirts as carefully as I can with one hand while holding my dinner plate aloft with the other.

"I'm glad you both came," I say, looking between them and summoning a pleasant smile. "Though I'm sorry to have to drag you away from your families."

"You didn't drag," Torre says, shaking his head. "We offered. And it sounds like good fun, doesn't it? A quest into monstrous lands to rescue a princess and claim a throne? What could be more fun?"

Is that how our objective has been twisted as it's been whispered among the ranks? That we are going to Lyonesse to rescue Guinevere? She wouldn't like hearing *that* at all, but I have to admit it's a good story, one that casts Arthur in a heroic light. It could be far worse.

"Besides," Lavaine adds, his eyes finding mine, heavy and knowing, "someone has to keep an eye out for you. You and Lady Morgana being the only women present . . . Father was worried and I think he was right to be."

I bite my lip. "There's nothing to worry about, Lavaine—"

"What's his name?" he interrupts. "The knight from earlier, with the dark hair."

I pause to take a sip of my ale, relishing its bitterness and the fact that it buys me an extra few seconds.

"Lancelot," I say finally. "He grew up on Avalon, we've been friends for years. He isn't a knight yet, not properly, but he's one of the best warriors I've seen, and I'm sure Arthur will knight him as soon as he's crowned. He'll be the king's right-hand man."

I'm not sure why I say it, why I try to bolster Lancelot when doing so will only make them more suspicious of my feelings for him, but all I know is that I don't like the way Lavaine is discussing him, like a rat that has snuck into our camp.

Lavaine and Torre exchange looks.

"You've been away for a long time, Elaine," Torre says after a moment. "There are . . . certain things you should perhaps be aware of when having dealings with men. Certain things that happen between—"

"Oh, Maiden, Mother, and Crone, please stop," I manage to choke out before he gets any further. "I wasn't cloistered away beneath a rock, I was in Avalon. Believe me, the same sorts of things happen there, and people talk about them far more. I know exactly what certain things you're referring to, so please save us this embarrassment."

Torre's cheeks redden, but he looks relieved as well and nods.

"The point stands, though," Lavaine says. "I saw him touch you, and I've heard all about the fey, how they take certain liberties—"

"If you must know," I interrupt again before he can go into any further specifics about what those liberties are, "Lancelot isn't the uncouth rake you seem to think. In fact, he asked for my hand. I was the one who turned him down."

I don't tell him about what happened before we came to the mainland, how liberties have been taken and given by us both without much care. They may be little more than strangers, but they are still my brothers, and some things I'd rather die than discuss with them.

"Just as well," Torre says with a firm nod. "As you said, he isn't even a knight—if you were to angle right, I daresay you could marry a duke."

"Forget a duke," Lavaine snorts. "If we make it through this, she could marry a king."

"Arthur and I are friends as well," I say. "And if it would set your minds at ease, I've no desire to marry anyone just yet. There is far too much to do."

They exchange looks again, like they don't believe me. I sigh.

"And, I will have you know, I didn't reject Lancelot because of his background or his lack of status. He has more nobility in his ear than any duke I've met—aside from Father, that is."

I expect some arguments about that, but Lavaine only eyes me thoughtfully. "Then why did you?" he asks.

There is no good answer to that question, not one I can give them, at any rate. "Because I don't think that's where my happiness lies," I say, which at the very least isn't a falsehood. "But I do wish you would stop focusing on my lack of a love life and tell me about yourselves. When I left, you were two mud-caked rascals chasing each other with wooden swords. And now you're *married*. With *children*. Tell me about them."

They exchange yet another look, and I'm reminded how it felt growing up with them, always trailing at their heels while they seemed to exist in their own world. Sometimes it was like they spoke a language I could never hope to understand. After a moment Torre shakes his head.

"It all started with a greased pig," he tells me, his eyes brightening as he launches into the story of how he met his wife.

# 29

ARTHUR ROUSES US well before dawn, and judging by the look of him, he didn't get much sleep before that either. We're all worried about what will happen with Gwen, but I suppose Arthur has much more at stake than we do. As much as we love Gwen, he's the only one of us truly putting his heart on the line, facing a girl who broke it and giving her the chance to do it all over again. With an audience, no less.

"He knows what I'm like when I don't get my sleep," Morgana grumbles as we pack up our tent once more in the dim light of the dying fire. Arthur's tent is already packed, and now he walks around the camp, trying and failing to hurry the others along. "I swear to the Maiden, Mother, and Crone, if he comes over here—"

"I don't think you need to threaten," I tell her, struggling to keep my own body moving. Sleep still tugs at my limbs, and my hands feel useless with exhaustion, weak and clumsy as I try to roll the bedrolls. "I'm sure he was plenty frightened of waking you up this early. I just think in this one instance he's even *more* eager to see Gwen again."

"Eager for her to reject him?" Morgana grumbles.

I know she's tired and peevish, so I don't correct her. I only make sure Arthur is too far away to have heard her say it. He's still on the other side of camp, hurrying along my father's men while rolling back and forth on the balls of his feet, looking more like a child the morning of his birthday and less like anyone's idea of a king.

"Eager to get it over with," I say, tearing my attention away from him and going back to tying the bedrolls. "And maybe just eager to see her at all. He's in love. I don't think Gwen's letter did much to alter that."

At that, Morgana scoffs and rolls her eyes, folding the tent just a little tighter and smaller than I think she could have without a hint of magic. "I do hope he's planning on wooing her with more than love," she says. When I glare at her, she laughs. "I'm sorry, do you think I should have more faith in my brother?"

"I think you should have more faith in *me*," I tell her.

EVERY MUSCLE IN my body aches with each jostle of the horse. Three days of riding have worn me down. One more and I fear my whole body will be reduced to a wilted leaf. When a castle appears in the distance, I want to sob with relief. This far in the middle of nowhere, it has to be the Lyonessian castle. Maps of Lyonesse are tricky things, with few Albionian cartographers willing to venture into the land to chart it, but there are fewer castles here than in other countries.

It *has* to be it.

"Bit nightmarish, no?" Lancelot asks, squinting at it. The sun is high now and it is just shy of noon, I would guess, but the sky is overcast, filtering the daylight and turning it a moody gray.

The castle itself is, structurally at least, like my family's in Shalott—the same high towers and stone walls—but instead of the gray stone of Camelot or the white stone of Shalott, the Lyonessian castle is built from stone the color of a raven's wing, the kind of black that absorbs all the light around it.

"Just a bit," I say, which is an understatement. The sight of it fills me with a kind of bone-deep dread I can't put a name to.

"It must get awfully hot there during the summer," Gawain says, coming up on my other side, staring up at the castle in barefaced awe. "What's on that flag there . . . do you see it? Not the Lyonessian flag. The other one."

I have to squint to make it out. A five-pointed star caught between the two points of a crescent moon, circled by a flaming sun. The sight of it makes me smile, as inexplicable as its presence may be. "It's the symbol of the Goddess," I say. "The deity of Avalon—she's a threefold goddess, the Maiden, Mother, and Crone. She takes on different forms, depending on what is needed of her."

"That's sacrilegious," one of Arthur's original knights—Percival—says from behind us. "There is only one God, and his work is done through the king."

"Not in Avalon," Lancelot says, shrugging his shoulders.

"And apparently not in Lyonesse," Gawain says, nodding toward the castle and the flag. "What's it doing there?"

"That," I say, frowning, "is a very good question."

Morgana hears our conversation and rides up beside us, her eyes focused on the flag as well. "Do you think Gwen put it up when she arrived?" she asks.

Arthur, leading the group, turns and looks at us over his shoulder. "That doesn't make sense—Gwen was never religious on Avalon. She mostly just used it as a curse, the way Morgana does. *Maiden, Mother, and Crone.*"

"Oh," Gawain says, frowning at Morgana. "I'd heard you say that before, but I didn't know what it meant."

Lancelot nods and, for just a second, looks away from the castle and at Gawain, like he's still trying to make sense of him. When he catches me watching him, he sighs. "In Avalon, it's a common expression. But you could never say it in front of the elders, or they'd box your ears for offending the Goddess."

"A lesson you learned many times, all too well," I point out, making everyone laugh and Lancelot's face redden.

"Never really learned it, though, did I?" he asks with a sheepish grin. "Besides, Morgana said it three times as often as I did and she never got in trouble once."

"That's because I was smarter about it," Morgana says. "I always made sure the elders weren't around to hear me."

Gawain is quiet for a moment, thoughtful. "When I was a child, my nanny used to tell me stories about Avalon, but they were always horror stories, meant to scare me into being good for fear of getting sent there," he says. "She said the fey had pointed fangs and red eyes and they stole children out of their beds to make meals of them, but they would leave one of their own in the child's place, disguised, so the parents wouldn't even miss them."

I glance at Lancelot warily, remembering his reaction long ago when I'd confessed my own prejudiced notions about the fey. His mouth is pulled into a thin line, but he doesn't snap. Instead he shakes his head and sighs.

"That's a changeling," he says. "There was a seed of truth in your nanny's stories, but the practice was only ever used by a very small handful of fey who didn't understand or respect magic or life itself. No one trained on Avalon would dare use such a dangerous and corrupt spell. If they did, the Crone would strike them down on the spot."

Percival must still be listening because at that, he scoffs. "The fey *are* corrupt," he says, but there's no real malice in his voice. He's merely repeating something I don't doubt he's heard countless times before. Still, Lancelot's hands grip the reins tight enough that his knuckles turn white.

"I thought so too," I jump in before he says something he'll regret. "I was raised on the same stories, I heard the same folklore from my own nanny. I'd even heard tell of fay women who lived in villages on the outskirts of Shalott, brewing poisons with children's bones and luring husbands away from their wives with love potions. I heard stories about those women being hunted down and slaughtered like animals. At the time, I might even have been a little glad for it—I imagined them as the villains in my nanny's stories. But seeing Avalon . . ." I trail off, biting my lip. "I'm not going to tell you there aren't evil fey. I'm sure there are, though I never met one I would call that. But there are evil people as well, aren't there?"

"The difference is," Percival says, "one evil fay can wreak far more havoc than one evil man. My father said—"

"Shut it," Lancelot breaks in, pulling his horse to a stop.

"How dare you—"

"Hush," Lancelot says, louder, holding up a hand. Percival flinches like Lancelot is throwing some sort of spell at him. He doesn't know, though, that Lancelot isn't capable of magic.

As soon as I think it, Lancelot straightens up. "Attack!" he cries out, throwing himself sideways into Arthur, knocking him off his horse, and sending them both tumbling to the ground the instant before an arrow hisses through the air where Arthur sat just a second before.

A breath later, everyone is drawing their weapons from scabbards, and Gawain, Percival, and Galahad bring their horses in front of Morgana and me, shielding us.

A twig cracks, and a single figure emerges from behind a thicket of trees, bow already nocked with another arrow. Though the hood is drawn up, hiding the person's face, I recognize the bow right away—fay-made with a gold filigreed handhold.

"Gwen," I call out. "Stop. It's us."

Even in the chaos between us, I hear her sigh. "Yes, I know it's you," she says, shaking the hood back from her face without lowering her bow. It's still trained on Arthur, though he's mostly hidden behind Lancelot. It would take a truly exceptional shot to hit him, but I don't doubt Gwen could do it. If she wanted to. "You're still trespassing," she says. "What are you doing here, Elaine?"

Though she addresses me, her eyes stay locked on Arthur.

"We seek an audience with King Leodegrance," I say, choosing my words carefully. I'm sure that Gwen wouldn't shoot Arthur. *Mostly* sure, at least. But as Nimue said, Gwen has always been a variable, and her unpredictability is one thing that can be counted upon.

"You didn't send a letter beforehand?" she asks, narrowing her eyes.

"Well, your last letter left something to be desired, didn't it?" Morgana interrupts. "You're hardly much of a wordsmith."

Gwen's eyes narrow as they dart to Morgana for just an instant. Her mouth quirks into a smile, and she lowers her bow.

"I'm disappointed in you, Lance," she says, clicking her tongue. "You've gotten sloppy over the last couple of weeks. I was tracking you half a mile and you didn't even notice."

Lancelot glowers at her, but he steps away from Arthur. "Unfamiliar terrain," he grumbles. "And I was distracted."

"Excuses, excuses," she says. She looks at Arthur for a moment like she wants to say something, but the words never form. Finally, she looks back at me. "You can stay the night," she says. "My father will speak with you, but tomorrow you'll head home. Disappointed."

"You don't even know what we've come for," I point out.

She shrugs. "I can guess well enough," she says before pausing. "It's good to see you again," she continues, and though she looks only at me when she says it, I know she's speaking to the others as well, and to Arthur in particular. "Follow me. You don't want to be stuck in these woods after dark."

She turns and starts back into the woods, trusting us to follow. As Arthur and Lancelot mount their horses, Gawain leans toward me.

"That woman tried to assassinate the king," he whispers. "Why the hell are we following her?"

"That woman," I tell Gawain, "is Princess Guinevere, King Leodegrance's only daughter and heir to his crown. She is also our only chance of succeeding in this quest."

"But she tried to kill him," Gawain repeats. "I'd say our chances aren't good."

"Believe me, if Gwen wanted to kill Arthur, she would have. That was merely . . . a cheeky hello."

Gawain glances at me, skeptical, but doesn't comment. Beside me, Arthur keeps his own gaze straight ahead. To most, his expression would appear inscrutable, but not to me.

"You unnerved her," I tell him as we start to ride again. "You know how rare that is. There is something at play here we don't understand yet."

Arthur nods, but his expression doesn't clear. "You should take the lead with her," he says after a moment. "You and Morgana. I'll talk to Leodegrance, but with Gwen . . . well, she seems more open to talking with you."

DAYS STRETCHED INTO weeks stretched into months and years on Avalon, and time often felt infinite. We never forgot about the world outside the island, but most days, it felt like another world entirely, a land from the pages of Arthur's books. Even my own memories of Albion and Camelot began to feel like something that had happened to someone else, more story and less memory.

Most days, we didn't talk about the future at all. The present seemed limitless, and that was more than enough for us—a life composed of sun-drenched days and star-strewn nights. Sometimes, I could even forget about the future myself, the visions I spent hours poring over feeling distant and disconnected from me.

But sometimes, the future would press in, a bucket of cold water thrown onto someone mid-nap.

"I wonder if they've forgotten me in Lyonesse," Gwen said once, while she, Morgana, and I trekked through the woods after night had fallen. Gwen had summoned little balls of light for each of us to hold in order to light our path, the orbs just bright enough to show what lay a few paces ahead of us and cast our faces in a warm, golden glow.

"How could they?" Morgana had asked. "You're their princess, and one day you'll be their queen."

Gwen made a noise in the back of her throat and shook her head. "Maybe that's fair logic to use with Arthur, but things work differently in Lyonesse—no one gives you a throne because your bloodline demands they do. And having a crown on your head and a throne beneath your arse means far less too. For all I know, my father is no longer king. In Lyonesse, anyone can take a throne at any time, so long as they fight tooth and claw for it. My father is no longer a young man."

"Surely, Nimue would have told you if that were the case," I said.

Gwen shrugged her shoulders, but her eyes were still troubled. "The time will come when we have to leave here," she said.

"*You'll* have to leave here," Morgana corrected. "Elaine and I will stay here, won't we?" she asked, looking at me.

I looked away, focusing my attention toward the ball of light in my hands and watching it flicker in time to the beat of my heart. "Arthur will need me," I told her. "And my family is still in Albion. I imagine when Arthur leaves, I will too."

A silence stretched over us for a moment, and I knew they were both thinking of my mother. Gwen knew all about her by that point, but this was before word had reached me of her death. This was when I imagined a homecoming that included her, for better or worse.

"I suppose that makes sense," Morgana admitted, though there was an edge to her voice that planted guilt in my belly. "I'll miss you both," she added after a second, though the words seemed to come out despite her best efforts to keep them unsaid.

I bumped my shoulder against hers and shot her a smile. "No need to get so mopey," I told her. "When Arthur is king and peace is restored between Avalon and Albion, we can visit so often it will be like we never left. Right, Gwen?"

"Yes, exactly," she said, her grin broadening. "I miss Lyonesse quite terribly, I'll admit, but there is nowhere I can find cakes as good as the ones here. I'd come back for that alone, but your company will be a welcome bonus."

Morgana smiled slightly before shaking her head. "Still, I don't like the thought of it," she said. "You'll be alone in Lyonesse with your literal monsters, Elaine will be alone in Camelot with figurative ones, and I'll be here, all by myself."

"You'll have Lancelot, won't you?" Gwen asked. "And Elaine will have Arthur. And you know I'm more ferocious than any monster in Lyonesse." She grinned, but there was something unfamiliar lurking beneath it—a touch of unease.

"It's not the same, and you know it," Morgana said, shaking her head.

"No," Gwen admitted, her grin fading to something smaller, sadder. "But we have worlds to conquer, don't we? I've a country to rule, and Elaine will help Arthur rule—he'll need her. And you'll be Lady of the Lake when Nimue's gone."

She said it so simply, but the words still carried the weight of something forbidden. But no one, not even Nimue, could live forever, and it seemed an accepted fact that when Nimue did die, Morgana would be her successor. She'd been groomed for the position, raised to believe it was hers. I'd heard it said that Morgana's power might be greater even than Nimue's.

Morgana's smile was brittle.

"Who would have thought power would be so lonely?" she asked with a sigh.

"Everyone," Gwen said, her voice sobering. "There is no power without loneliness, Morgana. It isn't fair, but it's the truth."

Silence stretched over us again, but this time it was the uncomfortable kind, like scratchy linen rubbing against raw skin. When it became unbearable, I slipped an arm through Morgana's and rested my head against her shoulder.

"There's no need to worry about it now," I told her. "We are here and we are together and whatever future may come, it's ages away."

Morgana let out a long, low exhale before nodding, slipping her free arm through Gwen's.

"It's ages away," she echoed.

HERE WE ARE now, and ages have passed quicker than any of us imagined, but we're still together. But as I think about Gwen's expression in the woods, the way she looked at me with that cold distance, like we were strangers, I hear her words echo through my mind again and again.

*There is no power without loneliness*, she said. I should have wondered how she knew that already, though with Gwen, I learned it's best not to question most things.

But that was just it, the look she gave me in the woods, the way she refused to look at Arthur, the way she spoke with coldness and authority I'd never heard in her voice before.

I never thought to worry about her when we went our separate ways, when all of us went off together to Camelot while she left for Lyonesse alone. It was Gwen—she could handle herself, after all. Why should I have worried?

Now, though, I am worried. For us, but also for her. This new Gwen is well acquainted with power, that much is clear, but she knows loneliness as well, and that realization lodges in my heart like a splinter.

# 30

THE INSIDE OF Lyonesse Castle is even more bleak than the outside, with few windows, dark stone hallways, and heavy iron sconces that do little to mitigate all the darkness. The walls are bare, without the ornate tapestries and framed paintings that hang in Camelot. Even the floors are unadorned with rugs, the sound of boots on bare stone echoing like a thunderstorm as the four of us follow Guinevere down the hall.

The rest of our party stayed outside the castle, seeing to the horses, which I am grateful for. Circumstances aside, there is something nice about being just the five of us again—not Prince Arthur and his entourage—just us, as we were on Avalon.

But that is an illusion that shatters the instant Guinevere speaks.

"You shouldn't have come," she says without turning around. "It was a mistake."

Though she doesn't speak to anyone in particular, the words feel directed at Arthur, and in the dim lighting I can just make out his frown. He stands a little straighter.

"Of course I came, Gwen," he says, his voice soft but steady. "Quest aside, I would have come. You know me—you should have known that."

For a moment, she doesn't say anything. "I hoped I was wrong. Lyonesse . . . it isn't a place for you. Any of you."

"But it is for you?" Lancelot asks.

She shrugs but doesn't look back at us. "It's my home. It's a part of me. There is no escaping that. I belong here."

"And we belong with you," I say, though I sound more sure than I feel. The chill in the air has worked its way into my bones, and I have a feeling no hot bath, no pile of blankets, no warm fire will be enough to get it out again until we leave. "We're a team, Gwen. You said that."

"And I meant it," she says, each word clipped. "*Then*. But things have changed. I have changed."

"What do you mean?" Morgana asks.

Instead of answering, Gwen pushes open a door and ushers us inside.

Like the rest of the castle, the room is dim, cast in a pall of gray-tinged light emitting from a single small brass chandelier that doesn't look like it's been polished in many years. Cobwebs hang from the arms like a dreary garland. Though the room is large enough for a full audience, only five figures stand before a single tall chair that could, perhaps, be called a throne, though it has none of the splendor of the one in Camelot. Instead of being molded from gold, this one is carved from wood with a rough hand.

Sitting on the throne is a man in his eighties with a balding head and a bent back, making him so hunched over that I can't see his face. At our approach, though, he looks up, and my breath hitches.

Because he is not a man—at least not entirely. His features are human enough, with two eyes, a nose, a mouth. His arms and legs look, at first glance, like any man's, but something about him isn't quite right, though it takes me a moment to realize why that is.

He looks the way a fay child might have drawn a human, if they had never seen one before.

Gwen crosses to stand at his side, leaving us in the middle of the room. She places a hand on his frail shoulder and he smiles at her, covering her hand with his own. But in the light of the moon shining through the windows, his hand is not a hand. It is closer to a claw, with long, jagged talons instead of fingers.

The others must see it, too, but no one reacts immediately. There were stranger things in Avalon, after all. But we aren't in Avalon.

"King Leodegrance," Arthur says, his voice filling the cavernous room. He bows, and the rest of us follow suit, Lancelot bowing awkwardly while Morgana and I dip into curtsies. "I am grateful for your hospitality, and for your speaking with me tonight. I believe we can both help each other—"

Before Arthur can get any further, Leodegrance laughs, the sound thin and wheezing. "You're a brave one, boy, I'll give you that much. Braver than your father, who never set foot in Lyonesse. Braver than his knights, who ran before the moon managed to fully rise. But brave as you might be, you're a fool all the same. Stay the night—my daughter insists upon it—but you'll be gone first thing in the morning."

Arthur glances at me, brow furrowed, before looking back at Leodegrance.

"I was hoping we could speak about an arrangement that could benefit us both—"

"At my age, boy, you learn to value the time you have left, which means not bandying about having the same conversations I've had already. There will be no alliance. You might think to change my mind, but I assure you that many souls wiser than you have tried." He waves a dismissive hand—*claw*. "Gwen can show you to your rooms for the night, but as I said, you will be gone tomorrow, whether you go willingly or not. Am I understood?"

Arthur doesn't move, not even when Gwen comes toward him, her eyes pleading but her mouth set firm as stone. Instead, he holds his ground, looking only at Leodegrance.

"There is something you want, though," he says after a second.

"I beg your pardon," Leodegrance says, leaning forward in his throne.

"There must be," Arthur says, pushing forward. "You won't meet with me because you see it as a waste of time, but you met with others. Because you did want something then. They wouldn't give it to you. But I could."

"Arthur," Gwen says, her voice low and dangerous, but he ignores her, all his attention focused on her father.

"Uther thought my request a mad one," Leodegrance says. "His council did as well. Every person who dared come this far to meet me said the same thing—it was undoable. The king would not yield. And here you are, a boy—not even a king! What makes you think you'll be any different?"

Arthur considers it for a moment. "Because I am, as you seem keen on reminding me, a boy. Not a king—not yet. Which means that I need this alliance more than my father did. I have more to lose by not securing it. I will be willing to part with more to ensure it happens. I make no promises," he adds quickly. "But I think it would be worth hearing each other out. We are both in a position to help each other, after all."

At that, Leodegrance laughs again. "You mean to help *me*," he scoffs. "You have no country to offer and a scant hundred men at your back."

"And yet you do want something," Arthur says. "I can't help you unless we discuss terms."

For a moment, Leodegrance says nothing. "Very well, princeling," he says finally. "Perhaps this won't be a waste of time—at the very least, you amuse me, so there's that. Stay until sundown tomorrow. We will have lunch together and, should you be particularly amusing, perhaps you'll stay for supper as well."

Arthur inclines his head, but I can tell he's bristling at the term *amusing*. Still, we got what we wanted.

GUINEVERE LEADS US down the maze of narrow hallways to our rooms, but as soon as we are far enough from the throne room, she spins around to face us, her freckles standing out starkly against furious red cheeks, apparent even in the dim lighting.

"You great buffoon," she snaps at Arthur. "Do you have any idea what you've done?"

Arthur, to his credit, doesn't wither beneath Gwen's glare. He holds it. "No, frankly," he says, his voice calm. "I haven't the slightest idea what I've done because all you've done is offer up vague warnings and ill omens."

"To *protect* you all," she says. "I told you, you shouldn't have come. And now, you should leave at dawn. Go home and never come back."

"Why?" I ask.

Gwen shakes her head. "I can't talk about it," she says, glancing around the empty hallway. "But after everything, I would think I've earned your trust. Trust me when I say you won't find what you want here. *Go home.*"

Morgana laughs, the sound sharp and bitter. "What home, Gwen?" she asks. "Avalon won't have us—you know that—and Camelot . . ." She trails off.

I jump in. "Camelot won't have Arthur as its king unless we can solidify an alliance with Lyonesse. If we return with nothing, there is no home for us there either."

"Royalty is overrated," Gwen says, glancing away. "You can still return, even if there's no crown waiting for you."

Arthur stares at her for a moment. "No, Gwen," he says. "If I fail, Mordred takes the throne. And he will drive Albion into the ground—and I doubt he would stop at Lyonesse's borders either."

I freeze, worried that I said something I shouldn't have about my visions, but I know I didn't. Arthur doesn't know what I've seen about Mordred, but he doesn't need to—he's seen the truth of it just as clearly without glimpsing the future.

"I didn't come for me," he continues. "And I didn't come for you either. I came for Camelot, for Albion. I came because it's the only way to protect my people, and I won't leave until I've done that."

Guinevere chews so hard on her bottom lip that I worry she might draw blood. After a moment, she straightens up, squaring her shoulders.

"Then it seems what is best for your country and what is best for mine are at odds with each other," she says, her voice cold. "If you're determined to stay this path, I can't stop you, but believe me when I say it won't end well. For any of us."


GUINEVERE LEADS ARTHUR and Lancelot to their room first, and when she closes the door, she draws a heavy iron key from the pocket of her skirt, turning it in the lock with a heavy click that I feel in the marrow of my bones. It doesn't feel quite like fear, but it is close. Trepidation, perhaps. Foreboding.

"And here I thought you wanted us gone," I say, keeping my eyes on the key as she tucks it back into her pocket. "Why lock them in?"

Gwen glances at me with wary eyes, pressing her lips together in a thin line. "I'm not locking them in. I'm locking the others out," she says.

"The others?" Morgana asks slowly. "What others?"

Gwen doesn't answer, instead leading us farther down the hall to the next room. She pushes open the door and ushers us through.

"You know I can unlock that door without a key," Morgana says to her.

"You won't need to," Gwen says, drawing the key out from her skirt once more and pressing it into Morgana's hand. "But you shouldn't. Not until sunrise."

Morgana rolls her eyes. "Come on, Gwen," she says. "You know me. You know right now that I'm tempted to do exactly the opposite of what you ask, just because. I need a better reason not to."

Gwen glances over her shoulder into the empty, dark hall. When she looks back at us, her eyes are heavy. "I can't," she says through gritted teeth. "Just stay here. Please. No matter what you hear. I wouldn't ask you if it weren't important. *Please.*"

Morgana and I exchange a look, and I know we're both thinking the same thing—Gwen never says please. She never begs. Whatever she's hiding, it's important.

"Fine," Morgana says, practically biting out the word. But when Gwen starts to close the door, Morgana stops her, holding the door open with a white-knuckled hand. "I thought our friendship meant more to you than this, Gwen," she says, her voice low. "Break Arthur's heart if you have to. He's asking a lot of you, and I would never blame you if it was too much. But we were friends, and I thought that meant something."

"We *are* friends," Gwen says. "And Arthur—"

"I don't care," Morgana says. "Friends don't do this to one another."

At that, Gwen laughs, but there is no mirth in the sound. "You don't even understand what *this* is," she says. "You don't even understand that I am trying to *help you.*"

"If you want to help us, *talk to us,*" I say.

Gwen looks back and forth between us, opening her mouth to speak, then closing it again. She shakes her head. "I can't. Just . . . stay here. Lock the door behind me. Promise me that."

"You don't deserve any promises from me," Morgana says, her voice heavy with scorn.

For a second, I think Gwen might push the issue, but eventually she shakes her head and casts a pleading look at me, but I keep my expression placid.

"Fine then," she snaps. "Do whatever you like. See if I care when all that's left of you is blood-soaked bones and rotting flesh."

She slams the door so hard it echoes throughout the room. Morgana and I stay still, listening for her footsteps, but the sound never comes. Instead, Gwen lingers outside our door, her shadow dancing beneath the doorjamb. When her light steps do finally fade down the hallway, Morgana turns to me, fury still simmering off her like oil in a hot pan.

"Well," she says to me. "Your plan of pleading friendship didn't get us very far, did it?"

I open my mouth to remind her that it wasn't *my* plan, that she agreed with it, that Gwen was her friend too. But I know Morgana well enough by now to know that when she gives in to anger, she is unreasonable, and there is nothing I can say to quell her temper. Instead, I shrug my shoulders.

"She's afraid of something," I say. "Perhaps you should lock the door."

Morgana laughs, shaking her head. "Gwen is afraid of nothing," she says. "It's the most frustrating thing about her. Do you remember when Lancelot dared her to dive into the kraken's lagoon and steal a bit of its treasure? She didn't even hesitate before plunging in."

I consider it for a moment. "Gwen told me once that only fools are fearless, that it was the difference between her bravery and Arthur's—Arthur was wise enough to know what to fear but did the right thing anyway, but fear never reached her in the first place."

"So you see?" Morgana says. "She's not afraid then."

I shake my head. "Everyone's afraid of something. And the way she looked at us . . . she's not afraid of what's outside."

Morgana looks at me like I've grown a second head. "You think she's afraid of us?" she says slowly.

"I don't know," I say. "But I think you ought to lock the door, Morgana."

THOUGH IT WOULD have been impossible to bring my whole loom with me on this journey, I don't need it. I find the skein of oracle thread in my satchel, and with Morgana's help, I loop the thread under and over my left fingers and the fingers of both her hands, knitting them together and creating a small loom—too small to be able to stitch any actual images, but enough that I will be able to catch a glimpse of whatever there is to be Seen.

"Will I See anything?" Morgana asks me when I explain it to her.

"I don't think so," I say, frowning. The only times I've done this have been with Nimue, and sometimes I did See things then, but Nimue assured me it was only my own sensitivity as an oracle. Someone without the gift, like Morgana, shouldn't be able to glimpse anything.

*Shouldn't* would have to be enough.

As we sit on the large velvet-draped bed, facing each other with our hands bound, though, a feral shriek pierces the air outside our window, followed by another, and then more and more until the sound fills the air.

"It sounds like howling," Morgana says quietly, looking toward the window, though we both know there will be nothing to see outside in the dark.

I swallow. "Gwen said there would be noises. She said to ignore them."

Morgana rolls her eyes. "Gwen said a lot of things," she points out. "None of them terribly helpful."

Still, she doesn't get off the bed. When the howls fade to silence, she bites her lip. "I hope Arthur and Lancelot heed her words," she says.

It's all too easy to imagine them doing just the opposite, finding a way out of their room and charging into the bleak night with no idea of what they're going to face, no idea how to fight it, but foolishly determined to try anyway.

I don't need to scry to know how that would end for them.

The howls begin again, louder this time. I try to concentrate on the loom stretched between Morgana's fingers and my own, on threading the white silk, on keeping my mind blank, but it proves more difficult than I imagined. I'm too aware of the sounds, how I can feel the howls deep in my bones; I'm too aware of Arthur and Lancelot down the hall and what must be going through their heads; I'm too aware of Morgana just inches from me, her fear and worry eating her alive.

"Did you see Leodegrance's claws?" I ask her, unweaving my progress for the third time to start fresh.

Morgana nods, her eyes far away. "He's not human," she says. "But he's not fey either. I don't know what he is."

I hesitate, winding the yarn back up into a skein. "And Gwen?" I ask.

"Gwen doesn't have claws," Morgana says quietly. "There's nothing monstrous about her. She's just a girl—a girl with power, yes, but not like this."

She sounds so sure of it, so sure of Gwen. I imagine it must be nice, to be sure of someone like that. To not constantly have to think of all the facets of a person that exist, how they are constantly in flux, how impossible it is to truly know anyone—even and maybe especially the people we love.

The howls outside the window start up again, but this time they are different, tinged with laughter—human laughter—and then . . . there, so clear it turns my whole body to ice. The sound of a human scream, anguished and terrified.

But not Arthur's. Not Lancelot's. I assure myself of this over and over again as the screams continue, as they are joined by the screams of others, as those screams are drowned out by howls and laughter, pain and mania and joy mingled in a way that is not quite human and not quite animalistic but something wholly other.

I try again to empty my mind and focus on nothing beyond the shimmering thread, but the sounds outside mingled with my own mounting frustration make it impossible. I let out a frustrated groan and rewind the skein once more, my movements angry and jerky. Morgana covers my hands with hers, squeezing them so tight it hurts.

"You're going to drive yourself mad like this," she says.

"I'm going to drive myself mad if I don't try," I reply, shaking my head. "Besides, it isn't like we'll be able to get any sleep."

Morgana looks toward the window for a moment before pulling her hand from mine and waving it toward the walls. The effect is immediate, a heavy curtain falling and blocking out all sound except for our own breathing.

But even though I can't hear the screams anymore, I know they're out there. I know they're going on and on. I swear that I can feel them in my bones.

Still, I try to smile at Morgana. "Thank you," I tell her.

She tries to smile back, but I don't think either of us are comforted. But we try to be. We lie down together and hold each other tight and try to pretend there is nothing happening outside this room.

I MUST MANAGE TO fall asleep at some point because suddenly, I'm aware of Morgana shaking me awake and a hazy yellow predawn light filtering in through the window.

"It's morning?" I ask, my voice coming out rough and groggy. Going by the dark circles under Morgana's heavy eyes, I doubt she managed to sleep at all.

"Not quite, but someone's outside," she says, nodding toward the door. Sure enough, the light of a candle slips beneath the door, flickering wildly like a living thing. "I'm going to lower the spell, but I didn't want it to frighten you if it's still . . . if it's still going."

I nod, sitting up and watching as she waves her hand again, letting the outside world back in. I brace for the screams and howls to return, but instead only silence greets us, pierced by the occasional chirp of birdsong. The quiet and idyllic atmosphere is strangely disconcerting, juxtaposed with the chaos and horror that swarmed only a few hours ago.

"Hello?" Morgana calls toward the door.

For a moment, there's no response.

"It's me," a voice says finally, thin and tired.

Gwen.

I start to get out of bed to let her in, but Morgana stops me, her hand on my arm.

"What do you want?" she demands.

Gwen doesn't reply for a moment. "Please can I come in," she says.

Something in her voice wraps its hands around my stomach, twisting. It's the *please* again. Never in more than a decade did I hear Gwen beg for anything. Now it seems she does nothing *but* beg.

Morgana looks at me, lifting an eyebrow. I nod.

There's a beat of silence as Morgana climbs out of bed and crosses to the door, key in hand. She slides it into the lock and turns, the sound of metal grinding against metal filling the silent room. I lean back against the headboard and pull the quilt up to my chin to block out the early-morning chill as Gwen steps inside, holding a candle that casts a pale gold glow about.

She looks like one of the frescoes that covered the walls in Avalon, with candle-warmed skin and wild red hair down to her waist in tangled curls. Her nightgown is torn in places, more dirt streaked than white, and . . . my eyes catch on the stains that stand out, crimson splotches on her nightgown, on her skin, in her hair.

"Is that blood?" I blurt out. "Gwen, what *happened* last night?"

Before Gwen can answer, Morgana jumps in. "It's not hers," she says, surveying Gwen with cold eyes. "There's not a scratch on her."

She's right—dirty and blood streaked as she may be, her skin is unblemished. No scratches, no scrapes, no cuts.

"What happened?" I ask again, but this time my voice quivers.

Because as much as I have seen of Gwen, of all the terrible choices she can make, all the coldness she's capable of, all her stubborn pride and rash decisions, I never thought her capable of actually hurting someone. I think of the screams last night and I want to be sick. I can't look at her—every time I try to meet her gaze, I have to look away.

"It wasn't me," she says quietly.

At that, I force myself to look at her. Relief sings through me for an instant before she speaks again.

"I mean, it *was* me. But it also wasn't. I don't . . . I don't know how to explain how both can be true, but they are."

"Who was killed?" Morgana asks, her voice somehow coming out level. "If it was any of our men—"

"It wasn't," Gwen interrupts before swallowing. "One was a farmer who mistreated his animals. Another was an earl who bedded his servant without her consent—several servants, actually. The third was a seamstress who stole from her patrons."

"Criminals," I say, and Gwen nods.

"It's the punishment here," she says. "For any and all crimes. Lyonesse demands her sacrifices, however she can get them."

"What happened?" I ask, for the third time.

Gwen comes toward us and sets the candle on the table beside the bed before crawling into it. She doesn't touch Morgana or me and keeps a careful distance between us, but for a second, it feels like we're back in Avalon, too exhausted after a bonfire to go back to our separate rooms and instead just curling up together in the same bed, drunk and giggling and talking until we fall asleep one after another.

But this is nothing like those nights. I focus on the blood on Gwen's hands to remind myself of that.

"Something . . . happens in Lyonesse," Gwen says carefully, her voice shaking. "I remembered part of it, but in my mind it was different. I suppose I didn't see the worst of it as a child. I thought the ceremony wild and exciting. And it is, in a way, but I . . ."

"Gwen," Morgana says, every bit of her remaining patience disappearing. "What happens in Lyonesse?"

Gwen swallows, biting her bottom lip. "It's the moon," she says. "When it rises, it . . . takes hold of the people here—only those born here. It changes us. You saw my father yesterday—his claws. In his old age, it takes hold of him earlier than most. In a few years, he will have only mere hours of humanity a day."

"We saw you under the moon in Avalon plenty," I point out. "You never . . . changed."

Gwen shakes her head. "Not there, no. It has to be here. It has to be under the light of the Lyonessian moon. But even in Avalon, I *felt* it. I could rarely sleep and only when the moon was thin or gone altogether. I might not have changed outwardly, but I did inside. I felt restless and hungry and *angry* and

I couldn't stop it, I couldn't quench it. It wasn't until I came back here and participated in the first ritual that I realized what it meant, what it made me."

She presses her lips together tightly, drawing her legs up to her chest and hugging them tight. She doesn't want to say more, but Morgana leans toward her.

"What does it make you, Gwen?" she asks, her voice soft but still dangerous.

Gwen meets her gaze, hazel eyes unwavering. "It makes me monstrous," she says slowly.

"You wrote Arthur then," I say, drawing her attention to me. "It's why you broke off your engagement, why you wouldn't tell us what was happening."

"I didn't want you to know," she says, shaking her head. "I didn't want you to remember me like this. But you cannot stay here another day, do you understand? You have to convince Arthur to leave today, before dark."

"Why?" I ask. "If you come back with us to Camelot, the curse won't take hold of you anymore. You'll be like you were in Avalon."

Gwen doesn't answer, but after a second, Morgana does.

"Because she doesn't want to be like she was in Avalon," she says softly. "Because she likes being monstrous."

I wait for Gwen to deny it, but she doesn't.

"Gwen," I say. "You're taking lives."

"*Bad* lives." She shakes her head. "You don't get it, you don't understand how it feels—you couldn't possibly. You should see me, Elaine . . . under the light of the moon, with my claws and fangs and *hunger*. I am powerful and unstoppable and my fury takes over, drives me, consumes me and everything around me. And it feels *good*. It feels *great*. It feels *right*. I can't give that up for a life in stiff corsets, spouting pretty words over tea in Camelot. I can't. I won't."

Her voice breaks on the last word, splintering into shards sharp enough to cut.

Morgana looks at her again, but now there is no malice in her eyes. There is only understanding, an unspoken peace between them. I understand it, too, even without Gwen's claws and fangs or Morgana's bubbling fury. I understand the desire to destroy, to *take* something instead of always giving, giving, giving. There are too many days to count when I wouldn't mind being a little monstrous myself.

But not all of us have the luxury of hiding in the wild and offering our bodies up to the moon. Not all of us can afford to tear the world to shreds. Some of us have to live in that world. We have to survive it.

"We could change Camelot," I say after a moment. They both look at me like I've gone mad. "You're right, Gwen. It's a terrible place, restricting and shallow. It is not a place for women like us—women at *all*. It is a place shaped by men for men to thrive in, and that is all. But together we could cultivate enough power to change it. We could shape it. We can break their world and make our own in its stead."

"Elaine—" Gwen starts, but I don't let her get any further.

"We could," I say, louder. "Together. But we can't do it without Arthur on the throne. Please, Gwen."

Gwen shakes her head. "An alliance with Albion won't stand. If the people there learned what we are—"

"They would set out to destroy you," Morgana interjects with a shrug of her shoulders. "It would be a bloodbath, our numbers against your monsters. But make no mistake, that bloodbath would end in Albion's victory. If it were just Camelot, you might stand a chance, but with the entire continent . . . there would be no hope."

Guinevere's mouth pulls down into a frown. "Is that a threat, Morgana?" she asks, her voice dangerous.

"I don't threaten, Gwen," she says, rolling her eyes. "It's a fact. And one you can't dispute."

Gwen crosses her arms over her chest. "I'm assuming you think you have a better option?" she asks.

"Elaine's right," Morgana says, nodding toward me. "If you come to Camelot, if you stand at Arthur's side, we can change not just the country but all of Albion, including Lyonesse."

"That's exactly what I *don't* want," Gwen says. "For Albion to try to change Lyonesse, to tame it."

"Lyonesse needs a good taming," Morgana says with a hard and mirthless laugh. "You know it as well as I do—what happened last night was barbaric. Not the monsters, no, but the bloodshed itself. The ritualistic murder."

"They were criminals," Gwen says.

"That doesn't mean they all deserved death," Morgana counters. "You know that, Gwen. You looked sick when you came in here. You still do."

"The ritual is older than memory," Gwen says. "If you want to change that, the people will revolt."

"But *I* won't be changing it. You will be—as queen of not only Camelot, not only Albion, but Lyonesse as well. You once said that power trumps all in Lyonesse—you would have the power. Lyonesse wants to revolt? Let them. You'll have the power of the continent behind you, and no one could take that away."

Gwen is quiet for a moment, considering it. "You're forgetting one thing," she says finally. "A queen of Albion has no power of her own. She is a charming smile and an elegant gown and a body meant for bearing children. Nothing more."

"That might have been true, before," I say. "But we are in an unprecedented time, and it just so happens that you have something Arthur and Albion desperately want. It just so happens that you are in a position to make demands. So demand."

Gwen purses her lips, but I know I have her. I can see it in the set of her jaw, in her thoughtful eyes—Gwen is never one to be consumed by thought. She acts first and thinks later, makes decisions quickly and without regrets. But not this time. This time she is considering it, weighing it, thinking about the outcomes. If she's pausing, she's wavering. If she's wavering, I've won.

"My father has his own demands," she says finally. "And he is still the king here. I am only the princess."

Morgana smiles, and though she was not born here under this cursed moon, I can almost imagine she has fangs of her own.

"You have your father's ear, though," she says with a shrug. "I suggest you lead him by it."

"It won't be that easy," Gwen says, shaking her head. "You don't know what my father will ask of Arthur, what no other envoy of Uther's or his father's or his father's before him would agree to. Arthur won't agree to it, either, I promise you."

"And what is that?" Morgana asks.

Gwen levels a look at her, and for just an instant, something soft flickers behind her eyes before she steels herself once more.

"Prey."

# 31

MORGANA UNLOCKS THE door to Arthur and Lancelot's room, and we meet them in the hallway once they're dressed and ready. Judging by their glazed-over eyes and haggard appearance, they didn't sleep last night. Understandable, since they didn't have Morgana to block out the sound of the screams. When Arthur sees the three of us, though, his shoulders sag.

"Thank the Maiden, Mother, and Crone," he says, rubbing his tired eyes absently. "With all of that screaming . . . well, we worried."

"You think I would have let that happen?" Gwen snaps.

For a beat, Arthur doesn't answer, but then he shakes his head. "I don't know anymore, Gwen. They were *someone's* screams, weren't they?"

"The screams of criminals," she says, crossing her arms over her chest.

"Some more than others," I say quietly, thinking of the seamstress who had stolen from her patrons. A crime, yes, but not one on the same level as abusing animals or rape. I can't begin to say with any kind of certainty who deserves life and who doesn't, but the whole affair sits queasily in my stomach.

Lancelot looks at me, then back at Gwen. "Would someone like to explain what is happening?" he asks.

As quickly as possible, the three of us fill them in on what Gwen said this morning and what Arthur should expect going into his audience with King Leodegrance. When we finish, Arthur and Lancelot wear matching perplexed expressions that would be funny under other circumstances, but today I just want to shake them until they understand.

After a moment, Arthur clears his throat and gives a decisive nod. "Good," he says.

"Good?" Morgana asks with a sharp laugh. "What about this is *good*? You can't seriously be willing to agree to those terms. And even if you did want to, you know it wouldn't hold once the rest of Albion hears of it."

"It's good that we know what we're going into," Arthur amends. "It's good to know what Leodegrance's cards are, what he wants." He looks at me. "What cards do we have?" he asks.

I shake my head. "None," I say. "There's nothing we have that he wants, beside lives. Opening trade would benefit him, but I don't think he cares about that. Having his daughter be queen of Albion isn't a bargaining chip—he would much rather keep her here."

"Please don't speak of me as a bargaining chip," Gwen says.

"I'm only saying, there's nothing we can offer."

Arthur nods, his brow creased. "Then we are like every envoy that has come before us," he says. "And we'll leave empty-handed, just as they did, if we make the same attempts."

Something in his voice gives me pause. It isn't the practiced, thoughtful voice Arthur usually uses when discussing strategies, not his king's voice, either, all full and round and demanding attention. No, this is something else, something rough at the edges, and wild. Something desperate.

"Arthur," Lancelot says, his hand coming down on his shoulder. "What are you thinking?"

Arthur blinks, like he's pulling himself out of sleep. When he looks around at us, his expression is set.

"I'm thinking that bargaining will get us nowhere. Offering will get us nowhere. Trading will get us nowhere. If we want to return to Camelot victorious, it will take force."

"We don't have their numbers," Lancelot says. "Not to mention last night—"

"No, a full-out battle would be impossible," Arthur agrees. "But there's another way." He looks at Gwen, his eyes leveling on hers.

"You can't be part of this, Gwen," he says, not unkindly but unflinchingly. "You made your choice, you chose your side. I'm grateful for your help, but unless you're prepared to stand against your father and your people, you need to go."

For an instant, Gwen hesitates, her eyes darting around the hall before they find mine. In the dim candlelight, they glow amber ever so slightly, like a cat's. For an instant, I can imagine her roaming the woods beneath the Lyonessian moon, her fine hands curled into claws, her teeth sharp as daggers, her spine bent low to the ground.

"He's my father, Arthur," she says, her voice soft. "This is my country."

"I know," he says. "And I'm not asking you to betray them. I wouldn't. But I'd also be a fool to put you in a position to betray us."

Gwen looks at him like she's been slapped, her mouth gaping open slightly. "I wouldn't . . . I didn't . . ." She trails off, the realization settling on her shoulders. There is no neutral ground, not anymore. It is two halves of her heart, and that is a terrible choice to have to make.

So Arthur is removing the choice. Maybe he thinks it's the noble thing to do, the kind thing, but Gwen doesn't feel the kindness, and she's never had any patience for nobility.

"Fine," she says, her emotions sealing themselves away behind her eyes once more. She straightens up, squaring her shoulders. "My father will receive you in the throne room when you're ready to make your appeal."

She turns to go, but Arthur reaches out, catching her elbow. He hesitates before bending his head toward hers, a few murmured words slipping past his lips and into her ear, too quiet for me to hear them.

Gwen lingers for a fraction of an instant, then pulls away from him, surveying the rest of us with a look so distant, she might as well be looking at strangers. She gives one decisive nod.

"Best of luck to you," she says, her voice cold. "Believe me, you'll need it."

THIS TIME, KING Leodegrance isn't alone in the throne room. Now, in the cold frosted light coming in through slatted windows, he is surrounded by his court in all their wild glory. The women wear their hair loose and tangled, their gowns cut off at the knee. Before Avalon, the sight of their bare legs would have scandalized me, but now I understand the practicality of it. They are women who have not been raised to stand idly and curtsy and twirl around a dance floor elegantly. These are women like Guinevere—women who have been raised to run.

The men are similarly unkempt, with scraggly, overgrown beards that cover half of their faces, and loose shirts in need of a good wash and mend. Many of them are barefoot, and those who do wear shoes look uncomfortable in them, shifting their weight from one foot to the other.

At the center of it all, King Leodegrance sits on his rough-hewn throne, hands resting on the arms of it with his talons curving over the edges. As we step closer, I notice the dark color staining the tips of them, how it is also wedged beneath his nail beds. I cannot tell if it is dirt or blood, and I'm not sure I want to know.

I think of the visions I had of this day, of Arthur dying at the claws of beasts. Arthur is smarter than that, I tell myself, but it gives me little comfort. After all, there were several versions of Arthur that *weren't* smarter than that.

"Tell me, Prince Arthur, how did you sleep?" King Leodegrance asks as we approach, Arthur at the forefront with Lancelot, Morgana, and me a step behind.

Though the question itself is innocuous enough, the sort of question any courteous host would ask of his guest, there is nothing innocuous or courteous in Leodegrance's smile. It is a curling, smug thing, a question he knows the answer to. It is a challenge, but it is a challenge Arthur rises to with a smile of his own.

"The bed was very comfortable, Your Grace. I daresay I've never slept in its equal," he says, his voice calm and level. As if he actually had slept. As if he hadn't even heard the screams or, if he had, they didn't unnerve him the way King Leodegrance expected they would.

"I'm glad to hear it," Leodegrance says, looking anything but glad. "Are you ready to discuss my terms?"

Arthur pauses, as if considering it even though he knows exactly what those terms are. He takes a step toward Leodegrance, and the men on either side of him growl low in their throats as they crouch, as if ready to pounce on Arthur at any moment. Beside me, Lancelot sees this, and his own hand goes to the pommel of his sword.

"I don't need to hear your terms," Arthur says, stopping a few feet before the king. "You want men, sacrifices for your blood sport."

"Don't be ridiculous," Leodegrance says with a laugh. "We don't share Albion's gender prejudices—we will accept women as well as men."

Around him, his court bursts into titters, but the sound isn't human. It reminds me of the hyenas that lived in the caves at the west end of Avalon, how their laughter would echo throughout the mountains on quiet nights, haunting and bloodcurdling.

"Then I'm afraid you were correct that no peaceful treaty can be reached between us with words," Arthur says.

"Well, you did try," Leodegrance says with a pitying smirk. "And let it be known, you got much further than other men have dared."

"Oh, I'm not done," Arthur says, straightening up. "There is one last recourse for a peaceful treaty. I hereby challenge you, King Leodegrance, to a duel."

"A *duel*," Leodegrance says, derision dripping from the word. "Such an Albionian concept—a fight without blood, without risk, without death. All show, no real action. All that can be lost is dignity."

"Then we'll make it a duel to the death, though if you were to offer surrender, I might show mercy," Arthur says with a shrug. "The terms would be simple—I've brought with me over a hundred men. Should you win, they are your prisoners to do with what you wish."

Leodegrance arches a gray eyebrow. "You would offer the lives of your men?" he asks.

"They knew the risks when they agreed to join me here," Arthur says, though I know this part of the decision troubled him.

"What of the witch and the oracle?" Leodegrance asks, glancing at Morgana and me. At the term *oracle*, I jump, which makes him laugh. "Oh yes, I knew what you were the second you stepped into my castle. I've heard that ingesting oracle flesh gives one the Sight, though it's been centuries since we were lucky enough to have one in Lyonesse."

I can't suppress the shudder that racks through me, and Morgana places a steadying hand on my back.

"That isn't part of the—"

"It's a deal," I say, my voice coming out thin but sharp.

A murmur breaks out among the court, and I try not to hear them, try not to listen to the strangers speculating about eating my flesh. I have to have faith in Arthur. He will not fail. He *can't* fail. But then, I didn't foresee any outcome of a duel between him and King Leodegrance.

"Interesting," King Leodegrance says, leaning back in his throne to survey us thoughtfully. "And what is to stop me from simply taking your men and your women prisoner without any duel?" he asks, directing the question to Arthur, though I am the one who answers.

"Because I am Elaine Astolat, Lady of Shalott, and if any harm comes to me in these lands, my father will rally his armies and the armies of his many allies, and he will attack Lyonesse until there is nothing left of this land but razed earth."

At that, Leodegrance sneers at me. "You think I fear your human armies?"

"I think you're wise enough to know that what powers you have are dependent on the strength of the moon, and that fangs and claws are only so powerful when facing armies that outnumber you thrice over," I say.

King Leodegrance sucks his teeth, the sound loud in the otherwise silent room.

"And if you happen to win this duel, Prince?" he asks Arthur. "What would you demand in return? An alliance written on paper?"

"An alliance written in blood," Arthur says. "The sons and daughters of your court—let us say twenty-five—will be sent to the great houses of Albion to solidify the alliance, as husbands or wives, if they desire it, or wards and knights. Should you decide to break our alliance, their lives will be forfeit."

Leodegrance grunts, but I can tell he's impressed. The way he's looking at Arthur is different from last night. I doubt he will call him *boy* now.

"And would your own marriage be part of this deal?" he asks, looking sideways at Gwen, where she stands at his right side, her eyes downcast.

Arthur shakes his head. "I have made my intentions clear to your daughter, Your Grace, but I would not have an unwilling bride. The terms as they stand are enough for me."

"And will you let me set the time of this duel?" Leodegrance asks.

"Of course," Arthur says, nonplussed. "I assume you will want it to take place after nightfall?"

"Under the light of the moon, yes," Leodegrance says. "But even with that advantage, I am an old man, Prince Arthur. To expect me to fight a warrior as young and virile as you . . . well, that isn't fair, is it?"

Arthur's smile is tight. "I think you are selling yourself far too short, Your Grace. I'm sure we would be evenly matched in a duel."

"You are kind," he says. "But you won't begrudge an old man such as me the opportunity to choose a surrogate for this battle in order to make things more fair?"

"I would not," Arthur says. "Choose your surrogate. I will gladly fight whoever will stand in your place."

King Leodegrance's grin is a sprung trap. "Very well," he says, voice smug and gleeful as he glances to his right, where Gwen already looks sick. Because she knows her father, I realize. She knows his mind. She knew where this would lead even before he did. "Then you will fight my daughter, Princess Guinevere."

WHEN THE CROWD in the throne room dissipates and I move to follow Arthur out, Gwen grabs my arm, pulling me to the side of the room while everyone else pushes past us. When we are the only two left, I wrench my arm from her grasp.

"Arthur shouldn't have challenged him," Gwen says, her eyes flittering around the room. Her voice, for all of its crisp edges, wobbles in the middle like a half-baked cake. "Was that at your advice?"

"Your father gave him no choice," I reply. "Did you expect him to sacrifice his people, Gwen? Or return home empty-handed and let his bastard half brother drive Albion into the ground? He found a third choice, and if you expected anything else of him, you don't know Arthur at all."

She takes a step back from me, pressing her lips together in a thin line.

"What is wrong with you, Gwen?" I ask her. "You know your father is wrong, you don't like what he's doing." I pause. "You know he's mad."

Gwen flinches from the word but doesn't deny it.

"He's my father," she says quietly. "I am all he has in the world, and he is all I have."

"You have us," I remind her.

She shakes her head. "I saw your face this morning, El. Yours and Morgana's. I saw the horror in your eyes when you realized what I was, what I was capable of. Arthur will look at me the same way tonight, and whatever regard he thinks he holds for me will fall away quicker than he will be able to draw his sword, quicker even than I will pounce on him with bared teeth and claws. You don't have to be an oracle to know how it will end."

I swallow, but I can't deny she's right. Even when they face each other on an even field, with matched weapons, Gwen has always been able to beat Arthur handily nine times out of ten. And the tenth, it was usually agreed, was mercy on Gwen's behalf.

"You would really kill him?" I ask her. "You would kill him and doom all of us?"

This time, Gwen doesn't flinch. She looks at me with a level gaze that chills me to my bones.

"Better to have my hands bloodied than bound in chains," she says. "There's still time for Arthur to leave. As his adviser, you should encourage it."


I WAS SURPRISED BY how quickly the others accepted me on Avalon, how seamlessly I became a part of their lives and they of mine. In so many ways, Avalon felt like an exhale, like until I'd set foot on her shores, I'd been holding my breath, waiting and waiting and dying in the process. I worried that coming back to Albion would mean going back to that, but it hasn't. Now, I realize it wasn't the place—not entirely, at least; it was the people. Morgana and Arthur and Lancelot and, despite everything, Gwen.

There were moments, though, when I still felt like an outsider, even there, with them. Arthur and Lancelot were often on their own plane, making jokes no one else understood or challenging each other to any number of physical contests—races and duels, yes, but also things like seeing who could eat the most cherry tarts at dinner before they got sick. And then there was Morgana and Gwen, who bickered as often as they didn't and would sometimes go days without speaking, until they couldn't remember what they were fighting about to begin with.

But they also had magic, the kind that I couldn't understand any more than they could understand my visions, and sometimes it felt like that magic formed a glass wall, one I could see through but never fully breach.

"In theory—" Morgana said one day over lunch. We'd arrived at the dining hall late, and it was otherwise empty, with only scraps left over for us to eat. Perhaps that would have been a bad thing if we were anywhere else, but scraps from Avalon's kitchens could have made for a feast in Albion.

"Theories are useless," Gwen had cut in before Morgana could say anything more. She took a bite of toasted bread, piled high with fruit and cheese. "If you can't perform it in person, there isn't a point."

Morgana made a low noise in the back of her throat that might have been a grumble if her mouth weren't occupied with a bite of apple. She swallowed and leaned forward, elbows on the table and loose black hair spilling down, threatening to drag through the open pot of peach preserves.

"A theory is the first step," she said, shaking her head. "It's the dreaming of a thing—"

"And don't even *start* about dreams," Gwen replied. "Do remember who you're arguing with."

Morgana rolled her eyes. "Not literal dreams, not always at least. But ideas, musings. Surely you've had those, Gwen."

Gwen didn't respond, but she waved a hand for Morgana to continue.

"If we didn't theorize, how would we ever test our limits? We would never know more than what we're taught, never expand our horizons, never try something new. *Theories* are the basis of discovery."

Gwen swallowed and set her half-eaten toast aside. "Fine," she said. "What are you theorizing about today?"

At that, Morgana's smile stretched into a grin, and she glanced around the empty dining hall. "Something quite scandalous," she said, lowering her voice. "Something Nimue would certainly not approve of."

And then her gaze finally slid to me, like she'd forgotten I was there. I didn't blame her—when the two of them got to talking about magic, I often forgot I was there too.

"Don't mind me," I said, taking a sip of my tea. "I don't understand half of what the two of you say anyway, and I wouldn't repeat it if I did. Carry on with your scandalous theorizing."

Morgana shook her head, looking back at Gwen, and just like that, I faded from the conversation once more while they bent their heads together and murmured about impossible possibilities, the ways they sought to stretch their powers, just how they might go about doing so.

They must have had dozens of conversations like that, around me alone, and I meant what I said to Morgana—I only ever understood half of what they talked about. The rules and laws of magic were complex and fragile as a spider's web, and there was only so much I could hear of them before my mind began to fray and my eyes glazed over. I imagined it was the same way they would have looked if I'd tried to explain my Sight to them.

But one thing I understood was this: Fragile and complex as the rules of magic might have been, they were also flexible, and Morgana had all sorts of ideas about how to bend them to suit their will.

I FIND MORGANA IN the hall, waiting for me. In the shadowed castle hallway, her eyes are heavy and guarded—uncertain, though that is a look I am unfamiliar with from Morgana. When I approach, she forces a tight-lipped smile and links her arm through mine, her grip firmer than it usually is.

"Whatever happens tonight . . ." she starts, but she doesn't seem to know how to finish that sentence.

"Whatever happens tonight, we lose," I finish. "We lose Arthur and our own lives and everything Nimue has been working toward for centuries. Or we lose Gwen."

Morgana nods, her eyes focused forward. "I thought she would come around," she says after a moment. "I thought it would be like it always has been—we argue and bicker and throw our tantrums, but at the end of the day, we come back to one another."

"I think . . . I think she tried to come back," I say, biting my lip. "But so much has changed these last weeks, for all of us. I think she forgot the way."

Morgana stops short, turning to face me and forcing me to meet her gaze. "Elaine," she says, her voice low. "Tell me there's a way through this. For all of us."

My throat tightens. "The last time I was able to scry, there was one chance in dozens. A sliver of hope. We're past many of those possibilities now—there won't be a battle, no duel for Gwen's hand—but I didn't see this outcome. I don't think I need to scry to see that there is no happy way through. No matter what, we will lose something."

Morgana nods, her lips pressed tightly together.

"But I've been thinking," I say, the words slow and careful. "I've been thinking about your magic theories, the ones you and Gwen used to talk about—what I understood of them, at least. You're capable of a great deal, Morgana. But if your limits were stretched, if you pushed the boundaries of your power . . ."

I trail off, but Morgana's eyes spark with understanding.

"It isn't a simple thing," she says.

"I know," I tell her. "As I said, no matter what we do, we will lose something."

"Will we lose Arthur? Gwen?" she asks.

"I don't know," I tell her honestly. "But the more I turn this over in my mind, the more I think it's our best chance to leave this place, whole and together. I've seen a future, a glimpse of a choice you make that I never understood before. It never made sense to me, but I think maybe it does now. But it requires big magic—the kind of magic that would make Nimue furious. The kind of magic that might break you."

Morgana's shoulders square, but I can see the fear lurking beneath the surface. Still, she holds my gaze and smiles.

"I'd like to see it try," she says. "What do I have to do?"

# 32

WHEN THE SUN goes down, we gather in the courtyard, Morgana and me on either side of Arthur while Lancelot stands just behind, dwarfing us all in his shadow. The Lyonessian court is already there, fanned around King Leodegrance in their tattered and dirty finery. At first, I thought they looked sad, even destitute, but now there is nothing pitiable about them, and the sight raises goose bumps on my arms that refuse to go away no matter how I rub them.

"You alright, Shalott?" Lancelot asks, his voice low, meant only for me. Though he tries to sound nonchalant, I hear his own fear lurking beneath the surface.

He knows as well as I do that no matter what happens, there is no coming out of this night in total triumph. If Arthur somehow manages to win, we lose Gwen. And even if my plan with Morgana works, that will have its consequences as well.

Arthur's knights wait on the other side of the courtyard, armor on but helmets held at their sides. I'm not sure what they've seen or heard from their own lodgings, but it must have been enough to spook them. They don't look at us as we approach, not even Gawain, who stands beside his brother with a hand on his shoulder. For his part, Gareth looks even younger than his fifteen years, bright eyes large and sunken, mouth thin.

Seeing him sends a pang of guilt through me. He came along looking for adventure, searching for a purpose. Instead we have led him—led all of them—into the claws of monsters.

We come to a stop, and I step toward Arthur, helping him put his helmet on. As I do, I meet Gwen's eyes across the courtyard. Her red hair is down again, wild and tangled with dirt. Her freckled face is smeared with lines of red across her cheekbones, and I don't want to ask what that red might be.

But it isn't Gwen. Not really. She has already sealed herself away, sealed everything away that would interfere with what she feels she has to do. Sealed away her love for Arthur and for all of us. For just a moment, though, there is a flicker of something that might be remorse.

Remorse. Not conscience. Because no matter how guilty she might feel about it, her mind is made up and there is no changing it.

"She will kill you," I tell Arthur, adjusting his helmet.

Through the eye slit, he meets my gaze, his dark blue eyes steady.

"I know," he says. "And I'm sorry for putting us into this mess. I should have seen—I should have listened."

"You weren't the only one," I tell him.

Arthur shakes his head. "That's just it, though. I understand it, understand her. She is protecting her father, protecting her country. I can't think badly of her for that—I'm not sure I would have done differently if I was given the chance."

"Your father sent you to Avalon for your own protection, even though it cost him," I say. "For all of Uther's faults, he would never have demanded you sacrifice yourself for his pride."

"But she loves him," he says. "And that is not a thing of logic."

"Arthur," Morgana says, her voice low and desperate. "You have to fight back. Please."

He looks at her, surprised. "Of course I'll be fighting back," he says. "I'm going to fight with everything I have."

Lancelot glances between Morgana and me before his eyes settle on Arthur. "We all just assumed that you would . . . have problems with that. Because . . . well, it's Gwen."

Arthur lifts his helm. "I do have problems with it. Normally I would never . . . but, well, it's her or you three. Her or all the men who followed me into this wasteland. Her or all of Camelot, all of Albion. And she's made her choice. So I will do what I have to, and if it comes down to it, I'll defeat her."

"You'll kill her," I correct. "Because that's what it is, Arthur. It isn't just another practice duel on Avalon. It isn't about defeat. It's a fight to the death, and you know she will not ask for mercy. She dies, or you do, and all of us with you."

He flinches but then nods. "I'll kill her," he says, and despite everything, he does sound certain.

Morgana catches my eye, her expression set and eyes hard. We both hope it won't come down to that, but theories are only ever just that. We can't get his hopes up, not until we know for sure.

I smile and kiss his cheek before putting his visor back down. Morgana hugs him next, so tightly that I think she might manage to break his bones even through the armor. Lancelot merely claps him on the shoulder, but the gesture is somehow just as intimate.

And then Arthur turns away from us and steps into the center of the courtyard to face Gwen.

At first, they appear woefully mismatched—Arthur in his armor with his sword in one hand and shield in the other, Gwen in nothing but a tattered gown, with no weapons but her own two hands.

Behind me, I can almost feel the relief of the knights. They must think this will be easy, that it will be over in mere seconds, that we are safe and victorious before a single blow is dealt.

"Strike first," I murmur under my breath. "Strike now."

But of course, that is too much to ask of Arthur. He stands, shoulders squared and ready, facing Guinevere and waiting.

Morgana takes hold of my hand, squeezing it tightly in hers. I squeeze back, readying myself.

The clouds shift overhead, and moonlight shines down on us, pale and silver, and in that moment, there is fear in Gwen's eyes. For an instant, she looks like she wants to run. But the second passes and then she falls to the ground on all fours, her back showing through her ripped gown. Her spine ripples underneath her skin like something with a life all its own.

Her scream pierces the air, guttural and savage. She isn't the only one screaming, the only one changing. All of the Lyonessians are shifting beneath the moonlight. But Gwen is the only one of them who also sounds frightened. I didn't think Gwen capable of fear, but suddenly it is all I see in her. Not a monster, not even when her nail beds pull back and give birth to claws sharp as knives. Not even when she bares her teeth and they are filed into fangs. All I can see is a girl afraid.

Afraid of Arthur.

*I didn't want you to know,* she'd said. *I didn't want you to remember me like this.*

But Arthur doesn't step away from her, not even when she begins to snarl. He doesn't lift his weapon or ready to attack. He just looks at her the same way he always has, like she's still just Gwen.

And that is his first mistake. Because she is not just Gwen anymore.

*It* was *me. But it also wasn't. I don't . . . I don't know how to explain how both can be true, but they are.*

I didn't know, either, but now I understand it a bit better. I can see the battle behind Gwen's eyes, I can see that she is not alone in her own mind, that there is a creature battling for control. I can see the moment she lets it go.

Quicker than a flash of lightning, she pounces and pins Arthur to the ground, causing the Lyonessians to erupt in something caught halfway between cheers and howls. For an instant, I think it is already over, and I squeeze Morgana's hand back, feeling my nails digging into her skin.

*Do it now,* I beg her, but there is no pull yet, no smell of jasmine and fresh-sliced oranges. I glance sideways at her to see her eyes not on the fight but higher, focused on the moon itself, hanging full and bright in the sky. Lancelot puts his arms around both of us, as if he can somehow protect us.

But Arthur promised he would fight back, and he is nothing if not a man of his word. In a single strike, he throws her off him with his shield, though he barely has a chance to get back on his feet before she springs for him again. This time he is ready. He meets her with his sword drawn.

I watched Arthur and Gwen duel often enough on Avalon. They practiced sparring and tried out new techniques with each other, and it was always interesting to watch—more like a dance than a fight, with each of them moving together and in sync, anticipating the other's moves an instant before they made them.

This isn't that kind of duel, though. Now, they aren't coming together in a dance as equals and friends. Now, there is nothing elegant about their movements. It is all desperation and hunger and fury and blood. So much blood I don't know whose is whose, and I find I don't care either. Every time one of them gets a hit in, every time one of them gets hurt, I flinch. I cry out. I hold Morgana and Lancelot tighter, and they hold me tighter in turn. Every time they hurt, I hurt.

"Morgana, it's time," I tell her. "Please."

Her expression wavers, but after a moment she nods, once. "Brace yourself. Lancelot, keep her upright."

"What?" Lancelot asks. "What are you—"

"Trust me," she tells him, and just like that the choice is made. It isn't a question, not even a request. It's a demand, but one we all agreed to long ago.

I nod and Morgana squeezes my hand again, but this time, there is something more to it than comfort. This time, the scent of jasmine and oranges floods the air, and I feel her drain me, feel her pulling magic from me. I sway on my feet, steadied only by Lancelot before Morgana takes hold of him too.

As she draws on both of our energies—both of our lives—the sky above begins to darken. At first, I think I'm seeing things, but I'm not. The moon itself is actually *shrinking*. The howls of the Lyonessians turn pained and Gwen shudders, stumbling back from Arthur and throwing her arms over her head. The claws recede back into nails, her spine straightens, and she becomes Gwen again, out of breath and wild-eyed but Gwen. Arthur steps toward her, bewildered and dazed but with his sword raised high and ready to strike, ready to end it.

"Wait," Morgana cries out, letting go of my hand and Lance's.

My mind is such a blur that it takes some effort to focus on her, to reckon with what I'm seeing in front of me. Morgana, her hands held up before her, holding a glowing silver orb the size of her head. It hurts to look at it, but it is impossible to look away. It is the moon itself, brought down from the sky and shrunken.

I've already Seen this in flashes, the image of her with the moon in her hands. It seemed absurd at the time, the sort of abstract vision that was half-dream, the kind I'd long ago dismissed as an impossibility. But it wasn't. It was a glimpse of salvation and horror. A glimpse I would need. And I was right—Morgana was capable, but not alone. Not without me and Lance, not without our own power, our own lives.

It will have its consequences, I see that in the way Arthur's men look at her, in the way her own hands begin to shake, the way even Lancelot looks un-nerved.

Morgana must know this. She never asked what the consequences would be and I didn't tell her, but she must have realized. Even if she did, even if she made the choice willingly, it doesn't ease my guilt. I have seen what Morgana becomes, severed from her humanity, from us, and now I have pushed her down that path.

"Without this, you are weak," Morgana says, her booming voice carrying across the courtyard. "If I were to break it, you would never be strong again. You would die weak."

"We would all die," Leodegrance says. In the small moon's dim light, he looks like the old man he is, not the monstrous creature I've come to see him as. "Everyone would, even Albion and Avalon would perish without a moon. You wouldn't do that."

Morgana laughs, sounding unhinged altogether. It's the way she laughed in my visions of her far in the future. Or maybe not so far after all. "You think I wouldn't?" she asks, her grip on the moon tightening. In her hands, it looks as fragile as a ball of thin blown glass. It could break beneath her touch alone.

"I assure you, Leodegrance, everyone I love in this world is here, and they will die no matter what. I am not my brother—I don't care a whit about anyone outside."

For a moment, he looks like he wants to call her bluff. Even I, as well as I know Morgana, am not entirely sure whether she's earnest.

*You're all variables,* Nimue told me. But Morgana might be the biggest variable of us all.

"She'll do it," Gwen says before spitting out a mouthful of blood and wiping her lips with the back of her hand, leaving a smear of blood across her jaw. "I wouldn't underestimate her, Father. She will doom the world to save a few."

"And what do you say to that, noble prince?" Leodegrance sneers at Arthur, but he is too winded still to answer, still stuck staring at Morgana in a mix of horror and wonder.

"He doesn't have to say anything to it," Morgana says, her eyes never leaving the king. "He will live to see tomorrow and that is enough. Do we have a deal, King Leodegrance, or would you like to test my will against yours?"

They stare hard at each other for a moment, but Leodegrance is the first to look away. "Your terms?" he asks.

"Your head," she says without missing a beat. "Our safety. The alliance we came for and one of our people on your throne to ensure the alliance holds. Nothing less."

"You make steep demands," Leodegrance says.

"I hold a steep cost if you refuse," Morgana replies evenly.

Leodegrance thinks it over for only a moment, mouth pursed and eyes lingering on the moon in Morgana's hands. "Gwen," he says, his voice softening as he looks at his daughter. "Bring a sword and make it quick."

Gwen looks at her father, aghast. "No. I . . . I can't—"

"You can and you will," he snaps. "The moon isn't meant to be out of the sky. She will wither to nothing if she isn't returned soon."

With small and weary steps, Gwen walks toward him. When she passes Arthur, he hands her his sword and she takes it without looking at him. She comes to stand before her father, and her hands only shake slightly before she lifts Arthur's sword.

He whispers something to her that no one else can hear, and she nods once before drawing the blade across his throat.

Though the Lyonessians are confined to their human forms without the moon, when King Leodegrance's blood spills, the court erupts in a chorus of feral howls that shake me to my core.

# 33

PART OF ME fears that when Morgana returns the moon to the sky, there will be nothing to keep our arrangement in place, nothing to keep the Lyonessians from attacking and ripping us to shreds before we even have time to scream.

But they don't, and it isn't until Arthur, Morgana, Lancelot, and I are returning to our rooms in the castle that I understand why that is. They're afraid of us—they're afraid of Morgana specifically. Because what she did once she can do again, at any time, at her slightest whim. For all their fearsomeness, they fear her. And they aren't the only ones.

I saw how the Albion soldiers looked at her—or rather, how they didn't look at her at all. They didn't thank her. They kept their eyes downcast when she walked past them, their faces paler than the moon she held in her own two hands. The image of King Leodegrance bleeding to death is what should stay with me, or even Morgana holding the moon, but it's the fear in those men's eyes that I can't get out of my mind. Fear like that will not be rationalized with, it will only grow wild and untamed, spreading further each day.

"We knew there would be a price to pay," I say to her when we are alone in our room once more. "It would seem to be your reputation."

She looks at me, unsurprised and nonplussed. She shrugs her shoulders.

"An easy sacrifice then," she says, flopping back on the bed and staring up at the ceiling. "You know I didn't have much of one to begin with."

I shake my head. "It's more than that. Word will spread throughout Albion," I say, pacing the length of the room. Outside the window, I catch sight of the moon, back in the sky where it belongs, hanging full and round amid a star-littered sky like nothing ever happened to it at all. "They'll call you a witch, paint you as evil. You'll be their villain."

She doesn't say anything for a moment. "I saved their lives—all of our lives. You said it yourself—there was no other option."

"You know that and I know that, but it isn't about truths. It's about stories, remember? They won't like that story, and so it will cease to be the truth. You will be their villain because they will want you to be, truth be damned."

"Yes," Morgana says after a moment, though she doesn't sound bothered by that notion. She sits up slightly, resting on her elbows. "But Arthur is alive, Gwen is alive, you and Lancelot as well. We are alive and safe and I did that. You told me there would be a cost and I didn't care—I still don't care. I'd do it over again if I had to."

I pause in my pacing, a realization dawning. "You made yourself a villain so that Arthur could remain a hero."

She glances away, out the window. "Nimue would be awfully proud, wouldn't she?" she asks, her voice brittle as frozen glass. "Arthur before all."

I can't form words. I try a couple of times, though I don't know quite where to begin. I don't know how I can possibly tell her that in saving Arthur today, she's doomed him in the future. *We* have doomed him. Because even though Morgana chose the path, I led her right to it. And if I hadn't—if *we*—hadn't? Arthur would be dead right at this moment. It was the right choice, wasn't it? But the more I think about it, the more my mind ties itself into knots that I doubt I'll ever be able to undo.

I don't know how to explain to Morgana that this will be the beginning of the end, the first fracture between her and Arthur that will soon widen into an uncrossable chasm. I don't know how to say that the sacrifice she made today will eventually drive her mad with resentment, how it will eventually make her hate Arthur so much she would see him dead. I don't know how to apologize for my own part in it.

There is no saying any of that, even if I could find the words to express it. To tell Morgana anything I've Seen would break all my vows and could make things infinitely worse. There is nothing to say, no reply to make at all.

So instead, I can only laugh, and it is some time before I stop.

ARTHUR AND LANCELOT join us in our room just before the moon slips out of the sky, both with the same sleepless and haunted look in their eyes. Arthur's wounds have been shoddily patched up, his left arm wrapped in a makeshift sling and bandages stretching over the right side of his face. He doesn't seem to be in much pain, though that might just be Arthur's stubborn bravery.

"Do you want me to . . ." Morgana asks him, gesturing to his arm.

Arthur shakes his head, the movement causing him to wince. "I think you've done enough for one day." Though he says the words mildly enough, Morgana still flinches away from them.

"It wouldn't kill you to thank me, you know," she says, not just to Arthur but to Lancelot as well. "If I didn't do what needed to be done, we would all be dead."

"Of course everyone is grateful," I cut in. "It just . . . it wasn't how any of us imagined it going."

At that, Morgana laughs. "No, because Arthur thought he would show up with his righteous ideals and swoony sentiments and Gwen would fall all over herself to marry him and everything would be tied up in a neat bow. That was never going to happen."

Arthur finally forces himself to look at his sister.

"Would you have done it?" he asks her quietly. "If it had come down to it, would you have really destroyed the world?"

Morgana doesn't answer right away. Instead, she picks at a thread in the comforter, her eyes focused on that so she doesn't have to meet his gaze.

"I didn't have to make that choice, so what does it matter?" she says.

"It matters," he tells her, because to Arthur, it's the only thing that does.

She lets out a slow exhale before drawing her eyes up to his. "Yes, I would have done it," she says, her voice so low I barely hear her. "Cast the entire world into darkness. And why not? What good is a world without you in it? It would have fallen to darkness anyway."

Arthur has nothing to say to that, but nothing needs to be said. A thousand words lie in the way he looks away from her, in the way the corners of his mouth turn down, in the furrow of his brow. Morgana sees it as clearly as I do, and she shrinks in on herself in response.

She might have prepared for the world to fear her, she might have steeled herself against their hate and misunderstanding. But she never in a thousand years expected it from Arthur.

"I saved us," she says, to him and to herself. Her voice is thread thin, lost to the night as it fades into a new dawn. "And I will not apologize for finishing what you didn't have the stomach to."

Arthur has no response to that, and Morgana doesn't seem to expect one from him. She turns and walks out of the room without a glance over her shoulder. The door shuts behind her with a slam.

Though part of me wants to, I don't go after her, and neither does Arthur or Lancelot. After all, in a land of monsters, Morgana is still the most fearsome creature around.

WITH HIS INJURIES, Arthur needs sleep more than Lancelot and me, so I give him a dose of the sleeping draught Morgana and I packed, and in a matter of minutes he is fast asleep in the bed. His snores are loud, but I'm grateful for something to fill the silence that hangs in the air between Lancelot and me as we sit on the sheepskin rug stretched out before the dying fire.

The air is cold, so I draw my knees up to my chest, hugging them tighter beneath the threadbare blanket. For his part, Lancelot seems unbothered by the chill, though he does seem to be unbothered by most things. When he sees me shivering, he hands me the only blanket without a word.

"Did you See it ending like this?" Lancelot asks after a while, though his gaze is focused on the flames burning low in the fireplace.

"I Saw a dozen different versions of it," I say. "A dozen different ways our journey here would end. The only good one I Saw was us returning to Camelot triumphant, but I never Saw how. There was another vision, though, some time ago, of Morgana holding the moon in her hands. I never knew what to make of it—I thought it was some abstract dream, nothing as literal as what happened. But the more I thought about the problem before us, how big a part the moon played, the more I thought about that vision. So I suggested it to Morgana, if she could get enough power to do it."

"And, of course, Morgana took that as a challenge," he says, exhaling loudly.

"But I've Seen other things," I add, unsure of why I'm saying the words until they're out of my mouth. Lancelot is surprised as well, his eyes darting from the fire to rest on me. "Things I think we're getting closer to now more than ever, that I've pushed us toward tonight. Worse things."

"Worse than being eaten by Lyonessian beasts?" he asks.

I pause before nodding. "I can't say more," I say.

"I know," he says, and he does, better than the others. Unlike them, he's never asked about my visions, not even in jest. Because he was born and raised on Avalon, among the oracles. He knows the rules as deeply as I know which type of fork to use for dessert. "I wish you could, though."

I shake my head. "Everyone always says that, but it's a heavier burden than you would think, to know the fates of the people you love."

For a moment, he doesn't say anything. "I'm sure it is," he says finally. "That's why I wish you could share it. So that you wouldn't have to shoulder the burden alone."

He goes back to staring at the fire, but I let myself look at him, taking in the sharp planes of his face, the intensity of his green-gold eyes. After a moment, I inch closer to him, opening the blanket up to share it with him, wrapping us both in its warmth. He settles an arm around my shoulders, and I don't know if it's meant as a gesture of comfort or one of romance, but I find I don't care either way because whatever it is, it feels good. It feels right.

No one will mention Morgana's name at the round table. No one will clamor to fill the empty seat at Guinevere's left, one place away from Arthur himself, though I'd imagine most would like to. No one will so much as look at it. Though only Morgana herself will have been banished, it will feel like her name has been outlawed as well. Saying it would be a curse on all of us. A bad omen we certainly will not need, what with war brewing at our doorstep.

In the chair next to hers, Gawain will fidget, staring at his hands bundled in his lap. He will not have slept, and violent dark circles will stand out starkly against umber skin. He must feel my eyes on him because for an instant, he will look up and hold my gaze. Gawain always sees the best in people, long after they stop deserving it, and Morgana will be no exception to that. He will have a harder time than the rest of us wrapping his mind around what she will have tried to do to Arthur—whether it will be poison or a dagger or a dark spell that wraps itself around his neck and tightens.

Those details tend to vary, but the intended result does not. Sometimes, though, she succeeds, and the futures that spider out from that outcome are very different indeed.

The polished white stone of the table will glint with veins of gold in the candlelight, carved into a perfect circle—it will have been a gift from Avalon to celebrate Arthur's coronation. Even here, a world away, it will crackle with a hint of magic.

Over the last months, Arthur will have been dividing up the great houses of Albion, laying them out on the table like pieces on a board before the game—before the *war*—begins. Each house has its sigil carved from stone, the size proportional to the size of the army it brings with it, from the crescent moon that spans the distance from my thumb to my pinkie, to the fleur-de-lis the size of an apple. The houses he can count on pile on his side of the table—the Lyonessian moon and the Shalott fleur-de-lis among them—and on the other side, near Gareth, he keeps those who will swear allegiance to Mordred should he decide to declare war.

Mordred's pile grows bigger every day. Before long, it will become a fair fight.

Silence will constrict the room when Arthur walks in. If Morgana's absence bothers him, he will hide it well beneath a placid exterior, his expression hard and smooth as the table itself.

Without saying a word, he will take the stone raven from his side and place it on Mordred's. With Morgana gone, wanted for treason against the crown, Tintagel will fall to Morgause without a fight.

Though Tintagel isn't nearly as big as the Lyonessian moon, it will be a significant loss. It will bring us one step closer to a war we will not survive.

Guinevere will be the one to finally break the silence.

"It still isn't enough," she will say, reaching out to rest a long-fingered hand on Arthur's. Her nails will be even more ragged than I've ever seen them, bitten to the quick, the cuticles torn and raw.

"We can persuade Carrendish back," she will continue, reaching for a horse figure on Mordred's side and nudging it toward the middle. It is about half the size of the Tintagel raven.

"Not without bowing to the serf laws they want, and I won't do that," Arthur will say, pushing the horse back to Mordred's pile. "It's practically slavery."

If Morgana were still here, she would tell Arthur that idealism didn't win wars and compromise is necessary. She hated Lord Carrendish as much as anyone and would have rather swallowed spiders than give in to his antiquated serf laws, but she was always the one willing to suggest what no one else could, even if she proceeded to kill the idea herself.

Someone will need to fill that gap, to make the difficult suggestions, to call Arthur a fool when he's being one, but no one does.

"The chimera," Lancelot will suggest instead from his place next to me. He will nod toward a figure on the outskirts of Mordred's group. He will open his mouth but close it again quickly, face reddening.

"Lord Perdell," I will whisper to him, earning a bashful smile.

"Lord Perdell," he will echo. "He's easily flattered, desperate to feel validated.

He feels forgotten way out in the borderlands, and Mordred won his favor easily. You could win it back."

Arthur's brow will crease as he stares at the pieces, a puzzle he cannot solve. "How?" he will ask after a moment.

"His favorite daughter just came to court," Lancelot will say before hesitating. "If she were to marry into your family . . ." He will break off, but he really doesn't need to say any more. With Gareth newly wed, there is only one eligible family member Arthur has left.

All eyes will turn to Gawain, who will try to sink down lower in his chair, as if wishing it would swallow him whole.

Arthur will rake his hair back from his eyes, looking truly tired for the first time. "I would never ask that of you, Gawain," he will say.

"You don't have to ask," Gawain will reply, somber dark brown eyes heavy on Arthur. "Of course I'll do it. Lancelot's right—it will win back Lord Perdell, and a bond like that will keep him loyal."

For an instant, I will expect Arthur to say no, that it isn't worth it. Once, an age ago, he would have. His friend's personal happiness would have meant more. But that Arthur was an idealist with a rigid moral compass. That Arthur had Morgana to balance him, to make the difficult decisions. Without Morgana, he will be off-kilter. So instead, he will rub a hand over his forehead before nodding.

"Do it fast," he will tell Gawain. "I fear we're coming up quickly to the breaking point."

# 34

THE DOOR CREAKS open just as the sun crests over the horizon. At first, I think it's Morgana, but instead Gwen slips through, in the same tattered white dress as earlier, now even dirtier and stained with King Leodegrance's blood—her father's blood.

Her eyes meet mine, and I steel myself for her rage, for her fury, for her blame. Lancelot goes tense beside me, readying for the same. But when Gwen speaks, her voice is level and calm.

"There are things to discuss," she says, her eyes going to Arthur's sleeping form. "We should wake him up."

"It's not a natural sleep," I say, forcing myself to get to my feet, though my body protests the loss of the blanket's warmth, of the security of Lancelot's arm around my shoulders. "After everything, he couldn't fall asleep, but with his injuries, rest was necessary."

In the dim light of the mostly dead fire, it's impossible to see her face clearly, but I could almost swear she flinches.

"She wouldn't heal him?" Though she doesn't say Morgana's name, there is so much vehemence in that single syllable that it knocks the breath from me. I understand it, I can't even hold it against her, after what Morgana did—what *we* did—but still everything has fallen apart so quickly I can hardly wrap my mind around it. Even yesterday morning, the three of us still stood on the same side of things. And now that has been ripped to pieces I fear will never mend.

"He wouldn't let her," I say. "You aren't the only one angry with her. It was all I could do to convince him to take the sleeping draught."

"How long will he be out?" she asks, the edges of her words crisping.

"Hard to say. Could be any moment, could be another hour."

Gwen nods, looking around the room. "And where is she?"

"She needed some air," Lancelot says. "What she did was weighing heavily on her."

He says it so smoothly I know I would believe him myself if I hadn't seen Morgana's unrepentant righteousness with my own eyes. Still, it isn't enough to appease Gwen.

"Not as heavily as my hands at her throat will weigh when I see her next," she bites out, crossing her arms over her chest.

"There wasn't another choice," I say softly.

Gwen whirls on me, eyes blazing. "And you," she says. "I should have known you had a hand in this too—you have a hand in everything, don't you?"

"I presented her with options—"

"You knew she was capable of it? No one should be capable of that."

"No one is," I say, glancing at Lancelot. "Not on her own, at least. She pulled from us to do it. It was all I could do not to pass out then and there. One of her theories—I'm sure you remember them. Circumstances were dire enough that she—*we*—saw fit to put them to the test."

Gwen's eyes widen. "She drew on your lives to amplify her own power," she says slowly. "It never occurred to me she would actually try—" She breaks off, shaking her head. When she speaks again, her voice is whisper soft. "Do you know what this means? What she's capable of? If using the two of you like that allowed her to pull the moon itself from the sky . . ."

"With enough lives to draw from, there is nothing she couldn't do and no one who could stop her," Lancelot finishes.

"Not to mention the fact that she could have killed the two of you," Gwen adds.

My stomach twists into knots until I feel like I'm going to be sick. I swallow it down. "She did it to save us," I say when I find my voice. "You know, Gwen, that there was no other way to do it. You were going to kill Arthur, even if you didn't want to. I saw it—that wasn't entirely you. There was something in your body with you, and that *thing* would have killed him, and all of us would have died shortly after. What Morgana did was horrifying—I won't deny that, even if I did give her the idea—but it is the only reason all of us are still here, able to have this conversation."

Gwen sets her jaw, glaring at me, but there is no argument she can make. She knows I'm right, though she would rather die than admit it. Instead, she stalks toward Arthur's bedside, reaching a hand out to him.

"Don't," I snap before she can touch him. To my surprise, she stops short, though her hand is still extended out, fingertips inches from Arthur's forehead.

"There's no time to waste," she says.

"He needs to rest."

"*We* need a next step. This isn't over yet, and with the power of Lyonesse in flux, it is a more dangerous place than ever."

"But *you* have power over Lyonesse," I point out.

She laughs, shaking her head. "I might have," she says through clenched teeth. "But there is only one way to hold power here, and I lost it the second I forfeited in combat."

"You didn't—"

"I did," she says, each word pointed. "It might not have been a traditional outcome, but there was a clear winner and a clear loser in that battle, and it is very clear which side I fell on. My court will never forgive or forget that, and so I doubt they will be my court for much longer. If you want this treaty to hold, we need to act quickly."

She doesn't give me a chance to protest, though she does look remorseful for an instant before she presses the pad of her thumb to Arthur's forehead, drawing him out of his deep sleep with a wrenching cry of pain that I feel in my bones.

"Shhh," Gwen says, moving her hand to his cheek.

"Gwen?" he asks, voice anguished. "What's—"

"This is going to hurt," she tells him before closing her eyes and letting magic flow through her fingertips, into him.

Arthur's body goes stiff and he hisses in agony, and though he doesn't scream or cry out, I know he wants to. Healing is one of the few intersections of Morgana's and Gwen's powers, though it is different for each of them. Morgana's way is easier, a mending of bones and muscle and skin, each piece inanimate on its own, but Gwen's way is to control the living pieces, to use a person's life, their blood, their pain. I remember her healing a twisted ankle for me once, how I felt like every inch of my body was swallowed up by pain. I'm sure whatever Arthur is feeling is worse.

It is over as quickly as it came about, and when Gwen steps back, Arthur collapses against the pillows, breathing heavily. Slowly, he removes the bandages from the right side of his face, his left arm now able to move without pain. When the bandages come off, the skin of his face is smooth once more, as if the earlier fight never happened at all.

"I suppose I ought to thank you," he says to Gwen, watching her warily, like she might attack him again at any moment.

She sees this and looks away. "There's no need," she says. "You must be afraid of me now."

At that, Arthur laughs, sitting up straighter in bed. "I've always been a bit afraid of you, Gwen," he says. "Nothing's changed in that regard."

Her eyes snap back to him. "You don't hate me," she says slowly.

He frowns. "There's nothing you did that I wouldn't have done in your place," he says. "Well, maybe that's not true. But I believe that's more my failing than yours. We were both trying to do what was best for our people."

*And so was Morgana*, I want to say, but I hold my tongue. The difference is that all of Morgana's people are here in this room.

Gwen says nothing for a moment. Instead, she sits down at the edge of the bed, looking down at her hands, the dirt crescents beneath her fingernails, the dried blood spattered against her pale skin, nearly indistinguishable from her freckles in this light.

"I had thought that when you saw me for what I was you would hate me," she says, her voice thread thin. "It was part of why I wanted you to leave so badly, so that it wouldn't come to this and you could always remember me as I was on Avalon."

Arthur starts to reach his hand toward hers but pauses halfway. "There is little difference to me," he says after a moment. "Who you are is who you have always been. My feelings for you haven't changed. I can't imagine they ever will."

"Then you would still have me?" she asks quietly. "A monster for a wife, a heathen for a queen?"

Arthur doesn't move for a moment. "I . . ."

"We should give you two some space," I say, placing a hand on Lancelot's arm to lead him away, but Gwen shakes her head.

"Not much of a point in that," she says with a sigh, her eyes still on Arthur. "Little of our lives together will be private from here on out, after all, and this does concern you."

She has a point there, but it still feels like such a private moment between them that it's uncomfortable to stand there, waiting for Arthur's answer. Beside me, Lancelot shifts his weight from foot to foot.

"I would have you, Gwen, in all of your iterations, if I thought it would make you happy. But we both know it wouldn't."

"You do make me happy," she says quietly.

"I do, maybe," he says, shaking his head. "But Camelot wouldn't. The court there wouldn't. That crown is a different one entirely from the one here. You would hate it, and you would hate me, too, eventually."

"You're wrong," she says, and in that instant, her eyes do find mine, and I remember what we discussed our first night here. *We could change Camelot*, I told her, and she truly means to try. "And beyond that, I can't remain here. They will dethrone me before the moon is full again in the sky, I'm sure of it. The only hope for our alliance is if I join you in Camelot as your queen and we rule Lyonesse remotely."

"Will the alliance hold when we are gone?" I ask.

Gwen considers it for a second and nods. "Your demand for Lyonessian children was a smart one, using them as hostages."

"They'll be treated well," I say quickly, but Gwen waves that away.

"Of course they will be, I'll see to that myself if I have to. But it was a smart move. I have an uncle who can act as regent in our stead, and I've been assured he will honor the alliance. He won't have a hard time of it, what with Morgana's threats. Even when she's gone, they will know that she can return. She'll haunt their nightmares."

"Not just hers," Lancelot says quietly. "You saw the knights, how they looked at her."

"She's made herself a villain in this story," I agree. "Even if she wasn't."

Gwen scoffs like she might argue that point, but after a moment she decides to hold her tongue.

"After what she did, she cannot make a life in Camelot," Gwen says. "You know that as well as I do, Elaine. Better, even. You've seen their cruelty first-hand. I've only heard stories of it."

"We'll have to keep her close," I say.

"Close," Gwen presses. "Or very, very far."

She wants to banish Morgana, I realize. Send her far away, and not for entirely selfless reasons. Of course she wouldn't want to look at Morgana every day—how could she without seeing her father's death again and again?

"We need Morgana," I say, my voice firm.

"Elaine," she starts, but I shake my head.

"It was my decision too—I gave her the idea," I say. "If you want to banish her, banish me as well. But you need both of us, and you know it. I'm not saying you have to forgive her, Gwen, and I'm certain she hasn't forgiven you, either, but banishment isn't the answer."

Gwen's jaw clenches, and she looks away.

"What would you have us do, then?" Arthur asks softly. "You've orchestrated this so far, Elaine. How does it end?"

I expect venom in his voice, or at least some measure of blame, but he asks the question simply.

"Gwen is right," I say, shrugging my shoulders. Already, I can see how this will play out without even visions to guide me. "Your men saw what she did, they'll understand what she's capable of. As soon as we return, they'll tell their families, their friends, their neighbors. And as great and terrible as her powers are, the rumors of them will only grow wilder. Your people will fear her and turn on her, and if she is standing at your side, they will turn on you as well."

I have long been told that Morgana will destroy Arthur, I have seen visions of her slipping poison into his drink, burying a dagger between his ribs, but this would destroy him as well. Morgana herself would become the poison, turning whatever she touches to ruin. Unless. Gwen is right, there is one way to stop it.

"Which means we have the duration of our journey back to Camelot to tell them a better story," I continue. "Specifically, we have Shalott."

"What sort of a story?" Arthur asks.

"One where Morgana did not take the moon from the sky. One where it was little more than an optical illusion." I swallow and look at each of them in turn. "One where Morgana is powerless and docile."

MORGANA RETURNS NOT long after, a black wool shawl drawn tight around her shoulders and her violet eyes sunken and tired. When she sees us all gathered, she deflates for an instant before straightening up again, taking in the sight of us. Arthur up and dressed, his wounds healed. Gwen in a fresh gown, her hair and skin cleaned of the dirt and blood that caked them. Lancelot still in his armor as if expecting an attack at any moment. And me . . . when she looks at me, I look away and hate myself for it.

"I can't say I'm sorry for what I did," Morgana says before anyone else can speak. She sounds like she's practiced the words while she walked, how to apologize without actually apologizing. "I'm not. I would do it all over again if I had to. But I am sorry I had to do it. And I'm sorry you don't understand that."

"We do," Arthur says, no longer angry but only tired. Only resigned. "Give us the room, please."

Gwen and Lancelot start toward the door without looking at Morgana, as if fearing that meeting her gaze will reduce them to ash on the spot. When I move to follow them, Arthur stops me with a hand on my elbow.

"Would you stay, Elaine?" he asks quietly. "Your guidance has always been true, for both of us. I think we could benefit from it now."

I nod and close the door, stepping fully back into the room, though part of me hates that I have to stay for this. But this is my mess as well, as much as it is Morgana's.

"Is this a conversation or a meeting?" she asks Arthur. "Am I speaking to my brother or my future king?"

Despite the venom leaking into her voice, Arthur holds firm. "You're speaking to both," he says. "Since what you did, you did as my sister and my adviser. What you did does not reflect on only you anymore."

"What we did," Morgana says, her eyes falling to me.

"What you both did," Arthur amends.

"What we did is the only reason you will have a crown to claim when we get back to Camelot, if you can even manage the third task," she says. "You weren't going to win against the Lyonessians with your logic and your books and your pure heart. You needed to be ruthless. You needed to take power rather than ask for it.

"You will be a great king, Arthur, I believe that with every ounce of me, but you will never get the chance if you can't take the throne, if you can't hold it against the enemies who would see you dead. And you don't have what it takes to do those things. So I did what I always do, what I have always done. I protected you, no matter the cost."

Arthur looks away, focusing out the window.

He doesn't have the heart to say it, I realize. He knows he has to, but Morgana is right: At the end of the day, he can't make the difficult decisions. He can't hurt people, especially not the people he loves.

"Gwen's agreed to marry Arthur, to accompany us to Camelot and take the throne beside him," I say. "It's only a matter of time before what happened tonight is known throughout Albion, and when that story is told, you will be the villain."

"I know that," she snaps. "I did what I had to do. You said it yourself, there would be a cost. I agreed to pay it, and so I will."

"But it doesn't have to be that way," I say. "We have a few days to change the narrative, to make a heroine of you, and to preserve Arthur's reputation in the process."

Morgana looks between Arthur and me, brow furrowed. "How?" she asks.

"They hated me before this, before they knew what I was capable of. They'll hate me more now."

"Not if they think you are incapable of anything," Arthur says.

"They saw—"

"They saw what they needed to see. A bit of smoke and mirrors you employed to convince the Lyonessians to surrender. Clouds that shifted to cover the moon entirely, a candle you held in your hand. You could have faked it all," he says.

"But I didn't," Morgana says.

"But you did," I say, my voice firm. "Please, Morgana, this is the only way."

She shakes her head. "They won't believe it," she says. "They know I have magic, they know—"

"You won't have magic," Arthur cuts in.

Silence follows the declaration, and I find myself holding my breath, waiting for her response. I expect fury, bewilderment, protests. Instead, Morgana laughs.

"Of course I'll have magic," she says. "You could sooner drain my body of blood, my mind of thoughts."

"It's a simple spell," I say, my voice softer than Arthur's was, but that doesn't make the words any less bitter. "A binding. Easy to apply and easy to remove, when the time comes."

"When the time comes," she echoes. "And when would that be?"

"When Arthur is secure on the throne," I say. "When the alliance with Avalon is made official and the boundaries between our worlds have fallen, when magic is seen no longer as a curse but as a gift. When what you did can be appreciated."

"A few years, perhaps," Arthur adds, but he doesn't look at her when he says it.

"No," she says. "Absolutely not. I just . . . won't use magic anymore. You have my word."

I shake my head. "You said it yourself—it's part of you. How long until you forget, until you slip up?"

"I won't," she says.

"You will," I say, softening my voice. "You know it, Morgana. You can't go a full day without magic, let alone years."

"No," she says again, her voice firmer.

"The alternative is banishment," I tell her.

Morgana looks between Arthur and me, mouth slack. "You cannot be serious," she says, her voice dropping to a hoarse whisper. "This is my punishment?"

"It isn't a punishment," I say before Arthur can speak. "We are trying to control the situation, and we can only do that if you are no longer a target. These are the only two ways to accomplish that."

"*We*," Morgana spits out. "Please. Yesterday I was a part of that *we*. And now you're treating me like an enemy, seeking to bind me. And why? Because I saved the lot of us?"

"Because I can't trust you," Arthur says, all but yelling. "Because you put the world at risk to save a mere handful of us."

"Who else matters?" Morgana asks him. "What world would it be without you?"

"It would survive, at least," he says, shaking his head. "Someone else would rise up. The world would go on. I am not more important than anyone else who breathes on this earth, human or fay. And I cannot trust an adviser who doesn't understand that, who holds the world on an imbalanced scale, who has that kind of power at her fingertips."

"Then call this what it is," Morgana says, her voice rising. "A punishment." She chokes out a laugh, collapsing to sit on the bed, her spine curved and shoulders hunched. "I don't know why I should be surprised, though. This is how it's always been. Ever since we were children, I've had to sacrifice so that you could flourish, Arthur. Protecting you has always fallen to me, no matter the cost I endured, and you've finally found a cost that is too high."

"That's unfair—"

"Is it?" she snaps. "Then why aren't I on Avalon right now? Why did I have to follow you to this goddess-forsaken land? If I had any say in it, I would have stayed in Avalon, I would have been happy there. But no—as always, I had to trail after you. And now even you won't have me, not all of me, just some chained and docile version you can control. Where is the fairness in that?"

Arthur doesn't have an answer. All he can do is stare at his sister, wounded and shaken.

"There is no going back, Morgana," I say, when he can't bring himself to speak. "There is only going forward. You can do it alone, or you can join us. And it will only be temporary—"

"And you?" she demands, turning toward me. "Will your powers be bound? This was your doing as well, you had the vision—"

"Elaine's power isn't threatening," Arthur says.

"And Gwen's?" she presses. "Those same knights saw Gwen turn monstrous, saw her try to kill you."

"A curse Arthur broke," I say softly. "That is how they will see it—a beautiful girl made monster by evil magic, a spell broken by a valiant young prince. And so long as she is in Camelot, away from the Lyonessian moon, that story will hold."

"She still has magic," Morgana points out.

"Yes," I agree, glancing at Arthur. "But no one knows that. No one even suspects it. No one fears her."

"So you trust that *she'll* be able to hide it?" Morgana asks with a scoff.

"Yes," Arthur says, unflinching.

Morgana shakes her head, speechless for a moment. "Let them fear me. Let them cower and whisper and plot my destruction—they will fail."

"But what kind of a life would that mean for you?" I ask her. "A lonely one."

"Not if I had you," she says, but her voice breaks over the last word.

"Of course you have us," I say, even as I feel her slipping further and further away. "But when you saved us, you toppled a tree in a crowded forest. I told you there would be consequences and here they are. You agreed to risk them, and one day, people will see what a hero you were. But that day isn't today. Today you are a monster to them—those are the seeds that Morgause will all-too-happily plant and water until the vines of fear and hate grow thick enough to strangle us all."

"Not once Arthur returns to Camelot, once he completes this third quest and is crowned king—"

"Kings can be overthrown," I say. "And the ties that hold Albion together are already fraying. War will be on us before next winter's frost. Arthur needs to hold on to as many allies as he can if we want to stand a chance when that happens, and he can't do it if your shadow is cast over him."

Morgana and Arthur both stare at me. It's the most I've ever told them about the future, and maybe it was an error, but I need her to understand what is really at stake here—I need them both to understand.

After a long moment, Morgana smooths her rumpled gown over her legs and gets to her feet.

"It is something of a relief, to finally understand," she says, her voice stiff.

"I would have told you sooner, but it's dangerous—"

"Oh no, I don't care about that," Morgana says. "I meant that it's a relief to understand that our loyalties are so imbalanced."

"Morgana—" Arthur starts, but she holds up a hand to silence him.

"I have spent my life in your shadow, Arthur, and I have done it willingly because I love you and I want the world to unfurl at your feet," she says quietly. "But I never imagined my own shadow would be such a burden for you. I'll have my power bound, but not until we're out of Lyonesse. To do so before would put us in danger, and then everything I did would have been for nothing."

She doesn't give either of us the chance to respond before turning on her heel and walking out of the room, slamming the door behind her.

# 35

ARTHUR AND GWEN marry that night, in a small ceremony—more private than the one they will have in Camelot after Arthur's coronation, but both are spectacles in their own ways. This one is for Lyonesse, for the family Gwen has left, an attempt to spin the murder of a king into a triumph, the joining of the country with Albion as a victory for all.

It works better than I expected. Gwen was right—Lyonesse respects power above all, and we have that. They fall in line with surprising ease.

I didn't think that Morgana would make an appearance at the wedding, but she arrived on time in a fine black gown with lace overlay and sweeping trumpet sleeves. She pastes a smile over her face and stands at Arthur's side with Gawain to represent his family, and when the ceremony is done and Arthur and Gwen are husband and wife, she embraces Gwen and kisses her cheek to welcome her as a sister.

No one would know that there was anything rotten between them. No one would know how they acted against each other.

"Cheer up, Shalott," Lancelot says, coming to stand at my side as the crowd breaks off to celebrate with food and wine and dancing. He hands me a heavy gilded goblet filled with red wine. "It's a happy occasion, after all."

"You could have fooled me," I tell him, still watching Morgana warily. I know her too well to believe the facade. I know her too well to believe she can hold it up for long. "She agreed to the binding, but it isn't over."

"She'll still be Morgana, even without her magic," he says softly.

"I know that," I say, taking a sip of wine. "But she doesn't. That's the problem."

Lancelot looks at me like he wants to ask why, but he doesn't and for that I'm grateful. "It's still meant to be a happy night," he says. "I'll be honest, I didn't think Arthur and Gwen would ever get here."

I laugh. "There were times I doubted it," I say. "Especially after the last week."

"You think it's possible, for them to forgive each other for everything?" he asks, watching them.

I don't answer for a moment. Instead, I follow his gaze. Both of them are tall enough to stand above the crowd. Her arm is linked through his as they speak to a Lyonessian lady I don't know. They look right together, side by side; it is easy to forget that just yesterday they were literally at each other's throats.

"I think they already have," I tell him. "I think they're the same, at heart. They understand why the other acted the way they did—they would likely have done the same if they'd had to. And they love each other. That love is a difficult thing to break."

Lancelot doesn't say anything. Instead, he holds a hand out to me as the musicians in the corner strike up a song.

"Lance—" I start.

"Come on, Shalott," he says with a smirk. "It's bad luck to not dance at a wedding."

I raise my eyebrows. "I've never heard that superstition."

"It's a fay thing," he says.

"Fey don't have weddings," I point out.

"Fine," he says. "It's my superstition. Starting now. But do you really want to risk it? It seems like we need all the good fortune we can scavenge."

Despite the world falling to pieces around us, I take hold of his hand and let him lead me to the middle of the dance floor.

"You might have to help me out here," he murmurs, placing a hand low on my hip. "I don't know any of these mainland dances."

"Well, for starters," I say, moving his hand up a few inches so it is on my waist, just like a lifetime ago when we danced in front of a bonfire. "And you're quite lucky it's only a dievité and not a clommende, or you would have gotten positively trampled in the commotion."

"Don't look so disappointed, Shalott. The night is young and there is plenty of time for me to get trampled during the next dance."

We begin to move together and he carefully follows my steps, one step back, two to the left, a quick twirl under his arm. His eyes are stuck on his feet, so I take the opportunity to look him over—the half-moon shadows beneath his green eyes, the dark stubble along his jawline, the tension he holds in his mouth. Beneath the gilded veneer of sarcasm and stoicism, he's as anxious as I am.

"You don't have to do that," I say.

"Am I not doing it right?" he asks, looking up from his feet, perplexed. "The steps are complicated—"

"You don't have to keep me distracted," I clarify.

His mouth bows into a smile, but not a true one. When Lancelot smiles fully, it's a blinding thing. This one is about as bright as a dying candle in a sunlit room.

"Did it ever occur to you that I'm not trying to distract just you? It's been a bad day for all of us," he says, his gaze trailing to Morgana again. "I wish I could do something that would fix it all."

The words make my heart lurch. "Me too," I tell him. "But I don't think there's anything to do."

He looks at me, and in that instant of distraction, he stumbles, tripping over my foot and grabbing my elbow. It's all I can do to keep us both upright.

"Sorry," he says, his cheeks reddening.

It's strange to see him like this, so out of his depth. He is always poised and confident, as graceful in the middle of a duel as he is walking down a hallway. Now, though, he is unsure, as clumsy as a colt taking its first steps across fracturing ice.

"It's alright," I say, looking around the room. No one is watching us. Most eyes are on Arthur and Gwen as they do their own twirls across the dance floor. The only pair of eyes I meet are Morgana's, but as soon as I do, she glances away and turns to the man standing beside her, whispering something low in his ear.

He looks up, and when his eyes meet mine, the earth shifts beneath my feet and it's my turn to stumble. Lancelot steadies me, but I'm barely aware of him. I can't take my eyes off the man—a stranger, but a stranger I know. A stranger I have seen.

*A young man will stand beside Morgana, dark-eyed and sullen, his face all hard angles, sharp enough to cut. Though he will look like he would bite someone for looking at him the wrong way, his hands will shake, his eyes anxiously darting around the scene. He won't reach for the sword, though desire for it will be clearly etched into his expression.*

Accolon. That was what Nimue called him. Just a boy in Lyonesse, a second cousin of Gwen's, hungry but powerless. Nothing to worry about, she said. But I have seen him with Morgana, I have seen what they are capable of when they stand side by side, determined to kill Arthur.

*"Just this one thing, Accolon," she will tell him, her voice weaving around him like a spell, though there is no magic in the air. "Then I'll take you to Avalon, just as I promised, and we can be together always."*

*She will paint a dream he will want so desperately to come true, no matter what he will have to do to get there.*

*"Always," he will repeat, his voice reverent. He will take the sword from her, holding it aloft so the midday sun glints off the blade. It will look wrong in his hands.*

No.

I don't realize I've said the word out loud until Lancelot looks at me, brow furrowed.

"Did I do something wrong—"

"No," I say, tearing my gaze away from Accolon. I open my mouth, then close it again. I wish I could tell him what I've seen. He said himself that it was a heavy burden, and now more than ever I want to share it. But I can't, so instead all I can do is laugh. The sound erupts past my lips before I know what it is, and once it comes on there is no stopping it, not even when tears begin to stream down my cheeks and the people around us begin to stare.

Lancelot leads me away from the dance floor and out of the room, his hand on the small of my back, anchoring me. People stare as we pass, and distantly, I know I'm making a scene, but it doesn't matter. What does matter, truly, in the face of fate?

When we step into the empty corridor outside the banquet hall, Lancelot leans back against the rough stone wall, leveling his gaze on me and waiting. Waiting for me to stop laughing hysterically, but he'll be waiting awhile yet. The laughter shows no signs of dying down, and every time I think I'm starting to get hold of myself, the laughter claws its way around me and starts anew.

"What's wrong with her?" a voice asks, and I turn to see Morgana slipping through the door, closing it firmly behind her. She's alone now, with no sign of the sullen boy from earlier. Accolon.

The sight of her sobers me instantly, and I straighten up, steadying myself against the wall.

"Nothing," I say quickly. Too quickly.

Morgana narrows her eyes and opens her mouth to speak, but before she can, Lancelot interrupts.

"No more fighting," he says, looking between us. "It's been a long day—a long fortnight, in fact. We'll face what we have to tomorrow, but let's call a cease-fire tonight."

Morgana closes her mouth and glances away, crossing her arms over her chest.

"Who was he?" I ask her after a moment. "The man you were talking to? The one with the dark hair."

She blinks at me. Whatever she was expecting me to say, it wasn't that.

"Sir Accolon," she says. "Gwen's second cousin."

It's no more than Nimue already told me, but the unease in my stomach only grows.

*Stay away from him*, I want to tell her, but I hold my tongue. Only trouble would come from that, and Lancelot is right—tonight should not be spent fighting.

Instead, I nod my head.

"I am sorry for everything," I tell her. "I'm sorry it came to this. I'm sorry about binding your powers. But it will be reversible."

Morgana looks at me for a moment, her expression inscrutable. She hesitates. "I do understand, you know," she says finally. "I understand the why of it. It's a brilliant move to make."

"You were brilliant too," I point out. "What you were capable of . . . the power you possess. You saved us. Arthur knows it, too, but . . ."

"He's soft," Morgana supplies. "It isn't a bad thing. It's one of the things I love about him. But that kind of softness can only survive if it's surrounded by thorns. I was those thorns; now you'll have to do that."

"You will still be thorny, magic or no," I say, but Morgana doesn't look so sure.

"I don't know who I am without my magic," she says after a moment. "It's always been the thing that defined me—first in Camelot as a curse, then on Avalon as a gift. It's as much a part of me as my heartbeat. The thought of living without it . . . I don't know how to do that."

"We'll figure it out, then," I say. "Together. And one day, maybe you won't be angry anymore." The words almost sound true, as if I can make them so if I say them enough times.

"I'm not angry, not really," Morgana says, shrugging, but I see the truth in her eyes. The anger might be only simmering now, but if we don't kill it, it will boil over.

"You are," I say, before taking a deep breath. "And I've Seen what that anger will do to us, to the world."

Morgana doesn't look surprised by the revelation. Maybe a part of her has already felt it take root, felt it begin to fester. I think about what she said to Arthur earlier. *I have spent my life in your shadow.* I never saw that resentment brewing, but maybe I was so busy looking for the big break on the horizon that I ignored all the minuscule tensions that led up to it, that made it easy.

She looks at me, pursing her lips, and in her eyes I see some small hope, some part of her not yet lost, some part that can maybe—maybe—find her way back to us. If not now, then someday. Hopefully before it's too late.

"Meet us in the courtyard," I say to Morgana. "Oh, and see if you can steal a bottle of wine. Or three."

MY FIRST MONTHS on Avalon passed like breaths. I inhaled days scrying in the cave with Nimue and exhaled afternoons and evenings exploring Avalon with Morgana, Arthur, Guinevere, and sometimes Lancelot. The field of thorns between him and me didn't soften, but for everyone else's sake, we tried to avoid fighting—and therefore spoke to each other as little as possible. It was easy enough, when it was the five of us.

I began to grow accustomed to the fey as well, though I still am not sure when or how that happened. One day I was forcing myself not to stare at them, and the next I managed an entire conversation about the weather with a woman before noticing her moth wings or the antennas protruding from her forehead. The fey who dominated the horror stories I heard as a child slowly receded from my memory, replaced with the fey I saw every day, who laughed with their friends and ate the same food I did and had families they loved.

I thought that if the people back in Albion could understand that the fey were more like them than not, maybe there wouldn't have had to be so much bloodshed. But perhaps that was naive. Perhaps we would always see differences before similarities. Perhaps we would always look for reasons to fight instead of reasons to coexist.

I could only measure passing time in the waxing and waning of the moon, in the bonfire that would take place every time the moon hung round and full in the sky.

At first, we were all too young to attend. We would have to stay up in our rooms, listening to the revelry and imagining what it was like. But after we turned sixteen one by one—first Morgana, then Lancelot, then Guinevere, with Arthur and me coming last only a few months apart.

I lost count of how many bonfires I attended over the years that followed, but that first was always my favorite because it still felt forbidden, in a way. It shone with a kind of illicit novelty. Attending felt like we were getting away with something.

Gwen smuggled a bottle of wine out of the cellar below the great hall, but back then even the sight of it made me nervous. I half expected Nimue to sweep out of nowhere with disappointed eyes and snatch it away from us, sending us back to our beds with a click of her tongue.

When Morgana passed me the bottle, I very nearly passed it on to Guinevere without taking a sip, but a daring light had been cast over the evening. Refusing seemed childish, and as one of the youngest, I always felt like too much of a child anyway. So I lifted the bottle to my lips and took a gulp.

I'd had wine before, but only tiny, ladylike sips from delicate crystal glasses at banquets when toasts were called for. This was not that sort of wine.

It burned down my throat and made me cough violently until Morgana gave me a none-too-gentle thud on the back. Lancelot roared with laughter that made my cheeks grow warm.

"It's strong stuff," Guinevere told me with a laugh of her own, though hers wasn't mocking. "You should have seen Lancelot the first time he had it—he actually spit it out all over the girl he was trying so hard to impress," she added with a sharp but charmingly dimpled grin at him.

Lancelot glowered at that, but I smiled my thanks, passing her the bottle of wine.

"It's stronger than Camelot wine," I said, shaking my head.

Morgana nodded, turning her gaze out to the horizon, where the last sliver of the setting sun hovered just over the shimmering sea. "Everything is stronger here," she said. "It's like Avalon is the rest of the world, distilled."

"More and more, it feels like Camelot was a shadow world, painted all in muted grays. Like I was sleepwalking until I came here, but now I'm awake."

Morgana looked at me thoughtfully.

"Do you ever miss it?" she asked me.

I didn't know how to answer that. The truth was a complicated beast, too messy and sticky to begin to give voice to. *Of course I don't miss it*, I wanted to say, but the words tasted like ash, like the lie they were.

"I miss my mother," I said, another sliver of truth that had shades of lies to it as well, because more and more I didn't miss her at all. "And the roasted pheasant."

"Maiden, Mother, and Crone, I forgot all about the pheasant," Morgana said with a laugh. "That's a fair point—I do miss the pheasant, but don't tell anyone I said so. I heard that when you offend the cooks here, you wind up with food that turns to dirt in your mouth."

"What *is* pheasant?" Lancelot asked, frowning.

"It's a bird," I said, taking pleasure in the fact that for once, I knew something he didn't. "Have you never had pheasant?"

"They aren't native here," Morgana said. "But they're like . . ." She trailed off. "Do you know what they look like?" she asked me.

I frowned. "No, actually. I've only had them when they've already been plucked and cooked. Like a chicken, maybe?"

"Well, we have plenty of chickens here," Guinevere pointed out, taking another swig of wine. "I don't see what the fuss is about."

"It's different, though," I said, trying to put it into words. "It tastes different. Better."

But I couldn't say quite how. It had been a little over three years since I came to Avalon, and I realized I'd forgotten not just what pheasant tasted like but other things as well. The way the air smelled in our tower. The sound of an orchestra's crescendo echoing in the great hall. Even the shape of my mother's face.

Before I could think too hard about it, though, Morgana stood. "Come on, the bonfire will be starting soon and it's a bit of a trek," she said, offering one hand to me and one to Guinevere. She pulled us both to our feet before starting into the woods at a run, still hand in hand with Gwen and me.

"It's not a race, Morgana," Arthur called after her, but he sounded amused.

Morgana laughed, the sound echoing through the woods, scaring a flock of birds and sending them flying out from the trees. "You only say that because you're losing," she said.

The thunder of footsteps behind us picked up until Lancelot and Arthur were right beside us.

Suddenly, the world was only big enough for the five of us. The stars flickering into sight shone only on us, the air was only ours to breathe. There was no Albion lingering on the outskirts of our minds, waiting to draw us back to her, there was no Nimue watching with wary and worried eyes, there was no Cave of Prophecies with our destinies scrawled on its walls.

There was only us, only laughter, only a hazy world full of nothing but golden possibilities.

I wish I could have found a way to bottle that night up, to live in it for an eternity. I wish there were a way to get it back now, when it feels like everything is fraying apart in my hands.

But maybe this will be the next best thing.

MORGANA AND LANCELOT worked quickly while I went to invite Gwen and Arthur. The courtyard has been utterly transformed, a small fire now burning in the center and a large, thick sheet of canvas stretching overhead to block out the light of the moon. A plaid blanket has been spread out over the damp ground, set with two sea-green bottles of wine.

It isn't anything like Avalon—there is no rhythmic crashing of waves, no magic making the air heavy and honey-scented, no crowd of fey twirling, no music working its way under your skin. It is, if anything, a pale imitation. But still, it brings a smile to my lips.

"It's perfect," I say.

"We were lucky with the tarp," Lancelot says with a wry smile. "Apparently, there are times when even the Lyonessians tire of their moon-selves."

That doesn't surprise me. I'd seen the exhaustion in Gwen's eyes after her nights in her monstrous form—the others might be more accustomed to it, but it's difficult to imagine that it didn't take its toll on them as well.

"The wine's good too," Morgana says, holding a third bottle, uncorked. She takes a swig before wiping the remnant off on the back of her hand. "It's not Avalon wine, of course, but by mainland standards, it isn't bad. Better than the swill they serve in Camelot, certainly."

After half an hour and one bottle already gone among the three of us, Arthur appears in the archway that frames the entrance to the castle. I've seen Arthur draw attention to himself with no effort at all—seen people's eyes go to him first in a crowd. It's a kind of human magic I've never been able to understand. Now, though, he all but fades into the darkness of the castle hallway behind him. His hands are shoved in his pockets, shoulders stooped. When he meets my gaze, his smile is tense and hard at the edges.

"Mind if I join?" he asks.

I look over his shoulder for Gwen, but he's alone. My stomach tightens, but I can't bring myself to be surprised. The wounds between Morgana and Gwen are not from principles or morals; they are deep and personal, the kind that may never heal.

Still, I hoped, and now that hope deflates in my chest.

"You were invited," I remind him, pushing my disappointment aside.

Lancelot uncorks the second bottle with the edge of his sword before holding the bottle out to Arthur.

Relief falls over Arthur's expression like a velvet curtain, and he steps toward us, taking the bottle from Lancelot. It's only then that he looks at Morgana.

I don't know what I expect to pass between them—apologies and pleas for forgiveness are not in character for either of them—but all they do is eye each other for a moment. Arthur nods once, taking a swig of wine.

"What you did was reckless and immoral in more ways than I can name," he says, each word measured. Morgana flinches, opening her mouth, but before she can argue, Arthur holds his hand up to stop her. "But without your actions, none of us would be here tonight. And even Gwen . . . she would have never forgiven herself for it. None of us could have done what you did, and though I don't agree with it—though I can never condone it—I would be lying if I said that I wasn't grateful for it."

It's not an apology, but it's as close as he'll come. Morgana presses her lips together and glances away.

"I can't regret it," she says quietly. "But I hate that it's ruined us."

Arthur takes a step toward her. "It hasn't ruined us," he says. "You're my sister—"

"And you will never look at me the same way," she finishes, her voice breaking. "When you were little, even before we went to Avalon, you always looked at me with stars in your eyes, Arthur. Even when you got older, when people started to look to you for reassurance, you always looked to me. And whether you like it or not, that's ruined now."

I wait for Arthur to correct her, but he doesn't. "You're my sister," he says again. "You could burn down the world and I would still love you, whether I wanted to or not."

It's a sweet sentiment, but in it I can't help but hear my mother's prophecy—*she'll burn the world to ash and flame*. I can't help but think that someday soon, it won't be hyperbole.

Morgana opens her mouth to respond, then closes it again, her eyes traveling over Arthur's shoulder to the archway, where Guinevere stands in her twilight-blue wedding gown. She looks uncomfortable in it, tugging at the full skirt awkwardly.

"Late, as always," Lancelot says.

I shoot him a glare, but Guinevere surprises us all by laughing. It's not her full laugh, not as loud, but it's a laugh all the same. She looks shocked by it as well.

"You should try getting from one side of the castle to the other in this monstrosity," she says, shaking her head. "What did I miss?"

The question is directed at Lancelot and only him. She doesn't spare so much as a glance at Morgana, but Morgana is the one who responds.

"Just talking about me burning the world down," she says, though the words have a wryness to them, a familiarity I haven't felt among all of us since we left Avalon.

Even Guinevere isn't immune to it. Her forehead pleats as she nods her head, stepping more fully into the courtyard, the frilled hem of her gown dragging along the ground behind her like she's trailing the ocean with her.

"You could do that without magic," she says after a moment, a small smile playing on her lips. It's the closest she'll come to an apology, and Morgana seems to realize that as well.

"I don't suppose you want me to help you change into something more comfortable?" she asks. "While I still can?"

Gwen bites her lip before nodding. "If you don't mind."

Morgana waves a hand in Gwen's direction, and the air around her shimmers as her gown transforms into a simple cotton tunic and leather leggings. Gwen takes a full breath, reveling in the feeling of her lungs full, her torso unrestrained by the bone and laces of her corset.

"That's better," she says before considering her next words. I watch her fight against them, against herself, but eventually they come through. "Thank you."

In a past life, Morgana might have reveled in Gwen's gratitude, might have grown smug over it. She might have held it over her head, adding it to the tally between them. Now, though, she only nods.

"I'm sorry for your loss," she tells her—an apology not for her actions but for the outcome of them. It is the closest she will come. Gwen must know that as well.

"My father wasn't a good man," she says after a pensive moment. "He wasn't a good king, either, beloved as he might have been by the court he gave free rein to. I left for Avalon when I was so young—he was still a shining idol to me, a god who could never do anything wrong. When I returned, it was difficult not to feel the same way, to see him through a child's eyes. But I was starting to, even before you came. It was why I wanted you to stay away—so you wouldn't see it. So you wouldn't see me."

"No one thinks less of you because of your blood," Arthur says. "Even when you changed, Gwen, you were still you at heart."

She shakes her head. "Not that. Not *just* that. I thought you would think badly of me for my father's actions, for the fact that I didn't stop him."

Gwen looks at Morgana, her eyes level and somber, shining in the light of the fire with tears that she won't cry, not even now, when she's only among friends.

"He was my father, and I loved him, and for that I can't forgive what you did," she says. "But I also know that when the goddess of death comes to collect her debt, she will not hold his murder against you."

THE NIGHT DWINDLES on as the fire burns out and the five of us find familiar conversations, about Albion and Nimue and the other fey, about Camelot and what Gwen can expect. It is not like those nights we spent on

Avalon's shores, talking together with ease and laughter. Sometimes the words still strain. Sometimes anger leaks in. The cast of the night before hangs over us always.

It is something, though. It is a step closer to who we were once, and even if we are never those people again, maybe there is a kind of peace in this.

*I wish I could do something that would fix it all*, Lancelot said.

But some things can't be fixed, they can't be glued back together as they were. Sometimes, all you can do is find the beauty in the broken. All you can do is figure out how to put the pieces together as best you can, to make something new out of them.

# 36

WE LEAVE AT sunrise but still have to stop for the night just past the
Shalott border, in a clearing in the woods. No one's happy about it,
but it can't be avoided. As everyone sets up camp, I can see Morgana's fingers
itching with magic, anxious to use it to help, but I take hold of her hand to
stop her.

Gwen stands on her other side, just as powerless. She might not be of any
use with the tents, but the fire is a living thing, and she could get one started
in an instant. She could hunt faster and more efficiently than those tasked
with that as well, lure deer to her and end their lives as humanely as possible.

We all know this, and Arthur and Lancelot must as well, but we all stay
quiet. We've already planted the rumors among the men, with Gawain's help,
sowing the story of Morgana's great illusion, her true powerlessness. It should
surprise me how quickly it's caught on, how ready these men are to believe
the transparent lie over the truth they saw with their own eyes, but it doesn't.
It's easier for them to believe Morgana is docile, so of course they don't question it.

And as for Gwen, well, it's easier for them to believe their future queen is
only a pretty girl, saved from a monstrous curse by their noble prince. They
don't look too closely at her, except in appreciation.

And so we stand together, watching Gareth try to light the fire with only clumsy fingers and flint. Every time he fails, Gwen's hands twitch at her sides. Finally, she balls them into fists and turns away from the scene.

"This is my life now, I suppose," she says, each syllable enunciated by bitterness.

"Our lives," Morgana corrects. "I think I'm almost looking forward to binding my power when we get to the castle. Somehow, this is even more torturous—being able to use magic but stopping myself."

"It won't be so bad," I say, but the words come out hollow. They give no indication, but I know that part of them hates me for saying it. After all, what do I know? My power is passive and nonintrusive. No one will ever take that away from me.

*But they have before*, a voice whispers, and I think about my mother and her potion. I understand better than I'd like to, which is why I hold my tongue now and allow them their bitter fury.

"Morgana once referred to Camelot as *a gem-encrusted wasteland devoid of intellectual stimulation*," Gwen points out.

"I meant it," Morgana says.

"It isn't so bad anymore," I say.

"It's worse," Morgana cuts in. "Somehow, it's worse. Maybe because I've seen beyond it. You can't argue that, Elaine. Not to us."

My mouth tightens, but she's right. I can't argue it. So I don't.

"Gem-encrusted wasteland it may be, but it will be *your* gem-encrusted wasteland, Gwen, and when that crown is on your head, we can make real change, just as we planned. Get Arthur on the throne, secure him there, bring magic back, and unbind Morgana's powers. As soon as we can."

Gwen shakes her head. "You know it won't be that easy," she says. "Their reaction to Morgana was proof enough of that. Nimue prepared us for a lot of things, but she never prepared us for the truth about men—they see you as either something fearsome to be cowed or something docile to be shielded, but either way, they don't respect us."

"Not all men," I point out. "Arthur and Lancelot respect us. And you haven't spoken with Gawain, but he's always been respectful."

Morgana scoffs, but Gwen speaks first.

"Not all men, fine, but enough of them. Enough to drown out the few good ones. More than enough to ruin the whole damned world."

I DON'T HEAR EXACTLY what Sir Lamorak says over dinner—only Morgana's name underscored with venom and distaste, only the laughter of the men around him. Cruel laughter, ugly laughter, the kind that sets my teeth on edge. And I don't need to hear exactly what was said to know the gist of it, to know its intent.

I feel myself go tense. Morgana and Gwen must hear it, too, but they don't acknowledge it, both of them keeping their eyes on their food. The only sign of Morgana's displeasure is the narrowing of her nostrils, the tightening of her shoulders.

A defense rises up in my throat, but Gwen's hand on my arm stops me, reminds me of what's at stake. Her other hand goes to rest on Morgana's, an instinctual gesture that goes beyond their differences and their arguments. It is something deeper, an acknowledgment that no matter what happened, when it comes to this, they are together.

Arthur, however, doesn't have to restrain himself. His spine goes ramrod straight as he turns toward the knight, goblet of water halfway to his lips. He pauses, lowering it.

"Say that again, Lamorak," he says, the words a dangerous dare.

Lamorak glances around the fire, his smile uncertain. "It was a joke, Your Highness," he says.

"A joke about my sister," he says. "Whose clever trick saved your life. So why don't you repeat it?"

"Arthur," I say, a warning, but he ignores me, keeping his gaze steady on Lamorak.

"It was nothing, truly," Lamorak insists. His eyes dart to Morgana briefly, before settling again on Arthur. "I only said that perhaps Lady Morgana would have been happier in Lyonesse."

"That wasn't all," Gawain says, his voice soft but with a hard edge to it. "Say the rest. You seemed to think yourself clever enough, why not repeat it now?"

Lamorak's mouth settles into a thin, firm line, but he doesn't back down from the challenge. "I said I thought she would have fit in well there, I've heard it said all their women have thorns between their legs."

The words are barely out of Lamorak's mouth before Arthur is lunging toward him, but Lancelot gets there first, his fist colliding with Lamorak's jaw so hard that a sharp crack echoes throughout the clearing, followed by a cry of pain. The other men erupt into gasps and murmurs, and Arthur takes the moment of distraction to gather himself, sealing away his raw emotions beneath the veneer of a future king.

"There's no need for violence," he says, though I almost think he smiles at Lancelot as he says it. "But, Sir Lamorak, you have now insulted both my sister and my wife, your future queen, and I will have an apology from you."

"But, Your Highness," Sir Galahad interrupts. "You saw with your own eyes—"

"I saw a clever trick," he says. "I saw my very clever sister take advantage of the clouds covering the moon, saw her use her reputation as a sorceress to hold a lit candle in her hands and pretend it was the moon to cow the Lyonessians into a surrender. Without her ploy, we would not be here, drinking wine and making jokes, and I trust that when you tell the story of what happened in Lyonesse, you will remember that part."

Lamorak lets out another cry of pain, touching his bleeding jaw delicately. "I think it's broken," he cries out, looking at Lancelot in disbelief before turning to Arthur for help. "He broke my jaw."

Arthur's eyes immediately go to Gwen and Morgana, ready to ask for their help healing it before he remembers himself.

"Yes, well, perhaps it will serve as a reminder," he says.

He gets to his feet, setting aside his mostly full plate. "I think I'll head to bed, and I suggest the rest of you do the same—tomorrow will be a long day."

After he leaves, the rest of the camp hastens to clean up and help Lamorak bandage his jaw, but in the chaos, I see Lancelot slip into the woods and I follow him, running to catch up.

"Let me see it," I say when I fall into step beside him.

He pauses, holding up his hand between us, though he won't look at me. His green-gold eyes almost seem to glow in the moonlight, a rolling thunderstorm lurking behind them.

"You're going to tell me it was foolish," he says, the edges of the words hard.

I look at his hand, the knuckles red and slick, but—upon further inspection—not with his own blood.

"It would have been more foolish if Arthur had done it," I say. "Or if Gwen or Morgana had been provoked to use their magic. Or me, for that matter, I wouldn't have minded a shot at him. All of us wanted to do it, Lance. But you were the only one who could get away with it. So I would say that it was impulsive and violent, yes. But I wouldn't call it foolish."

We walk together until we find a stream, and I help him wash his hand, ensuring there are no cuts or scrapes or breaks that will need tending to, but there is nothing but smooth gold skin. Whether it's fay blood or just dumb luck, he's entirely unharmed.

"If Morgana could have," he says, sitting down beside the stream to roll up his pant legs above his knees, "she would have done far worse. Made his hair fall out, maybe."

"Transfigured his shirt into a swarm of bees," I add with a smile.

He laughs. "Set his pants on fire," he counters.

That gives me pause. I clasp my hands in front of me tightly. "Actually, the first time I met Morgana, she set a whole room on fire to spite her sister," I tell him. "It was the first magic I'd seen up close. I remember thinking, *How extraordinary it must be, to bend the world to your will like that.* It didn't occur to me then how the world would snap back, how it would punish her for it. All I saw was the glamour and the glory. All I wanted was to be just like her."

Lancelot eases his way into the stream. The water comes up only to his calves.

"It's funny you say that," he says after a moment. "I often thought she felt the same way about you."

"Me?" I repeat, unable to hold back a laugh. The idea of it is ridiculous—a great oak tree doesn't idolize its shadow.

Lancelot shrugs. "Yes, you. Especially after we left Avalon—she could force her way through any situation—Lyonesse is proof enough of that—but she's like a cannonball, destroying everything in her path. Normally, I don't think that bothers her. In Avalon, she got away with it easily enough, but on the mainland . . . I think she envies you your ability to maneuver through difficult situations like a dagger, precise and sharp. You both solve problems in your own ways, you're both frighteningly good at it. It's just that you tend to leave less collateral damage in the process."

I shake my head. "Maybe you just can't see all of my collateral damage yet," I say, thinking of the futures, how they are narrowing down now, how paths are being chosen.

I shake my head again, pushing the thought from my mind, but Lancelot watches me as if he can read my thoughts.

"I've been doing some asking around, with the men your father sent," he says slowly. "Some of them are old enough to have fought in the Fay War with my father."

I blink, trying to follow the change in subject. "And?" I ask. "Did you find anything?"

He nods once. "A name. A soldier lost in a shipwreck, only to return home again some months later. The timing lines up. Banwick."

A memory slides into place. "Lord Banwick," I say. "I remember. He was a friend of my father's. His son, Ector, was friends with Lavaine . . ." I trail off, realizing what Lancelot must have already put together. "Ector's two years older than you are."

Lancelot nods. "He had a wife when he met my mother," he says. "And a baby. He went back to them. It was a choice."

He says the words impassively, reporting simple facts, but I see the emotion flickering beneath the surface. I want to reach out to him, but instead I wrap my arms tighter around myself.

"I'm sorry," I tell him.

He shrugs. "We both knew there was a good chance it would end like this," he says. "But I had to know."

I swallow. "And now that you do?" I ask.

"I can't say that it feels good," he says, and I can tell he's choosing his words carefully. "But it does feel finished. And I think that's enough."

I don't know what to say to that. I keep thinking about how it will feel for me one day, when the future has become the past. Will it be enough, for it to simply be finished, for better or worse?

"Well?" Lancelot says, drawing me out of my thoughts. He takes a step deeper into the stream so the water rushes up to his knees, reaching his rolled-up pants. "Are you going to come in or not?"

I laugh, tucking my arms tighter around myself. "It's freezing," I point out. "And *I* had the good sense not to get all blood soaked, so what's the point?"

He shrugs, a familiar smile curling at his lips. "Actually, the water is warm—there must be a hot spring upstream. See?" Without warning, he splashes me, sending a wave of water that I don't quite manage to step back quickly enough to miss.

"Hey!" I say, shooting him a glare. But he's right—the water seeps through the wool of my dress, warm against my skin. Still, I hold my ground. "I don't feel like it," I tell him.

He eyes me for a moment. "You don't think . . ." he says, trailing off. "You don't think you'll drown?"

He knows all about my drowning visions. Even after I learned to channel my Sight through the loom, my drowning dreams persisted. He would be there sometimes, when I woke up thrashing and panicked, feeling like I couldn't breathe. He always held me and stroked my hair until I calmed down.

He didn't press me for details at first, but eventually I told him about the vision, as much as I dared. He tried to help, offered to teach me how to swim, but I refused. I didn't know how to explain that, in my vision, I didn't even try to swim, how it wouldn't make a difference if I could.

I hesitate now. "No," I say, biting my lip. "I don't think I will. But . . . well, I can never be sure, can I? And I've done so much to see Arthur take that throne. I'll be damned if I'm going to die before I get to see him sit in it. At this point, close as we are, I'm not about to take any chances."

He considers this, stepping back to the center of the river where it's the deepest, the water now all the way up to his waist.

"Your pants are soaked now," I tell him.

He waves away my concern. "Morgana can—" he says, before catching himself, his smile growing rueful. "Ah. I keep forgetting."

"I know," I say. "It's a hard habit to break."

He steps back to the edge of the river, until he stands on its bank, only a foot away from me, holding a hand out.

"Come on," he says, with a smile full of mischief, the same one he always wore during bonfire nights on Avalon, the same one that never fails to set my stomach aflutter. "I won't let you drown. I swear to the Maiden, Mother, and Crone."

I regret it the second I pull my dress over my head and drop it on the dry grass, leaving me in only a thin cotton shift that ends at my knees. He's seen me in far less—seen me in nothing at all—but the way his eyes darken and his mouth goes slack feels like liquor rushing through my veins. It makes me bolder. I take his hand and let him draw me into the rushing river until we are standing together in the deepest part.

"You see?" he says with a grin. "I've got you. You aren't drowning on my watch, Shalott."

It is a difficult thing, for an oracle to trust. I have seen Lancelot betray me a hundred different times, seen him let me drown, if not literally then figuratively at least. I have seen us rot on the vine, seen us poisoned, seen us rip each other to shreds. Trusting him isn't only foolish, it's masochistic. It is stepping into a riptide and hoping that it doesn't drag me under.

And yet . . . I do trust him. The woman I am now trusts who he is. Not who he has been, not who he will be, but him in this moment. And despite everything, that feels like enough.

"In Camelot," I say, my voice suddenly dry, "you asked me to marry you. Do you remember?"

"Of course," he says, wincing. "A worse proposal has never been made—even Arthur and Gwen managed it better than I did, and she still had her father's blood on her dress."

I laugh, taking a step closer to him so that we are only an inch apart. "Maybe so, but I find I've changed my mind. If the offer still stands."

It is not an easy thing, to surprise Lancelot, but I've done it. He stares at me, mouth agog.

"Why?" he manages to ask after a moment of floundering.

I shrug my shoulders. "Because you've never let me drown," I tell him. "I mean, not in water, but also not in myself. Not in futures, even when they begin to close in and smother me. Not in hopelessness, whenever that begins to creep in. You have never let me drown, and I don't believe you ever will."

*No matter what I've seen*, I add silently.

He kisses me then, warm water rushing around us, and his arms secure around me. And even though the rest of the world feels wrong, even though Lyonesse still haunts me, even though I am already haunted by the prospect of binding Morgana's magic and what that might lead to—this here and now is right. And that feels like enough.

I WILL BE LED through the halls by a guard, through the royal wing, lined with paintings of the royal family, of Arthur as a child, standing with his mother and father, of King Uther at his coronation. There are no pictures of Morgana, but there are others that I haven't seen before—Arthur, wearing his father's crown and sitting on his father's throne. A wedding portrait of him standing with Guinevere. In her white lace dress and gold crown she is effulgent, but her eyes are unsure, an animal in the seconds before the trap is sprung.

The guard will push open the door to the library, ushering me inside. As I pass, I will see something in his eyes that I've never seen directed at me before: fear. It's the same way I've seen people look at Morgana. This man will be afraid of me.

The door will close firmly, and it will take my eyes a moment to adjust to the dim lighting.

"Elaine," a voice will say, unmistakably Arthur's. Not his public voice, booming and clear, but not quite the soft voice he uses when only with friends either. Now, there will be a rawness to his voice, a sleepless haggardness that breaks something deep in my chest.

He will be sitting in one of the high-backed chairs by the fire, the body of a bejeweled golden goblet as tall as my forearm cradled in his hand. "Come, sit."

He will be older, but not by much. A year, maybe two, still with the same boyish roundness to his face. There will be violet circles under his eyes and stubble covering his jaw that age him further, and not in a pleasant way. Like this, he certainly won't look like a king, though his shoulders will be straight and square, and his head will still be held high, even though he will be angry and brooding and deep in his cups.

Something will be wrong. Not only with Arthur, but with me as well— with the world itself; it will seem darker, swathed in gray chiffon. My own mind will feel dull and far away, not quite present. Not quite awake. It will be like moving through a fog.

Still, when I come sit down in the chair across from him, Arthur will reach his free hand out to take mine, clutching it so hard in his that his knuckles turn white. And I will return the grip just as tightly. We will cling to each other like shipwrecked sailors in a storm. We will be all we have left.

"I'm sorry for dragging you over here at this time of night. I know this isn't easy on you either." It will be his diplomatic voice, the one he uses when addressing a crowd or his knights before a battle. The voice that charms subjects and negotiates treaties, not one that he uses when it is only the two of us.

My throat will feel too tight to form words. Arthur will realize this because without being asked he will pass me his goblet of wine.

A lifetime ago, we drank wine together on Avalon's beach, from far less ornate goblets, both of us by turns giddy and melancholy, in love with people we thought would never love us back. We will have laughed about that at my wedding, I will remember, both of us triumphant and happy and in love. Even for me, this future felt unfathomable.

But maybe we had the right of it back on Avalon. Maybe they never did love us back. Maybe it was all cursed from the very start. We should have known, should have let it be and walked away when we still could. After all, wine and dancing will not be enough to mend our broken hearts this time.

"Did you know?" he will ask me as I take a tight-lipped swig. His voice will be casual, but there will be an edge as well. He will be looking for someone to blame. Even with Gwen in the dungeon and Lancelot banished from Camelot, he will hunger for something more, for something to ease his pain.

I will hold his gaze, taking a longer drink before passing the goblet back to him. "It was a possibility," I will say, choosing my words carefully. "There are many possibilities, Arthur. But Gwen and Lancelot—there was a future where you fell off a cliff after being set upon by dozens of butterflies, and even *that* seemed more likely than the two of them . . ."

My voice will break, and Arthur's expression will soften. "I'm sorry. I didn't ask you here to talk about your visions," he will say, shaking his head. "When we left Avalon, I thought that I was surrounded by people I could trust with my life. It turns out I was wrong in every respect, except for you. You are the only person I can trust, El."

I will take a breath, steadying myself in a way I've never had to with Arthur before. "Are we speaking now as friends, or are you my king and I your oracle?" I will ask tentatively.

"Friends," he will answer without hesitation. "I haven't . . . I haven't wanted to see anyone at court since it happened. The way they all look at me . . ." He will trail off and shake his head. "Friends," he will repeat, more emphatically.

"Morgana once told me to guard my heart with iron and steel, above all else. She said if a person has your heart, they have all of you, and love is never a steady force. It is always changing."

He will laugh, the sound sharp and bitter, but beneath that there will be something else, a hint of fondness. "That sounds like her, doesn't it?"

Despite myself, a laugh will burble up in my throat. "It was advice I never truly knew how to take," I will say, holding my hand out for the goblet again. He will give it to me. "Gwen was always better at it. She tried for so long to resist giving you her heart."

He will scoff at that. "I never had Gwen's heart," he will say. "I don't think she even has one to give."

For a few seconds, I won't say anything. If Morgana were here . . . if Gwen were here . . . if Lancelot were here . . . but no else will be here now. No one will be left to tell him the truth, no one will be left to confront him. No one will be left who dares speak to their king that way. There will only be me. So I will dare.

"Gwen loved you as much as she could."

His expression will turn stormy. "She told me I expected too much of her," he will say, his own voice breaking. "But what did I ask for that was so difficult to give, Elaine? Love? Faithfulness? Loyalty?"

"And what of your faithfulness, Arthur? Your loyalty?" I will ask, so quietly the crackle of the dying fire will threaten to drown out my words.

He will hear them, though. With a strangled cry, he will throw the goblet into the fire, causing it to flare up. I won't jump; I won't flinch. I will keep my eyes level on him until he finally looks away. The door will open, and the guard will look in questioningly, but Arthur will impatiently wave him away.

"I never would have if she hadn't pushed me away," he will say when the door closes once more. "She was never herself after we came to Camelot, after we left Avalon even."

"None of us were the same," I will say.

I will reach forward and take his hand in mine. It will shake, but it slows in my grip. He will turn his head to look at me, blue eyes glowing in the dim light. Bringing my hand to his lips, he will brush a kiss over my knuckles, his stubble scratching me. It will hardly be an intimate gesture, but it will still bring tears forth all over again. I will feel them sliding down my cheeks. I will be surprised I have any left after the past few days.

"Do you remember that night on the beach on Avalon, when you danced with me to try to cheer me up? You wore that green dress."

"I remember," I will say, a smile struggling to break through.

"I thought for a moment that night that I might kiss you. I wanted to. A real kiss, not like the first one. Because I wanted to, not just to prove something."

"Arthur—" I will start, but he will interrupt.

"No, I did. I thought: *I could fall in love with her. She's lovely and kind, and talking with her always makes me smile.* And I wanted to kiss you. What a lot of trouble that would have saved us. We would have made a better match, Elaine. We never would have broken each other like this."

"We wouldn't have broken each other," I will agree, squeezing his hand. "But, Arthur, we wouldn't have made each other great either. Whatever you will say about Gwen—and I'm sure you have said a great many things these past days—she made you a better ruler, even a better person. You did the same for her."

He will see where I'm going, and he will pull back from me. "El . . ."

"Let her go, Arthur," I will say. "This execution business—you can't truly mean to kill her—"

"What she did was treason," he will say, his voice sharpening. "The punishment for treason is death. Lancelot would be facing the same if he hadn't run like a coward."

"You can't mean to kill her, though. It's *Gwen*."

"She doesn't deserve your loyalty."

"She doesn't deserve to die either," I will say. "And we both know that if you truly wanted Lancelot found, he would have been by now."

Arthur won't say anything for a moment, his gaze focused on the dying fire. "Granting her clemency would be a sign of weakness," he will say slowly. "They are already calling me weak, you know. How weak I must be to be made a cuckold by my own knight. I can't have that, Elaine. Rebellion is already growing—if more families defect to Mordred's side, Camelot will fall. Gwen made the same choice about me once, if you remember. In Lyonesse, she would have let me die to protect her country."

"But that's not you, Arthur," I will say. "You might not be able to grant her clemency, but we both know Gwen, don't we? If she were to escape the dungeon, none of your men would be able to find her again. Your hands would be clean, your authority would hold."

His face will contort into a grimace. "I can't, Elaine."

"You won't have to," I will say. "Just let me handle it."

Still, he will hesitate.

"If you go through with this, Arthur, the decision will haunt you for the rest of your days. The guilt will drive you mad. You will hate yourself for it every minute of every day."

"Oh?" he will say. "Did you See that as well?"

He will be mocking me, but I will ignore it. "I don't have to See it," I will say. "I just know you. I know your heart. It is not made for this kind of cruelty, Arthur."

His eyes will find mine again, and after a moment, he will nod, his eyes dropping away to focus on the ground. "You have never led me astray, Elaine," he will say. "I trust you. Do what you will, but if she is caught in Albion, I will have no choice."

As I leave, I will hear Arthur call out behind me for more wine.

# 37

LANCELOT AND I tell no one of our engagement. I say it's because I want to talk to my father first, that I am his only daughter, and as Lancelot has no title, no land, that makes things trickier than they should be. It is the truth, but it is not the whole truth.

The vision lingers on the outskirts of my mind as we ride across the border and into Albion. It is an old vision, mostly, but more solid now, with references to Lyonesse.

*Lancelot and Gwen.*

It was true, what I said to Arthur—what I *will* say—though I'd seen visions of their affair and the aftermath, I have never seriously believed any of them. In all the years that I've known them, there has never been a hint of anything romantic between them, not even on Avalon, when Lancelot went through girls as often as he changed clothes.

They are too similar, I told myself. They looked at each other the same way Arthur and Morgana did, with love, but the familial kind. Anything else had seemed unfathomable.

And yet.

And yet that future seems to be fleshing out now, no longer tendrils of smoke but solid roots taking hold in my mind.

Why, though, is the question. Why now? Is it because of Lancelot's and my new engagement? No, that can't be it—there have been so many visions of life after that, in all different directions, some pleasant but most not.

I look up, searching for Gwen in the crowd of riders. She's a ways ahead, riding beside Arthur, her posture ramrod straight and her eyes set directly ahead.

*She was never herself after we came to Camelot*, Arthur said in my vision. I also remember the painting I'd passed in the hall, of what will be their wedding portrait. I remember the look in her eyes, that of a caged animal searching for escape.

Perhaps the cage will grow smaller and smaller. Perhaps she will find the only escape she can.

DO YOU THINK it will hurt?" Morgana asks as we cross into the woods around my father's castle later that afternoon.

She, Gwen, and I ride together, me in the middle and them on either side. For once, Gwen is the one slowing us down, her horse's gait awkward and a pleat of concentration between her brows as she struggles not to fall off the horse entirely. Every so often, she mutters a curse under her breath and tries to adjust herself, to get comfortable, but there is no help for it.

Gwen is not used to riding sidesaddle.

Of the three of us, I'm the only one with any breadth of experience at it, but Morgana managed to get the feel of it on our journey out. Gwen, however, is hopeless at it, and with every step her horse takes, she grows more frustrated.

"Will what hurt?" she asks, dragging her attention from her horse to Morgana. "Apart from my arse, that is," she adds, wincing. "Who decided this was more comfortable than the regular way?"

"I don't think it's meant to be about comfort," I say, shrugging my shoulders. "But it wouldn't do for ladies to go about straddling horses, now would it?"

Gwen rolls her eyes skyward. "Maiden, Mother, and Crone, save me from the obligation of modesty," she says.

"They won't," Morgana says. "They're the ones who sent us here."

Neither Gwen nor I know what to say to that, and after a second, Morgana shakes her head as if she can rid herself of the thought.

"I meant the binding," she says. "Do you think that will hurt?"

The mere mention of it sets me on edge, but there is no one to overhear. Gwen is moving so slowly that we've fallen behind the rest of our party. I can still hear them ahead of us, but that is only because they aren't making an effort to be quiet. Some of them have even taken to singing folk songs to pass the time.

"I don't know," I tell her, frowning. Morgana hasn't mentioned the binding since we left Lyonesse, and though it's been weighing heavily on my mind, I've been glad for her silence on it. It's almost felt like something I imagined, something we will not actually have to go through with.

"I've been good about keeping myself from using magic," she says after a second. "It hasn't been easy, but I've managed it. I could keep managing it."

"Morgana," Gwen says, and though I think she tries to soften her voice, there is still a hard edge to it.

"It just takes one slip," I say, before Gwen can make it worse. "And you know your sister—she will do whatever it takes to provoke it from you. And if word gets out before Arthur has had the chance to make a treaty with the fey and lift the ban on magic . . ." I trail off.

"You've spread pitch everywhere," Gwen continues. "And maybe we've managed to convince people that you haven't, that there's no pitch at all, only their imaginations. But all it will take is one spark, Morgana, and we will all go up in flames."

I don't think this is anything Morgana doesn't already know, but she needs to hear it all the same.

"I need a guarantee that you will lift it," she says after a moment.

"You have my word," Gwen says.

Morgana snorts. "Arthur had your word, too, didn't he? You still would have killed him if you could have."

Gwen doesn't retort. "What sort of security would you like?"

"You'll be taking something of mine," she says. "I'd like something of yours in turn."

I hold my breath, readying for another fight, but I think Gwen is as tired of fighting as I am because she doesn't argue. Instead she looks at Morgana with a single eyebrow raised.

"Very well. I won't insult you by assuming you don't have a suggestion for what that might be," Gwen says.

Morgana's smile is tight but there. "It'll be an even trade," she says. "I'm binding my magic, so you should bind yours as well."

"Morgana," I say, my voice a warning.

Gwen shakes her head, laughing. "My magic is practically inconsequential compared to yours," she says. "It's tied to my emotions, yes, but what is the worst that can happen? I get angry enough to cause a light rain? I'm incandescently happy, and bunnies and birds begin to follow me everywhere?"

"She's right," I say. "Gwen's magic isn't harmful. If anything, it's a good way of acquainting the people with the concept of it. Get their feet wet in lukewarm water instead of plunging them into the deep end of a freezing-cold lake."

"No, hear me out," Morgana says, holding up a hand. "If my use of magic will reflect back on Arthur, then so will hers, harmless or not."

"Yes, but I've never used my magic to threaten to destroy the world," Gwen says. "And I think I've given up enough, don't you? I left Lyonesse."

There it is, the bitterness already seeded deep within her, already taking root.

"I think that you're the one strong enough to take my magic," Morgana says, ignoring her question. "And I think you won't give it back willingly when the time comes."

Gwen opens her mouth to answer but quickly shuts it again.

"What is your plan then?" I ask Morgana. "You take Gwen's magic? Then there is no one to take yours."

"I take Gwen's magic," she says. "And then I give *you* both of our powers."

I pause, frowning. "Can you do that?" I ask.

Morgana shrugs her shoulders. "Theoretically," she says. "A bit like with the moon—I can take Gwen's powers and then, using both my physical magic and her nature magic, I should be able to instill my powers in you. It would be a mix of both, you see."

"So you want us to make you *more* powerful," Gwen says with a scoff.

"For a moment—only long enough to give both powers to Elaine," she says.

"And what would that do to me?" I ask, not because I have any intention of going along with this mad plan, but because I'm mildly curious.

"Again, this is theoretical," Morgana says with a sigh. "But *theoretically*, you wouldn't feel differently. Think of it as me placing our magic in a metal box and locking it with a key. Then giving you both the box and the key. You'll have the power to unlock the box anytime you like."

"And when I do?"

Again, Morgana shrugs. "I don't know, but I wouldn't recommend it. That much power, loose in someone who isn't used to it . . . it very well may consume you. When you unlock it, it should only be when it's time to give our powers back."

"You trust her more than you trust me," Gwen says, not sounding surprised, but a little hurt nonetheless.

"I killed your father, Gwen," Morgana says. "And you tried to kill my brother. Trust is more than a little broken between us at the moment."

Gwen doesn't argue with that, instead frowning ahead, her gaze focused on nothing in particular.

"No," I say, before she can respond. "It's unnecessary, Morgana, and I fear it will do more harm than—"

"Done," Gwen says, before I can finish. "Take it. It isn't as if I'll need it, is it? And fair is fair."

"Gwen!" I say.

She only fixes me with a cool look. "Careful, or we'll lock yours up too."

"Nimue would kill us," Morgana says, spurring her horse to walk faster, Gwen right beside her. "Elaine was always her favorite."

"That isn't true!" I say, struggling to keep up.

Gwen laughs, and as happy as I am to hear that sound, to see the two of them laughing together again, I wish it were under different circumstances. And I wish they weren't laughing at me.

"And what if I die before unlocking your powers?" I ask.

"Actually, if my theorizing is correct, your death would unleash our powers. So try not to tempt me to murder, will you?"

Gwen laughs again, and I scoff.

"This is a terrible idea," I tell both of them.

"Says the one of us not sacrificing anything," Gwen calls over her shoulder.

I have to bite my lip to keep from retorting. She's right, after all. They've both been forced from their homes now, and soon, they'll have their magic bound. I can't imagine how that will feel, and I'll never have to imagine it. No one will ever take my power from me.

"Besides, no one is going to die," Gwen says, shaking her head. "The two of you are so dramatic. We'll do both bindings tonight, when we're somewhere safe and sequestered at the castle."

A heavy silence falls over our trio at that, and I know both of their thoughts have traveled down paths mine cannot follow.

"Lancelot asked me to marry him," I blurt out before I can stop myself. "Well, maybe this time I asked him. But either way, we're betrothed."

For a moment, neither of them speaks, but after what feels like an eon, Morgana laughs.

"You owe me," she tells Gwen.

"That doesn't count!" Gwen protests. "We were on Avalon when we made that bet—where am I supposed to find fay wine in Albion?"

"I don't know, but a bet is a bet," Morgana says.

"You *bet* on me?" I ask, looking between them.

Gwen shrugs her shoulders. "You couldn't have made your vows on Avalon and helped me win?"

"How long has this bet been going on?" I ask.

Morgana and Gwen exchange a look. "Oh, two years now?" Morgana says. "It was only a matter of time, and we decided to make it interesting." She pauses and glances sideways at me. "And not that I'm not glad to win this bet, but why now, El? Before, you seemed to think . . . well, you had fears about the future. Did those . . . dissipate?"

She tries so hard to dance around saying exactly what she means, but for once I actually want to speak plainly.

"No," I say. "The visions I had of Lancelot and me breaking each other's hearts are still very much there, very much possibilities. But it was breaking my heart to keep my distance. I just figured that this way, at least we have a chance."

I try not to look at Gwen when I say it—I swear I do. I try not to think about the visions I've had of her and Lancelot, of the heartbreak that follows, strong enough to rupture an entire continent. But I don't quite manage it. Gwen must feel my eyes on her, and I suspect she knows me well enough to know there is something beneath the surface of my words. Part of me wants her to hear it, to know what I've seen and to promise me that it will never happen. But that won't help anything at all, so I push the thoughts aside.

"We'll marry before we leave Shalott, once my father gives his approval."

"You sound certain he will," Morgana says carefully. "Lancelot is a half-fay bastard—not exactly what most noblemen hope for in a son-in-law."

"I know," I say. "And I have a plan."

"Of course you do," Gwen says, shaking her head with a fond smile on her lips. "Elaine Astolat, Lady of Shalott, always has a plan."

MY FATHER GREETS us at the gate to the castle near midnight, his eyes tired but a smile on his face that broadens when I step into his embrace. My brothers were part of the first group to arrive, and now they stand with him, flanking him on either side.

When he holds me, his grip is strong and true, his hand secure on my back.

"One day," he says softly to me, "I hope I can begin to expect your return rather than merely hope for it."

I kiss his cheek and step back, making way for the others.

Arthur dismounts behind me and starts to bow before my father shakes his hand and clasps him firmly by the shoulder.

"You return to me triumphant," he says.

"Word travels very quickly indeed," Arthur says with a bashful smile.

"Word didn't travel at all," my father quips. "But seeing as how you're alive, it's easy to surmise."

Arthur's smile wavers, but he turns to help Gwen off her horse, though we both know she doesn't need the assistance. She accepts it, though, letting him hand her down with a demure smile, playing the role she needs to.

"And may I present my wife, Princess Guinevere of Lyonesse," he says.

I'm sure my brothers have already told him all about Gwen and the circumstances of their wedding, but my father looks at Gwen much the same way he looked at Arthur, taking her hand and lifting it to his lips for a chivalrous kiss as he bows before her.

"We are honored by your presence, Your Highness," he says, before turning to Morgana, dismounting last. "And Lady Morgana, as well," he says with a pleasant smile. "You left several of my men lovesick when you left—I'm glad you've returned. It should serve to lift spirits."

"Your Grace," Morgana says with a dimpled smile. "If you were a younger man, I would think you were flirting."

My father laughs. "If I were a younger man, I might be. Sadly, I am not. But there are plenty of men who are up to the task, I'm sure."

Suddenly, I realize how strange it is that my father hasn't remarried. It's been three years now since my mother's death and even then, they'd been estranged for some time before that. But he shows no signs of even considering it.

My father clasps his hands together, the important greetings out of the way. "Now, it is late. Please, come inside and we'll show you to the rooms we've set up."

"Actually," I say, taking everyone by surprise. I clear my throat and gesture to Lancelot, where he stands with the rest of the knights. Tentatively, he comes forward, eyeing my father with a strange expression I've never seen on his face before. I think it might be fear.

"You remember Sir Lancelot," I say.

"Of course," my father says, frowning. He might dimly recall Lancelot, but a knight with no family to speak of wouldn't have left much of an impression.

"Before we retire, we would like to have a word with you."

My father is a sharp man. I see the pieces fall into place before his eyes— his daughter, a young woman of marriageable age, introducing him to a handsome upstart knight by name, seeking an audience. There is really only one thing this could concern.

He nods.

"Very well," he says, "I'll have tea brought to my study. I'm sure you would like the chance to freshen up after your journey—meet me there when you're ready."

Lancelot nods, only just finding his voice. "Thank you, my lord," he says, bowing his head.

As we make our way into the castle, my brothers fall into step beside me, Torre on my left, Lavaine on my right, both of them amused.

"It seems our little Lily Maid has caught herself a fish after all," Lavaine whispers.

"Quite a small one, though," Torre replies jovially. "Perhaps you should throw this one back—catch yourself a duke or an earl instead."

Playfully as the barb might be, it is still a barb, though it is one I am ready for.

"Sir Lancelot is the best swordsman in all of Albion, and he will be the right hand of our new king," I tell them, lifting my chin. "I daresay I've caught myself a bigger fish than either of your wives can claim."

That surprises them both to silence, though it is short lived. After a moment, Lavaine laughs, shaking his head.

"Our little Lily Maid has teeth," he says, looking to Torre with amusement flashing in his eyes.

"And claws to match," Torre adds, putting a hand on my shoulder and giving it a squeeze.


A TOURNAMENT," MY FATHER says slowly, giving the word an extra syllable. He, Lancelot, and I sit in his study, porcelain cups of steaming tea before us.

Lancelot hasn't said more than a word after he proclaimed his intention to my father, instead quietly sipping his tea and letting me discuss the logistics he still doesn't fully understand.

"A tournament for my hand as well as a parcel of Shalott land that would serve as my dowry," I say.

"You would like to be given away with a parcel of land?" my father asks with a laugh. "I wish I'd known. There are plenty of wellborn men who have written to ask for your hand over the last week. I turned them all down because you said you wouldn't have a husband."

"I won't have *any* husband," I say. "It will be Lancelot or it will be no one."

As I say the words, something twists in my stomach, and I see my vision once again, Arthur and I heartbroken, Lancelot gone, Gwen imprisoned. I push it aside. The future is still wide enough to change, and I meant what I said to Lancelot last night—I trust him. I trust him more than a hazy future in flux. I even trust him more than my visions.

"But a tournament leaves it to chance," my father says, shaking his head. "Anyone can win. And you would be giving your word—you would have to marry whoever won. And a prize like this—not only your hand, but land as well—the competition will be fierce, with swordsmen far more experienced and well trained than your boy."

Lancelot sets his cup down on the table beside him, leaning forward in his chair. "All due respect, my lord, but though I lack experience and what you call training, there is no one who is my equal with a sword."

"And you," my father says, turning on Lancelot with a raised finger. "Do not get me started on you. What sort of a noble knight do you imagine yourself? You were meant to be serving your prince—your future king—not seducing a defenseless maiden."

"It isn't like that," I say, heat rising to my cheeks. "He asked me to marry him in Camelot, and we've been in love long before that. We know that it will be a tricky road to navigate, that people will talk, that they'll say exactly what you just did and far worse. But I've thought it through. He makes me happy."

"For now," he says, and those two words knock the breath from me.

He doesn't know, he can't know. He's only speaking of the future he imagines, with both of us poor and disgraced, our love turned to rot in the face of reality. Still, it hurts.

"I'm sure of him," I tell my father, my voice firm. "And I will marry him with or without your blessing, with or without land or a title to make it palatable to the court in Camelot. But I would hope, as my father, you would seek to make the road I walk as smooth as you can."

That gives him pause. He reaches for his cup of tea, taking a deep sip while he considers it. "A tournament," he says finally. "And you will marry whoever is victorious. You swear it."

A brittle smile comes to my face—not because I've won, but because he thinks he has, and that is more or less the same thing. So I swear it.

# 38

WHEN LANCELOT AND I leave my father's study, my limbs are heavy with exhaustion and I'm longing for my bed, but the night is not over yet, and the most unpleasant task still looms large. But it is a necessary thing.

A powerless Morgana will not be able to summon a sword from a river. She will not be able to brew poisons—not the kind I've seen her brew, at least. A powerless Morgana will mean a Morgana who is less a danger to Arthur. I don't need Nimue to convince me it is the right choice.

And, if navigated correctly, a powerless Gwen has advantages as well. As she is, she will still be too wild for the Camelot court. There will still be whispers and those who seek to bring her and Arthur down. But without magic and separated from Lyonesse, Gwen will have no choice but to adapt to court life. Though I hate myself for thinking it, I have to wonder if we all won't be better off if she does, if she becomes the queen Camelot expects—docile, sweet, ladylike.

*You must protect Arthur at all costs*, Nimue told me once, and at the time I'd thought that was a simple thing. Of course I would protect Arthur. There is not a price I wouldn't pay to keep him safe. But when I made that vow, I never imagined the price wouldn't be mine.

But Gwen and Morgana grew up with Nimue's words in their ears as well. They made the same vows, and they have agreed to this willingly.

The others are already at work when Lancelot and I step into my room. Arthur is thumbing through one of Morgana's spell books while Gwen bustles around the room, twisting at the length of rope in her hands. It isn't long—just enough to loop around our wrists to provide a physical bond.

For her part, Morgana sits utterly still in the chair by the window, her hands folded in her lap in a way that might be described as prim if it were anyone else. It's only on closer examination that I notice how tightly her hands are clasped—so tight her knuckles have gone white.

*Perhaps we should discuss this,* I want to say, but I hold my tongue.

We *have* discussed this, so many times I know exactly how the conversation will go. And I know how it will end. There is no point in pretending otherwise.

"Did you find the spell?" I ask Arthur.

He flips back a few pages and nods. It gives me some comfort to see his own hesitation. Petty as it feels, I want this to hurt him. I want him to know exactly what his sister and his wife are sacrificing for him.

"And they caught you up on their agreement?" I ask.

Again, Arthur nods. "It's a fair agreement," he says, but it isn't his usual Arthur voice—it's his future king voice, the one usually reserved for meetings and proclamations and speeches, not for friends.

Morgana gives a loud snort. "Nothing about this is fair," she says. "Let's get it over with before I change my mind."

I'm not entirely sure she's joking.

"What do you need from me?" I ask.

"It's big magic, these bindings," Morgana says. "Not as big as the moon, but more than either of us are capable of on our own. I've gone over the specifics of how I took power from you with Gwen—it didn't have any lasting consequences, did it?"

I shake my head. "I was exhausted afterward, but after a good night's sleep I was fine."

"Good," Gwen says. "This won't be as bad as that, but we'll make sure you get your rest afterward."

"Luckily we're already in your room," Morgana adds with a wry smile that doesn't quite manage to hide the tension lurking underneath. "Once it's done, we'll get you tucked into bed, snug as a bug."

I shouldn't laugh, but I can't help it. That seems to have been Morgana's goal, because she looks quite pleased with herself.

"Arthur, Lance, you'll want to stand back. Whatever you do, don't interrupt the spells—this kind of magic might be painful, we might fight it, but if the spell is interrupted, it might not ever be able to be undone."

Arthur looks green at that, but he nods once, passing the open book to Morgana and joining Lancelot on the far side of the room.

Gwen loops the rope around her wrist and Morgana's, binding them together before Morgana uses her unbound hand to take mine, pressing our palms flush together.

It shouldn't be easy, the spell to bind Gwen's magic. It is a spell that alters her body, her mind, and her soul—alters the very marrow of what makes Gwen who she is. It should be complicated. But it isn't. In the end, when I've felt Morgana's power mingle with mine and the smell of jasmine and oranges floods the air around us, the only reaction from Gwen is a small gasp of air, like she's stubbed her toe or realized she forgot to pull the kettle from the fire. And then it is over.

"Did it work?" Arthur asks.

Gwen's brow is furrowed, but she nods. She looks like a child who suddenly finds herself lost in a vast and unfamiliar forest. "I . . . yes. Yes, it did. I don't know how to explain it, but I feel it."

"You'll get it back," Morgana reminds her, but Gwen waves the words away.

"I know that and it's fine, really. It didn't hurt as much as I thought."

I know that she's lying, and the others must as well. Gwen unties the rope, freeing her wrist from Morgana's. Without a word, Arthur reaches out a hand to her and she takes it, like a drowning woman grabbing hold of a raft. She lets him pull her to his side, his arm going around her shoulders. Like a brace, or perhaps a vise. It is difficult to say which.

"El," Morgana says, her hands going beneath my arms to keep me from falling. I realize a second too late that I'm dizzy, that I was a mere second from collapsing to the ground. I shake my head and force a smile.

"I'm fine," I say, stepping out of her grip and taking hold of her hand once more. This time, she uses the rope to bind our hands together. By the time she's done, my dizziness has gone, leaving behind a ghost of a headache.

"We can take a break," Lancelot says. "Give you a second to rest."

"I'd rather not," I say, shaking my head though I give him a small smile. "Better to get it over with quickly, I think."

"If you're sure," Morgana says.

"I am," I say, and I think it's the truth right up until Morgana begins drawing on my magic for her spell. Once it begins, I am not sure of anything at all.

Jasmine and oranges flood the room again, but now there is something else added—the scent of Gwen's magic: grass after a rainstorm and crushed rosemary leaves. The mix of fragrances is heavy and cloying and so overwhelming I feel like I might be sick with it.

Morgana doesn't gasp. She doesn't make any sound at all. Her eyes stay locked on mine the entire time, a single tear tracing its way down her cheek.

When it's done and Morgana pulls the rope's knot free, my lungs are greedy for the fresh air. I swallow down breaths of it like it will never be enough, like I could gorge on the air around me. My head swims and blurs until I can no longer remember where I am or how I got here. All I know are the hands at my back, on my arms, arms scooping me up and carrying me, setting me down on a soft bed, tucking the quilt up to my chin.

I hear voices dimly, a murmur more than words. But as the world around me fades to black, I hear Morgana's voice, quiet and fragile.

"I can't feel it anymore," she whispers. "It's gone. It's really gone."

I COME TO CONSCIOUSNESS again when the sun is just starting to rise in the sky, the light coming through my window a yellow so pale and soft that it takes me a moment to remember where I am and what happened last night. It takes me a moment longer to realize that I'm not alone.

Morgana lies on one side of me, Gwen on the other, and neither of them are sleeping.

I sit up slowly, waiting for the stabbing headache to return, but now there is only a dull thud.

"Elaine?" Morgana asks, sitting up with me, a beat before Gwen does the same.

"Are you alright?" Gwen asks.

"I'm fine, I promise," I say, looking at Morgana. "How are you?" I ask her.

She opens her mouth but quickly closes it again, and I can see her weighing her answer, weighing just how much she wants to lie to me.

"That bad?" I ask her.

She sinks back into the pillows and stares up at the ceiling.

"Do you remember on Avalon when we had to hollow out those gourds to make lanterns for the solstice?" she asks after a moment. "We spooned out all of their seeds and guts and carved holes into them so that candlelight could shine through from within?"

"I remember," I say. On my other side, Gwen is silent, but I feel her presence, her nimble fingers picking at the edge of the quilt.

"It doesn't feel like that, exactly," she says. "Like my insides have been scooped out. I think that's what I expected. It's like . . . like after the solstice, when the candles were extinguished and the gourds began to rot. That's what I feel like—like there's nothing inside me anymore, no guts, no lights, no seeds, nothing but rot and decay."

"It's temporary," I say again, reaching for her hand. She doesn't pull away from me, but she doesn't hold me back either. Instead her hand is limp in mine. "And it was for your own good too. One slip, Morgana, and they'd have killed you."

For a long moment, Morgana doesn't say anything, but when she does speak, her voice is hollow, just like those gourds we carved up a lifetime ago.

"I think I'd have preferred that," she says finally. Then she places my hand back in my own lap and climbs out of bed. "I'll let Arthur and Lance know you're alright—they were worried, but it wouldn't do for them to be caught here."

I didn't think there was anything worse than Morgana's voice in my visions, the hard-edged rasp, laced with fury and hatred. I was wrong. The way Morgana speaks now isn't hard—there is no feeling to it at all. It is like talking to someone who is still half asleep.

She slips out of the room without another word, closing the door firmly behind her.

"And you?" I ask Gwen, already fearing the answer. "Do you feel rotten as well?"

Gwen doesn't answer right away. "I don't share Morgana's flair for the dramatic," she says finally. "Nor do I share her connection to her power. Don't misunderstand me—I love my magic and I do feel the loss of it keenly, but it's nothing like how I felt when I decided to leave Lyonesse."

I swallow. Somehow, that answer is even worse. Morgana and Gwen will get their magic back someday, but Gwen will never return home.

"I'm no oracle," she says a moment later, her own voice exhausted and wary. "But I haven't been able to sleep all night. I keep thinking . . . I keep thinking that this was a mistake."

I roll over to face her, drawing the quilt up to my chin.

"The thing I learned from my training on Avalon is that there are few good choices," I tell her quietly. "There were no good choices here, Gwen. We made the only choice we could live with. Maybe it was a bad one, but all we can do now is make the best of it."

"How?" she asks.

I swallow and force a smile. "By sticking to the plan," I tell her. "We get Arthur on the throne, seal the treaty with Avalon. And the instant magic is no longer outlawed, I give you your magic back."

Gwen looks like she wants to argue, but after a moment she nods. "Then we'll stick to the plan," she says.

Morgana, don't do this, please."

The voice isn't mine, but it will be one day, panicked and desperate and frightened. The small room will be made from shadow and stone, lit only by a few scattered candles, burning down to little more than puddles of wax. In the dim light, the pupils of Morgana's eyes will be huge, making her look manic as she flits around her room, pulling bottles down from their shelves and uncorking them to sniff or pinch or dump completely into the bubbling cauldron. Her ink-black hair will be unbound and wild, following her around like a storm cloud. Whenever a piece of it drifts into her face, she will blow it away in an annoyed huff, but that will be the only sound she makes. She won't speak to me. She won't even look at me.

Cold air will bite at my skin, the smell of sulfur seeping into the air from the potion brewing. Without a word, I know that whatever potion Morgana is brewing isn't only dangerous, it's lethal.

"Morgana," I will try again, my voice cracking over her name. Still, she won't acknowledge me. Not until I touch her shoulder. She will flinch away, but at least she will look at me, violet eyes hard and distant even when they meet mine.

She will not be the Morgana I know now, the Morgana who was my first friend, who has stood by my side unfalteringly since I was thirteen years old.

"This cannot stand, Elaine." Her voice will be calm and resolved, at odds with the chaos in her body, the storm in her expression. "The things Arthur has done—"

"He has done what he believes best." It's a line that will feel familiar on my tongue, like I have spoken it many times. I will believe the words with every part of me.

Morgana will pull away from me, making a sound that is half-laugh and half-sob.

"Then you think Arthur a fool, Elaine? You think he didn't know exactly what he was doing? What is worse—to have a foolish king or a cruel one?"

Her eyes on mine will burn until I have to look away, unable to defend Arthur for the first time in my life.

"Which do you think it was?" she will continue, and I realize the question isn't rhetorical. She will want an answer. "Is he stupidly noble, or is there a conniving side under all of that quiet erudition?"

"Arthur loves you," I will say, because I won't know what other answer to give. It will be one of the only true things I will know, but that doesn't mean it makes her beliefs untrue. I don't know how the two things can be unassailable facts, but somehow, they are.

She will scoff and turn away from me, unstoppering a bottle and letting the shadow of a serpent slither out into the sizzling cauldron. It will die with a shriek that echoes in the silence between us.

"And you?" I will ask her when I find my voice again. "He's your brother, and I know you love him. How can you even consider doing this to him?"

She will begin to turn away, but I will grab her hands in mine, holding tight and forcing her to look at me.

"The boy you teased mercilessly when his voice began to change? The one who still turns red in the cheeks every time Gwen smiles at him? The one who has taken your side against every courtier in this palace who wanted you banished or worse? If you do this, Morgana, there is no coming back. I have Seen this path, I have Seen this moment, and I am begging you not to do it, not to break us into pieces that we will never be able to mend."

Her hands will go slack in mine, and she will falter. For an instant, she will look once more like the Morgana I have always known, her vulnerabilities like sunlight slatting through a boarded-up window.

She will open her mouth to speak and—

I'm prepared for the vision to end, as it always does, but this time is different. This time there is a breath, an inhale, an exhale, and then it continues.

She will open her mouth to speak, and her voice will come out cold. "Would you take his side over mine?" she will ask quietly.

"This is not about sides," I will tell her. "You are talking about killing him. *Arthur.*"

"Such loyalty." She will pull her hands away, and her mouth will twist into a cruel, mocking smile. "How quickly you forget, Elaine. Without me, Arthur wouldn't even know you exist. You certainly wouldn't be his adviser. You would be home in Shalott just as mad as your mother, without any friends and a family that resents you. Without me, you wouldn't have control of your power, or Nimue's favor, or Lancelot's love. Without me, you would be nothing. So I will ask you again: Whose side are you on?"

Her words will be cruel, but they will be crueler still because they will be the truth. I will have thought them myself too many times to fault her for saying them once. No matter how far I will have come, I will always be the lonely girl in the tower. Without Morgana, I will always be nothing.

"Yours," I will say, because it is the only answer. "I am always on yours."

Her smile will become feral as she takes my hands again and pulls me toward the cauldron. It will not be a gesture of friendship or comfort, as I first thought. I will be able to feel magic tingling under the skin of my palms, unfamiliar but itching to be used. Once, I had to summon it, twisting out each drop like juice from a stubborn lemon, but more and more often it will always be there, always waiting to be called on. It should be a relief, but instead it will frighten me.

"Then help me," Morgana will say.

The words themselves will be innocent, but there will also be a layer of venom beneath them that will sink beneath my skin. After all, she wouldn't need my help if I hadn't rendered her helpless. It will be a debt that will have grown wider between us no matter how I try to atone. What I did to her will be unforgivable. The familiar scent of rotten oranges and wilted jasmine in the air is reminder enough of that.

But what she will ask me to do is unforgivable as well, isn't it? Even with the vise of her friendship wrapped tight around me, I will know it. Even as the magic weeps from my skin and into the potion, turning it lethal, I will know it. Even when Morgana thanks me and embraces me and tells me we will go down in the legends as heroes, I will know it.

I will know it and know what I must do, but that won't make it any easier to betray Morgana a second time.

I SIT BACK AGAINST my pillows and look at the small tapestry set over my miniature loom. It is the first time I've tried to scry since I failed in Lyonesse, and I was afraid I would see more of Lancelot and Gwen's betrayal, but this is worse.

It is only the second time I have seen a vision expand, after the first one Nimue showed me in the Cave of Prophecies. Still, I remember what Nimue told me then, how she'd explained it. A choice had been made. A path forged. The world shifted beneath our feet.

The last time it happened because Morgana brought me to Avalon, because she saved me.

Now it's happened because I couldn't do the same for her.

Gwen was right. The binding was a mistake. For a second, I contemplate breaking it now and unleashing their magic once more, but as tempting as that is, I also know that wouldn't solve anything. The reasons for the binding are still there, still strong. And the alternatives are every bit as unbearable.

No, Gwen might have been right, but I was as well. There is no turning back. We stick to the plan and work to undo Morgana's binding as soon as we feasibly can. All I can do is hope that she isn't too far gone by the time we get there.

# 39

THOUGH HE ONLY has a day to put together the tournament, my father manages it spectacularly. In addition to most of Arthur's knights and my brothers—who won't be competing for my hand but for their own pride and the land our father promised—there are five sons sent from the surrounding lands with haste. One suitor, Sir Pellinor, arrives mere minutes before the tournament begins.

As the men line up before my father's spectator box, where he and I are to sit with Arthur, Guinevere, Morgana, and the scant few knights who will not be competing, my father looks sideways at me, trying to gauge my reaction, though I am careful not to give him one.

It is easy, in the crowd of hulking men, to lose Lancelot completely. I'd always thought him tall, which I suppose he is compared to Arthur and the rest of us, but many of these men are giants, with broad shoulders and arms thick with corded muscles. Beside them, Lancelot looks almost diminutive.

"It isn't too late," my father says to me, a challenge in his eyes.

Lancelot meets my gaze, his own nerves plain on his face. He nods once, expression grim but determined, and that is enough to anchor me.

"We'll need to leave for Camelot at dawn if we're to make good time, and I'd like a decent night's sleep," I tell my father with a smile. "Let's get on with it, shall we?"

My father raises his eyebrows at me, bemused, but motions for the tournament to begin.

"I hope you know what you're doing," Arthur murmurs to me as the first matches are set up. The tournament ground has been sectioned into smaller squares where early matches will go on simultaneously until the number of victors has been narrowed to four. Then the four will be set against one another as a group, the last man standing the winner.

"Have you ever seen a greater swordsman?" I ask him.

"No," Arthur admits. "But I don't claim to have seen very many. And the look of those men is enough to cause me some concern. But then, I don't have to marry one of them if this goes poorly."

The thought pools like oil in my stomach.

"You could have told us what you were planning, you know," Gwen says, though her eyes are fixed on the first set of matches. "Arthur could have given him a title as soon as he's crowned, there was no need for the spectacle."

Lancelot isn't in this group, but Gawain is, matched up with a man I don't know, with angry eyes and a thick scar over his left cheek. I realize I've never seen Gawain fight before, but he is better than I would have thought, with his quiet demeanor. His movements are deliberate and precise. He doesn't waste energy with theatrics, unlike his opponent, who quickly runs himself ragged with his overextended movements and extra footwork.

I shake my head. "It isn't enough to just give him a title. It might even make things worse—you saw how he and Lamorak already clashed. They would say you favored a half-fay knight over your own men."

"Lancelot *is* one of my own men."

"I know that," I tell him. "They don't. But this will ensure they at least respect him."

"So long as he wins, you mean," Arthur adds.

"He will," Gwen says, giving me a tentative but reassuring smile.

Gawain falls to the ground in his match, his sword landing a few feet away from him, just out of reach. A few seats down from me, Gareth winces, his eyes glued on his older brother as his opponent crosses toward him, victory already shining in his eyes.

"It's not over yet," I tell Gareth, though even I don't see a way out for Gawain.

His opponent raises his sword, ready to lift it to Gawain's chest to declare victory, but in the instant before he does, Gawain uses a final burst of energy to kick the sword out of his opponent's hand, taking him by surprise and giving Gawain the few seconds he needs to retrieve his own sword and point it at his opponent's throat, all in what looks to be one fluid movement.

"See?" I say to Gareth. "He did it."

The boy's relief is followed quickly by a petulant sigh. "I don't see why I couldn't compete as well. I'm sixteen in a few weeks—it should have counted."

"Your turn for glory will come," I tell him. "Quests and triumph and damsels in distress—all that and more. You just have to be patient."

The promise must sound hollow to him, the sort of condescending thing adults often say to children, because he lets out another sigh.

"I didn't think you wanted to marry Elaine this badly, Gareth," Arthur teases gently, making his cousin's cheeks turn bright red.

"I don't," he insists, his expression sour. "I just want to fight—to show that I'm just as good as Gawain. Better, even."

"Well, I don't know about that," I say. "But your time will come. And you'll know it's here when you hear the name Lynette. Can you remember that?"

He looks at me, brow furrowing. "Lynette," he repeats, but he no longer looks annoyed. Instead, he looks curious. "What does that have to do with anything?"

I shrug my shoulders, unable to let myself say more, but Gwen jumps in.

"It's a Lyonessian name," she offers. "Maybe you'll return there one day, on some noble quest."

"I hope not," Gareth blurts out before catching himself. "No offense, Your Highness."

"None taken," Gwen says with a smile, though her attention is not fully on Gareth, or in the box at all; it is on the field, watching the one remaining match dwindle to its end. Her eyes follow each strike and movement, sometimes before they are even made, and there is something akin to longing in her eyes.

"Lucky you can't compete," I say, trying to make light of the situation. "I think Albion might frown on a polyamorous queen."

That earns a laugh. "Shame, though," she says, glancing at me with a mischievous twinkle in her eyes that I haven't seen there since Avalon. "We would have made quite a formidable couple, don't you think?"

"Oh, undoubtedly," I say, returning her laugh. For just a second, I forget about my visions of her and Lancelot, but all too soon I hear my mother's voice in my mind, the prophecy I never quite understood until now.

*Trust not the girl with the golden crown, she'll take what's yours and watch you drown.*

"I am right here, you know," Arthur says mildly, drawing me back to the present. He's looking at Gwen with an amused smile. "And we're married now—I don't think you're supposed to flirt so shamelessly in front of me."

"Well, *that* certainly wasn't in our wedding vows, was it?"

He laughs before his attention is drawn back to the field. "Oh, look, here comes Lance. Morgana, Lance is up."

Morgana moves like a shade, coming to sit next to her brother without a word.

I force myself not to look at her, instead turning back to the field, where the first group is exiting and the new group is coming out. Lancelot catches my eyes right away and I get to my feet, walking toward the railing and beckoning him over. He quickly looks to where the other competitors are settling into their spaces before jogging toward me, his helmet at his side.

In the spectator box, I tower over him by more than a foot, and I have to lean well over the railing to speak with him.

"I have something for you," I tell him.

His eyes brighten, and a grin works its way past his nerves. "A favor?" he asks, remembering my stories about how tournaments work. He'd been so fascinated by Albion traditions back on Avalon, though he usually called them all ridiculous. The tradition of favors was no exception—he'd laughed at the idea of a scrap of silk protecting a knight, but now that we are here, he actually looks excited about it.

I take the ribbon that binds the end of my braid. Without it, my hair comes loose around my shoulders, blowing in the gentle wind. It will be the last day I will be able to wear my hair down like this, I realize with a pang of sadness. I have not been a true maiden in several years now, but according to society I still am, at least until I'm wed.

"Here," I say, holding the ribbon out. "Let me see the hilt of your sword."

He holds it up to me, gripping the blade in his gloved hands so that I can tie the green silk ribbon around the handle.

"The Maiden, Mother, and Crone smile on you," I tell him.

"*You* smile on me," he says. "That is all the good fortune I need."

In the end, I'm not sure how much he even needs that. His match is over in an instant, in a single movement that brings his tower of an opponent down to the ground with a thud that echoes throughout the space and brings several other matches to a pause.

At my side, my father leans forward, his eyes locked on Lancelot and wide with shock. After a second he looks to me, mouth gaping open.

I shrug my shoulders, unable to suppress a grin. "I told you," I say. "He's the best swordsman in the country, the world even."

My father scoffs at the bold claim, but there is wariness in his eyes now. What sounded ridiculous last night suddenly has a measure of credibility to it.

"Well," he says, leaning back in his seat and steepling his fingers on his lap. "That is only the first round."

It HAPPENS QUICKLY. One moment, the semifinal round of jousts is going well, with Lancelot fighting against Galahad. It should have been an easy match—Galahad is good but not anywhere close to Lancelot. Still, I see the moment when Lancelot slips, when his movement is just a breath too slow, when Galahad's blade makes its way past Lancelot's shield and in between the chainmail that covers his torso.

It is a lucky hit—one even Galahad looks surprised by—but that doesn't make it any less effective.

Lancelot falls to the ground slowly. I'm not sure if Gwen reaches for me or me for her, but suddenly her hand is in mine, clutched so tight it's painful. I reach for Morgana's hand as well, but it is weak in my grip. She does lean forward, though. Seeing Lancelot hurt shakes loose some part of her; I can see it in her eyes. She lets out a shudder of a breath.

On the field, Galahad blinks out of his surprise and advances toward Lancelot, ready to strike the defeating blow, but that instant of shock, of hesitation, is all Lancelot needs. With a final burst of energy, he launches himself up once more, throwing Galahad to the ground instead and positioning his blade at his throat.

I let out a breath of relief, but Gwen's grip on my hand doesn't loosen.

"Elaine, his side," she whispers to me.

I follow her gaze to where Lancelot stands, helping Galahad up. He winces at even that small effort, his free hand clutching his side where blood stains his chainmail red.

"He can't fight like that," Gwen continues, her voice low in my ear as dread pools in my stomach.

"I've never seen him hit," Arthur says, sounding dazed. "Not seriously, at least."

I shake my head, trying to quell my panic. "Come on," I say, getting to my feet and pulling Gwen with me.

"Morgana," I start, before hesitating. She won't be of any use now, not without her magic, and I worry her presence will only make things more difficult. "Stay with Arthur, send word when we're needed back."

Morgana looks like she might argue, but after a second, she sinks back into her seat and nods, looking back at the field. "Alright," she says.

As Gwen and I pass Arthur on our way out of the spectator box, he leans in.

"Please help him," he whispers again, an edge of worry in his voice. "And remind him that he's supposed to *avoid* getting stabbed."

As soon as Gwen and I are out of the box, we break into a run toward the tents where the contestants are being held.

"Wait, Elaine," Gwen says, pulling me to a stop. "We can't just burst in there. I'm their future queen, and *you're* meant to be their prize. What would you say to explain?"

"I don't know," I say, my voice cracking. I know she's right, but it is strange to have Gwen arguing for caution instead of the other way around. I force myself to take a deep breath. "He can't lose, Gwen," I say.

"I know," she tells me, glancing at the tent and the copse of woods just behind it.

"Go, wait there," she tells me, nodding toward the edge of the trees. "I have an idea."

I open my mouth to argue, but the trumpets sound again from the tournament field, indicating that another match has ended, and quickly too. There are only two more now, and hopefully they go on much longer than the last.

"Hurry," I tell her, before lifting my skirts and running toward the edge of the field and out of sight.

From the edge of the trees, I watch Gwen lurk near the entrance of the tent, never setting foot inside. When the two competitors make their way back from the field, she motions them toward her.

Gawain and Kay, neither hurt but both smiling and happy—for them, this is nothing more than a game, I suppose. Gwen speaks to both of them for a moment, wringing her hands in front of her and biting her lip. She gestures over to me, and both of them look before glancing back at her. After a moment, Gawain nods.

The two of them disappear into the tent, and Gwen runs over to me.

"Gawain will bring him here," she says. "Didn't take much convincing—most of the men like Lancelot. They can't stand Lamorak, so their fight made him some new friends."

"You told them I was here?" I ask her. "But—"

"Relax," she says. "The two of them have been traveling with us long enough to see the affection between you and Lance. You aren't exactly subtle. I'd imagine for them, this tournament is for fun. Here they come."

She nods toward the tent, and I follow her gaze to where Gawain is helping Lancelot walk toward us, though each step makes him wince.

As soon as they make it to the tree line, I help Gawain sit him down so he can lean against a trunk while Gwen gets to work examining the wound.

"It's not as bad as it looks, really," Lancelot says through clenched teeth.

Gwen shoots him a contemptuous look. "You've lost so much blood, it's surprising you're still awake," she tells him. "So kindly shut up and let me fix it."

"You can't fix it," I remind her, my voice soft.

Gwen flinches. "I forgot," she says, her voice hoarse. "I can't believe I forgot already."

"It was an accident," Gawain says, paying our whispering no mind. "Galahad felt terrible about it. He didn't even want to compete this morning, but I told him I thought it would be fun."

"Are there any herbs?" I ask Gwen. "Any medicines that might help?"

She looks at the wound for a few more seconds before looking at me. "I can bandage him up and stop the blood. Gawain, can you find some hallowroot for the pain? It's a blue flower with yellowish leaves, and I thought I saw some in the woods."

Gawain nods and starts deeper into the woods, and Gwen turns to me. "It won't be good as new. I'm worried there's more damage inside."

She pauses.

"If I had my magic . . ." she starts.

I bite my lip, temptation to agree rising up. I could give her the magic back. What was it Morgana said? I have the locked box and the key, all I have to do is unlock it. I don't even hesitate before nodding.

"How?" I ask.

She shrugs her shoulders. "The same way you took it to begin with," she says.

I use a scrap of my skirt, torn where no one will notice, to bind Gwen's hand with mine, and I remember how Morgana bound the power, how she described it to me—a locked box with the key. I imagine myself using that key, feel the box open, the magic just within reach. I smell oranges and jasmine and grass and rosemary . . . but the more I try to channel it back to Gwen, the more fruitless it feels.

After a moment, I open my eyes.

"Anything?" I ask her.

She shakes her head, her brow furrowed.

"It should be easy to undo," I say.

"In theory," Gwen replies softly. I hear what she doesn't say, that all of this has been in theory and those theories have held so far, but now? It is possible what's been done can't be undone. And what will that mean?

Lancelot pushes himself to sit up, looking between the two of us. "We'll figure it out later," he says. "Gwen, fix what you can with bandages and herbs—it'll have to be enough. I'm still half-fay—my body will heal quickly. By tonight, I'll be fully healed *and* have won."

"Not if you breathe the wrong way and your spleen ruptures," she tells him, pushing him back against the tree trunk once more. "You can't fight—it's too dangerous."

Lancelot glances at me, then at Gwen. "You can't be serious," he says, his voice low. "You want me to forfeit? You know what that means, Gwen."

"Of course I do," she snaps. "But if you go out there, you could very well die. Would you rather that?"

"No, she's right," I say before Lancelot can protest. "You can't fight. It's too dangerous."

Lancelot stares at me. "Elaine . . . if someone else wins—"

I cross my arms tightly over my chest. "I would rather marry someone else than see you dead."

He shakes his head. "We never should have made this deal. It was foolish."

"It wasn't foolish," I say, swallowing. "It was a calculated risk—you should have beaten every one of these men with ease nine hundred and ninety-nine times out of a thousand."

"The Maiden, Mother, and Crone just have a cruel sense of humor then," Lancelot says, wincing as Gwen gives his wound a prod.

"It's already starting to heal," she says. I follow her gaze, watching as the bleeding stops before my eyes. Gwen uses a wet rag to wipe away the blood. It's neatly closed, without so much as a scar. To look at him, he wouldn't appear hurt at all, but she's right—he's still in pain.

Gawain returns with the flowers Gwen requested, and she immediately holds them up to Lancelot's mouth.

"Eat them," she says.

He frowns. "Leaves too?"

"Leaves especially," she says. "I don't know how much good it will do, though."

Lancelot groans, but does as she says, stuffing the flowers into his mouth and chewing, wincing as he does.

"So it's over?" Gawain asks, looking between us all. "He can't fight?"

Gwen presses her lips together into a thin line and shakes her head.

"Not without putting his own life at great risk," she says.

"I'm in the final as well," Gawain says. "What if I were to keep the others away from Lance? Keep him from getting hit again? Then in the end, he can give me one good hit and I'll fall and he'll win. Easy."

"It's still too much of a risk," I say. "Even if he moves the wrong way, if he sneezes—his fay blood might have begun to repair the superficial injury, but the rest of it will take longer."

As if on cue, the third match ends with the blare of the trumpet and a burst of cheers.

"Help me up," Lancelot says. "I have to get back in the tent to give my spot up to Galahad before the round ends."

Lancelot being only half-fay means he can lie, but he's never been particularly good at it.

"You aren't going to resign, are you?" I ask him.

He lifts his eyes to meet mine. "No," he says plainly. "I will fight, I will win, and I will be fine. If this is a test from the Maiden, Mother, and Crone, it is a test I will pass."

Gwen picks up a rock from the ground. "If I hit him just right, I can knock him unconscious without causing any real damage," she tells me.

"Don't you dare," he says to her, before looking back to me. He reaches for my hand, holding it tightly in his. "This is our chance, Elaine," he says, his voice raw but determined. "What happens if you end up with a husband who wants to keep you in some country palace like a doll on a shelf? Without you, Arthur will fail. You know it as well as I do."

"I could win," Gawain says quietly. "If I do, nothing will change. I won't even marry her if she won't have me."

"If," Lancelot echoes. "That is a large risk to take. You don't need to search your futures to see that, Elaine. I need to fight."

I close my eyes and bite my lip. If I concentrate, I can feel the power inside me—Morgana's and Gwen's together. Folded away neatly in a box, just as Morgana said. I felt it, there at my fingertips. And I couldn't give it back, but that doesn't mean I can't use it myself.

I think about the vision I saw last night, the extended scene with Morgana. In that scene, I was able to use her magic, to call upon it as easily as if it were my own.

I prod at the borrowed magic like a child with a new tooth growing in, exploring the unfamiliar surface. I don't know how to use magic, not this kind of magic, but if I could . . .

"Lancelot needs to fight," I say slowly. When I open my eyes again, Gwen and Gawain are staring at me, mouths agog.

"He could *die,* Elaine," Gwen says.

"He won't," I say. "Gawain, go get his shield."

Gawain doesn't wait for further instruction, running toward the tent as quickly as he can.

"He won't fight on that field, but Lancelot will," I say.

Lancelot's frown deepens. "What on earth is that supposed to mean?"

"Healing is a complicated thing, you told me it took you years to learn. But illusion charms are easy, aren't they?" I ask Gwen. "There were toddlers on Avalon who could craft them, and it was one of the rare spells both you and Morgana could do."

"Easy, yes," Gwen says, looking even more bewildered. "But still entirely beyond me now. I couldn't cast a spell to disguise my pinkie nail, let alone anything bigger."

"But what if I could?" I ask, looking to Gwen. "I don't trust myself to try healing, but what if I could place an illusion charm on the shield? So whoever wields it will look like Lance, even if they aren't. Even if *you* aren't."

Gwen's hands go still and she looks up at me. "You want me to take his place?" she asks, her eyes brightening for only an instant before she shakes her head. "I can't do that. Even in armor it would be obvious I'm not him."

"Hence the illusion charm," I say.

"You want to use Morgana's and my magic," she says slowly.

I swallow. "Normally, I would never," I say. It feels like a violation, like a theft. "But . . ."

Gwen takes a deep breath, not looking happy about it, but after a moment she nods. "Just this once," she says.

I nod, though if my vision is anything to go on, it is a promise already broken. "Just this once."

WHEN GAWAIN RETURNS with Lancelot's shield, Gwen has changed into Lancelot's armor. It's big on her, but she can still move in it, and a hindered Gwen is still more ferocious than anyone else I've seen.

"Can you manage it?" Lancelot asks her, his voice low with worry.

She gives a test lunge, sword held aloft.

"Yes," she says, leaving no room for hesitation.

"Anyone with eyes will know right away," Gawain says, shaking his head.

"Pass me the shield," I say.

Gawain does so without question, handing me the great plate of metal, painted Camelot red and gold.

"Elaine, are you sure you can do it?" Gwen asks.

She told me the basics while we waited for Gawain to return, how to feel the power in my fingertips, how to let it travel into the shield, powered by my intention.

*Visualize it*, she said. *See exactly what you want to happen. And then trust that it will.*

I don't answer her. I've never tried to use magic before; I don't even know where to begin with it. But, it turns out, the magic knows. It reacts instantly, sensing what I need of it and seeping from my fingertips before I can so much as move.

No wonder Morgana had such a difficult time controlling her magic—it is not something easily reined. It almost feels like it has a life of its own.

Gwen, Lance, and Gawain stare at me in silence as the smell of jasmine and oranges—Morgana's scent, but not quite right somehow—fills the woods, and the shield begins to quiver in my hands.

"Elaine," Lance says, his voice low.

I don't answer. Instead I shove the shield away from me, toward Gwen, who takes it without hesitation.

"Go on," I say. "Lift it."

Gwen looks at me like she's never seen me before, but she obeys, lifting the shield up as if she's blocking a blow.

The air around the shield shimmers for an instant, and her features shift and morph until her face is no longer hers. It's Lancelot's.

"You'll have the helmet on most of the time, but if you win—*when* you win—you'll have to remove it to claim your prize," I say.

No one speaks, not even Gawain, who must be terribly confused.

"Morgana can't know," I say, looking between them. "It would destroy her if she found out I used her magic. She would blame me."

"But it isn't your—"

"The moon trick was my idea," I say. "I didn't argue for her to keep her magic, I even helped with the spell. You think there isn't a part of her that will believe I wanted this?"

*I did want it*, I think, but I push that thought aside. I didn't want it like this.

"Elaine," Lancelot says, but before he can say more, the horn sounds again.

"It's time," I say, looking at Gwen. "Can you do this?"

Gwen looks at me with Lancelot's face for a long second before she nods, donning his helmet.

"Let's go," she says.

# 40

I MAKE MY WAY back to the spectator box just as the trumpets sound again to announce the start of the final tournament. Lancelot is still in the woods, as he couldn't return to the tent without someone noticing there were two of him, but as soon as we can get away, Gwen and I will return for him.

"Where did Gwen go?" Arthur asks as I retake my seat.

My father glances at me, and I know he's listening to the answer as well.

"Lady problems," I say carefully. "But I'm sure she'll be along soon—you know how she loves a good fight."

The last bit is meant for Arthur alone, but he frowns, not catching my meaning. Morgana notices something is amiss, though, and I feel her eyes on me as I focus on the field, trying not to let my guilt overwhelm me.

As soon as Gwen steps onto the field and begins to fight, Arthur knows her. The illusion is good enough to fool everyone else—they've never watched Gwen fight like Arthur has, not even Morgana, who always found watching their tournaments boring. Arthur recognizes the way she arcs her sword through the air, how her steps have a dancer's grace, how she is faster than Lancelot, her movements quicker.

"Elaine," he says to me, his voice low. "What did you do?"

I don't answer, but Arthur doesn't seem to expect me to. His eyes are glued to Gwen as she just barely ducks in time to miss a blow from Lamorak, using the momentum of his movement to let him tumble to the ground, touching her sword to his neck and disqualifying him in a single fluid motion.

"If she's found out—"

"She won't be," I say through gritted teeth.

"Your beau seems to have recovered well," my father says, drawing my attention to him. "I thought certainly that wound would have hindered his performance."

"He's tougher than he looks," I tell him with a smile.

"I've heard the fey heal quickly," he continues. "But this is something else entirely."

"Perhaps the wound wasn't as dire as it appeared," I say, shrugging my shoulders. "It's hard to tell with the chainmail, isn't it?"

"I suppose," my father says, but he doesn't sound convinced.

Gawain falls quickly after that, though I think he does it on purpose, because he glances at me just before he does, letting the other knight touch his blade to his throat to disqualify him before hurrying off the field.

"Curious," my father says. "I know many men placed good money on Sir Gawain. He was considered the favorite—I've heard rumors of his training in Tintagel. They say he's even more skilled than his father was, which is truly saying something."

"Well," I say, keeping my eyes on Gwen. "Everyone has an off day."

"Tell me, who is this last man?" I ask, eyeing Gwen's final opponent—a mountain of a man with a greasy scraggle of a beard bursting through the openings of his helmet.

"Ah," my father says. "That would be Lord Uhred. Nasty fighter, I've heard. He won the games in Camelot last fall, though there were some rumors of foul play."

As if on cue, Lord Uhred delivers an elbow to Gwen's face, knocking her helmet clear off, though she keeps a strong hold on the shield so at least the illusion holds, even as blood trickles from her clearly broken nose.

Arthur grabs my arm, squeezing it hard.

"It's alright," I assure him, keeping my voice quiet so that even Morgana can't hear me. "Gwen has withstood worse than that."

He shakes his head. "But if he won't play fair, then she stands no chance," he says.

"Gwen isn't you. If he won't play fair, neither will she," I say, nodding toward the field where Lord Uhred lunges toward Gwen again, but this time, she anticipates him. She steps out of his way, light as a cat, but leaves her foot sticking out. He trips, sprawling out on the ground with a groan so deep and loud it makes the earth quiver. His sword drops from his fingers, and Gwen kicks it away, out of his reach.

When he tries to get to his feet again, Gwen hits him—not with her shield, but with the pommel of her sword. It is not lost on me that she could have ended the fight then and there by placing her sword to his throat. No, she's toying with him now, paying him back for her broken nose.

"Careful, Sir Lancelot," my father bellows from his seat. "Another move like that and I'll have to disqualify you."

"Apologies, my lord," Gwen says, pitching her voice deeper in a frightfully good imitation of Lance's. "My sword slipped."

She doesn't even try to make it convincing, and I think I see a smile ghost at the corners of my father's lips.

*Just finish it*, I want to scream at her. Every instant she drags it on is another opportunity for the illusion to shatter.

But Gwen seems in no hurry, and it takes me a moment to understand why: This is the last time she'll get to do this, to fight out in the open, against someone who isn't afraid to hurt her. After this, she will go back to being a princess, soon to be queen. Soon, she will restrict herself to a life of gowns and diplomacy and good manners, but not today. Today, she gets to hit and stab and fight with every ounce of repressed fury she holds on to.

Lord Uhred doesn't stand a chance against that.

She fights circles around him, leaping and running and striking, her familiar smile stretched wide over Lancelot's face. She is a cat playing with a mouse, and when she eventually does pin him with her blade aimed lazily at his throat, part of me is sad to see it end. To see this part of her end.

I force my gaze away from Gwen, and only then do I realize that Morgana is no longer watching the fight—she's watching me, and I can see her put the pieces together. Lancelot would never have turned to unfair play, not even when confronted with it himself. And the voice Gwen used—close enough to fool most people, but not her. She knows it's magic, but it's a leap to the how of it.

It isn't a leap for Morgana, though. Maybe she feels the magic still thrumming in the air, pulling at her heart. Maybe the scent of jasmine and oranges lingers.

*I can't feel it anymore,* I remember her saying, her voice high and panicked. *It's gone. It's really gone.*

Surprise flickers over her expression, followed by disbelief, denial, and, finally, anger.

"Morgana," I start, but she's already gone, bolting out of her seat faster than I can blink and storming from our box without a word.

As SOON AS the match is called, Gwen dashes off the field, only for Lancelot to return a moment later, without a shield or a sword in hand. He still grimaces a bit when he walks, but I think I might be the only one to notice it. Even my father looks pleased.

"It seems you've given favor to the right man, Elaine," he tells me as Lancelot approaches our box, the crowd in a mad frenzy of cheers behind him.

"I did tell you as much," I say, getting to my feet.

When Lancelot comes to stand before us, he drops to one knee before my father until he motions for him to stand.

"You fought bravely, Sir Lancelot," my father says. "It is my great honor to offer you my daughter's hand in marriage, along with a dowry of fifty acres and fifteen thousand pieces of gold."

Lancelot bows his head, but his eyes linger on mine.

"If she will have me," he says, his voice low but clear, traveling all the way to the back of the crowd. It is a trick of Arthur's, I realize, though I didn't think it was one Lancelot had ever picked up on.

I try to fight a smile, but it is a losing battle. It blossoms and grows so broad it hurts my mouth, but I barely feel it at all, because Lancelot's smile matches mine, and despite all the people watching us, it feels like it is only him and me.

"I will have you," I tell him, and in front of the crowd I lean over the railing of the box and kiss him soundly.

The cheers grow deafening.

I SLIP AWAY FROM the crowd as soon as I can, leaving Lancelot to his new admirers, eager to offer up their congratulations. In some ways, this is what was taken from him on Avalon, when he lost the tournament to protect Arthur. I won't be the one to dampen his glory, but I also need to find Morgana.

She makes it easy on me. As soon as I approach the castle, I see her leaning against the stone wall beside the door, waiting.

"I did it because I had to," I tell her as soon as I'm close enough for her to hear me. "I didn't know if I could even manage it, small a spell as it was. I found out quite by accident."

Morgana shoves off the wall and closes the distance between us in a few quick paces.

"That's just it, Elaine—it's always an accident," she bites out. "You're always scheming and plotting and making decisions in favor of some unknowable future, performing your sacred duty. But here we are, *now*, and your actions have consequences. But not for you—never for you. You have everything you've ever wanted now. The status and power you craved when I first met you, but also love, Lancelot. And still it wasn't enough. Tell me, is my magic finally enough?"

I don't think the words could hurt more if she'd punctuated them with physical strikes. I reel back from her, stumbling slightly.

"You think so little of me," I say, but that only makes her laugh.

"Oh no, I assure you I think a great deal of you," she says. "You want things and you take them—Maiden, Mother, and Crone, I admire you for it. Perhaps I should be proud, I helped make you that, didn't I?"

I swallow and try again. "I didn't want this," I tell her. "I don't want your magic. Giving it to me was *your* idea. I used it today because it was necessary, but I promise I won't again. I'd give it back if I could—"

"No one's stopping you, Elaine," she says, taking a step closer to me, then another. "Come on, if you mean it, then go ahead."

"I can't," I say, before I can stop myself. I flinch as she searches my expression, reading every inch of me with no effort at all.

"You tried," she says, going still. "Of course you did, it would have been easier for Gwen to just heal him. You tried and you couldn't."

I don't deny it. "Maybe I did it wrong," I say, shaking my head.

She tilts her head to one side, her expression closed off. "Do you think you did?"

A *yes* rises up in my throat, but I know she will see the lie. I think I could get away with it if she were anyone else, but I cannot lie to Morgana. "No," I tell her, looking away. "No, I felt it. Visualized it, just as you said—a locked box and a key. But no matter how I tried, I couldn't release it back to her."

Morgana looks at me like I've struck her, shocked and wounded and betrayed all at once.

"I tried," I tell her. "But you said it yourself, it's all theoretical. Perhaps you miscalculated—"

"So it's my fault?"

"No," I say quickly. I bite my lip. "There must be a way. I'll ask Merlin about it when we get back to Camelot, I'll even reach out to Nimue. I'll read every magical text I can get my hands on, but I'll find a way to get it back to you, when it's safe."

"When it's safe," she echoes, each syllable dripping with disdain. "Was it safe when you used my magic today?"

"It was necessary," I say, shaking my head.

"And when I used it in Lyonesse? That wasn't necessary?" she asks, a question she already knows the answer to, though I give it to her anyway.

"Yes, but you were discovered. I wasn't, and I won't use it again. You have my word."

She doesn't say anything for a long moment, instead only looking at me with eyes that see too much.

"Do you want to know what I think?" she asks, and I know right away that I don't. I don't want to know what she thinks. But she doesn't wait for my answer. "I think the reason you can't release our magic is because deep down, you don't want to give it up. You *want* it."

"I don't," I say, but even as the words pass my lips, I know they're a lie. I have envied Morgana and Gwen their magic in the past, just as I've envied everything else about them, and now I have it. But that isn't why I can't give it back—not the entire reason, at any rate. "The reasons for binding your magic still stand—"

"No, not binding," Morgana cuts in. "Binding implies that it is still mine. It isn't. You didn't bind my magic, you stole it. It is not the same."

"Because you asked it of me," I say. "You think I forced your hand, that I orchestrated all of this? *You* made choices, Morgana, as much as I did. If you want to blame me, blame me. But all I have tried to do for almost half my life is—"

"Is keep Arthur safe," she finishes for me. "I know. How often have I heard it from you, from Nimue? Arthur must be kept safe at all costs. I'm so sick of it, sick of having to put him first every step of the way, no matter what it does to me, how it hurts me."

The bitterness in her voice should scare me. I should see it for what it is, a precursor to the hate from my visions, the resentment that will drive her mad. But that idea is a distant one, cast in the shadow of a much greater thought.

"That wasn't what I was going to say," I tell her, my voice softening. "All I have tried to do for almost half my life is keep *you* safe, Morgana. From yourself. From this simmering anger that will tear you to pieces if you let it."

She can only stare at me, so I force myself to continue.

"They aren't unrelated," I say, the words spilling forth now before I can stop them. "In protecting you, I protect Arthur, that much has always been known, since long before I came to Avalon. You will be either his bolster or his doom, Morgana. It has been foreseen, one way or another."

For a moment, Morgana only stares at me, and the air leaves her sails. She deflates. I shouldn't have said that, but before I can begin to regret the words, she finds her voice.

"Are those my choices then?" she asks quietly. "A villain or bolster? No matter what, my life is defined by his, reflected by his."

"Morgana," I say, but she holds a hand up to silence me.

"I love my brother," she tells me, her voice low. "In spite of everything, I love him more than anyone else in this world, you included. I didn't think there was anything I wouldn't give up for him, not even my magic. But I was wrong. I won't give up myself. That is my line."

I open my mouth to speak, to tell her she's wrong, but no words come out.

"I'm not returning to Camelot with you," she says. "You have my magic, you don't need me there. You'll keep him safe—I trust you with that much."

I try not to feel the sting of the words, but the splinter of them wedges beneath my skin, and I know I'll feel them for some time yet.

"Where will you go?" I ask her.

She shrugs, glancing away from me. "Avalon," she says, as if it should be obvious. "It's home. It's the only place I can get power back—even if it isn't my own power. And you Saw it, didn't you? Me, there."

*Us, there*, I want to say, but instead I only nod. I've already told her too much.

"Nimue won't welcome you back," I tell her.

"I don't intend to give her a choice," she tells me, and for the first time, I find I fear for Nimue. "Tell the others I said goodbye. I can't stomach it. Tell Arthur . . ." But she trails off, and her voice cracks.

I don't need her to finish the sentence, though.

"I will," I say.

Before I can overthink it, I step toward her, arms outstretched, but she stops me short, holding both of her hands out. Like I am a spirit she is trying to ward off. I blink away my tears and wrap my arms around myself instead, as if I can keep everything together that way when it seems so determined to fall apart.

"We'll see each other again," I tell her, and I'm not sure whether I mean the words as a reassurance or a threat.

She nods, blinking rapidly, and I realize she is holding back tears as well.

"I found my line, Elaine," she says softly. "Where is yours?"

She doesn't give me a chance to answer, instead turning and walking away from me. She doesn't walk back into the castle—I suppose there's nothing for her there anyway. Instead she disappears into the woods, never once looking back.

# 41

B Y THE TIME we start preparing for the wedding, Lancelot says he feels no pain at all, and after checking the place where his wound used to be, Gwen confirms that he is at least mostly healed. Fay blood indeed.

Gwen's nose is another issue, though. If she's seen in public with her face mottled and bruised, there will be questions—questions that none of us can provide believable answers for. In the end, I heal it with her own magic and promise, again, that it will be the last time I use it. She pretends to believe me.

As a handmaid helps me into a Shalott Blue gown that was hastily altered from one of my sister-in-laws' wedding gowns, Gwen watches with her head resting on her arm, her eyes threatening to droop closed at any second.

"Would a nap help?" I ask her. "The wedding won't be for another hour— plenty of time for a bit of rest. When was the last time you slept?"

Gwen scoffs, forcing herself to sit up straighter and blink the sleep from her eyes. "I don't nap," she says. "The rare occasions I do sleep, it's difficult to rouse me for at least half a day. No, give me something to do and I'll catch a second wind quickly enough."

A heavy cloak of silence falls over us, and I know we're both thinking the same thing, missing the same person who should be here.

When I told the others that Morgana was gone, no one was truly surprised. Arthur seemed shocked at first, but even that faded quickly.

"I suppose I should have expected it," he said, shaking his head. "She was never going to be happy here. Maybe now she can be."

I didn't tell him that in all my visions of Morgana's future, I've never seen her happy.

But now that it's only Gwen and me, I can't keep Morgana's words from echoing again and again in my mind.

*I found my line. Where's yours?*

Where's Gwen's line? I wonder.

"Gwen?" I say, my voice coming out softer than I intend, a fragile word that threatens to break as soon as it leaves my lips.

She looks up at me, blinking the exhaustion from her eyes. "Hmm?"

"Do you miss Lyonesse?" I ask her.

She leans back in her chair, considering the question for a moment.

"I do," she says finally. "Quite horribly, actually. I'm not sure why. I spent more of my life on Avalon—you would think leaving there would have been harder, but it wasn't. Leaving Lyonesse felt like . . . like the skin was being stripped from my bones. The feeling hasn't gone away yet."

"Then why are you here?" I ask her. "Because you love Arthur more?"

She frowns. "Maybe that's it, at least part of it," she says before shaking her head. "I made a choice, Elaine. If you're asking if I regret it like Morgana, I don't. There's no point in regrets like that, and pretending otherwise doesn't do anyone any good."

I believe her, but that isn't much of a balm. I believe she means it now, that she sees a future ahead of her that is wide with possibilities. But that future is an illusion—one I shoved her toward, one I convinced her was right.

*I found my line. Where's yours?*


LANCELOT AND I marry by the river where my mother and I used to play when I was a child. Traditionally, weddings are held indoors, but my father didn't put up a single protest when I asked for this—he feels her presence here, too, I think.

It is a traditional Shalott ceremony, where I walk arm in arm with my father down a path strewn with lilies, Gwen walking a few steps ahead. Lancelot approaches from the other path, running parallel to the river, walking just behind Arthur. Healed now, there is no pain in his smile when he sees me. His eyes lock on to mine, and all of a sudden, I see it—not the dozens of paths of pain that branch out from this moment, but the one glowing one, the single path that leads us to wrinkles and hair gone gray, to a house far from court where we can hear the sea each morning and fall asleep beside each other each night.

I see happiness, and I know that I will do whatever I must to keep us on that path.

*Where is your line, Elaine?*

I try to push Morgana's voice from my mind, but I don't quite manage it.

When we meet by the river, before the audience made up only of my family and Lancelot's fellow knights, my father passes my hand to Lancelot, and he holds it tight in both of his. He holds it like he never wants to let me go, and I hold him back just as tightly.

Arthur leaves Lancelot's side and comes to stand between us. As a prince of the realm, he has the power to oversee a marriage, and my father has relinquished that duty to him. There are phrases he's supposed to say, centuries-old words about marriage and duty and the joining of households, but I know before he even speaks that he will be veering far off course.

He clears his throat, looking between us with a grin before turning his attention to our gathered friends and family.

"It would be a lie to say that Elaine and Lancelot loved each other from the first time they met," he says. "No, the first time they met, they clashed. They argued and insulted and fought so constantly it drove me mad."

I press my lips together to keep from laughing while Lancelot shoots Arthur a dirty look.

"Really—Elaine is a very well-raised woman, sir," Arthur adds, looking at my father. "But I once heard her call this man *a gilded prat with an ego the size of the sun.*"

At that, Lancelot snorts, squeezing my hand.

"In my defense, he deserved it," I say.

"He more than likely did," Arthur allows, nudging Lancelot. "But all of that aside, I cannot truly say that I am surprised to be standing here today, celebrating them and the love that they have discovered and nurtured over the years. They have always challenged each other, and through that, they have shaped each other into the very best versions of themselves. I am so incredibly grateful to know both of them, and even more grateful that they have found each other. And so, in addition to your new land and your new titles as husband and wife, it would be my great honor to give you another title."

"Arthur," I say.

"Yes, I know, it is not done. Not by princes. But I am doing it, and if someone would like to stop me, they are welcome to try, but that is a problem for tomorrow. Today, though, I would like to pronounce you not just man and wife, but I would like to give you a family name to pass on to your children, and to their children after them. I hereby name you Sir Lancelot and Lady Elaine Du Lac, as a way to honor the lake and Avalon, the place that brought you—brought all of us—together."

Lancelot looks at Arthur for a moment, blinking. "Thank you," he says finally.

Arthur smiles. "Well, go on then. Kiss the bride before I change my mind."

It's a hollow threat, but Lancelot doesn't waste a second before pulling me toward him and sealing his mouth, his life, and his future irrevocably with mine.


THE TENT WILL be drafty and sparse, with only a thin bedroll, a change of clothes, a leather satchel, and a familiar sword and shield set against the side. And him, sitting on top of the bedroll and staring at me like I am a figment of a dream made real, and not a very pleasant one.

For an eternity of a moment, Lancelot and I will only look at each other. It will almost be easy, in the dim, candlelit tent, to pretend that the last few years haven't happened. He will almost seem twenty-five again, the way he looked when we stood beside that river and pledged ourselves to each other, when he was still hungry for a world he will never understand. But he will not be hungry for it anymore, only tired.

I won't know if it's standing in front of him again or something else, but I will feel tired as well, more than I think I've ever been. More than I ever will be again. I will wait for anger to come back to me—I would even welcome sorrow, but I will only feel old. Impossibly old.

Without saying a word, he will take a leather flask from his satchel, twist off the cap, and take a long swig before offering it to me. When I won't move to take it, he will frown.

"Can you still drink?" he will ask, before looking away, embarrassed.

"I don't know if it will have any effect," I will admit, but I'll take it anyway, careful not to touch his skin, though I will want to. I will miss how his warm, calloused hands felt against my skin; I will crave it. But I will not want him to touch me because I will not know what he will feel in turn.

The liquid will burn down my throat, but I won't mind it. It will be a relief to feel something.

"I don't suppose you came here for a friendly chat," he'll say after a moment.

"There isn't anything friendly left between us." The words will leave my mouth before I can stop them, but I won't be able to deny the bolt of pleasure his expression sends through me. He will look like I slapped him. He will look like he was hoping for worse.

"You won't see another sunset," I'll tell him. "But I think you already know that."

He will look away, staring over my shoulder with such determination it will be surprising that he doesn't singe a hole in the tent. "A lot of men will die tomorrow. Only a fool would think himself immune. Even if Death was once a friend."

"Morgana had no say in it," I'll protest.

He'll give me a reproachful look. "Morgana doesn't exist anymore, Elaine." It will be the way he used to talk to me back when I first came to Avalon, when I was naive and stupid and he seemed to know everything. But I will not be that girl anymore, and he certainly will not be the same shining, valiant hero I fell in love with.

"Elaine doesn't exist anymore either," I will tell him.

His eyes will rake over me; his expression will harden. "No. I suppose she doesn't. I am sorry about that."

I'll take another gulp of the liquor. This will not be the conversation I wanted to have with him. I will not want his apologies. But what did I expect? He will be a man facing death, and I will be his biggest regret. Of course he will want to make amends. Of course he will want to die forgiven.

But I won't know if I have forgiveness left in me.

"I came to take you home. To Avalon. It isn't too late," I will say.

Surprise will knock the air from him. Whatever he will have expected me to say, it will not be that. His eyes will flicker in the candlelight, and a smile will ghost across his face, gone too quickly.

"I have made a vow of loyalty twice in my life, El. Once to you and once to Arthur. I won't break both of them."

Something painful will writhe in my stomach, twisting around my chest like wild vines. I will have told myself I have come as a courtesy, because I will owe something to his mother, because even after everything, I will feel this is still a part of my duty. I might not have expected him to agree, but it won't be until now that I will realize how badly I wanted him to.

When I speak, my voice will be thread thin. "If you come home, we can fix things, fix our vows. I will forgive everything. Please, Lance."

Though he will stay upright, his body will seem to fold in on itself, shoulders sagging forward, head drooping. Green-gold eyes will finally meet mine. His hands will twitch, fighting the urge to reach out to me.

"I don't think you would," he will say. "So much rot already lies between us. Would you have Arthur's body join it?"

"I would have you on Avalon," I will tell him. "Safe and alive. I cannot save Arthur, but I can save you."

He will shake his head, but before he can protest again, I will interrupt.

"Morgana once asked me where my line was, the line I wouldn't cross, even for Arthur," I will tell him. "I didn't know how to answer her then. Where's your line, Lancelot?"

Lancelot will hold my gaze. "I haven't found it yet," he will tell me, his voice soft. "I don't think I'll find it tomorrow, either, not even in death. I'm not sure that line exists for me, Elaine."

A cry will strangle me, coming out mangled and not quite human, but Lancelot won't flinch from it. Instead, he will swallow, then hold a hand out toward me. At first, I will think he means to take the flask back, but when I hold it out, he will take hold of my wrist instead, pulling me toward him, and despite all of that rot between us, I will let him. Even though his skin will be so hot against mine that it burns, even though I imagine my own skin must feel like ice to him, like something not quite alive anymore.

But if he feels it, if he understands it, if he is at all repulsed, he will not show it. Instead, he will look at me the way he did a lifetime ago, like I am the sun in his universe and nothing else exists at all.

"If I am to die tomorrow," he will say, his voice a mere whisper between us, "will you stay with me tonight?

"Lancelot—"

"I have no right to ask it, none to expect it, but as I am a dying man, I will ask it anyway," he will say.

"You are dying because of your own stubbornness." The words will be rough edged, forcing their way past tears that will have risen in my throat. "And the right you had to ask anything of me died when you betrayed me—betrayed us—with Guinevere."

"That wasn't about you," he will say, before catching himself. "We never spoke of it, did we?"

"We didn't need to," I will say, yanking my hand out of his grip. "We still don't. I came to warn you, and I've done that. My duty is done."

"It wasn't to do with you," he will say, ignoring me. I suppose it will make sense, how he will want to unburden his soul in his last hours. How he will want to say what he will never again have the chance to say. "And it wasn't to do with Arthur, for Gwen's part. It wasn't even to do with each other, really. You and Arthur . . . you belonged there, in Camelot. You flourished. The two of you fit in so seamlessly."

"It was a duty," I will say. "His to lead Albion and mine to lead him. We were good at that duty. I didn't realize that was a bad thing."

"I'm not . . . I'm only trying to explain why," he will say. "I know they say I loved her, I've heard the poems and the songs, and I'm sure you have as well. But I didn't—*don't*. Not like that. You know that, know what is between us."

"The last time I saw the two of you together, there was absolutely nothing between you," I will say, taking some pleasure in the venom that leaks into my voice. "That was the problem."

"It was a mistake," he will say. "One I have regretted every moment since. And if that mistake haunts me into whatever next life I find, so be it. But I would not have it haunt you. I love you, Elaine. I made a mistake. There is nothing more to it than that. If you take anything from tonight, take that."

The venom simmering in me will dissipate. I will know that I should leave, know that I should leave things as they are, let my anger nourish me the way it has for the last year. But I won't. Instead, I will sit beside him.

"Are you afraid?" I will ask.

"Have you ever known me to be afraid?" he will reply.

"Yes. Plenty of times," I will say, staring straight ahead. "You are brave, Lance, but you aren't fearless."

He won't say anything for a moment, but when he speaks, his voice will be little more than a whisper.

"The thing of it that makes me afraid isn't the dying bit," he will say. "It isn't the bit where I don't know what happens next. It's an adventure, and I am always ready for a new adventure. What frightens me is that I know you won't be joining me on it. That wherever I go, you will not follow."

"Our paths diverged long ago," I will say.

"No, you have always haunted me, El. And a part of me has always believed that one day, we would find our way back to each other, when all of this madness is over. I thought I would come to you on Avalon, maybe, when the war was won. It was foolish, I know, but I believed it. Now . . . now there is no hope for forgiveness. Now our paths diverge for good. That is what frightens me, more than dying, more than whatever might come after. It is the first adventure I will embark on alone."

He won't reach for me—I think that if he did, I would leave and not look back. But he won't reach for me, and so I will reach for him. I will press myself against him the way I did the night we married, as if I will be able to bind myself to him through this life and the next.

Together, we will watch his last sunrise, but I will not let myself cry until I am back on Avalon and his soul has been claimed by Death.

I WAKE UP WITH cold sweat drenching my skin, my breathing heavy and labored. It takes a moment to recognize not just where I am—my childhood bedroom in Shalott—but that I am not sleeping here alone. Lancelot's chest presses against my back, skin against skin, and his arm is loose around my waist. When we fell asleep together last night, drunk on wine and giddiness and utterly spent, the arm around me had felt like a comfort, but now it is too much, too heavy, too hot.

I pull away from him, out of the bed, my bare feet cold against the stone floor. I barely make it to the chamber pot before I vomit.

Nothing has changed. That vision was even more solid than others I've had, full of more details, even recollections of our wedding. Last night, this path became more solid, not less. And the rest of it . . . Lancelot dying in battle at Arthur's side, Gwen betraying Arthur, mentions of Morgana as a goddess of death. All of those futures are closing in tighter now, no matter what I have tried to do to stop them.

I rise on shaky legs and dab my mouth with a towel before drawing a dressing gown around my body, tying the satin sash around my waist.

Lancelot stirs in bed, looking at me through tired, slitted eyes.

"It's barely dawn," he says. "Come back to bed."

Tempted as I am to do just that, to lose myself again to sleep and the blissful present, I know that if I close my eyes, all I will see is his guilt-stricken face, hear his voice telling me he is ready to die.

"I need water. I'll be right back." I'm surprised the lie comes so easily, but he believes it, giving me a sleep-laced smile before rolling away from me and burrowing deeper into the covers.

It's a strange sight, him stretched out in my childhood bed, naked except the band of gold around his left ring finger. Almost surreal.

*Yesterday was a good day*, I think. *This was a good choice.*

But I can't quite bring myself to believe that.

I grab the enamel hand mirror off my vanity and slip out of the bedroom, closing the door softly behind me.


NIMUE'S FACE RIPPLES into being, stretched over the surface of the mirror, skin smooth and eyes untroubled. She looks as she always does, as she always has, as—I suspect—she always will. She blinks her large gray eyes.

"Elaine?" she asks. "Is everything alright? We discussed this—mirror communications are only for the direst of emergencies."

I don't say anything for a moment, though a thousand words lodge in my throat. There is so much I want to say, so many questions I want to ask her, but none of that manages to push through first.

"Morgana is gone," I tell her.

For a moment, she doesn't speak. "We knew it would happen," she says finally. "This is sooner than we thought, perhaps, but Arthur is safe, isn't he? You did well."

"Arthur is safe," I agree. "He married Gwen three days ago. I married Lance just last night."

"I see," she says, her brow furrowing slightly, trying to see where I'm going with this. It is a comfort, I suppose, to see that she doesn't know everything.

I shake my head. "I thought I was so clever, Nimue," I say. "I thought I had found a way to keep us together, to keep us happy. Morgana agreed to have her magic bound—Gwen did as well, which I thought might end up making things easier. Neither of them were happy about it, but they knew it was for the best. And Gwen married Arthur by choice, was not cornered into it. We were returning to Camelot together, all of us. It should have been enough to keep us from that path. It should have been enough to keep us *us*. But it wasn't."

It's her turn to fall silent, though she no longer looks surprised. Instead, she only looks tired.

"Elaine," she says, like a warning. But this time, it is a warning I do not heed.

"You knew, didn't you?" I ask her.

"Most fates can be changed," she says carefully. "Some are more steadfast than others. When you are as old as I am, you learn the difference. You learn to see people differently as well, learn to see who they are, how they will grow, what choices they will make. You understand these things even before they do."

"Then why?" I ask her through gritted teeth. "Why would you bring us to Avalon at all? Why would you make me think I could change things, that I could save them?"

She doesn't have an answer to that, not right away. Instead, she glances just past the mirror and takes a deep breath.

"When Arthur and Morgana came to my shores, she was holding his hand in hers, tight and secure. When I stepped toward him, she thought me a threat, and do you know what she did? She stepped in front of him. That was her instinct—to shield him, even if she had to do it with her own body. She was six. And so I looked at her with her angry, mistrustful violet eyes and I hoped. It was foolish and I should have known better, but hope is a funny thing like that.

"And then Gwen came, all feral and restless, a monster of a girl, yes, but a monster who loved the two of them fiercely. Who would rip the world to shreds rather than see them hurt. Lancelot was next, the fay boy who was not afraid of humans, who saw them as his own. It became unthinkable to me, that those four would cause one another such hurt. You can understand that— it was an impossibility to you as well. And so my hope flourished. But then you came, and I understood the truth of it."

"Me?" I ask, taken aback.

She inclines her head, gray eyes intent on me, urging me to understand, but I don't.

"Tell me, Elaine, what happens after?" she asks. "After Morgana turns to darkness, after Lancelot and Guinevere have their affair, after Arthur is left alone on that battlefield, facing off against Mordred?"

I open my mouth, then close it again. "I don't know," I admit. "He dies—"

"You've Seen him die?" she asks.

I rake through my memories, searching. I have Seen Mordred's sword cut clean through Arthur's stomach. I have Seen Arthur hobbling toward a shore, leaning heavily on Gawain and bleeding.

But I have never Seen the life leave his eyes.

"That is what I realized when you came to me," Nimue continues when I don't answer. "That what is set in stone would come to pass, that there was little any of us could do to prevent it. But the after? That, we could still control. That, we can still save. At a cost."

I think of Lancelot as I Saw him, resigned to his fate. I think of Morgana in my vision from so long ago, washing a bloody shirt that I had sewn with my own hands.

"Lancelot will die," I say.

Nimue hesitates only an instant before nodding. "His life was never meant to extend beyond that day. If you were to deflect every sword point, an arrow would find him. If you managed to shield him from those, he would be struck by a stone falling from the sky. Lancelot is a hero, Elaine, and heroes do not live long lives."

"And Morgana will turn," I say.

Again, Nimue nods. "The turn is foretold," she agrees. "You've seen her on Avalon."

"As a goddess of death," I say.

"The cruelest punishment the Maiden, Mother, and Crone see fit to inflict on their children," Nimue agrees softly. "She and death will not be strangers by then, and her hands will be dripping with blood. She will owe a debt, and she will have to repay it."

I swallow. "And Gwen?" I ask her.

Nimue flinches. "Gwen will end up banished to a convent," she says, her voice low. "She will die there, powerless and alone and miserable. She will never ride a horse again, never lift a sword, never even feel the sun on her face or the grass beneath her feet. All she will know is walls of stone and stale air."

My stomach twists, and I think I will be sick all over again.

"But if Arthur survives," Nimue says, "it will be enough."

For an eternity of a moment, I can't speak. I can't begin to contemplate her words, the implications of them. I've *Seen* other futures, I want to tell her. I know I have. But she's right—those happier lives have always been woven with spider's thread—too fragile to exist.

"You should have told me," I tell her finally. "You shouldn't have let me believe I could change things, that I could make a difference."

"But you can," she says gently. "You already have. Perhaps I should have been more transparent about my plans, but you weren't ready to hear them. You weren't ready to see beyond the end, to what comes next. You would have seen all that death and destruction and given up, sunken into such a deep depression that nothing would have pulled you out again, and Arthur needs you too much for that."

*Where's your line, Elaine?*

"And what about what I need?" I ask her, my voice cracking on the last syllable.

Nimue's smile turns sad. "You need them," she says. "Which is why you are going to get up now and dry your tears and see that that crown ends up on Arthur's head."


THE SUN IS bleeding over the horizon when I slip back into the bedroom and let my dressing gown fall to the floor. I crawl into bed beside Lancelot and press my body against his, reveling in the warmth of his skin, in the way his arms come around me, gentle and secure, in the noise he makes, low in his throat, in the scratch of his stubbled cheek against my shoulder.

I close my eyes and press each sensation deep into my memory, careful not to let any tears fall.

When all is said and done, when the day comes when we are not on this earth together anymore, I will not remember the hurt to come, I will not remember the heartbreak or the betrayal. I will remember only this, and I will smile.

# 42

THE STORY OF our triumph in Lyonesse somehow arrives in Camelot before we do, and when we return, we are greeted by a crowd at least thrice as large as the one that saw us off, all cheering and waving. The crowd flusters Arthur, but he does a good job of hiding it, waving and smiling in turn as he rides in side by side with Gwen.

For her part, Gwen tries to look the part of the rescued damsel, demure and pretty, but the expectations are already chafing at her more than the sidesaddle she still hasn't gotten used to.

Merlin stands at the castle steps, waiting with Morgause and Mordred, who wear matching sour expressions. When we dismount and make our way toward them, Merlin inclines his head.

"I hear you return to us victorious, young prince," he says before turning to Gwen. "And married besides. And so you've done what your father and many others could not. But there is one task left, and it will be more difficult than the first two combined, though I am glad to say it will be much quicker, and not nearly so far away. Come."

Without another word, Merlin turns and walks into the castle, Mordred and Morgause at his heels and the rest of us falling in after.

MERLIN LEADS US through the castle halls and out into a small courtyard at the center. It is not the main one, always bustling with people, but a smaller one off to the east, barely big enough for a single beam of sunlight to shine down on a large, jagged gray stone. But it isn't the stone itself that stops me in my tracks.

"What is it?" Lancelot asks from beside me, but I barely hear him. All my attention is focused on the sword hilt sticking out from the top of the stone, embedded with rubies and glinting gold in the sunlight.

"Excalibur," I whisper, more to myself than to Lancelot, but somehow Merlin hears me, his eyebrows raising.

"Indeed, Lady Elaine," he says, stepping toward the sword. He places his ageless, bone-pale hands on the hilt of the sword and gives a sharp tug, but the sword doesn't budge from its place. "Legend says that Excalibur was the sword of the first king of Camelot, given to him as a gift from the Lady of the Lake at the time—Vivienne. Upon his death, Vivienne used her magic to bury it in this stone, proclaiming that only a true king of Camelot would be able to pull it from the stone. Though, since that day, every would-be king who has tried to pull it free has failed. Even your father couldn't manage it."

Arthur looks at the sword, brow furrowed. "So you have set me an impossible task," he says slowly. "Has Mordred tried to free it?" he asks, glancing at his glowering half brother.

"Several times, I believe," Merlin says mildly, making Mordred glare harder. "But in my view, Mordred's claim to the throne is still the stronger one. He is from Camelot, he has been trained for this. His loyalties are not in question. If you are to usurp that claim, it is on you to prove yourself. Pull the sword from the stone, and the crown is yours."

Arthur frowns. "Now?" he asks.

Merlin inclines his head toward the sword. "Give it a try," he says.

After everything in Lyonesse, this must seem easy to him. Only a few moments, a single movement, stand between him and what he has been working toward.

But Arthur is not an idiot, and he knows it is not that simple. I can see it in his expression, in the way he takes hold of the sword and braces his foot against the rock for leverage. He doesn't expect it will come free, but he tries anyway, pulling with all his might.

The sword doesn't budge.

Morgause is unable to keep a grin from spreading over her face as she clutches Mordred's arm, though his glower doesn't fade and he bats her away impatiently.

"It's impossible," Arthur says.

Merlin eyes him thoughtfully. "I don't believe it is, young prince," he says. "You have until tomorrow night at sundown to free the sword from the stone and claim your throne. If you cannot do it, the crown will go to Mordred instead."


WHEN THE CROWD disperses, I lose Arthur to a group of well-wishers, though many of them are the same ones who kept their sons from joining his last quest. I suppose now, with two challenges accomplished, they've decided to hedge their bets a little more evenly, impossible as this final task might seem.

I linger in the courtyard until everyone but Lancelot and Guinevere has gone. When it's only the three of us, I step toward the sword, taking hold of it myself and trying to pull it free. It isn't that I expect it to come loose for me, but I need to feel it myself, how firm the grip is, what that glittering hilt feels like in my own hands. And I am not the only one—as soon as I step back, Gwen tries her hand at it, then Lancelot. But it stays stuck.

"An impossible task," Gwen says, shaking her head.

"It seems that way," I say, biting my lip.

I've seen Arthur with this sword in hand, seen Morgana try to use it to kill him through Accolon, seen him fall on a battlefield with it clutched in his hand. This will be his sword—I know that as sure as I know my own name—but I don't know how to get it for him.

"Don't be too hard on yourself, Elaine," a familiar voice purrs.

Morgause is walking toward us from the courtyard entrance, her movements delicate and small. It will never not be strange to see Morgana's face on someone so different from her, I think.

"Arthur did better than anyone expected," she continues. "But no one can free that sword, and Merlin knows it. I doubt he could even do it with all his great power. He knows, though, who should sit on that throne."

"Mordred would bring destruction to this land," I say. "Though I respect your attempt to defend your husband . . . or your stepbrother? I'm sorry, the genealogy is so intertwined—which term would you prefer?"

Morgause's smile grows more simpering, tighter at the corners.

"If you had any sense, you would take your pretend prince and leave Camelot before Mordred is crowned—he wouldn't be the first king to execute a would-be usurper and his accomplices," she says.

"Well, you're quite lucky, then, that Arthur is far too noble to consider doing the same when he's crowned king," Gwen interjects with a smile of her own. "I don't think we've met, though I've heard so much about you I feel I know you like a sister. Morgana sends her regards, by the way."

At the mention of Morgana, Morgause's eyes glint. "Smart of you to leave her to the beasts, though I didn't think you had that sort of ruthlessness in you, Elaine. To abandon your friend like that . . ." She breaks off, clicking her tongue like a condescending schoolmarm.

"It must be tempting to breathe easier without your sister present," I tell her, trying to ignore the guilt her words spark in me. "But I wouldn't, if I were you. You don't frighten me anymore, Morgause."

She laughs, but it is tight-lipped. "Arthur will fail tomorrow, and you will fail with him," she says, her words sharp as a sewing needle. "And when I am queen, I will see the lot of you burned for your treasons. Perhaps I will even send an army to bring back my sister's head."

I don't doubt she means it, but I force a laugh. "You would send an army because you are too afraid to face her yourself," I tell her. "Little do you know though—I am every bit as fearsome as she is. I could snap your neck this instant, and I can assure you, I would feel no guilt over it."

Something like fear flickers behind Morgause's eyes. "You're lying."

I shrug my shoulders. "Maybe I am," I say. "If you would like to find out, then please—say Morgana's name once more. I beg of you."

For an instant, I think she might call my bluff, but instead she clenches her jaw and turns away, stalking back into the castle and leaving us alone once more.

"You couldn't really," Lancelot says, but all of a sudden, he doesn't sound sure.

I shrug my shoulders. "I suppose I could," I say. "But I meant what I said. No more magic—not until Arthur is secure on the throne and I can find a way to give it back to Gwen and Morgana. Morgause, however, doesn't need to know that."

"I didn't know you had it in you, Elaine," Gwen says, with something that might be akin to pride.

I shake my head, pushing the compliment away. It makes me wish Morgana were here to have seen it. She was right, after all. She made me.

"We have only a few hours to figure out how to get that sword from the stone," I say. "There's no time to waste. Meet me in my tower—I'll be along soon, but there's someone I must speak to first."

I FIND MERLIN IN the cloister that runs along the northern side of the courtyard, leaning back against one of the pillars with his arms crossed over his chest. For just an instant, he doesn't look ageless or ancient; he looks like an adolescent boy crushed by boredom. At least until he sees me. Then, he pushes away from the pillar and his eyes light.

"Lady Elaine," he says before pausing and tilting his head to one side. "I beg your pardon—Lady Du Lac. I hear congratulations are in order."

"Thank you," I say. "Would it be presumptuous to assume you were waiting for me?"

"Perhaps," he says, his mouth crooking into a smile. "But you would not be wrong. I assume you've been keeping Nimue apprised of your progress. Was she pleased to hear about your nuptials?"

I can't help but grimace at the mention of Nimue. In the days since I spoke to her, I've heard her words echo in my mind again and again, painting the picture of a future that is unavoidable—a future she has no desire to avoid. Lancelot dead, Morgana as a goddess of death, and Guinevere locked away somewhere, away from the sun and fresh air and everything that makes her Gwen.

And me? Where does that future leave me? I never asked Nimue. I forgot, I suppose. There was so much to process, after all. But I'm not sure that's the entire truth. I think part of me knew that if I asked, she would answer me with honesty, and I did not want that. I did not want to know.

"I don't want to talk about Nimue," I tell him, pushing the thought away. "It seems an impossible task that you've given Arthur."

He lifts a single dark eyebrow. "It seems that way, perhaps, but it isn't," he says. "I don't cheat, Elaine. If Arthur is a worthy king, I will do everything in my power to assist him. If he isn't, he has no business taking the throne."

"And Mordred does?" I ask him.

He doesn't answer, instead shaking his head. "Tell me, would Arthur have returned triumphant from Lyonesse without your counsel?" he asks. "I don't think he would have. I think he would have perished the second he set foot over the border."

My stomach tightens. "I'm his adviser," I say. "So is Lancelot. So was Morgana, for that matter. It is our duty to advise him."

"Ah yes," he says, something hard and knowing coming into his dark gaze. "Morgana. She didn't return with you, but I have had word that she left Lyonesse at your side. Dare I ask what transpired between there and here?"

*I found my line, Elaine. Where is yours?*

When I don't answer, his smile tightens. "It was always foretold," he says, his voice lowering. "You know that."

I don't say anything for a moment. "Nimue said it could be changed," I tell him finally. "I thought the fey couldn't lie, but she never really believed that."

He considers this. "Perhaps it could have been," he says. "Perhaps Nimue did not wish it changed. Perhaps she was perfectly happy with the path she had set you on."

*The path she'd set us on*, I think. A path that leads to ruin for all of us—all of us except Arthur, though he will be ruined in plenty of ways as well. He will merely be alive at the end of it, whatever that may be worth.

"Nimue wants magic back in Albion," I say. "You want to prevent that."

"And you?" he asks me. "What is it you want?"

It occurs to me that Nimue has never asked me that. As long as I have known her, it has not been a question worth pondering. It has always been Arthur above all, above everything and anything I have ever wanted for my-self. And that has never chafed, exactly. Not the way it did for Morgana or even for Gwen. But suddenly, it does.

"I want to protect the people I love," I tell him. "And that includes Mor-gana. Nimue believes that losing her—that losing Lancelot and Gwen and maybe even losing me—is an acceptable loss for reuniting Albion and Avalon. If you had asked me a fortnight ago, I'd have agreed."

"And now?" he asks.

"Now, I'm not sure." It's the first time I've said the words aloud, and part of me fears that lightning will strike me down for it. It feels so treasonous, so sacrilegious, that I should perish on the spot. But I don't.

He doesn't speak for a moment, instead nodding his head once. "There is new power in you, Elaine. I sense it. But it isn't yours."

I don't see the point in denying it. "It's Morgana's and Gwen's," I tell him. "We thought it best. Morgana was capable of frightening things, and Gwen . . . well, it seemed fair. They both agreed to it, on what was meant to be a tempo-rary basis."

"Meant to be?" he asks.

I hesitate only a second. I don't trust Merlin, but in this, I trust him more than Nimue. "I tried to give Gwen her power back. I couldn't."

For a moment, he doesn't speak. "You played with magic you didn't under-stand," he says, shaking his head. "Magic *I* don't understand. But one thing I do know is that magic like that has a cost."

"You don't think it can be undone," I say.

He shrugs. "I didn't say that. But the cost might not be something you're keen on paying," he says.

"More hypothesizing?" I ask him.

He shrugs. "I'm afraid I don't have the answers to questions that have never been asked before."

"That isn't comforting," I tell him.

"It isn't meant to be," he says. "But one thing I do know is that you possess power too great for one girl to hold. You didn't trust your friends with it; why do you trust yourself?"

For a moment, I don't reply. I promised I wouldn't use their magic, but it's a promise I've broken twice already in less than a week.

"There doesn't seem to be another choice," I say, instead of answering.

He smiles, a thin-lipped thing. "Perhaps there is a third option. I could bind your powers, and theirs along with them."

For a moment, I don't understand what he's saying, why he's saying it.

"You're mad," I tell him.

He shrugs his shoulders. "You aren't the first to say it," he says, unbothered. "But you've seen the future, Elaine, all kinds of futures, I'd imagine. Tell me, does magic ever do the lot of you any good? Does it prevent misery? Does it save the good, punish the evil? At the end of it all, when the world burns, does magic save anyone? Or does it merely strike the match?"

I open my mouth to answer but quickly shut it again. Because he might just be right. Everything I've seen, everything I've *Seen*—magic has caused problems, never solved them. Not without causing ten more in the process.

What if, in the end, magic is the ruin of us all?

"I don't need your answer now, Elaine," he says when I don't reply. "I've given you much to think on, I'm sure, but I want you to ask yourself if the road ahead would be simpler for you—for all of you—if you unburdened yourself."

I swallow, but he must sense my hesitation because he smiles.

"You're a newly wed woman, Elaine," he continues. "Your entire future is ahead of you, a future you can fill however you like. Imagine it—not having omens pressing in on you, not having to worry what horrors await you, not having to fear you will go as mad as your mother. Imagine how happy you could be."

And the worst thing is, I can imagine it. It is the same future my mother tried to force on me once, but then I wasn't ready. Then, I wasn't given a choice. Then, I didn't understand the gift beneath the cruelty.

"I will think on it," I tell him, hating myself for uttering the words.

But he only continues to smile and inclines his head toward me. "Then we'll speak again soon."

# 43

THERE IS NO future where Arthur pulls the sword from the stone.

I have sat at my loom for hours, Gwen, Arthur, and Lancelot with me in my tower. I have stared at the shimmering white Sight thread until my eyes have begun to cross and blur. Every time, though, it is the same.

Arthur will stand before the sword, the entire court crowded around him in the courtyard, watching from the windows that overlook it, shouting his name. He will take Excalibur's hilt in both of his hands, and for the briefest shining instant the world will align, it will feel right. Then he will pull with all his strength and . . .

Nothing.

Every single time I scry, I see Arthur fail.

"But you've seen him as king," Gwen says when I come to again, shaking my head.

"Yes," I say.

"And you've seen him with Excalibur," Lancelot adds.

"Yes," I say again.

"Then this doesn't make sense," Gwen says, frustration blooming in her voice.

Arthur is quiet, sitting near the window, his own expression thoughtful. When he feels my gaze, he turns to meet it.

"Merlin knows what you are," he says after a moment. "He knew you would use your gift to help me. So he's found a way to get around you."

I nod, picking the stitches from the loom once more. I didn't tell them about my conversation with him, but his words are still echoing through my mind. As I sit at the loom and weave futures, I wonder—could I give this up?

Once the answer would have been an emphatic no. Of course I couldn't give it up. It was like Morgana said, her magic was such a deep part of her that she didn't know who she would be without it. But she survived losing her magic. Gwen survived leaving Lyonesse. I could survive losing my Sight.

And life without it would have its advantages.

I push the thought aside and focus on the task at hand.

"I can't see the outcome of a choice until it's been made," I say. "Not until it's been at the very least considered. This is not an impossible task, but it is a riddle, and one designed so that my gift is useless."

Gwen shakes her head. "It doesn't make sense," she says. "How many people do you think have tried to lift that sword over the centuries? Thousands, millions even. Many, I'm sure, who were stronger than Arthur—no offense, Arthur."

"None taken," he says mildly. "You're right—not a single person has been able to do it."

Something in his words prickles at me.

"No," I say, sitting up. "No single person has been able to do it—you're right. But what if you *aren't* just a single person?"

"What is that supposed to mean?" Lancelot asks.

"Merlin's riddle is confusing enough, there's no need to add your own to the mix," Gwen says.

Only Arthur is silent, watching me with eyes bright.

"What are you thinking, El?" he asks.

I smile, gathering the Sight thread in my hands once more and beginning to warp the loom. "It will mean my using magic again," I say, with a wary glance at Gwen, who frowns. "But more than that, I'll have to draw on the rest of you—just as Morgana did in Lyonesse. But if I can do it, Arthur wouldn't be drawing Excalibur on his own, with only his own strength—he would have the strength of all of us together, and that—*that*—just might be enough."

It is a faint glimmer of a plan, full of too many hypotheticals to be at all solid. I wait for them to protest, to poke holes in it, but they don't. After a moment of consideration, Arthur nods slowly.

"Can it be done?" he asks me, wary eyes lingering on the loom.

I bite my lip. "If I try to scry the outcome of that spell, I should have an answer."

"No," Arthur says, surprising all of us. "No more scrying. If this plan succeeds, it succeeds, but at this point, there is no use knowing before we know. I trust you, Elaine."

THE BINDING SPELL will be too wide to hold for long, so it must be put off until the last possible moment, until we are all together in the courtyard, gathered around Arthur as he stands before Excalibur. Until his hand rests on the hilt, his grip on it white-knuckled.

That is when I let my magic—*Morgana's magic, Gwen's magic*, I remind myself—loose. I feel it stretching from my fingertips, feel it burning, like a hand reaching in to pull my very heart out.

Lancelot's hand comes to rest on the small of my back, to steady me or maybe to steady himself. On my other side, Gwen sways, digging her nails into her palms, her expression twisting like she has stomach pains. I'm sure my own face looks similar, but I bite my lip and try to mask the pain, keeping my gaze focused on Arthur.

The first time he pulls, Excalibur doesn't budge, but the second time—the second time it shifts, ever so slightly. Just enough to make the crowd pressing in around him lean in closer, just enough to elicit a few quiet gasps.

It's not enough, though. I need to take more. I send a silent apology to Lancelot and Gwen before I steel myself, forcing more power still, drawing on Gwen and Lance to support the spell. My knees go weak, Lancelot's grip on me becomes harder, like he's using it to keep himself upright instead of to steady me.

And Gwen—Gwen falls to the ground in a faint.

When the crowd turns toward her, though, Arthur pulls again, a third time, and Excalibur slips from the stone like a knife pulling from a pat of butter. He holds it in the air, triumphant, and the crowd erupts into cheers.

My strength comes back in a wave, rushing through me and making my skin buzz.

*We did it.*

Euphoria swims through my mind, making me dizzy and giddy even as Lancelot and I hold Gwen between us. She comes to, blinking wildly, and when she sees Arthur holding Excalibur, she smiles.

"It worked," she says, as if she can't quite believe it herself.

I squeeze her shoulder.

"It worked," I tell her. "We made a king."

# 44

THE GOLDEN CROWN hangs down low around Arthur's brow, still a touch too big. It makes him look even younger than his twenty-three years, like a child playing dress-up in his father's clothes. It isn't just the crown that gives that impression. He stands awkwardly on the dais of the throne room, fidgeting. In all the times we've rehearsed this speech, he was never sure what to do with his hands—no matter how many times I've told him to keep them still by his side, to hide his nerves. His russet hair sticks up in places, though five minutes before he stepped out onto the dais, I smoothed it down myself. I shouldn't have bothered—Arthur's hair never lies flat for more than a few minutes at a time—but I wanted him to look the part of a king.

Hundreds of courtiers have packed themselves into the humid, hot throne room to see him crowned today, hundreds of pairs of eyes dissecting him from head to toe—not just from Camelot but from all over Albion—each of them noticing every wrinkle in his suit, every bead of sweat forming on his forehead. He must feel each judgmental thought, each ill wish, but he doesn't cower beneath them, which is more than I might have managed in his place.

His eyes flicker around the room, landing briefly on me. I give him a nod and a smile of encouragement, but it doesn't do much to help. He still looks like he's going to be sick.

"If he passes out onstage, do I have to carry him out?" Lancelot asks from where he stands on my left.

I want to tell him not to be ridiculous, that of course Arthur won't pass out. But as soon as I think it, Arthur sways on his feet slightly, and though it might be the sunlight flickering through the stained glass windows, I think he actually turns a bit green.

"Yes," I tell him, not looking away from Arthur. "But you won't *carry him* carry him, Lance. Let him lean on you and make it look like he's holding himself up. He can't look weak, or that's how he'll always be remembered. Arthur Pendragon, the king who fainted as soon as the crown was placed on his head."

Sweat is beginning to show under Arthur's arms, staining the red velvet crimson, but Gwen is at his side, resplendent and confident enough to make him brighter by merely standing in her presence.

"Repeat after me," Merlin says. "'I, Arthur Pendragon, first of my name, vow to protect Camelot and Albion against all threats from both outside its borders and within them. I vow to reign fairly and justly. I vow to take care of all of my people, until my reign ends when I take my last breath.'"

Arthur repeats the words. His voice is loud but gentle as it weaves its own kind of spell around the courtiers gathered, making them forget all the petty, vain ways they think he's lacking as a king. No one could look at Arthur now and think him gawky or sloppy; no one would dare call him awkward. He has proven himself his father's son and then some, a uniter of kingdoms and a true king fit to rule over all of them. As soon as he starts speaking, he has them captive, in the thrall of his charisma.

I have my Sight. Gwen and Morgana had their magic. Lancelot has his agility and speed and strength. But Arthur—Arthur is the only one of us who is human through and through. This charisma is natural, yes, but also carefully cultivated and practiced. I can't imagine I will ever see anyone hold a crowd like he does now. It is, I think, its own kind of magic.

"I wish Morgana was here to see him," Lancelot says to me, the words like a punch. Try as I might, I can't get her voice out of my head. Over and over again, I hear her asking me where my line is.

"Me too," I tell Lancelot, which I find is true enough. Though our conversation haunts me, she should be here. She should see this. She should witness what she has given him. Maybe she would even be happy to see it, though I doubt it. One day, maybe, she will look on Arthur and smile, but that day is a long way away.

# 45

OW LONG DO you think it will be?" Gwen asks me when the coronation is done and the crowd descends on Arthur, full of flattery and congratulations. Even Gwen is quickly forgotten in the crush, the target of appraising smiles and lecherous leers, but none of the respect Arthur has commanded. She slipped away easily, finding Lancelot and me on the edge of the fray.

"Until what?" I ask her, tearing my gaze away from Arthur to look at her.

She blinks, her forehead furrowing. "Until the truce with Avalon," she says slowly. "You know, the whole point of this," she adds, gesturing to Arthur. "How long until magic is no longer banned, until Morgana and I get ours back?"

I bite my lip, thinking about my conversation with Merlin, how giving back their magic may require a higher price than I'm willing to pay. "I didn't realize you missed yours so much," I say carefully. Merlin's words have been swirling through my mind ever since our talk, and though I feel his gaze on me even now, I can't bring myself to meet it. I'm no closer now to an answer than I was when he suggested I give up my magic as well, that I consign all three of us to powerless lives.

*Happy lives, though*, a voice whispers through my mind. *At least, happier than the misery Nimue has herded you toward.*

Gwen shrugs her shoulders but doesn't look at me. "I didn't miss it at first," she admits. "But being here, it feels like I'm sealed away from everything I love—*most* of what I loved, at least. There's no sunshine, no fresh air except the occasional stroll through a minuscule garden. I haven't been able to go riding since we arrived, and when I asked my maid where I might procure a bow and arrow, she *laughed*. Like I'd made a joke."

"She likely thought you did," I say. "Ladies don't partake in archery, Gwen. I told you that."

"You also told me we would change things," she says.

*That was before*, I want to say. *That was when Morgana was still here and I thought we had a chance at happiness.*

"Not all at once," I say instead, trying on a smile that doesn't quite fit.

"But the treaty with Avalon?" she presses. "Surely that will be Arthur's first act now that he's king. And maybe when Morgana has her magic back . . ." She trails off, unable to finish the thought.

I glance at her, eyebrows raised. "And here I thought you'd sworn to never forgive her," I say. "I suppose I should have known better—you always forgive each other."

*But will you forgive me? If I can't give your magic back? If I give up my own as well? Will you forgive me if I don't, if you end up sealed away in a convent for the rest of your days? Will I forgive you?*

"We just need to give it time," I tell her, pushing those thoughts aside.

She exhales slowly, a sound I'm familiar with, one that's usually followed by an outburst, by a string of cruel words she never really means, by a stomping foot or a slamming door or some other tempestuous tantrum. Not this time, though. This time, she lets out that long, loud exhale and seems to deflate before my eyes, her shoulders slumping forward and her head falling.

"If you say so, Elaine," she says.

She drifts off into the crowd, making her way back toward Arthur, and when we're alone again, Lancelot reaches out, his hand touching the small of my back. He doesn't say anything, though I'm sure he has more than a few questions.

"What would you think of a world without magic?" I ask him softly. "Hypothetically. If Arthur didn't align us with Avalon. If I couldn't release Morgana's and Gwen's power?"

He frowns, but it isn't in anger. He's truly considering the question, as if it is truly hypothetical and I am not talking about barring him from his home, from his mother.

"I don't think you would be asking me if it weren't something you saw the appeal of," he says finally. "I'd imagine this isn't Nimue's idea."

"No," I agree. "Nimue seeks the union of Avalon and Albion—she's been working toward that end since before any of us were born. But I have reason to believe that she doesn't have our best interests at heart."

He doesn't appear surprised by the revelation, though I suppose he wouldn't be. He understands the fey better than anyone.

"And does Merlin?" he asks. I must look confused, because he smiles. "You went to speak with him before Arthur pulled the sword from the stone, and you've been quiet ever since. It doesn't take any kind of brilliance to connect the two, merely someone who pays attention to you."

"I'm not entirely sure what Merlin's intentions are, except that he wants to keep the humans and fey separate. I'm not sure that's for the best, though."

He considers this, his mouth drawn into a thin line. "Do you remember what I told you once, about the fey?"

"You will have to be more specific," I say. "You've said many things about the fey over the years."

"About the life spans," he clarifies. "The main difference between the fey and humans." When I nod, he continues. "Maybe Merlin isn't one of the fey, maybe he is. I haven't the slightest idea. But I do know that he's immortal. He and Nimue see the world the same way, at such a distance that the rest of us are little more than pieces on a board game."

I let out a slow breath, shaking my head. "I am growing tired of playing a game I don't understand the rules of," I tell him. "I don't even know whose side I'm meant to be on. Nimue's or Merlin's, the humans' or the fey's."

He considers this for a moment. "Why are those the only two options?" he asks.

THAT NIGHT, I don't dream of the future. Instead, I find my mother again, standing by the same river as before, the same river where just days ago I married Lancelot, but now the river is not peaceful. It is a wildly churning thing, and as I step toward it, I feel my own heart thunder in my chest.

"There you are, Little Lily," my mother says, like she's been waiting for me.

I push away my fear and come to stand at her side. After a moment, she tears her gaze from the waves and focuses on me instead, her eyes darting over my face as if she is charting a map.

"I wondered, before, what would be left of you when those you loved chipped away their pieces," she says, her cold fingers coming up to graze my cheek. I struggle not to flinch away from her touch, but also not to lean into it. "Tell me, have you discovered the answer?"

I close my eyes, as if blocking my sight will block out her truth, but it doesn't work. I feel it in my bones, a deep, aching knowledge that will not leave me anytime soon.

"I thought that Morgana made me," I say after a moment. "That she shaped me into something stronger, bolder, more powerful. And I suppose she did. So did Gwen—Gwen made me brave. Not fearless, never fearless, but braver than I ever thought I could be. You made me too. You bent me and broke me and made me a shadow of myself, until I was so afraid of everything and everyone that I didn't dare want anything at all."

I open my eyes again, to see if the words hurt her, but if they do, she doesn't show it. She wouldn't, I suppose. After all, she is not my mother, just the shadow of her that lives deep in my own mind, the ghost I can't get rid of.

"You all made me," I say. "And you've all hurt me, or you will. So what is left when those pieces are stripped away?"

I take a deep, steadying breath. The smell of the river is a comfort, the fresh air, the trees. For the first time in my memory, I feel entirely at peace.

"I'm left," I tell her. "Me. Everything I am, everything I've made myself. Maybe you have all shaped me, molded me like a vase, but when all is said and done, when everyone has chipped away their pieces, I will not break."

My mother watches me for a moment, and then she nods once, a small smile coming to her lips.

"Where is your line, Elaine?" she asks me, but her voice is no longer hers. It is Morgana's, and this time, I know what the answer is.

I don't give it to her, though. Instead I step into the rushing river and let the tide carry me away.

# 46

WHEN I WAKE, the moon is still high in the sky, and Lancelot's arm is flung over my waist, heavy and warm. In the quiet of the night, I'm aware of his heart beating where his chest presses against my back. I turn, rolling over so that I'm facing him. Though I try to move carefully, he still stirs, his eyes slitting open.

"It's not morning yet," he says, rolling onto his back and pulling me with him so I'm curled against him, my head on his chest. He sputters, bringing his other hand up to his face, brushing my hair down over my shoulders.

"Your hair got in my mouth," he says, and I laugh, even though doing so hurts something deep within me. It's such a normal moment. The easy kind, as if we have thousands of moments like this ahead of us. Because he believes we do.

I know what must be done now. He was right earlier; it is not about choosing between Nimue's plan for me and Merlin's, it has never truly been about either of them. But I can't bring myself to get up just yet. I can't make myself say goodbye.

*It's not goodbye*, I think. *I'll see him again, at least once more.* Nimue said his death was unavoidable, no matter what came, but now I know that when I see him again on that day, I will be the one apologizing.

"I love you," I tell him.

"Hmmm?" he says, already drifting back to sleep. "I should hope so, you did marry me, after all."

He believes it easily tonight, but when morning comes, he will doubt it. And there is nothing I can do to prevent that, to convince him that I am saving him, too, in a way. And I don't want to taint this last moment by trying.

Instead, I lift my head and kiss him, soft and slow. After a second of waking up, he kisses me back, his hand coming up to cradle my head. When he pulls away, his eyes scan my face.

"Everything alright?" he asks.

I smile. It isn't even forced. I smile because being here, with him, makes me happy, and for once that is a simple thing.

"Everything's fine," I say. Not a lie. "Just thirsty. I'll be back."

I slip out of his arms and out of the bed, and as I make my way to the door, I hear him roll over again, burrowing back into the pillow and reaching for sleep.

"We've got to start keeping a bedside pitcher for you," he says, already halfway to sleep again. "You're always thirsty."

I pause by the door and turn, just to look at him once more. The moonlight pouring through the window sharpens the angles of his face, making him look more fay than ever.

*Get back in bed*, a voice whispers. *It's not too late.*

But my mother's prophecy comes back to me, and the last line lingers: *She'll break them both and then she'll die.* I've been so worried about the first two parts, of Gwen's and Morgana's terrible acts to come, that I didn't realize that last part of it had already happened.

I'd broken Morgana and Gwen. Not intentionally, not maliciously, but I broke them all the same. But broken things can be put back together, and I know exactly where to start.

I know where my line is now. I've crossed it once, and I will not cross it again.

ARTHUR IS STILL awake, which doesn't surprise me. He sits in his study, still dressed in his coronation outfit, but now the jacket is undone and draped over the back of his chair, his hair mussed from his hands anxiously running through it. He is quite a spectacle from where I stand in the doorway.

The king that I made.

The king who, in many ways, made me too.

He looks up, and when he sees me, his eyes brighten.

"Hello," he says. "I thought you'd be long asleep. Maiden, Mother, and Crone know I should get to bed, too, but . . ."

He trails off, his eyes dancing over me, taking in the fact that I am not in my nightgown, not in my gown from earlier either. Now, I wear the simple cotton frock I wore when we arrived from Avalon, with a blue velvet cape over it.

"Are you going somewhere?" he asks, frowning. "At this hour? I know your father wanted you to visit Shalott, but surely—"

"I'm going back to Avalon," I tell him before he can finish.

For a moment, he just stares at me.

"You want to see if Morgana is safe," he says slowly.

I shake my head. "I'm not worried about Morgana's safety—I pity the creature that tries to cause her any kind of harm, magic or no."

He wavers, and I can practically see his thoughts working behind his eyes, trying to make sense of what is right before him.

"You'll come back, though," he says, his voice lowering.

"No," I say. "I won't."

Arthur scrambles to his feet, coming around his great desk to stand before me, his hands taking hold of my shoulders.

"You can't leave, too, El," he says. "I need you. There's the treaty with the fey to forge, and I'm not foolish enough to believe Lyonesse will stay docile for long. And then there's Mordred . . ."

There is a rawness to his voice that breaks my heart, but I hold steady, taking his hands in mine and squeezing them tight.

"You are king now," I tell him. "We've gotten you this far, Arthur, put you on this throne. But you are king now, and that is something you have to do yourself. You'll be brilliant at it."

He blinks. "A vision?" he asks.

"A truth," I say. "From someone who knows you better than just about anyone. You have challenges, and I won't pretend it will be easy, but I believe in you."

Arthur swallows, glancing away from me before closing his eyes tight. "Tell Morgana I'm sorry," he says when he looks at me again.

"Tell Lancelot the same for me," I say.

He nods. "And . . . we'll see each other again, won't we? One day?"

There's such hope in his voice that it feels like a vise tightening around my chest until I can scarcely breathe. I drop his hands and wrap my arms around him instead, holding him close.

"One day," I say, hoping that day isn't for a very long time. I pull back, fixing him with the brightest smile I can manage. "You are going to be a great king, Arthur. The greatest king. You don't need me for that."

I don't think he believes me, not really, and I can't blame him. I've grown so used to having him at my side—and Gwen, Morgana, and Lance as well—that I don't know if I can stand on my own two feet. But I'll have to. And so will Arthur.

He will fall. Nimue said as much. Another touchstone vision that will not change. Mordred will strike him and he will fall, it has been Seen. Nimue believes that he will need me if he hopes to recover, but I'm not so sure. I do know that I cannot sacrifice others to save him. If he is going to rise again, he will have to do it on his own.

So I kiss his cheek one last time and say goodbye.


GWEN FINDS ME in the stables, waiting for a horse to be saddled. She is in her nightgown with her feet bare and hair loose, looking so much like the Gwen I knew on Avalon that it makes my heart hurt. But I never saw Gwen cry on Avalon, and now there are silent tears tracing their way down her cheeks.

"You can't leave," she says when she sees me.

I knew she would come—not because of any visions but simply because it was impossible that she wouldn't.

"I have to," I tell her. "Before Morgana left, she said she found the line she wouldn't cross, not even for Arthur's sake. She wouldn't give herself up."

Gwen frowns, trying to make sense of the words. "And you don't want to give yourself up either?" she asks.

I shake my head. "No, I think I would have done that without a second thought," I say, not realizing until I say the words how true they are. I would have given myself for Arthur; I'm not sure I would have even thought it much of a sacrifice. "But Morgana asked me what my line was, and then tonight I realized that I'd already crossed it once, with her."

Her frown deepens. "What do you—"

"My line is you. You and Morgana and Lance. I would do anything for Arthur, but I will not hurt the three of you, I will not sacrifice your lives, your choices, your happiness for him. I crossed that line once, when I insisted Morgana give up her powers—maybe I crossed it when I convinced you to leave Lyonesse—"

"You didn't convince me," she says, shaking her head. "I made my choice."

"Maybe," I allow. "But it was the wrong choice. And I should have told you as much, no matter the cost to Arthur. His happiness, his life, is not worth more than yours."

Gwen blinks down at me, her expression perplexed.

"Arthur above all else," she says softly. "It's what Nimue always said."

"I don't care," I tell her, realizing suddenly how true that is. "I will not sacrifice you for him."

"You aren't sacrificing me," she says.

"Of course I am," I tell her. "I started sacrificing you the second I convinced you to come to Camelot, to marry Arthur and take up the mantle of queen. I convinced you it would be different here, that you would find some kind of happiness. In my defense, I believed it then."

For a long moment, Gwen doesn't speak.

"And now?" she asks quietly.

I look her square in the eye. "You should return to Lyonesse," I tell her. "Take your throne there, by force if needed—I know you have it in you. You can't make change here, but you can make change there."

She shakes her head. "I made vows to Arthur, I married him—"

"You returning to Lyonesse won't invalidate your vows," I say. "A four-day journey isn't so much distance. There are couples with oceans between them."

"Arthur won't—"

"Arthur wants you to be happy," I tell her. "And if you stay here, you won't be. You will be miserable and angry, and you will take it out on him. If you stay here, you will both suffer."

Gwen glances back over her shoulder, and though I can't see much of her face, I still catch the longing there.

"I don't want to leave him," she tells me, turning back around.

"Neither do I," I say. "Arthur or Lance. But I've found my line. And I think you've found yours too."

## 47

GWEN AND I ride through the night in silence, the only sound the hooves of her horse beating against the ground, echoing the beating of my heart. I didn't expect her to come with me tonight, but she'd made up her mind, and I know her too well to try to change it. She wants to see me to the lake before continuing on to Lyonesse, and I am grateful for her company.

I know, finally, what I have to do, what my whole life has been coming to. And more importantly, I know *why*.

Maybe I've always known. Maybe the truth has always been there, hidden beneath Nimue's ominous words, hidden in my own visions, hidden in my recurring nightmare about drowning. Maybe I just couldn't see it before because I didn't want to.

I still don't want to. I tighten my grip on Gwen's waist, clinging to her warmth, her life, her humanity.

"We're almost there," she tells me, over her shoulder.

I don't know if she means the words as a comfort or a warning, but I hear it as both, and I hold her tighter.

Nimue used to say that there was peace in knowing the future, but I have never felt that way. Knowing the future set me on edge, it made me act rashly, and I used it to drive wedges between myself and the people I loved. It did not bring me peace.

But going without my Sight, as Merlin wanted me to, wouldn't bring me peace either. And if I can't sacrifice what I asked Morgana and Gwen to, there is only one way to make things right.

Now, I understand what Nimue meant. There is peace in finally knowing what the world wants from me. There is peace in understanding the part I must play. I thought I would feel helpless, but instead purpose swells up in me. It is not a soothing thing, not a comfort of any kind, but Nimue was right: There is a sense of peace.

When we come to the shore, Gwen dismounts first before helping me down.

"How do you know they'll let you back?" she asks. "I don't see any boats."

"No," I say, but I don't look at her. Instead, I stare out at the black water, the black sky—almost inseparable from each other in the dead of night. Somewhere out there is Avalon. Somewhere out there is Morgana, waiting for vengeance, maybe. Or perhaps waiting for forgiveness. Waiting for me, at any rate. "I don't need a boat."

I look to Gwen and take her hands in mine, squeezing them. "We'll see each other again someday," I tell her.

Arthur accepted the promise as a comfort, but it doesn't give Gwen the same thing. She grips my hands so tightly I can feel my bones ache.

"There's no boat, El," she says again.

I smile and look at the water, its glittering waves churning wildly, though there is no storm, no wind. It looks hungry.

Gwen follows my gaze, takes in the lake with new eyes. Perhaps she is seeing what I see—the start of a vision so old it has always been a part of me.

"You can't," she says, her voice cracking. "Elaine, that's madness."

It isn't the first time I've been accused of madness, but it's the first time there has been truth in the claim.

"Maybe it is," I say, a laugh forcing its way out. "But it's the only way. I know it somehow, deep in my bones. The same way I knew about Morgana's magic. About the moon. I *know* it."

"You'll drown."

As soon as she says the words, I hear it dawn on her—the truth of what I will be doing. What it will mean. How it will end.

"You'll drown," she says again. "That's what you know. You've Seen it."

I smile, even as tears sting my eyes. "Yes," I tell her, because there is no way around it. I pull her close and wrap my arms around her as if I can imprint her on my memory that way, absorb a bit of her fearlessness into me. "I'll drown, and when I do, my hold on your magic—on Morgana's magic—will break. You will both have it back."

"There must be another way," Gwen says, shaking her head.

"There isn't," I say, my voice breaking. "I've fought fate for so long, Gwen. But there are some things I can't avoid. This is where my destiny leads me. It's where the Maiden, Mother, and Crone drew my path, and I am ready to fol-low it."

Gwen places her hands on either side of my face, pressing her forehead against mine. "Please don't go," she whispers. "Please don't leave me too."

I wish that this moment could go on forever, that we could stay just like this, suspended in time, safe.

*You were not raised to be safe*, Nimue said to me once. *You were raised to be heroes.*

Part of me bristles at that—I never chose to be a hero. But then I remember that it isn't entirely true. I did choose this path, just as I have chosen every-thing that led me to this moment. I chose Morgana, I chose Avalon, I chose Arthur and Lancelot and Gwen. I chose this, and I would choose it all again.

So I pull away from Gwen.

"I'll never leave you," I tell her softly. "Take care of Arthur and Lancelot. And take care of yourself, and your people. Alright?"

For an instant, I think Gwen might protest. Her hands are so tight around mine that I don't think I could wrest them from her grip if it came to it. She is stronger than me, after all. But after a moment, she nods, lips pressed into a tight line.

"And you . . ." She trails off, swallowing. "Wherever you go, if you see Morgana there . . . you'll tell her I'm sorry, won't you? For everything."

I nod, not trusting myself to speak, and she lets go of my hands.

My feet feel like lead as I step toward the shore, leaving my shoes behind one by one. When my bare feet touch wet sand, I stop and strip off my dress, leaving it in a puddle of white cotton. Next, I strip off my petticoat, my corset, my chemise, my stockings, until I am standing before the lake in nothing but my skin.

Though I can hear Gwen crying behind me, I don't turn back. If I even look over my shoulder, I will falter. I will change my mind. Instead, I put one foot in front of the other and step into the lake.

The water is like ice against my skin, but I barely feel it.

I'm up to my waist before the current takes hold. It wraps itself around my legs like fingers, pulling me farther in, tugging me down below the surface. That final breath before the water closes over my head tastes like honey and smoke. It tastes like change.

# 48

I DIE DROWNING—JUST AS it has always been known.

The water is cold against my skin. It rushes around me like a storm, tearing my hair in different directions until it clouds my vision. I can't see a thing. I want to kick up to the surface, to breathe the air I know is only a few meters away, but I stay frozen and sink lower and lower in my whirlpool until my feet finally touch soft sand. My eyes close, and everything around me will fade to darkness.

My lungs burn, burn, burn, until I fear they are going to burst. The surface is so close, I know I could reach it if I just kick up . . . but I don't. I don't want to.

Elaine Astolat, the Lady of Shalott, dies drowning. When she does, it is a choice.

# 49

IN THE DARK nothingness, Nimue waits for me. I can't bring myself to be surprised.

For her part, she is surprised, staring at me like I am a specter she summoned from her darkest nightmares, but after a moment, that passes and she lets out a sigh. I don't think I've ever heard a sound so full of bone-deep exhaustion before, but then, I suppose Nimue has been working longer and harder than anyone else I've ever known.

"I should have known it would be you," she says before pausing. "This won't change everything, you know."

"I know," I say. "Arthur will still fall on that field. He may not rise again."

"He won't," Nimue says. "Not without you."

My stomach twists at the thought of it, the images I've Seen of him dying, but I force myself to nod.

"I would give anything to save him," I tell her. "But some things are not mine to give."

She tilts her head to one side, watching me with guileless gray eyes.

"You must think me a monster," she says softly. "Raising children like goats to the slaughter."

"I think you loved us as much as you could," I tell her. "But it wasn't enough. The world may still plunge into darkness. Everything we've foretold may still come to pass. But you said yourself, that future narrowed when I arrived. Now I've removed myself from their story."

For a moment, Nimue only stares at me. Then she laughs.

"Oh, child," she says. "Is that what you think you've done?"

She comes toward me—though how I don't know. There are no steps—there is no ground at all; there is only nothingness. But then she is mere inches away from me, her hands clasping mine.

"You are not removed from their story, Elaine," she says to me quietly. "You are, more than ever, thoroughly enmeshed."

She turns my hands palm up and unfurls my fingers. I watch her, feeling far away from my own body. These are not my hands, I think. I am not even seeing them with my own eyes. I'm so distracted that it takes me a second to realize what she's trying to show me.

My palms—and they *are* mine—are smooth, free of any lines, just as hers are.

*See, there's your life line*, Morgana told me once when we were bored after lessons. She traced the line with her fingertip. *And there's your heart line. Your head line. Your soul line.*

But now there are no lines at all. And Nimue's hands, always cold as midwinter snow, no longer feel cold to me.

Before I can speak, Nimue folds my hands up once again and looks at me with a small smile.

"May I be the first to welcome the new Lady of the Lake," she says softly.

"But I'm not . . ." I trail off, shaking my head. Because of course I am. Suddenly it seems ludicrous that anything else would happen. Haven't I Seen myself with power, more than I ever thought myself capable of? I remember my last vision of Lancelot, his asking me if I could still drink, my worrying he would notice how cold my skin was.

"This isn't what I wanted," I tell her, shaking my head. "I only wanted to save them, to give Morgana and Gwen their power back, to give them a chance at happiness."

"You never asked me," she says. "You asked what their futures held, but you didn't ask about your own. It was always here, Elaine. Sooner or later, it was always here. You were meant to come after—after Morgana had tried and failed to kill Arthur, after Lancelot had fled a traitor, after Guinevere had broken Arthur's heart. You were always going to end up here. But never this soon, never as the person you are now, still full of love and hope."

I swallow. "What does that mean?" I ask her.

She doesn't answer for a moment, but when she does finally open her mouth, she laughs.

"Would you believe I don't know?" she asks. "For the first time in my memory, *I don't know*. And I confess, I'm disappointed I will never find out."

My throat tightens. I haven't forgiven her for her deceptions and I'm not sure I ever will, but she did shape me, she did nurture me and raise me, and I would not be the person I am now without her.

"I'm sorry," I tell her, my voice breaking. "I don't want you to die."

Her smile doesn't waver as she releases my hands, bringing her fingers up to touch my cheek. "I've lived a very long time, Elaine," she says, but she doesn't sound like herself anymore—not ageless or ephemeral. She sounds human. "And I am so very tired."

I place my hand over hers, holding her tight, but it makes no difference. She still fades away to nothing before my eyes, smiling all the while.

# 50

I OPEN MY EYES to blinding sunlight, a sky of clear, cloudless blue. The sand beneath me is warm, and water laps at my bare legs, but I barely feel any of that. I am only dimly aware of the grains of sand pressing into my skin, the cool water ebbing and flowing over me. But I don't *feel* it. Not really. It is as if I am covered head to toe in a sort of weightless armor—I feel the echoes of sensation, but nothing truly touches me.

*I'm dead*, I think, but no, I know that isn't right. Because this is not some mythical afterlife paradise, though it is close.

No, I know this shore as well as I know my own heart. Avalon.

As soon as I think it, a shadow falls over me, and I squint against the sun to make out topaz skin and a mess of black hair that still refuses to be tamed. Morgana looks down at me with bright violet eyes and a smile I know as well as my own.

Did I truly see her only a few days ago? It feels like a lifetime has passed in the interim.

I open my mouth to speak, but instead I cough, lifting myself up onto my elbows. I sputter water. As naturally as anything, Morgana crouches beside me, her hand steadying and warm on my back.

I might not feel anything else, but I feel that, her touch solid and anchoring.

"What happened?" I ask her. "I walked into the lake and—"

"And the lake brought you here," she says, as if it's that simple. She pulls the gray shawl from around her shoulders and drapes it over my naked body. Though I don't think she is moved by her own modesty so much as mine. I pull the corners of it tighter around me.

"I saw Nimue," I tell her, the pieces beginning to filter back.

"Yes, I expect you did," she says. "She had gifts for both of us, it seems."

I take her in, the strangeness and familiarity of her at once.

"You are not Death," I tell her. "When I Saw you here again, you were made a goddess of death—"

"A punishment by the Maiden, Mother, and Crone," she says, nodding. "A way of atoning for the bloodshed I caused myself."

"But you never caused bloodshed," I say, pieces falling into place. *You were always going to end up here. But never this soon.*

Morgana's smile falters slightly. "I don't fully understand it, though Nimue explained it to me as best she could before . . ." She trails off, her gaze drawn toward the now placid lake. "I made it to the lake after I left you, but she wouldn't let me back. There was no boat, no way to cross over. I waited for days, but there was nothing. Then, one night, she came to me."

"She left Avalon?" I ask, alarmed.

Morgana shrugs. "I'm not sure, to be honest. By then, I hadn't eaten in days. I don't know that I was in my right mind. But I saw her. I felt her. I heard her. She held a hand out toward me and . . . the next thing I knew, I was here, on this shore, with Nimue. She said that you would be coming soon and she would be gone, but there were things about my future I had to understand."

"She told you your future?" I ask, alarmed. "But—"

"It wasn't my future. It *isn't* at least. Not anymore. She told me as much and then she walked into the lake," she says before closing her eyes. "I felt it, Elaine. The moment my magic came back. I wanted to weep with relief. Thank you for that."

"Don't thank me," I tell her. "I should never have taken it in the first place. It was never mine to give back."

"But you did. And Gwen is returning to Lyonesse with her own power intact."

I nod. "It was the only thing to do," I say.

She looks at me. "No," she says. "It wasn't. But it was your choice, and in making it, you created a new path. Nimue said she didn't know what it held, but we are here now, together."

"I'm the Lady of the Lake," I say slowly, tasting the words.

Morgana takes hold of my hand and pulls me to my feet, and when we stand face-to-face, she smiles—a tentative thing, fleeting and uncertain.

So much between us feels tentative, the bridge that connects us rickety, but she squeezes my hand like she used to, and in that gesture, I find my friend once more. The girl who saved my life, who had built me to be strong enough to survive anything—to survive this.

"Long live Elaine, Lady of the Lake," she says, her voice dripping in sarcasm but also, I think, a bit of pride.

I shake my head. For so long, this was what she wanted, what she dreamt of becoming since she was a child. It feels like another thing I've taken from her. "I didn't ask for this, Morgana. Any of it."

"I know," she says. "But here we are, and there is much to do."

I take Morgana's hand in mine.

An eternity of life is a frightening thing and not a gift I would ever have asked for. But if I have to spend a long lifetime fighting, there is no one I would rather have at my side.

"Yes," I say to Morgana. "There is much to do."

# 51

AFTER THE WAR is over, after the final blow has been struck, after Arthur falls, our paths will converge once more.

Guinevere will bring a dying Arthur to the lake's shore. In my slim boat, Morgana and I will sail to shore, though there will be no wind in the air, no waves, no sound at all. Nothing but stillness as the world holds her breath.

"He's dying," Morgana will say, touching her brother's face. It won't matter that I passed his apology on to her, it won't matter that she forgave him a long time ago, there will still be a tension between them. A tension that will break the second she brushes her fingers over his skin. Suddenly, he will be her little brother again, the boy she protected with everything she had. Now, she will want to protect him again, but that will be beyond her.

"You can stop it, can't you?" Gwen will ask. For a moment, she will seem to be crying, but no, not Gwen. Gwen was not made for tears. Still, there will be something pulled taut in her, something fraying, something ready to snap.

Morgana and I will exchange a look, unsure which of us she's talking to. It won't matter. The answer will be the same, but neither of us will be able to say it.

"Death cannot be stopped," I will say after a moment.

Gwen will know this, she must know this, but as soon as I say it, she crumples. Though we will be far from Lyonesse, there will be something animalistic clawing to her surface, something desperate and feral and wild. The sound she makes will not quite be human.

"But perhaps," I will say, my own voice thin as thread. "Perhaps it can be paused."

Morgana will frown. It will take a moment for my words to make sense to her.

"Life is a debt only death can repay," she will say. "Arthur has lived, but now that debt must be claimed."

"And it will be," I will say, my own voice sounding strange. "But not now, not here, not like this."

I will let myself touch Arthur then, smoothing his russet hair away from his eyes—messy as always. For an instant, it will look like he is merely asleep. He will look peaceful and young, the way he did before the world tried to break us. But the second my fingertips brush his skin, I will feel nothing but darkness and death and a doomed world ready to consume us all.

"Come on," I will say. "Let's get him into the boat, back to Avalon."

Gwen will hasten to help me lift him, ready to act without question, ready to do whatever might have even the slightest chance of saving him, but Morgana will hesitate.

"El," she will say. The nickname is strange to my ears, a remnant of a life long gone, but it will twist something deep in me all the same.

"It's the only chance, Morgana. The only chance for him and the only chance for the world. Please," I will say.

"It's a cruel thing, to live a recycled life," she will say, a flash of anguish crossing her expression.

"There was a time you wished cruelty on him," Gwen will snap, and Morgana will stare at her like she's been hit.

"You don't want to talk about cruelties, Gwen," she will say, her voice dangerous. "Did you cry like this when Lancelot fell at your side—"

"Enough," I will interrupt, because I could not help Lancelot but I can help Arthur. "He would want it, no matter how cruel. He would want to do it all again, to fight for Albion. It's who he is."

"Who he was," Morgana will say, so quietly her voice will nearly be lost to the wind.

"Who he *is*," I will say. "He is not dead yet."

Morgana will shake her head, looking down at the ground. "He deserves peace, doesn't he?" she will ask softly. "After everything, shouldn't he have a little peace?"

"He should," I will say. "But what kind of peace would he find when he knows what hell he left behind?"

There will be nothing to say to that. Morgana will come to stand beside me, and the three of us will lift Arthur's body into the boat before climbing in ourselves.

Gwen will hold Arthur's head on her lap, her shoulders hunched over, her face hidden.

Morgana will take his hand in both of hers, holding it tight and murmuring words of comfort and remorse.

And I—I will sit at the bow, my gaze fixed on Avalon as I bring us home.

# → AFTERWORD ←

As a depressed teenager, when I first read Tennyson's "The Lady of Shalott," of course I connected to the image he paints of Elaine: locked away, alone in her tower, forced to view life secondhand through a mirror without ever actually participating in it. For me, that mirror was always fiction, and so at seventeen I started writing the first draft of *Half Sick of Shadows*.

It isn't surprising that Elaine of Shalott was such a popular cultural figure during the Victorian era, a favorite of poets like Tennyson and the Pre-Raphaelite painters. She was seen as the ideal woman, especially when compared to the evil Morgana and the traitorous Guinevere. She was passive and kind, she did as she was told, she was so wholly dependent on her husband that she *literally* couldn't live without him. She became a cursed woman in a tower, weaving at her loom day in and day out, a fairy-tale princess who could not be saved.

But here we are now, in the twenty-first century, and that is no longer the kind of heroine we want or need. The version of Elaine's story you've read is, I'm happy to say, completely unrecognizable from that first draft I wrote more than a decade ago, in large part because I did eventually realize just how problematic Tennyson's original poem is, and how inherently sexist Arthurian mythology is as a whole. The women in the canon are seductresses and manipulators, prizes to be won and sacrifices to be made.

As I grew up and my worldview shifted, so did my version of Elaine. She grew a backbone, she took on her own agency, she came into her own kind of power. She stopped living on the outskirts of someone else's story.

She left her tower.

Writing that journey has been a challenge, but an immensely gratifying one, and in many ways, Elaine and I grew up together. *Half Sick of Shadows* is the result of that growth and broadening perspective, and it is truly, as we writers like to say, the book of my heart. I hope you loved it as much as I do.

—*Laura Sebastian*

# ⟶ ACKNOWLEDGMENTS ⟵

All books are a labor of love, and at fourteen years, this book has been a particularly long labor. There are so many people who have had a hand in shaping it and getting it into your hands that I have to thank.

My agent, John Cusick, who didn't bat an eyelash when I told him I wanted to rewrite the book in three different tenses and who has always encouraged me to challenge myself. This book wouldn't exist without your invaluable support and guidance.

My editor, Anne Sowards, who fell in love with Elaine and her story and helped me tell it in the strongest way possible. I'm so grateful for your brilliant counsel and encouragement.

The lovely folks at Ace/Berkley and Penguin Random House at large for being the best publishing team I could ask for. Miranda Hill for always being a quick email away. Angelina Krahn for catching all my embarrassing little grammar, spelling, and continuity issues. Katie Anderson for designing a cover beyond my wildest dreams and Adam Auerbach for bringing it to life. Alexis Nixon and Brittanie Black for being the best publicists I could ask for.

And my friends and family who have given me endless love, peace, and generosity over the years. My dad and stepmom, who have been my rock and sounding board and place to land. My brother, Jerry, and sister-in-law, Jill, for the on-the-go chats and plenty of laughs. Aunt Kim, for the baking tips and award-worthy hugs. Jef Pollock, Deb Brown, Eden, and Jesse, for being my NYC family. Lexi Wangler, Cara and Alex Schaeffer, Arvin Ahmadi, Sarah Gerton, Cristina Arreola, Kamilla Benko, Adam Silvera, Jeremy and Jeffrey West, Victoria Lee, and Rory Power, for always being a text away when I've needed to rant or rave.

Finally, to whomever I forgot. I know there's always someone. If it's you, I owe you a drink.